nanny

Michael James

First published June 2005

R

Published by
Recognition Publishing
Yew Tree House
PO Box 243
KT8 0YE

A catalogue record for this title is available from
the British Library

ISBN 0 9537373 1 4

Design and typesetting by
Stuart Nichols, Web Graphics, Lyon Road, Walton-on-Thames, Surrey

Printed and bound by St. Edmundsbury Press,
Blenheim Industrial Park, Newmarket Road,
Bury St. Edmunds, Suffolk, IP33 3TU

Thanks to Stan, Nicki,
Stuart and Peter for advice
and comment, and to
Anne and John for support,
patience and trust.

Chapter 1

Lucy Marie's pink anorak sleeve plopped to the surface, and no matter how many times nanny thrust it, splashing back into the freezing water, it wouldn't stay submerged. It was typical of the girl to be so bloody awkward. Nanny pushed the reluctant body again. Deep into the frigid lake. Along under the thick ice. It should stay there, surely. But within a few seconds the child's lily hand, fingers close together, rigid, came rippling to the surface; followed by the shining bubble of an inflated pocket. And then, to nanny's horror, inches from the dead hand, accompanied by a rich slurp, emerged Barbie appropriately dressed in her fashionable pink bathing suit. Swimming on her back, blond hair carried in the swirl, floating carefree in the black water. She was a survivor.

Lucy Marie had held on to *Florida Barbie* as nanny chased her through the trees that bordered the frozen lake. Crazy and deadly. Despite the ill-fitting boots nanny was too fast; the little girl's frantic whirling legs slapping the air and smacking the foliage. All action but no progress. Nanny's long strides took her on to the fleeing girl without much of a chase and she dragged her quarry back with only the hint of breathlessness. It was a brutal yanking at the collar of her padded ski jacket. Lucy Marie sobbed. She didn't understand why nanny had left her daddy lying on the pine needles in the forest. Had left her mummy sprawled across the kitchen floor. Or why her brother screamed from the cupboard where nanny had thrown his pleading face and locked out the light. Nanny knew Tommy hated the dark.

At the edge of the lake where, that sultry summer, daddy had taught her to water-ski; where he always watched the sunset with a bottle of beer as his friend; nanny pressed her thumbs into Lucy Marie's Adam's Apple. And with a crunching grip squeezed the disobedient life out of her.

Killing Mr. John Roberts was easy. In fact it was enjoyable. Even more exciting than the times she had imagined it. Then of course she hadn't possessed a gun. He'd been the first. The whole family had to go after that. So, with all that money and all that power, he was brought down, level. Sucking the soft carpet of the forest floor. Blood soaking or trickling from the two wounds. One through his shirt and into his gut, that he had clutched at and that felled him as he desperately lunged at her. The other that he appeared to swallow with his cheek and must have gone through to his brain. He twitched twice but never moved after that. How low and insignificant he looked. Just a bundle in the woods. It pleased her. From there he couldn't moan or criticise her very English methods, or poke fun at her dour dresses. Nanny was right this time. Nanny was in control.

She had heard the shots. His wife. What a slag she was. It was messy but just as gratifying. Too much blood. Half her nose had come off when the bullet smashed into her face. She probably died before she hit the quarry tiles. Lying in the pool that seeped from her splattered face. How peaceful not to hear her whine. Telling nanny what she hadn't done, and how to treat her delightful children. Now nanny was being ever so naughty.

Tommy wasn't so bad. She had to think about him. He'd still been whimpering from the cupboard when she had charged out of the cottage after the escaping little shit, Lucy Marie. Even he knew at that age that nanny had been bad. And they would make him tell.

But for now Lucy Marie was being as tiresome as she had always been. Nanny scooped up the basking *Barbie* and stuffed it into her coat pocket. Again she bent down at the small exposure of water where the ballooning pink anorak refused to plunge. She lifted the wax hand, pulled at the elastic cuff. And nanny squeezed out the obstinate air that was trapped. With a levered thrust she sent the puppet body back down into the dark liquid. And in its rotation Lucy Marie's dead stare caught sight of her nanny peering into the deep pool, framed against the raw mountain sky. And there stuck on nanny's face was the satisfaction that the impudent dead girl was slipping out of sight.

Nanny gave it ten minutes. Just to make sure that the squawking child wasn't going to show her smug face again. There were only the meringue mountains and the icing-sugar dusted forest watching her. Only they could tell. In their majesty they were the dumb witnesses to her dreadful deed. Nanny gave them a threatening sneer from the corner of her mouth and narrowing eye. She would only spare that. More important was to scan the smooth surface of the water. Nanny couldn't feel her forearms, and pushed them inside her jacket. Thrashing about in the icy water had killed all feeling.

Tommy wasn't stirring when nanny swung through the mesh door into the main house, but the cupboard door remained locked. On the shelf in the kitchen the pistol was lying on its side. Once she had shot a whacking hole in Mrs. Stella Roberts' ridiculous grin she hadn't needed a weapon. It was some twenty minutes before she could pick it up again. Her fingers were aching stiff and wouldn't fit round the grip. It didn't have that secure feeling about it that she had enjoyed. Handling at night in her room and planning for that day. Three shots left. She could see the brass of the cartridge cases and the red indelible ink near where the hammer struck. How violent the recoil when she first fired it. She had needed two hands to hold it steady as he charged at her. It was etched in the straining lines of his face. He knew the fate of his family. Knew nanny was going to slaughter them all. For once he was correct.

Nanny rapped on the locked door with the barrel of the Smith and Wesson revolver. Gentle but rapid taps. But she didn't speak. From inside the cupboard a scratching sound and staccato sniffling indicated the boy had risen from the floor and was probably listening, petrified. Nanny placed her ear against the painted white wood and tried to picture Tommy only millimetres away. It wasn't difficult to imagine his wild, frightened, sparrow eyes and the condensation of his breath on the wood wall. Swimming, blind and terrified, in a thick black darkness. He had probably messed his pants.

Nanny couldn't watch his face. Such a trusting, impish face. Not unlike that of Rupert. But she wouldn't think about Rupert. That was in the past. An old ghost. Such phantoms had to be pushed well back in her head.

She knew Tommy's height. Every day she dressed his scrawny body; pulled the elastic waist band of his trousers over his extended tummy. Rubbed his milky skin and tickled him to make him give her that warm giggle. Oh! Tommy. If only she could let him go. Nanny held a finger on the door to show whereabouts his lean frame reached its full extension. Hard against the gloss paint she pushed the muzzle of her .38 handgun. Nanny turned her head. Fired. Tommy hissed quietly as the bullet ripped through the wood, and through his frail body. Nanny heard him slump to the floor, onto the broom heads and the buckets. She fired at where she expected him to be lying. Two more shots just to be sure. And then she waited. She wouldn't be able to open the cupboard to see his lifeless body heaped like garbage with the rags and dust-bags. It was a relief when a deep crimson wave of blood seeped from under the door and spread towards her. So much blood from such a slight boy.

Nanny backed away from the approaching thick fluid; sliding on her knees. They were all dead. Now she really had to think straight.

Chapter 2

Lyme Regis, or just Lyme as the locals refer to it, is now a tacky seaside resort favoured by neck-tattooed tourists sinking down from the midlands. It straddles the border between the counties of Dorset and Devon in southwest England. A hundred years ago it was probably a fashionable sanctuary for the puffed-up Victorians growing rich in the barricaded financial houses in London. Old and leaning buildings hang over strangled cobbled streets, and asymmetrical sash windows threaten to fall from rotting frames and crippled wooden buttresses. And then there are buildings like the Co-op and other domino shapes slung up in the name of contemporary architecture in the sixties and seventies.

At the water's edge gulls pose mid-air or torment chip-consuming families squeezing out of amusement arcades, or swoop at crisp-toting kids loitering at pub doors. The beach boasts some trapped sand accidentally deposited when the harbour walls were improved. But it is stones, harsh and inhospitable rock, lovingly referred to as 'pebbly'. And the sea, unhindered North Atlantic Drift, empties its anger, carried for thousands of miles, onto those who dare to bathe or fish in it. An ugly colour painted by the churning waters dislodging grey-green silts delivered by the rivers of Devon and Cornwall. Occasionally slimy and deceptive, stroking the shore; but mostly lashing out like a prickly beast at the soft cliffs and chasing, with stinging volleys, the promenading holidaymakers resigned to the atrocities of the English weather.

Sarah Bickles spent her childhood and beyond in Lyme Regis. A cluster of council houses set away from the town. Built in the thirties to house farmhands and other manual workers and their families. Sandy masonry paint splodged on the patchwork greens and punctuating browns spoiled the landscape painting and ensured the estate was deemed an eyesore.

There was just Sarah and her sister living with a permanently depressed mother. Her father had escaped a house of clucking women. So significant was his departure that not one of the household could recall exactly when he had left.

Sarah was an awkward child, a clumsy teenager and a thoroughly ungainly adult. She had no natural gift. Not that she lived in the shadow of her mother or sister, Debbie; neither of them shone. At school the children recognised her ineffectual personality and she suffered chronic bullying. And the teachers were quick to identify her cul-de-sac aspirations.

So Sarah plodded through. But only *she* was aware of the simmering resentment that her banal childhood and adolescence was cooking up. No one was certain what she would do after leaving school, least of all Sarah. In the event a family friend stepped in to suggest her for a menial position at Ruckley Manor, home of Sir Peter Bassnett, former Tory MP and Master of the Dorset Regent Hunt. It was a safe job, tucked away from guests and at arms length from the family. Kitchen skivvy, washing-up and washing down, plucking or disembowelling game that the valiant Sir Peter had chased to exhaustion or shot with a wide spray of lead pellets; and any humble task that irritable Cook decided Sarah should perform.

Sarah had a dingy closet of a room high in the eaves of the east wing of Ruckley Manor. An old iron bedstead and a peeling chest of drawers, a porthole window and rippling linoleum that threatened to wrap up her feet as she walked. The perfect incubator for her embryonic sullenness.

Sarah had suffered the drudgery of her tasks at the Manor for five months before the first recoil. Stewing hostility to Cook's regime was sufficient to trigger a simple yet effective retribution.

'Lord Maldering and his new wife, Nigel Plummer from The Times and his gentleman friend. Dinner for six.' Brampton the butler had informed Cook. 'Madam is eager to impress as always. She'll tell them that she was the architect of the meal. Make it a good one.' Brampton touched Cook delicately on the shoulder. Any firmer and she would have lashed out with the ladle in her hand. Even he knew how temperamental the portly woman could be. It was in his best interest to keep her sweet.

'Have I ever let her down? Made 'er look like a bloody gordon blue chef I 'ave. And still she pays me a bloody pittance.' Cook had climbed on to her high horse. Not an articulate woman, but a magician around her stove. 'Not appreciated, me. Got to be better positions than this.' Brampton was forced to listen to the same old diatribe. Yes, there were other jobs, but not many employers would stand for her drinking habits and mood swings.

He managed to sneak through the door still nodding his head and muttering the occasional *'quite agree'* and other comforting phrases. Cook carried on complaining to the piles of pots and the hanging pheasants even after Brampton had escaped.

Sarah was the ideal punch-bag for Cook to take out her frustrations on, and throughout the preparation of the dinner Cook yelled out orders and abuse at the stodge of a girl who loped about fetching and carrying. 'No, no, not that pot you twit of a girl. You're a real moron. Get me the one that I use for the roast.'

Sarah scuttled around, ever so servile. Ever so incensed by the brute of a woman. 'Yes, Cook. Of course Cook. Anything you wish Cook.' It would suit her purpose for Cook to think Sarah was even more pathetic than she acted.

Sarah had fumbled around in the shed in the walled garden, reading as much of the contents of the scattered containers as she could manage. There were some long words. Chemicals that she couldn't pronounce and had no idea of their effect. The moss killer seemed the best bet. Colourless, and as far as she was able to determine, very little smell. Sarah was an amateur at poisoning. Not out to kill. Make people sick. Get Cook into trouble. It was a simple act of repayment. The only way she knew. No lashing tongue or rapier cynicism.

And when Cook slipped off for a pee or to gulp down a tumbler of gin, Sarah opened the pan where the courgettes sat in a bath of butter and garlic prepared for the hob. Measurement was a problem. The bottle was poised, ready to pour. But, how much? Sarah tipped it, and a small quantity spilled into the pan. It wasn't enough. She tipped it again. It slurped onto the courgettes. Too much! Too bad. Sarah pushed the clear liquid into the butter and twisted the pan to swirl the excess until it was absorbed, or picked up enough grease to avoid detection.

Her victims were upstairs. She could hear the snorting laughter. Sarah was stuck at the sink, but her ears were tuned into the frenetic activity behind her. As she struggled with the heavily soiled pots and pans in the low stone basin, Cook was buzzing about her oven and hob. Chubby conjuror arms conducting the sizzling food and the pattering lids. Sarah scrutinised each serving that Cook loaded onto the maid's tray, until she recognised the silver dish that steamed with sliced courgettes. Now she could stare at the suds and the grey water. It was on its way up. In her mind she followed its progress. Up the stairs from the kitchen, deep in the bowels of the house, and along the short corridor to the splendid dining room. The maid would leave it on the mahogany serving-table, from where Brampton would waltz it along the guests with a cheesy grin and an exaggerated tipping of the platter. Sarah smiled for only the dirty crockery to see. They would be eating it by now.

Lady Penelope Bassnett was the only diner who didn't eat the salmon or the courgettes. She was the only diner who wasn't awake half the night throwing up. Watching her husband retching into the toilet bowl until the early hours, she was alert to the potential damage to her own reputation. As soon as was polite she was on the phone to the Malderings and Nigel Plummer. It was a disaster. Neither of the Malderings was well enough to talk to her and Nigel Plummer and his friend were at the hospital after coughing up blood.

It was never traced. Sarah had never washed up a pan, a serving dish and Sir Peter Bassnett's finest dinner service so well.

Sarah's first success. Cook had never been so insulted. *Nobody talked to her like that. Nuffin wrong with 'er food. There were plenty of jobs elsewhere.*

Her replacement was nowhere near as masterful in the kitchen, but she treated Sarah like a daughter or a slow sister. Recognised her vulnerability. Took her under her wing. Encouraged Sarah to take on more. Help her with some of the food preparation. Simple stuff at first. But it was as far as it went. The new cook detected Sarah's awkwardness and was quick to redirect her. With a little persuasion Brampton allowed Sarah to step in when a maid went sick. And that was as regular as periods. She was kept to cleaning duties and other domestic chores. Routine tasks that she was confident with. It meant a uniform and more exposure in the house. It also meant that she met Rupert for the first time.

Rupert, three years old, the only child of an elderly Sir Peter and his young wife, Penelope. A treasured son. Spoilt, and already making excessive and unreasonable requests readily assuaged by misguided and doting parents. A series of nurses and nannies had come and gone. All blamed for intolerance towards the wonderful heir apparent. Even at three Rupert was right. Always right and always accommodated.

Their first encounter. Sarah was cleaning a guest room, bent over, pushing a rattling Hoover between the cabriole legs of a chest of drawers. Rupert stood in the doorway bawling. It wasn't until she stamped on the off switch that she heard the distressed child. There was no maternal instinct. Two vacant souls examined each other; unsure of the person in their sights. Rupert looking for attention and Sarah struck inquisitive, but disinterested in the boy's plight. A little fellow. Sir Peter's son. Even she was recognising the networking possibilities of befriending the tearful chap.

'Hello.' A weak greeting. An attempt to smile. She wasn't

well practised and her face resisted as she tried to crease it. And when the smile was fixed it felt like it would stick there. A frozen lunatic grin.

Rupert's weeping went into idle. Just a heavy sniffing and a regular gulping sound accompanied his gaze. He hadn't seen this one before. She would be a fresh source of comfort. A new face to urge to satisfy his selfish demands. All the others had gone. Mummy had got rid of them. This was another disposable employee. Rupert stuck his finger in his mouth and chewed. He mumbled an acknowledgement that barely passed his gnawed digit. It was the beginning of a fatal association. He had met his killer.

A maid's retrieving hand pulled the boy from the doorway and rushed him back to the nursery. Sarah resumed mowing the carpet with the vacuum cleaner, and in her long runs up the room the boy sat in her head. She had stopped him crying. Perhaps she had a way with kids. He seemed to like her. Sarah imagined looking after him. Being in charge of Sir Peter's son. It was a way out of life downstairs. She could live in the house. Almost part of the family. Her daydream was broken by the resounding clatter of the Hoover eating a television cable. It was a silly idea anyway.

Sarah ran into Rupert on several occasions the following week. Wendy the maid who cleaned the west wing was pre-menstrual and Sarah was assigned to the guest suite and other bedrooms in that section. Rupert's rooms were a little further along the corridor from the limits of her jurisdiction. And a hastily recruited nanny pushed or pulled him screaming past the polishing or dusting Sarah. Their eyes often met and she tried to massage a friendship in those fleeting exchanges. Sarah was slow to pick things up, but once she started scheming she displayed a ruthless determination to succeed. Not a real plan. As seamless as she could manage.

She didn't have to wait long before she had close contact with the boy. Sarah was on a step-ladder reaching for a high leaded-light when a flustered agency nanny charged in. 'The little bastard has flooded the bathroom. Can you keep an eye on him while I sort out clearing it up. Bloody kid!'

Sarah descended cautiously as the nanny disappeared along the corridor. Duster still in hand she scurried down to the open door and explored the nursery. Rupert sat on his bed, pleased with his most recent act of sabotage. He pulled small feathers from a tiny hole in his pillow and blew them in the air, cooing as they floated and tumbled in shafts of light from the window. Sarah greeted him with a beaming face that certainly wasn't admonishing; almost encouraging. In the bathroom she paddled in about an inch of water. On the floor lay a sausage of sodden tissues that the nanny had pulled from the overflow. Rupert crept up behind her and felt for her hand that she held at her side. Sarah didn't resist his squeezing grip. He could sense Sarah wasn't condemning; possibly found it amusing. It was in the growing smirk filling her face.

'What's my little scallywag been up to now?' Rupert and Sarah were startled by the arrival of Rupert's mother. She gazed over his head at the mess in the bathroom. 'Trying to drown us all, are you?' Penelope smiled at Sarah. 'Holding the fort I assume?'

'Er...yes, ma'am.' Sarah held on to Rupert. A demonstration for Lady Bassnett.

'He's a little devil at times. Means well.' Penelope Bassnett looked down at Rupert's impish eyes, but made no attempt to hold him. Sarah was quite comfortable with this confrontation. She surprised herself by her seeming lack of nerves.

'Oh! I'm sorry about this, my Lady.' The flapping nanny rushed through the door and ran into her employer. A mop and bucket that she had struggled up the stairs with cluttered to the floor. Sarah crept past the embarrassed woman, now on her knees trying to recover some dignity in front of the intrigued Lady Penelope Bassnett.

It worked. Between the succession of agency nannies Sarah Bickles was chosen to step in and look after the terrible toddler, until they gave up trying to get one to stay, and allowed Sarah to suffer Rupert full time. She moved into the nursery suite. Absolute luxury compared to her attic room. Her bedroom was connected to Rupert's and the playroom. Every conceivable toy and contraption was available to the child. Sarah found it hard to recall if she ever had toys as a child. Certainly not more than one or two. She would enjoy exploring Rupert's cave of goodies.

They complemented each other; the spoilt brat and the gawky woman now established as nanny. His parents were pleased that there was stability at last and that their darling child was content with his minder, despite some apprehension about the sombre and bumbling woman.

Sarah was encouraged to learn to drive so that she could transport the little demon, who was not the favourite passenger of the family chauffeur. He was an elderly man who had been with the family a long time and had turned noticeably greyer since first driving *young Master Rupert.*

It wasn't easy for Sarah to cope with instruction. And perhaps it wasn't fair on her or her instructor. After several narrow escapes and a small shunt her goal was downgraded to mastering just an automatic. Even then there were occasions when her teacher was grateful for his seatbelt, as Sarah stamped on an imaginary clutch and hit the broad brake pedal with alarming force.

A honeymoon period followed. With a nanny reclaiming her childhood and a delinquent infant being incited to perpetrate all manner of devilish deeds. But a three year old doesn't keep the faith. Even a kindred spirit needs to be tested. Rupert increased his demands. Just small things to start with that inconvenienced Sarah and blew her off course. Much of the routine she had to learn, and for her retention didn't come as easy as it did to others. She remembered things methodically and found an altered course difficult to steer. The boy seemed to recognise anxiety and saw it as a splendid opportunity to have some fun. Half expecting his new friend to relish the challenge. Or during his vicious moods would jemmy open any crack he observed in Sarah's defence.

There were times when child and nanny got on fine. Soul mates in certain situations. But in truth it was a lethal cocktail. A wild and selfish kid running out of control and a precariously balanced woman prone to totter on a precipitous personal edge. No one read the dangers. And no one would suggest that a volatile relationship existed within the confines of the nursery suite, when house staff, family, friends and neighbours spoke after his death.

Not that she meant to kill him. She hadn't killed before. Perhaps if there had been the opportunity in the past she might have done someone in. And when she killed there wasn't real pleasure, only the relief. Sarah Bickles killed to escape an emotional ambush. A last resort to free herself when she was cornered. Rupert hadn't realised he was setting a trap. To him it was just an ordinary grouchy day.

'Bath!' Sarah shouted at a closed door. Rupert had shut it. He didn't want to wash that day. And certainly not that early in the morning.

Lady Penelope had insisted he was 'smelling like a skunk' and needed a thorough immersion. 'Preferably in a sheep dip,' she had joked.

It was up to nanny to spruce up Master Rupert. 'Bath,' she repeated. The door didn't open. And beyond he made sure she knew he was dragging out every imaginable game, that involved a cascade of littered contents for her to clear away. Small counters and plastic chips that she would have to peel up with her nails.

Nanny sat on the soft seat where she always stood Rupert, to wrap him up in the thick bath-sheet and hug him until he was dry, and warm enough to dress. Deep down the panic was welling. Lady Penelope maintained he was to be clean, but he was not going quietly into that bath. It was to be a fight all right.

Both listened for movement beyond their door. Rupert was throwing debris at the wall; regular pelting to let her know he was holding out. Sarah heard that. But in the dank bathroom she was sliding deeper into a stampeding concussion.

And when she burst into his room he sensed more than just annoyance. Narrowed eyes and a chin held firm. Hissing with anger. Nanny's face loomed above his; telescope huge. She grabbed at the collar of his pale blue shirt and tugged him by it into the bathroom. He began to sob. Nanny had never been this rough. He'd never been thrown around like this. Her nails dug into the skin of his neck.

Sarah didn't speak. She couldn't move her jaw in the purple, singing anger that held her head in a vice grip. Rupert's clothes were unceremoniously torn off and he stood shivering. Vulnerably naked. Sarah lifted him roughly into the bath, handed him a bar of soap and sat breathing out through her nose, watching him like an encircling vulture. Rupert had never washed himself. They always did it. He knew better than to ask, and pushed the soap across his belly, copying what he had watched them do. He did his utmost not to cry; sucking back the bubbling mucus and stretching his eyes wide to strangulate the tear duct.

A young boy has only so much control. He fought back such lusty bawling that was being signalled from his stomach; rocked with every heaving of his body...until he detonated. It was a terrible scream. Rupert pleaded to the world. An explosive cry for help. But along the hollow corridors and through evacuated rooms that were drowned by the ticking of old sentry clocks his cries were lost. Lost on the brocade and the ancient mahogany of the furniture and the dismissive fabric of time.

Nanny was not pleased. Why had he double-crossed her? Broken the pact? All she could see was the warbling throat, pink frightened eyes and magnolia skin. He'd wake the dead, he would. All that row. The missus would get rid of her; punish her for this. He shouldn't be making such a din. Been a bad boy. She'd have to stop him. It was no way to behave.

Her hands were quicker than she thought. Took hold of his wriggling arms; near the shoulder. One quick downward movement that sent the water gushing up and around his struggling body and filled his hailing mouth with grey suds. Then she yanked him upwards with such force that the top of his head slammed into the gold mixer tap outlet. Blood poured through his slick hair from the wound. As if going for a further rinse whilst washing at a river bank she thrust him down. The water was just deep enough to cover his nose and mouth. A huge globe of his breath rose from his rubber lips and smacked the surface. It was the last of his air. With arms at full extension she held him down. Pressed his frail torso against the rough bottom of the bathtub. Pinned by her locked elbows. Only his feet escaped. They floated as if detached from his dead, marooned body. Gently rocking in a placid, slimy swell. Rupert was quiet now. Sarah let him go. He bobbed to the surface. His head rolled uncomfortably towards her.

'I told you.' Sarah shook an accusing finger at his ghostly stare.

Chapter 3

'So, you left him in the bath?' The policeman's pad flapped open and he jotted down what information he could drag out of the distraught woman.

'In the bath 'e was. I...wasn't gone that...long.' Nanny sounded very upset. She choked on her words.

'How long?'

'Three, maybe four minutes. That's...all.'

'And when you got back, what did you see?'

'Master Rupert...he was lying on one side in the water. Not breathing, like.'

'That's when you pulled him out and tried to revive him, was it?'

'Yes. Learned it from the telly. Mouth to mouth and that.' Sarah was lying well.

'Doctor reckons there's a wound to his head and red marks on his upper arms. Can you explain them?'

'There was blood on 'is face when I saw 'im. Maybe I was rough, like. When I dragged 'im out. Desperate I was.' Sorrowful voice, deep Dorset.

'Um.' Detective Rundle scratched his head with his ballpoint pen. 'Distressing business this.' It wasn't making that much sense yet. 'You take a seat. I'll need to speak to you again.'

Sarah covered her face with her hands. And behind them she prayed. She wasn't sorry, but she was scared; scared they'd find out.

Rupert was upstairs. He lay pale and unmoving on the bath mat where she had left him. When she was sure he was dead. When he had learned his lesson. The plastic feet of the pathologist alongside, and almost as large as the foetal body.

Her story was that she had found him lying under the water

after leaving him playing in the bath. She had to get some clean underwear for him, from an airing cupboard down the hallway. 'Liked it warm from there, 'e did.' It was a scratchy story. 'Right lively 'e was. Bouncing around in the water. Full of life. Must've come up quick and banged 'is poor little head; poor soul.' She had thrown some of his rubber toys in the tub after killing the mite. 'Having a real ball with them 'e was.' Rolled his head over and wiped some of her saliva on his purple lips and into his pink mouth. 'Tried to get 'im back, but 'e was gone. It's all my fault. Shouldn't 'ave left 'im.'

Lady Penelope's wailing cries floated, haunting, from a nearby room. They wouldn't let her see him yet. There were forensic, rubber-gloved hands lifting his stubby arms and his doll legs, poking in his hair and in his mouth with intrusive swabs. Bath water samples were collected in sterilised plastic containers and microscopic particles of skin and hair taken from the gold taps. By the time she was able to hold him he was stiffening; ghostly white. A Victorian china doll in death. She stroked the congealed blood that stuck his hair to his forehead and spoke to his blank face and his dead eyes, as if telling him his last bedtime story.

'What have we got, Doc?' Rundle quizzed the departing pathologist.

'Gash on his head and marks on his upper arms. Appears that he drowned, but I'll know more when we get him on the slab.'

'No heart, you buggers.'

'Can't afford the sentiment.'

'Does it fit with her account?' Rundle enquired, his pen jabbing his chin.

'It's a difficult one. At a glance it shouts out foul play. But it's possible, as far as I can see on initial examination, that the kid hit his head on the tap and was stunned, fell back and suffocated in barely ten inches of water.'

'The marks on the arms?' Rundle questioned.

'There's slight bruising. If she pulled him out roughly when she returned then it's possible that's what caused the damage. I am going to have a closer look for you though.'

'Thanks. She doesn't seem the type to harm the lad, and there's no evidence she had a motive. That doesn't mean I'm drawing any conclusions yet.' Rundle needed to discuss his train of thought.

'You'll sort it out George.' The doctor tapped him on the head and escaped out of the door with a smile.

George Rundle turned back towards the nursery suite. Who should he talk to next? His gut feeling was that there wasn't much left of this. He would let a couple of the constables speak to the bulk of the staff. Brampton sat on one of the oak carvers in the panelled corridor. Even his impeccable composure had been imperilled by this dreadful event.

'Mr. Brampton, just a few minutes please.' Rundle beckoned him into an empty room. His notebook was flipped open again. 'You were where during this incident?'

'Laying out the silver downstairs. Getting it ready for the weekly clean. It's a real hassle. Spread newspaper out on the refectory table and line it all up. Have to do it myself in case it isn't perfect for them. I'd get the blame so it isn't worth trusting anyone else.' Brampton babbled on. He was trying to avoid mentioning the death of the young Master Rupert. He knew things would never be the same in the house again.

Detective Rundle could sense this was most probably a tragic accident and that he was merely trundling through the procedure. 'When were you alerted to the incident in the nursery?'

'She came running in. A terrible state. Screaming out and pulling at her hair.'

'The nanny?'

'Sarah. She was hysterical. It was quite a few seconds before I could tell what was wrong. I chased upstairs and found the poor soul.' Brampton rubbed his eyes. He could still see Master Rupert's blank face, his blackened eyes and his ivory body. He'd never seen the mischievous imp that still. Even when asleep his scheming face would twitch with devious planning that Brampton imagined his dreams thrived on.

'What time was this?' Rundle scribbled untidily. It was stupid. He always had trouble reading his own writing when he was in front of the typewriter at the station.

'Let me see.' Brampton would get it right. A man of clinical precision. 'I always set the silver out at eight. I'd just set out the dining room collection. Yes that's right.' Brampton was confirming his own mental calendar. 'So five past eight at the latest.' He beamed at Rundle. Happy that he had recalled it so precisely.

Rundle scratched at the pad again. 'So we have the nanny storming in on you at five after eight.' He used the end of his biro to scratch his ear. 'What time would the nanny usually bath the boy?'

It was out of Brampton's realm. He could only guess. Not on solid ground; not where he wanted to be. 'I'm not sure. Let's see. She brought him down for breakfast at eight thirty so I assume he was bathed between seven thirty and eight. Does that sound about right?'

'Can't see anything out of the ordinary,' Rundle mumbled. 'Routine sort of day by the sounds of it.' It was all fitting in. An awful accident. 'The nanny, Sarah Bickles?' The policeman chose a clean page on his wilting notepad. 'What can you tell me about her?'

'Not a lot. She worked in the kitchen when she first arrived. Quiet, dull sort really. I don't mean that in a critical way. Kept herself to herself. I suppose I was too busy to make the effort to get to know her well.'

'How did she get on with the boy? Was she strict with him? Pull him about at all?'

'Oh no. Nothing like that. The best he'd had. There have been dozens. Not many lasted long, you see. He was a bit of a handful. A real scamp at times. Sarah seemed to have a good relationship with him. Every time I saw them together they would be enjoying a prank or game. Laughed a lot. Got on well. Poor little devil.' Brampton gave Rundle a cheesy grin and a tilt of the head. He was close to tears.

'In your opinion Mr. Brampton, do you think this nanny would harm Rupert?'

'Not at all. Never saw her speaking sharply to him. No sign of her hurting the lad.'

'Thanks. I didn't think so.' George Rundle slapped his notebook shut, puffed through a thin opening between his lips and began rounding up the troops. It was time to move out. He had done all he could at the house.

Brampton had inadvertently provided Sarah with a glowing testament. He had brushed over the tracks of Rupert's brutal killer and allowed her to walk away from the senseless death of a spoiled brat, an innocent child.

One of the black-coated men from the undertakers carried the body like he was walking out of a Tesco store with a box of groceries. A white coffin that looked too small for Rupert's stiff, bloated corpse. The assembled police officers bowed their heads. Women clearly tearful.

Sarah sat in her room in the nursery suite. Her mouth was dropped open in dejection. She cursed her rash actions. It wasn't clear to her why she had drowned the boy. But she knew it was foolish. What was she going to do now? Crazy old Sarah Bickles. It was a sumptuous room with thicker carpet than she had ever walked on, and a plethora of convenient bedroom furniture that she could never hope to fill with her meagre possessions. Soon she would pack the drab, faded dresses and leave all this. What a stupid idiot she had been.

Rupert's death was quietly filed away as misadventure, whatever that really meant. Rundle and the forensic experts made certain that the inquest never even considered the barbarous murder of nanny's charge by a mentally unbalanced woman. If they had they may have saved others. Nanny was still on the loose even though she would be laying low for the time being.

You don't get a decent reference when you have carelessly allowed a child to die. So Sarah had to find something else. Not that there was much she could do. Sixty miles further north. Nearer to the smoke. A Job Centre vacancy at Skiffers wine bar in the village of Thames Ditton was an inconspicuous excursion away from the perils of caring for children. Sarah took to the job despite her morose visage, which her employers certainly had reservations about. However, Sarah proved reliable and industrious. More than could be said of the young impetuous waitresses that *Skiffers* had seen come and go with frequent monotony. Yes, Sarah would provide the stability this bistro needed.

And so Sarah Bickles slid away. In hiding. So low she almost disappeared. When she wasn't working she hibernated in her bed-sit up the road, amidst the anonymous converted Victorian town houses of Surbiton. Bowed and inconspicuous she sneaked in and out of the dank flat. It was no hardship. Unnoticed and unrecognised. Just the job.

Shortly before closing time one Tuesday evening Sarah was surprised to be confronted by Jack Gibbs, owner of the bistro. His beaming eyes quickly putting her at ease.

'Sarah. I wouldn't normally bother you. I know you keep yourself to yourself, and you can tell me to forget it, but I need a favour.'

Sarah listened but didn't look at his face. She folded and twisted a napkin in her hand.

'Carol. Do you know Carol?'

Sarah shook her head slowly, but didn't speak.

'She's the girlfriend. You've probably seen her here. Blond and leggy.'

Sarah had seen her. She did know that she was his tart. A stupid bitch.

'Well...we've been invited to a big do after work this evening. Carol's got a little girl, Stephanie. She's four. No trouble. Lovely lass.' Jack was getting there. 'See, Carol can't get her normal babysitter to sit in for a couple of hours. I just wondered if you were able...?' Jack shrugged his shoulders and asked again with a friendly grin and pleading eyes. 'Help us out a lot. Won't be for long. Got a big telly there.' He was adding some incentive. About every carrot he could think of. 'We've tried about everyone we know.'

Sarah felt the phantoms stirring. Panic screwed up her stomach. Look after a little girl? It would be nice. Adults she could do without, but a sleepy little girl smelling of talcum and toothpaste.

A nod of the head and a softly murmured agreement sent Jack sailing away to let Carol know that they were off to party.

'Thanks, Sarah.' His voice trailed behind him.

'Really appreciate this.' Carol spoke to Sarah's reflection as she touched up her lip gloss. 'There's drinks in that unit and we've got Sky so there's plenty to watch on the box. Stephie's in there. Little darling is fast asleep. Shouldn't trouble you.' Carol smoothed her minute red skirt over her thighs and twirled to check her arse looked okay. 'Anything you need to ask?' She turned and smiled at the real Sarah.

'No.' Sarah was looking along to the room where the girl was sleeping, ignoring Carol's wide grin.

'See you later. Won't be too late. You're a *real* angel. Got us out of a spot.' Carol was hauled out of the door by Jack's dragging grip.

Sarah waited until she heard the car speed away before she moved. Stephanie's door was ajar. What a glorious smell. A little girl's freshly laundered dresses and the sweet aroma of shampoo. The light spreading from the opening door chased across the bed and lit the bundle of blond hair sunk deep in the col of the soft pillow.

That's how she liked them. That was how children should be. Sarah was happy with that. She was safe when they were snuggled up in their bed. And so was the child.

Sarah tip-toed round the bed to the white chest of drawers crammed with tilting photographs of Stephie at play, marooned in a paddling pool and at a wedding, looking like

the cake. Sarah touched the frames and the lace doilies that
they sat upon. She touched the pouches of the thick curtains
and the wicker basket smelling of Stephie's soiled clothes. And
she stayed in that bedroom for most of the evening, breathing
in the luscious ambience of the little girl's room. Such a
contrast to the dismal, barren room she had shared with her
sister. And as she sat in the misty light seeping in from the
corridor she imagined that she was a child once more, and this
delicious bedroom filled with soft smells and populated by
leaning dolls and slumped teddy bears was where she and
Debbie had spent their childhood.

Jack and the tart were late. They fell into the house. Carol
was cackling and Jack complaining that she had flirted the
whole evening.

'Weren't nothing. Just having fun. You're an old misery.
Come on loosen up.' Carol was stumbling around. Words that
would be forgotten in the morning slipping with the saliva
from her mouth.

'You don't have to dance so close. You were giving the
fucking come on to those young lads. Saw you.' Jack had said
it all before.

Sarah crept from Stephie's room. The squabbling couple
didn't see her at first.

'Oh, Sarah.' Jack had forgotten she was there. 'Sorry we're
late. Tried to get away. You know how it is. Done us a real
good favour. Appreciate it. Everything okay?'

Sarah nodded and fought to produce a smile.

'Bit pissed to drive you back. Get you a taxi?'

'I'll walk.' Sarah didn't want to hang around.

'You sure, dear?' Carol managed, almost crumpled up on
the sofa. She didn't really care a fuck; she was past it.

It had been a good evening, and nanny had got the taste
once again.

Despite Jack and Carol's poor time-keeping and appalling
behaviour, Sarah was ready to re-enter the heavenly world of
that sleeping child. Almost a drug. Soft, creamy aromas and

the porridge smell of a pampered girl. It was too much. She couldn't resist. Sarah chose to babysit for the couple whenever they asked, whenever Stephie was left alone, and the bed rose and sunk with the contented breathing of the little girl.

It didn't come as much of a surprise when an American couple, keen to make a base in the United Kingdom, were guided in the direction of Sarah Bickles. It would only be a temporary arrangement. Spend some time in the UK before visiting their property in the US, a lakeside cottage, and then take the kids to the Caribbean. Full time but not a permanent agreement.

Mr. and Mrs. John Roberts were less than astute New Yorkers, and about to make the biggest mistake of their lives. Rugged and often unscrupulous business dealings in the Big Apple netted John Roberts millions of dollars but it did nothing to improve his common sense, and found him devoid of conscience or charisma. Stella Roberts loved the wealth and rarely stopped giggling every time she studied their bank balance.

Roberts had made the move to England to escape punitive taxation in the States. Jack had befriended him at a function. Jack could smell the money. He was glad to be able to recommend Sarah. 'She's a wonder with the kid. Real golden lass her. She'd do a grand job for you.'

Sarah was summoned to meet John and Stella Roberts at their grandiose Wentworth home. As if they knew what to look for.

At the gate that wouldn't budge at her shoving hand she waited, expecting someone to trundle down from the house to open it for her. Sarah was oblivious to the tinny voice that crackled from the electronic grill on the wall. Eventually Stella Roberts spotted the heavily wrapped form of the new nanny on the video entry screen and let her in with the stab of a button.

Sarah watched, like a retarded yokel, the swinging gates that magically invited her to enter. She treated them with caution as she scrambled onto the gravel drive beyond the wrought iron entrance. You couldn't trust things that move without anyone touching them. In Sarah's book this was a very mystical happening. It was amazing the similarity between employer and employee.

Stella Roberts greeted Sarah, and displaying a glued smile showed her to a Charles II reproduction chair in the lounge overlooking an Italian Garden.

'We have heard a lot about you, Sarah,' Mrs. Roberts started.

'Oh,' Sarah mumbled. Her head was bowed. She dodged the compliment.

'It appears you have made quite an impression with the couple you baby-sit for. You obviously have dealt with many youngsters. Looked after kids that is.' If only Stella Roberts had known.

'I done some.' Sarah was only going that far.

'We have two adorable kids. You'll get on well with these guys, I can tell.' Stella Roberts reached for some photographs decorating a nearby coffee table. 'Of course they're at school right now. Tommy in reception and Lucy Marie year two at the pre prep school in the village. Do you know it?'

Sarah knew very little. 'I seen some little'uns coming through. Not sure where it is like.'

'Never mind.' Stella Roberts wasn't getting to grips with the Dorset dialect. She moved on. The photos were almost lost in her hands. 'Ah, yes, look here.' She pushed them towards Sarah.

Sarah took them as if they were tickets for the Underground, ready to pocket them without looking.

'That's Tommy on his bike. He can't ride it yet without the training wheels. Only four and a half. Always gives you a big smile. He's a very happy boy.'

Sarah held up the picture of the boy. She saw Rupert staring back. She tried to look away from the dead glare.

'And Lucy Marie is a pretty thing as you can see.'

Sarah was quick to shuffle the pack and send Rupert's accusing grin to the back.

'She's seven. Has the sweetest face. She's her Daddy's little princess. He adores his daughter.' There was a hint of jealousy in Stella's words. Disappointment but nothing malicious.

Sarah grunted softly. The girl was older than Stephie. Perhaps she would be more difficult to deal with. Sarah hadn't handled a girl of that age. Her head swayed from side to side as she looked deep into the eyes of the beaming child. Sarah was telling Lucy Marie's photograph that she had better be good. Not cause any trouble. Nanny wouldn't like that. Wouldn't want to have to deal with her.

'I am sure you will be as equally delighted by them both. We are very proud parents. Such wonderful children. Don't you agree, Sarah?'

Sarah looked up, screwed her eyes tightly closed and reopened them. Stella Roberts waited. She wanted to hear the confirmation.

'Nice children.' It was soft enough to sound convincing. 'Nice children.' Sarah repeated it, but she didn't know why. Probably to fill the silence. There was nothing else she could think of saying and Stella Roberts' moon face was seeking more.

'Now I'll call John and we can discuss all the dates and money side. He's better at that than me.'

John Roberts wasn't pleased being hailed from his phone conversation. There was money to be made on the New York Stock Exchange and he was just about to swoop on some ailing stock that he was certain would make him more than just a few bucks. He'd sell it later that week when the market picked up. He relished the game. A real vulture. He could recognise a sick company limping along Wall Street even though he had exiled himself to this miserable corner of Surrey, England.

'Yes?' He would let Stella know he was none too pleased by this intrusion. 'What's the damn urgency?' He nodded to acknowledge Sarah and clamped his eyes on his wife.

'John, this is Sarah; Sarah Bickles, the nanny.' She tried to deflect his stare. 'I think she is going to be fine. Comes recommended. I've shown her the guys' photos. Told her about the angels we've got.' Stella Roberts was babbling on and dancing around her steaming husband.

'Yeah, I know the deal. Have you sorted it all out? I really haven't got the time to be involved with the finer arrangements.' There was still time to get the deal done. He could reach his broker in time. 'Surely you can manage that.'

'There's the salary and locations to finalise. You always say you'll deal with it, now ...'

'Yeah, okay.' He had constantly insisted on being in control of the purse strings. He couldn't worm his way out of this. 'I'll take over.' With reluctance he let those easy pickings in New York slide away, and sat at the table. He wanted to smash it with his fist. He hated losing money.

'How much were you earning with your last employer?' It was more inquisition than inquiry.

Sarah stumbled. 'Well ... I were.' Did he mean Sir Peter Bassnett or Jack Gibbs? 'It were ...' Stupidly she gave her bistro wage. '... about £220 a week.'

'Weekly pay? That seems funny.' John Roberts tugged at his chin. 'Typical Brits, no wonder we are always underwriting the damn dolts.'

'John, that's not nice in front of Sarah.' Stella attempted to cushion the insult.

Sarah hadn't understood it.

'Look, Sarah, let's start off with a probation period. We'll pay you three hundred pounds a week, and see how it goes.' He was eager to get back to plucking some lame duck company with an inflated market value. 'How does that suit you?'

'Okay.' Sarah spoke without looking at him.

'Fine.' That was sorted out. John Roberts wasn't used to such mundane negotiation. 'Stella will fill you in with the dates. She's a wizard at that.'

Stella sat nearer to Sarah, aware that her husband hadn't actually given off the right vibes. 'We do travel a lot. Nice places. Do you like the sun? Do you ski?' Stella's eyes lit up.

Sarah scowled within. She wasn't keen on hot places and she had no idea how to ski. 'I ain't really done it.'

'Never mind. You might get the opportunity. Be nice to learn, eh?'

Sarah managed a feeble acknowledgement.

'Right. We are heading off to our place in the States the week after next. If you start on Wednesday then there will be time to get to know the kids before we go.' Stella studied her notepad on her knees. 'We have a cottage in New Hampshire.' A quick glance at Sarah's expression prompted her to explain. 'It's in New England, the North-East. A real wild place. Nothing for miles except mountains and trees. John likes the seclusion. Likes to be away in a secret place. Back to nature. In the summer we have boats he plays with, but this time of year we go for the snow.' It wasn't necessary to go on. Stella could see that Sarah would need to experience it for herself. It was a concept difficult for Sarah to grasp. The North American vacation notion. 'We would go for longer but John has his days to consider.' There was no way John Roberts was going to be forced into filing a tax return by staying beyond his allowance.

Sarah felt for her bag. She thought it was time for her to leave.

'And a few weeks after that we are off to the sun.' Stella grinned broadly. She loved the sun. 'Down to the Caribbean. British Virgin Islands. Have you heard of them?'

Sarah's mouth hung open. She had no idea where these islands were. 'Nope,' she uttered, still rummaging through her handbag and showing very little interest in what the woman was prattling on about. She simply wanted to be with the children. Sarah could cope with their language, but this woman had lost her. She needed to escape.

'I know this is a lot to assimilate now, but you'll get to grips with it once we are in the swing. We are a crazy family aren't we?'

There was no response from Sarah.

'Do you have a passport?' Stella quizzed.

Passport? Sarah's eyes flicked and darted.

'You haven't, have you?' Stella was reading the scared rabbit expression.

'No. I ain't got one.' Sarah's eyes were searching. *Was this going to lose her the job?*

'Get a form from the post office. John has a lawyer friend who can speed these things through. Reckons he can get them within days. Birth certificate and some photographs I think is all he'll need,' Stella instructed. 'So we will see you next Wednesday. I'm certain this is going to be enjoyable for all of us.' Stella Roberts was not as convinced as she sounded.

Sarah scooped up her coat and fled from the room. She didn't bother to put it on or hang her bag from her shoulder. Her head was buzzing and sizzling with confusion as she scurried up the drive. A determined absconder.

When Sarah returned on the Wednesday morning she carried just one soft bag. It was all she had. In it was the sum of her life. Plain clothes of subdued colours and crushed cotton underwear. There was no jewellery or the onerous paraphernalia of a complicated life. It hadn't taken her long to remove her meagre possessions from the crummy flat in Surbiton.

Stella Roberts had kept the children home so that they could meet their new nanny. She was quick to haul Sarah from the front door into a room that had obviously been jettisoned as living quarters and invaded by the most notorious demolition squad. It was a disaster zone. An excess of expensive toys were scattered over every inch of the floor. Some in the pattern of a discarded game that had long since been trodden on as another, more vigorous, activity had overrun it. Besides the general battlefield debris there were dolls tossed about like contorted corpses and lengths of toy train track spearing cardboard boxes. Boxes that seemed more of a delight than the presents that had arrived in them. And it was in these boxes, or at least nestling beneath a small mountain of them that the muffled sound of chortling children could be heard. Voices of mischief and conspiracy.

Sarah picked out a path between the strewn playthings as she followed behind the waddling backside of Stella Roberts.

'Hello! Where are you guys?' She pulled at some of the lower boxes. 'The rascals are having a game with us.' Stella spoke to Sarah through puffing breath. 'Come on out you little horrors.' A playful phrase so near the truth.

Sarah did nothing to help and let the American struggle to extract her little brats.

The first out was a small, wiry boy. He lashed at his mother's dragging arms. 'We were playing. You've spoilt our game,' he groaned.

From inside the barricade a voice reiterated the complaint. 'Yeah! We were having fun. You always ruin it.'

Stella lunged at the girl's waving arm that protruded from the pile of cardboard and pulled a protesting daughter from her hideaway.

Without speaking, but with the facial expression of an executioner, Stella smoothed the crumpled clothing of the two reluctant children and pushed them towards Sarah.

She was forced to speak. Her hands were clasped, and her head bowed so that her eyes were barely level with their heads. 'Hello, my name is...er...Sarah.' It was as if she had a problem remembering her identity.

The children swapped knowing glances. They were both receiving the same message. A nanny that was easy meat. It could mean a whole new ballgame.

'This is Tommy.' Stella had regained some composure and pushed the boy gently forward. 'And this young lady is Lucy Marie.'

Lucy Marie brushed her mother's hand aside. She wasn't going to be forced towards the dreary woman. In fact she wasn't going to be forced to do anything.

A nodding of the head displayed Sarah's acknowledgement of the two children. Their responses were grim stares. They were used to retaliation.

'Now, if you would like to spend an hour or so with them in here, just to get to know each other, then I will show you to your room afterwards. How's that?' Stella knew it wasn't a smooth start and was retreating as gracefully as possible.

In silence they stood; the two terrors and their pitiful minder. There was no battle of the eyes. Sarah was surveying the room, getting her bearings.

Lucy Marie broke the calm. 'What did you say your name was?' An unpleasant questioning.

It could have been war straight away. Fortunately Sarah resisted a strong urge to discipline her.

'I'm your nanny. You can call me nanny.' That's what she wanted. It was necessary. There was more status in that. Sarah was a dull name that was part of her other life where she was the butt of jokes. Now she was nanny and that was what these kids would call her.

'Nanny?' questioned Lucy Marie to herself.

Tommy held on to his sister's arm and looked into her face. They swapped nonchalant expressions and pulled each other back towards their game in the iceberg of cardboard boxes. They would talk about the nanny later. Far more important was to immerse themselves in the protective pockets they had hewed from the beige packing cases. Their spaces and places in a drama that only a child's imagination could stage.

Sarah moved cagily, inspecting the discarded toys and the impedimenta of their childhood. Her own dismal years as a kid flashing through her mind. She picked up the occasional separated limb and pushed it back into the gaping socket of the disabled doll. Lucy Marie took a delight in ripping off the arms and legs of even her most expensive toys during some memorably violent games.

For the most part Sarah was ignored. Her slow progress from Wendy house to wooden garage, from a Lego explosion to a teddy bears' graveyard neither observed nor an excursion of interest.

It was about half an hour before the voices ceased and the scratching from inside the cardboard heap subsided. Sarah had stopped and crouched at a jumble of books, arranging them neatly on a low pine bookshelf.

'What you doing? That's our stuff.' Lucy Marie ruled the playroom. This was her patch and she was going to exert her authority.

Sarah looked up. The child had her hands on her hips and legs astride. Her gaze was steely and her intention sculpting her rigid lips. Tommy was a lieutenant close behind her; his arms crossed and his head nodding.

Nothing was said. They watched their nanny rise from her haunches and stretch herself tall. Sarah was not the brightest button but she knew it was now that she had to establish the pecking order. She pinched her face by tightening the muscles around her mouth, and aimed missile eyes at the disobedient children.

It was Tommy who was first alert to the danger. He stepped back and lowered his arms. Lucy Marie remained outwardly defiant, but her stomach was telling her that this nanny was no push over.

'The books were untidy. A mess. I don't like messes.' It was a mechanical voice, the product of deep-seated annoyance. 'I don't want messes, I don't.'

Lucy Marie played with her nails, picking viciously at her left thumb. Now her head was tilted and her shoulders slumped. The wind visibly removed from her sails.

The children were near to tears when their mother returned.

'What a great picture this would make.' Stella Roberts was pleased to see her unruly children quelled and she was happy that they weren't an embarrassment. 'Well, you seem to have got to know each other. Sarah, come this way and I'll show you where you'll be staying.'

The children watched their mother guide Sarah gently through the door and deep into the house. They stood in silence, awkward about their feebleness. For the rest of the day their play would be subdued and apologetic. Something near trauma.

Sarah's room was bright and clean with a pleasant view over the rear garden; guest accommodation not far from the children's rooms.

'The bathroom's in there, and here you can hang your clothes.' Stella pulled at a sliding door to expose a roomy wardrobe. She glanced at Sarah's meagre bag, thought a lot but said nothing.

Later, when the house was quiet, Sarah would smuggle her tired clothes into the hanging space and shut the door on them.

Chapter 4

In the short time Sarah spent in the Roberts' Wentworth house she was able to form a fairly reliable impression of her new employers and their *adorable* children. Established were the long lists, on both sides, of mannerisms and attitudes that were found to range from simply tiresome to downright frustrating.

John Roberts was permanently on the phone. A threatening, barking voice erupting from his office. No one pulled the wool over his eyes, no one sold him short. It was a tough world out there and he'd tamed his precinct and now he wasn't allowing anyone to muscle in on territory so fiercely fought over. Even thousands of miles from the rectilinear thoroughfares of New York he was a dirty street fighter, unrelenting in his pursuit of the easy buck. Undeterred by the casualties left in the wake of his financial manoeuvres. And unforgiving in his criticism of his adopted country.

Stella Roberts didn't show her wealth by dripping in fabulous jewellery. She wasn't pretty enough, nor did she have the body to exhibit her seedy affluence like a mannequin. Unrestricted use of a gold credit card and frequent sorties to Oxford Street and *By Appointment* stores in the hinterland was her way of raising the profile. Motherhood hadn't quite been the joy she had expected, and although she loved Lucy Marie and little Tommy very much she somehow felt she wasn't in control; a lost soul, perhaps not bright enough to grasp her role in parenting. The children in turn had grabbed the initiative and were certainly at the helm. They had poor Stella just where they wanted. They were the puppet masters.

The Roberts were quick to discover that their new nanny wasn't a bundle of fun. In fact a little too dour in their opinion. Not that it really mattered, they weren't going to socialise, and as long as she did her job efficiently they were quite happy. As long as she kept the kids out of mischief and out of their hair she would be fine. An English nanny was still a status symbol to take to the States despite some recent bad press. It took away the pressure, a shock absorber. They could pretend that they were perfect parents from that distance. Even fool themselves.

Sarah was quick to get into a routine. There was a stand off situation at first, with Lucy Marie withdrawn and Tommy fidgety and insecure. But it didn't take long before new parameters were established. The children weren't going to cross their nanny; they would save any devilment for their mother.

Nanny watched them as they dressed. Pointed them to the bathroom. Beckoned them to breakfast. Hardly a word was said. Pushed them into the car. Ran them to nursery and school. Lucy Marie directing a woefully disorientated nanny along a maze of country roads.

'I'll know it soon.' Sarah broke the silence. She needed the girl now. It was important she didn't cock things up.

'Yes, I expect so.' Lucy Marie meant *I bet you don't you bitch!* but it was a time for seeming to talk peace.

Even Tommy was joining in the polite exchange. 'You know, my school is just down there,' he said, pointing to an approaching turning.

Stella Roberts was a little concerned when Sarah hadn't arrived back by eleven that morning. Without her navigator the return trip had been a mystery tour around the narrow lanes of rural Berkshire. At the best of times Sarah Bickles was a lousy driver, but the combination of this inadequacy and the tricky outward journey had completely bamboozled nanny on her initial outing in the family's Mercedes. And lack of familiarity with the geography of the area didn't help.

A concerned mother ran to meet the arriving car when it eventually found home close to midday.

'Are you all right? Where have you been all this time?'

Stella wanted to say, *Is the car okay? Boy, you are late,* but chose an outwardly more caring approach.

'I got lost. It's a bit strange round here. Not sure where I was, like.' Sarah felt foolish and she didn't enjoy having to explain her stupidity to the hunting eyes of her employer.

'Easily done. But you should have phoned. I was concerned, Sarah.' In other words, *wake up on the communications front, dear.* Stella was not pleased by this incident.

Dinner that evening was the first meal that Sarah ate with the whole family. Stella had accompanied Sarah when she went to collect the children from school, so ensuring there was no repeat of the morning incident and that they would all be present at dinnertime.

John Roberts ruled mealtimes. A real bully. He sat at the head of the table where he could control every aspect and every diner.

'So, Sarah, how was your day?' In his bunker he had been busy viewing the gains on his stock and was unaware of the morning's circuitous school run. 'Settling in?' John Roberts hailed the first course of the meal with a swinging arm. Stella went running.

'Good. I'm getting to know things.' Sarah poked at her salad and didn't look up. Her voice trapped between her mouth and the table.

'And the kids, how have they been?' Both children lifted their heads and gave their father a beaming smile, which he returned with interest. 'They're little darlin's aren't they.' A further exchange of grins.

'They've been fine.' Another mumbled reply into her starter.

'Unfortunately Sarah got lost this morning.' Stella used the opportunity to say what she really thought. 'Had me a little worried, I can tell you.' Her eyes opened wide and her head nodded.

'Lost?' John Roberts pricked up. 'What, with the guys on board?'

'No, when I left them, like.' With her voice a little louder the

Dorset twang seeped through.

'I'm a great believer in safety. When the children are in the car you have got to be vigilant, Sarah. You must take care in everything you do.' It was the beginning of a lecture that his wife supported with frequent but gentle nods of the head and pouted lips. 'They're precious to us, these youngsters. We feed them the right food and make sure they get the right vitamins.' He looked to Tommy and Lucy Marie as if asking for a big *thank you* from them for the cardboard flavour of soya milk and time spent chewing broccoli stalks. It wasn't acknowledged. 'Don't we, guys?' No contribution from either of them. He continued undaunted. 'So, when they're with you it is important to think *safety* at all times. Don't you agree, Sarah?'

Knowing that she better had, Sarah concurred with a nod. 'Yes.'

'I know you English aren't always as diligent as us Americans. Possibly a historical explanation.' John Roberts could sense he was speeding into Anglophobe mode and pulled off at an escape road. 'Only kidding.' His face filled with false apology.

For the rest of the meal everyone sat in silence except for the jolting pronouncements of John Roberts, who was describing in fine detail to Stella his present bible of wise consumption. Some quasi-medical book about eating according to your blood type.

Sarah and the children scratched at their plates as John Roberts continued through a fresh fruit dessert. He was on to the prospect of a world catastrophe as a result of pollution in the old Soviet Union, and other unrelated topics such as the beneficial qualities of Ginko trees. And decaffeinated coffee was sipped to his predictions of success and failure of emerging software firms on the Nasdaq.

Stella Roberts was from simple stock. An Appalachian girl from a huge family crammed into a ridge-top shack. Inbreeding had sentenced many of her brothers and sisters to fits, sickly childhoods and lives of poverty. Stella stood out. A relatively pretty thing who didn't have special needs at school. Getting out of the mountains and heading for New Jersey was her best move. But there was no escaping the raw truth. She was pretty dumb. And whatever her husband said, she believed. She was his disciple. Any proclamation by this bumptious man was given extra kudos by his wife. Her adoption of an opinion was taken to a degree of fanaticism. So if he reckoned a certain B vitamin combated lung infection she spread the gospel. No one was allowed to hold a contradictory or doubting position.

There were no worse people to invite to a dinner party or even a casual evening drink. The Roberts were asked on many occasions. Invitations were readily sent in the beginning. But only the once by each couple. Never to be repeated. The bore and the fixated adherent. Neither was smart enough to realise the nature of the hostility. They put it down to a further indication of the unfriendliness of the English. *Cold nation filled with cold people, quite different from the North American culture,* John would muse. But he'd left that club before he could be thrown out. He fooled himself if he thought that he would have a posse of friends back in the States. There were few people who could stomach the arrogant business shark and his parrot wife.

In the next few days Sarah would discover that the children were equally disliked. She may not have worked it out that this was caused by the frequent exposure to *the world according to John Roberts* and the fan club devotion of their mother; plus a completely incompetent attempt at parenthood. But she knew she had her work cut out.

Lucy Marie had been spoilt since birth, and was fully established as a selfish little madam. Of course it didn't help when the chosen one who had been worshipped above all else was betrayed by the birth of her brother, Tommy. Tommy had tantrums on occasions but he wasn't really a match for his belligerent sister. He had escaped the worst excesses of Lucy

Marie, and given a fresh start, away from the contaminating family, he would have had a good chance of turning out relatively free of the Roberts' curse.

Out of school time Sarah was required to supervise their play, prepare meals and to attend to all matters relating to getting them in and out of bed. Whenever she was in their company there was the atmosphere of an uneasy truce. Particularly where lines had originally been drawn; the playroom. There was no longer the frivolous abandon of previous amusement. Like nervous birds wary of a growing shadow, the children sat close together. Safer like that. Some comfort in your sibling being there. And like self-conscious starlings they tinkered with small plastic toys such as farmyard animals and the cast of a dispersed board game that happened to be lying there. It wasn't a real activity. No purpose, save avoiding the wrath of nanny. No attempt was made to take on extravagant physical gestures, or bound from one elaborate game to another. Soft, muffled, penitent sounds replaced the riotous yells of the old recreation. A poisonous silence kept them in place.

Sarah's commands were single words, emphasised by an accompanying facial expression that spoke louder than the utterance. She had the children where she wanted them. They, however, were treading water. It wasn't over yet. Sarah shouldn't have been complacent.

For the rest of the time the Roberts family were in England nothing changed. Every evening meal was dominated by the decrees of John Roberts and the encores of Stella Roberts, and nanny dealt with two apparently docile kids; much to the relief of their mother. Nanny was doing well.

Sarah pressed the swelling children's winter clothes in the hard shells of the suitcases and pushed her miserable belongings into her soft bag. The taxi would collect them at eight in the morning. When the children slept she picked open the tight pages of her new passport. She put it to her nose. It smelled of Government offices. At the back she studied her grim face; sour and complaining beneath the imprisoning plastic.

The prospect of her first flight and visiting the United States kept Sarah tracing the folds in the bedroom curtains and thumping her pillow into knotted bundles, until the sliding grey of morning crept into her room.

Chapter 5

It was as if you were stepping into the picture adorning the tin-lid of a tacky assortment of Christmas biscuits. A photograph filling one wall in a 1970s semi-detached. Drama for a grey urban monotony.

Forest, mountain and lake grew out of each other and filled every inch of land below a thin line of watery-blue sky. Greens crashed with steel-greys, and deep, hollow browns were stuck shadows cast by strident black basalts. A thug of a landscape.

Noises of an unseen army of creatures spun from the heavy foliage. Sometimes spilling out of barricade undergrowth or soaring away from guardian pines like dark missiles.

The White Mountains, New Hampshire, USA. Pick-up truck and baseball cap country. Defiant people proudly displaying *Live Free or Die* on their registration plates. A cross section from affluence to poverty, though not always apparent from their dress sense. Baggy denim dungarees and their winter coat of thick check shirts; a uniform for this area of New England.

The Roberts' cottage that was marooned at a lake edge wasn't a cottage at all. It was a large estate, and consisted of numerous buildings that covered an area equal to four football pitches. John Roberts had bought neighbouring properties to extend his original holiday home and to ensure anybody he hadn't sanctioned wasn't going to live next door to him. Best of all, for John Roberts, was the isolation. Well away from the pollution and the threat of kidnapping. His lovely children were safe there.

A main house, Camp Falcon, occupied a prominent position on Buttress Headland amidst sporadic pines, and below it was a timber boathouse topped by the Stars and Stripes. As you moved away from the house the other buildings gradually got shabbier and less important. A chopped-wood store was the last structure before the thick forest that was the boundary of the property. Such a dispersed arrangement and the separating landscape demanded year-round upkeep. There was a caretaker, Bobby Clayman.

Bobby met them at the heavy wooden gates when they arrived from the airport. John Roberts had driven the Suburban from Boston with Stella in the front and Lucy Marie, Tommy and nanny in the back. The highways were good but it was a six mile motor-cross track to reach the property. And at this time of year the dirt track was deeply rutted and covered with an icing of fresh snow over the frozen mud ridges. A journey that threw the occupants about like a fairground ride. Staggering travellers lurched from the vehicle when it arrived.

'Hi there Bobby.' John Roberts greeted his employee. 'How are things?' An enquiry out of habit, not concern.

'Just dandy, boss.' Bobby was a good worker, but the lights were dim. He'd missed out on education after some spasmodic early schooling. 'You had a fine journey? Hello there ma'am.' Bobby welcomed Stella as she rounded the car, treading carefully to avoid some dark pools of muddy water. 'Good to see you.'

'This damn place is always wet. Look at the state of my shoes. These cost me a lot of money.' There was no reciprocation of the greeting. Bobby was a buffoon and she was more interested in getting inside the house and out of the sticky quagmire.

'Grab these cases, Bobby.' John Roberts was organising the unloading of the Suburban. 'Just stuff them in the entrance hall and I'll deal with them later on or in the morning.' He tugged luggage from the back of the vehicle and loaded up his caretaker.

Tip-toeing round the car, leading two comatose children, Sarah was nearly floored by the bustling Bobby Clayman struggling under the weight of Stella's wardrobe suitcase.

'Sorry ma'am.' He tottered on the spot; the heavy load

unsteady in his arms.

Sarah swayed with him, as if hypnotised by his movement. She watched his startled face and examined his alien dress; a red scarf round his throat, braces drawing lines across his felt shirt and tight jeans stuck into calf-length leather boots. And a huge deerskin-handled Bowie knife at his waist. Topped at the end by a large silver teardrop. As big as a short sword. Like someone out of an old cowboy film, she thought. Davy Crocket.

'Didn't startle you did I?' Bobby stood a little steadier, but obviously precariously balanced.

'No. We're all right.' Sarah was sheepish. This man was a handsome fellow in her book, and he seemed very concerned about her.

'Oh, this is the new nanny, Bobby. Sarah meet Bobby. He does a good job round here. Looks after the place.' John Roberts had come from the boot and interrupted the stand-off.

'Sarah. That's a good name. One of my cousins in Wisconsin goes by the name of Sarah. Right fine-looking woman I recall.' Bobby shifted a foot to keep the case from slipping. 'I best get this baggage stacked. See you about the place. Nice meeting you.' Bobby tilted as he tried to remove a boot now stuck fast in the mud. The case rocked. With a slurp he was free and lumbering forward. He lifted his right hand to attempt a farewell salute. A fatal move. The weighty case slid sideways, slammed into the bog and embedded itself upright in the stiff sludge. A ridiculous monolith in the fading light.

Everyone slept beyond sunrise. There was no real noise to wake them. The scurrying of the squirrels through the pine needle debris and the quarrelling twitter of fickle finches disturbed no one. Even John Roberts wasn't up and on the hunt; chasing a crippled dog of a company, ready to pounce on its ailing stock values. It had been a tiring journey and the usual alarm clocks in the house, the children, were still thrown about their beds like rag dolls when Sarah went to organise them and thrust them into their snow suits.

It was late morning before the house was filled with the sounds of cursing adults and giggling children. Sarah was getting her bearings whilst the kids played in camps and fantasy caves that they had built or invented during their last trip. Stella and John were busy in conference in the kitchen, complaining about all the things that Bobby hadn't done in their absence. Upstairs Sarah sneaked into the master bedroom. The bed linen was crumpled like a chain of fold mountains, creamy white, snow-covered ripples smoothed by millenniums of weathering. Clothes lay where they had been scattered in the desperation of exhaustion, abandoned in haphazard creased piles. Sarah poked her head into the bathroom. Towels had received the same treatment as the discarded clothes; dollops of mashed potato on chairs and floor. Lingering in the damp air was the sour aroma of *Freedom by Tommy*. Stella hadn't gone through the whole routine but she had made certain she smelled like a woman with taste. A walk-in wardrobe displayed the corrugated edge of Stella Roberts impeccable line of dresses. Sarah touched the shoulders of some as she stole past. Usually the ones that glittered, or silky ones made of satin. His trousers and jackets hung there too. They were dull suits; greys and browns. Sarah moved past them quickly. She was reminded of him. Could see his milky eyes. Could feel the cold stare. She raised and lowered her head like an elevator as she followed the rows of shelves. Surveying all their belongings. So many clothes. So much money spent dressing themselves up. She thought of her own miserable garments. It hurt.

Lucy Marie and Tommy were back on familiar territory and reasserting themselves. This was their patch. Every tree and shadowy nook and cranny they had explored. Nanny was the newcomer. Off guard. There were opportunities here to get one over on the cow. And in a conspiratorial huddle, in a snow-banked lair, they dreamed up some surprises for their nanny.

'...spoils all our fun. It's not been the same since she came.' Lucy Marie undressed a doll in the wooden camp while Tommy poked at the soil with a stick.

He didn't look at his sister, but he barked his agreement. 'Yeah!'

'So, we need to get our own back. Have you seen the way she looks at us? It's weird, really weird.' Lucy Marie tugged at the doll's dress.

'Yeah.' Tommy tried to write his name in the earth as he grunted his concurrence. 'What we goin' t'do, then?' He could only fit the first two letters on the patch of bare ground, so he decided to thrash at the walls where some honeysuckle had pushed through in the summer and was now bone brittle.

'I'm thinking. Bound to be something we can do that'll give her a fright, eh?' Lucy Marie yanked at an obstinate sleeve that her doll appeared to be holding on to. 'I've got a few ideas. We'll need to plan it. Make sure it works.' Her eyes were small now. Pin pricks on her screwed-up face. 'Get her back. That's what we'll do.'

Tommy recognised the viciousness in his sister. He'd seen it before, when she had chased him like a wild cat and hit him repeatedly with a log, and when she had been cruel to a neighbour's rabbit; poking it with a metal tent peg through the wire netting of its cage until the white fur turned pink with escaping blood. But it was her laughter that haunted him, the apparent enjoyment. He gulped quietly and concentrated on the end of his stabbing stick. Tommy couldn't chase the rabbit incident away. His lips quivered. Lucy Marie had had that look then. More than just menace.

Bobby Clayman's truck swerved onto the property just as Sarah was looking for the children. They weren't coming to her call and were still plotting in the camp. Nanny would make them regret being troublesome.

'Hi there Sarah.' Bobby touched the brim of his hat. A subservient greeting.

'Hello.' It was broad Dorset. The final letter was dragged out and completed with high note escaping from rounded lips. No one had given her such attention before.

'You lookin' for them youngsters? Real rascals them kids.'

Bobby wanted to talk. He found it difficult to approach women, but this awkward chicken from England was as gawky as him. It was almost chemistry.

'I'll find 'em, in the end.' Sarah too was warming to the caretaker. Even her missing delinquent charges weren't urgently sought. 'You dry now? Bit of a mud bath wasn't it?' Sarah reminded him of his comic act the previous night. This was a speech compared to her normal economy of words.

'Oh, yeah, done m'self up real well.' Bobby stuck a gormless look on his face, pressing his lips together in a sort of pout and raising his eyebrows in the shape of rainbows. 'Bet you thought I was a darn fool.'

'Just an accident. Not your fault.' Sarah smiled with her chin and her eyes. She wasn't used to that. It felt foreign.

'Nice of you ma'am. Don't feel so bad. You're a good soul.' Bobby touched his hat brim and strolled off towards the main house, turning several times to exchange glances with Sarah, who watched his progress, harbouring an extraordinary warmth for the man.

When she found the children in their hiding place she almost forgot to be surly, and didn't even frogmarch them back to their meal. Lucy Marie sensed the change, and thought nanny had some idea about the planned campaign that she and Tommy had been plotting.

John and Stella Roberts had very different agendas. John had been brought up with summers spent around boats at the family cottage on a lake. He was going through the motions of being a boy again, except he could now boast an assortment of high-powered motorboats.

Stella travelled in the opposite direction. She headed, as soon as possible, for town. Turning her back on the lake and her husband's ridiculous pastime of messing about with his fleet of watercraft. There were fascinating stores to explore. A magnetism that Stella's urges would not repel. A clinging attraction. It was pure therapy.

With the parents out of the way Sarah could relax. In their

presence she would ensure she maintained a version of the dutiful nanny. Now, in their absence, she could stalk the children at the meal table, glower at their appalling manners, make threatening gestures at any lack of appetite and promise a thoroughly gruesome time if rules weren't obeyed.

For Lucy Marie it fuelled her hostility towards nanny and reinforced her commitment to vengeance. She would talk to Tommy after they had been put to bed. Creep into his room before the young boy had fallen asleep. He usually drifted off quickly so there would be only a narrow crevasse of opportunity. She had a plan. It was from a book that her father had shown her. The way they captured bears in that area long ago. There was that or the bridge.

Stella and John Roberts were not back before Sarah demanded that the miscreant kids got ready for bed. She snatched the dirty garments from the children as soon as they were tugged off. A quick hand almost tore their hair as it swung and grabbed the lifted clothing. Sarah could sit down in the den and flick through the maze of channels once she had ordered Lucy Marie and Tommy upstairs. With their parents not present there was no need to accompany them with the gentle encouragement that Sarah usually murmured as she took them to their rooms. A guiding hand. A nanny who cared. No need to act it out now.

Sarah zapped from incomprehensible adverts to American football to quiz games to soap operas. An absorbing fantasy at the stab of a button. She was giggling at sudden faces appearing, the flashes of programmes and their instant demise. She had the power to choose. She was in charge. Now Sarah would wait until a character's close-up face spoke and then she would cut him off in mid sentence and throw up the swinging arm of a baseball striker's scything shot, or into the earnest explanation of a wonder tool that achieved everything and was guaranteed for ever.

In the mountains the weather can suddenly change. Ask any guide who has seen sunshine and endless blue skies become the most hostile and terrifying maelstrom he has ever encountered. At the cottage the next morning the sitting snow and ice were warmed by a frontal system that threatened to flood much of the low-lying areas.

'We get these melts some times ma'am,' Bobby explained to Sarah as she goaded the children out through the screen door the following morning. 'Temperature really rockets. Like summer over night.'

'Nice not to freeze,' Sarah brightly responded, and wrapped her arms round herself to imitate the motion of keeping warm.

'Next time you're feeling kinda cold ma'am you can count on me to supply some heat.' Bobby gulped, not meaning to be that forward.

Sarah smiled with her eyes and tilted her head. She was flattered. It was the first time anyone had even hinted at being interested in her. No, she must be imagining it, misconstrued what Bobby was saying. She would need more evidence than this to believe Bobby Clayman was chatting her up.

'Want to keep me warm?' It was bold and out of character. Sarah looked at the floor and waited.

'Sure do ma'am,' he spluttered.

'I see.' Sarah walked away, leaving Bobby with the most ridiculous grin stuck on his face. She had said things that she would need to sort through, away from the drooling cowboy.

The children had disappeared again by the time Sarah had shuffled away from the amorous caretaker. They had some serious scheming to do and used the opportunity of this encounter to slide off into favourite corners of the property to begin their project.

'This will do,' announced Lucy Marie, halting in her tracks and laying down the snow shovel.

'Where?' questioned Tommy as he beat more long dry grass with another stick.

'Just here,' she added, drawing a large circle over the ground with her finger. 'About this size should do. That ugly cow would fit in this big a hole.'

'So we got to dig it out. Just us? It'll be hard.' Tommy wasn't enthusiastic.

'Ground's all mushy now, shouldn't be too bad.' She grabbed his stick and dug it into the soil and pulled it clear with a sucking gurgle. Lucy Marie attempted to encourage him. 'See, goes in great.'

She made the first cut with the shovel, removing a large piece of turf and exposing the black soil. This somehow motivated Tommy. He could see the vulnerable nature of this dark pulp and grabbed the long handle of the implement. There were lusty jabs at the soil at first, but these became weak pokes, and there was little effort to scrape out the loosened earth.

'Let me have a go.' Lucy Marie stepped in when she saw her brother was flagging. But even she didn't last long at the task, and was soon sitting on the lip of the hole sighing with the tedium of exertion.

By lunchtime they had barely achieved a shallow depression, but had managed to cover most of their clothes, engrain their hands and embed their fingernails with the dark soil.

'Wash up,' their mother told them when she saw her grubby children. Soft encouraging words that recognised the energy of mischief. Sarah spoke her annoyance with her eyes. Stella would blame her for the state of the children. They'd pay for that.

'What on earth have you been doing?' John Roberts bumped into Lucy Marie and Tommy heading for the bathroom. 'Looks like you've been mining.' He too shook his head with a kind of acknowledgement and condoning.

Both children fended off Sarah's steady glare throughout the meal and were invigorated by a greasy fare of chicken wings and beans. And when Sarah trundled out with dishes and helped Stella load the dishwasher, they escaped again.

'Shot out of here like bullets,' announced John Roberts when nanny came back with searching eyes and fallen chin.

'They're little rascals today, eh?'

'Yes.' John Roberts didn't detect Sarah's lethal tone.

Lunch seemed to have made the difference. Tommy dug like a miner and Lucy Marie efficiently shovelled out the loose material. She didn't appreciate the success until she felt herself now leaning precariously downwards to reach the mushy soil, and the hole seemingly eating up her brother's spindly legs.

'Big, sharp sticks. That's what they have.' Lucy Marie spoke as she tilted forward for more soil. 'To get the bears. Long and pointed.' She mused to herself.

'Sticks? What for?' Tommy parked the spade and quizzed his sister.

'To catch bears, you dink. When they fall in the pit the sharpened sticks go into them. That's how they catch bears.' Lucy Marie was proud of her hunting knowledge.

'So we're going to catch us a nanny is that right?' Tommy's smirking face asked.

'Sort of. Best we don't use those sticks though, eh?' Lucy Marie wasn't totally convinced that keeping the sticks was a bad idea.

'What then?' Tommy's head was the only part of him protruding from the pit. 'If we ain't going to use the sticks what can we use.'

'I'm thinking.' Lucy Marie was half lying down on the ground, supporting her head with a bent arm. 'It's got to be something nasty, something that she don't like.'

In the house Sarah had finished helping Stella and gone up to her room. The Roberts were going into town so she decided that she would have a short nap. The kids were around and being awkward but they were safe enough. Sure, if their parents were about she would have to be out there with them or looking for them. But now she could take it easy.

Her room was pleasant enough, and as she lay on the soft quilt cupping the back of her head with her hands she surveyed it once more. Sleep hijacked her inspection.

'Look!' shouted Lucy Marie.

Tommy jerked his head upward and followed Lucy Marie's finger. 'What?'

Through a gap in the trees, that separated the Roberts' property from the Goldman's, their neighbour's golden Labrador was arched-backed and straining, his back legs slightly overtaking his front ones as he forced. A facial expression that urged it out. Like the smooth exit of toothpaste from its tube, the turd was delivered, and in its landing promptly curled up into a perfect coil, the last pointed inch slapping down flat with the rest.

'That's disgusting,' announced Tommy, his fingers pinching his nose.

'Yeah, I know. It really is gross.' Lucy Marie tried to smother her laughter. 'But, think of this, a pit full of all that dog shit. Now, it wouldn't be nice to fall in that would it, Tommy?'

'No, that would make me sick.'

'Think of nanny falling in, Tommy, think of that.' The laughter escaped. A harsh and impish cackle.

Tommy laughed as well. His low and nervous; a doubting laugh quite unlike his demonic sister.

'Keep digging, Tommy, and then we can go and collect all the dog shit we can.' Lucy Marie was enthusiastic about her plan.

'You sure about this,' Tommy asked, as he dug slowly at the bottom of the hole. His imagination getting the better of him he danced with his feet as if to avoid stinking excrement.

'Yeah. We only need a few more inches and then we can collect the dog stuff and put the top on.'

'Top?' enquired Tommy.

'Got to make it look normal haven't we, dummy?' Lucy Marie sensed Tommy wasn't one hundred percent behind the scheme. 'Just some thin branches and a scattering of leaves and grass should do it.'

The last couple of inches took a long time. Tommy had slowed right down and sloppy with his spadework.

Sarah didn't hear the door of her room open, but when he

stepped on the creaky floorboard the groaning noise woke her up.

'What you want?' Sarah shot up into a sitting position and confronted the intruder.

'Sorry ma'am, really am, so sorry.' Bobby grabbed at his hat and held it to his chest and gave a quick tilt forward like a bow.

'What you doing in here?' Sarah asked, leaning on an elbow and creasing her brow.

'Mr. Roberts wanted me to check this there wiring going down the upstairs level, ma'am. Didn't know you was in bed like.' Bobby felt for the door handle behind him. A crimson hue stung his cheeks. 'Right sorry for the intrusion.'

'It's all right. Not your fault.' Sarah managed a smile. It was a new emotion.

'It's right lonesome for you out here isn't it ma'am? I mean the land's mighty handsome all right, but now'n' again you need some life. Don't you agree?' It was a crude attempt at chatting her up.

'What do you mean?' Sarah wasn't quick at detecting his motive.

'Well, for me, I can go back to the town and have myself a drink and listen to a band on a Saturday night. Get away from the forest noises. Hear some of those human sounds. You though, you're stuck here.'

'Suppose so. Don't really think about it.'

Bobby summoned up the courage. 'How about coming to town next Saturday? I'll show you around. Take you to the club.'

Sarah smiled a thin-lipped grin of resignation and nodded her assent.

'Great. I'll pick you up at seven. You sure the Roberts are goin' to okay it?'

Sarah nodded again. She would make sure that Stella let her out. They kept her cooped up enough as it was. There was no way they could stop her going out once. What an adventure.

Bobby smiled to himself as he left the room and strode down the corridor. He was proud of his audacity. Asked her out and she had accepted. Quite a guy.

Lucy Marie and Tommy trudged back to the house even dirtier than they were in the morning. They too took pride in their achievement. The trap had been finished. On their clothes was the debris of undergrowth, and clinging to their shoes the dark soil and some lighter smooth edges of glued dog excrement. No matter how much they tried to avoid the curled piles in the field they had managed to stomp on some stray faeces lurking beneath leaning grasses.

Sarah wasn't as hard on them as they expected. She had some good news. A date. Bobby was taking her out on Saturday and that was going to fill her week. The devilish little children would be no more than a nagging inconvenience for a few days.

She pushed them in the shower, saw them to bed and closed the door on their wary eyes. They were almost invisible. Sarah had other images to deal with.

Occasionally that evening as she fumbled with some embroidery Stella Roberts noticed the beginnings of a smirk on the nanny's face. And as Sarah turned at the door before heading upstairs told her astonished employer of her tryst with Bobby Clayman.

Tommy and Lucy Marie slept soundly after their strenuous day, but were busy in discussion as soon as they woke. Now they had to plan the next part of their dastardly scheme.

'We go out for a walk. Appear friendly like.' Lucy Marie explained.

'Ugh!' responded Tommy. 'Nanny is a pig, nanny is a pig,' he sang with mischievous eyes and snarling teeth.

'Make her look up when we get near the trap. At a squirrel or 'coon; even the tree top.'

'Yeah!' Tommy was getting the picture. 'Splosh! Straight in to the doggy poo.' Tommy was delighted with his mental snapshot.

'We do it 'safternoon, okay?' Lucy Marie rubbed her hands. 'Before the leaves and stuff go brown.' Even she was surprised at her own intuition.

There was no mad scramble after lunch. No escape attempt. Nanny should have been curious about that. Lucy Marie and Tommy loitered by the door that led to the depths of the forest. That led to the simmering layer of dog shit that these two children were lovingly going to deposit their nanny in.

No matter how nonchalant they tried to appear, a casual observer would have easily detected the signs of excitement tinged with apprehension. Tommy with stuttering tiptoes followed the same circle on the decking just outside the door, watching every one of his own tripping steps. Lucy Marie sat on an Adirondack bench and tugged at a loose sliver of nail that obstinately refused to budge.

Nanny pushed through the screen door and surveyed her charges. From one to the other she spied; her eyes screwed up and her lips pursed as if trying to read their minds.

'What are you two doing?' Sarah asked.

Lucy Marie looked up and Tommy came to a halt.

'Can we go for a walk?' Lucy Marie ventured.

'Walk? Where to?' Nanny was confused. 'You don't usually ask me when you go walking. Just push off and I has to find you. That's the normal. Walk?'

'Thought we'd show you things. Dad's told us 'bout the wildlife and things. Lots of stuff like that.' Lucy Marie made a fair effort to sound convincing. She had a lurking fancy that she might be an actress some day.

Nanny wasn't comfortable with the offer. She squeezed her eyes together and enquired through the tight slits. Her head shook slowly from side to side. 'S'pose so.' But nanny was far from certain.

Lucy Marie led the way. She jumped the last step down from the decking. Tommy scampered after her. Nanny, with movement nowhere near as sprightly or with the same enthusiasm, followed behind.

Back in the house John and Stella Roberts shuffled around the kitchen. The stock market wasn't open, no bones to pick, and most of the shops in town were shut. So their pastimes were hit badly, and neither could think of what to do. Their movements were those of retired people in a residential home; aimless and lumbering. Stella moved things around in the kitchen as if in a wacky game of chess, and John surveyed from the window the first shoots of grass and the last remnants of the spring snow.

It was just like the wildlife to let her down. Lucy Marie was cringing at the lack of activity from the trees, and the silence from the normally twitching undergrowth. Tommy hadn't seen anything either. Surely a chipmunk would venture out. Nanny plodded on, watching her own feet at every step.

'Look! Look!' Tommy shouted, as a small bird alighted from a huge spruce.

'Yeah. Did you see that?' Lucy Marie joined in, welcoming the first sight of fauna. 'Rare one that,' she added.

Nanny puffed. She hadn't seen anything; she was too busy negotiating a muddy patch beneath the tree. And if she had, all she would have spied would have been a very ordinary finch fluttering away.

Where they had stopped was not far from the trap. Tommy couldn't stop grinning to himself. He was already picturing nanny sprawling in the doggy poo. Lucy Marie remained tense. She could sense nanny's lack of interest in the expedition. It needed to happen soon.

'Follow me, I know where there's a racoon's home.' She motioned an encouraging hand and started off. 'It's just along here.'

They were on the final stretch. Lucy Marie knew nothing of racoons and no idea where they made their homes, but she did know where there was a deep pit full of the foulest dog shit, and where she wanted her awful nanny to spend her afternoon wallowing.

It was the merest corridor of trees. Bordered by the cut back forest. Tommy could see where they had spread the leaves and scattered the grass. It seemed to shout out a warning. A definite patch; easily visible. Nanny would surely see it. Know what was up. He searched for his sister's face. Lucy Marie was holding back a smirk; her pace was quickening.

They were only twenty metres from the stinking pit, when John Roberts leapt from the forest edge.

'Hi! guys.' He yelled, smiling broadly.

'Dad?' Tommy braked, and rubbed his head. 'What you doing here?' His voice was low and he questioned his own vision. Why was his father now strolling towards them?

'Thought I'd find you kids. Nothing much happening indoors.'

Lucy Marie strained to speak. Nothing came out. It was too late anyway.

First he was there strutting forwards, and then he was no more – felled by his sinking foot that found no firm ground; that plummeted through the crisp wood and the loose covering that concealed the hideous trap. His body was thrown forward and down. Slamming through the rest of the camouflage and taking him, with a heavy splat, into the reeking shit.

Nanny only saw the last moments of his toppling body slide from view. She didn't grasp immediately what had happened.

Lucy Marie and Tommy knew only too well what their father had fallen headlong into. Their eyes were stuck wide open, and their mouths chasms that strangled urgent silent cries.

Nanny waddled forward peering at the broken earth, and listening to John Roberts' strangled groaning. The children remained statues. When she reached the pit she was still baffled by her employer's sudden disappearance, couldn't understand why there was a hole in the ground and was puzzled by the awful stench.

'Christ almighty! What happened?' John Roberts' heavily

stained head scraped through the broken twigs. A large, bewildered face smeared with several different shades of excrement. Tommy, as far away as he was, recognised the pale beige clinging to his father's left cheek. It was the very fluid diarrhoea that he had painstakingly scooped up with some pieces of bark, when his sister thought it too liquid to be any good for their prank.

It still hadn't dawned on Sarah what had happened. She looked at John Roberts standing with arms out wide wishing he had somewhere to hide. Wishing there was a body of water a pace away that he could plunge into. Nanny's eyes drifted to the broken material that had hidden the pit, then to the children struck dumb, then back to her employer reeking of shit. And it dawned. Her temperature rose and her face glowed. Her eyes shouted brutal retribution and she headed, burrowing, shoulders rounded, for the two children; their eyes twitching, their feet cement.

John Roberts sensed her mission. 'Sarah!' It was a determined call from only a slit of a mouth. He dare not open it any wider, there was dog shit sliding perilously close down his cheek. 'I'll deal with it. Don't blame them yet.' The words were strangled to a fine whistle as he sought to reduce the opening even more.

Nanny stormed straight past the kids. They felt her expelling air and the sting of her stare. Back to the cottage she flew, steam powered.

John Roberts arrived back quite a while after his fuming nanny. His journey slower and at a more deliberate pace. He walked like Dr. Frankenstein's monster. As if he had those giant leaden boots. Lucy Marie and Tommy were close behind him. Not too close, they couldn't bear that. Their father smelled like a cesspit.

The children were sent to bed early without their nanny's attendance. She was in her room from where there was no sound. John Roberts decided on a rescue mission, and once he was well showered scheduled the children for activities that he and Stella would orchestrate until the weekend.

When Bobby Clayman called late Saturday afternoon, Sarah was still fizzing with indignation and had only left her room to eat. Silent meals where she threw stiletto stares at Lucy Marie and Tommy, and where John Roberts had failed to subtly ricochet nanny's icicle gaze with talk of sudden sell-offs on the Nasdaq.

Bobby stood in the hallway nursing his baseball cap that he had removed when Stella Roberts opened the door.

'Your date's here, Sarah,' Stella announced to the closed bedroom door. 'He's waiting downstairs for you.' Stella hid her amusement with a girlish yet encouraging voice. It was a weak attempt to build bridges.

'Right.' Sarah snapped. She had felt like cancelling the night out with Bobby but concluded that at least it would take her out of the house and away from those little brats. She waited until she heard Stella leave the landing and then squeezed through the narrow gap of the door she had opened, as if it were a secret tunnel entrance. Sarah floated down the stairs clutching her handbag; her head watching her feet. Like an old lady wishing she was invisible. Her pale blue frock kissing each flight as she glided.

'You sure are looking fine.' Bobby had a simple charm.

Sarah kept her head bowed and looked at him through a gap in her fringe. Shy eyes like those of a teenager on her first date.

'Takin' you somewhere grand tonight.' Bobby was exuding pride. He slapped his cap against his chest. A guiding hand was put on Sarah's shoulder as he ushered her through the door and towards his pick-up truck outside. Hardly a coach to the ball, yet Sarah wasn't fussed about the state of the vehicle. Bobby did the gentlemanly thing and opened the passenger door for her, and then scuttled around the bonnet to take his place in the driver's seat. He tried to make it feel she was chauffeur-driven even in that wreck. He beamed at his date when he had donned his cap and was ready to transport her.

She made an effort at a smile.

Bobby had heard from John Roberts about the 'shit pit' incident but wasn't going to raise it with Sarah. So he kept her amused with tales of his work that week and eagerly pointing out houses of people he knew. Not intellectual stuff but enough to keep Sarah from revisiting her bitterness.

Once at the end of the dirt track, which served the lakeside properties, they turned north towards the small town of Clipper Lake. A smooth, uncluttered highway that carved through blasted rock outcrops and tightly packed white-pine forest. In the cab Bobby continued to monopolise the conversation; sunny smile and jaunty gesticulations.

Sarah had seen cowboy frontier towns on the television, Hollywood mock-ups that were flimsy facades, but she had no idea she would be visiting a real one that evening. Clipper Lake only lacked the dusty main street and the duelling gunmen. But there were the porches and the side alleys, the single storey buildings with shop signs perched on the roof; where snipers hid, rocking chairs accommodating street-side philosophers and the clacking and tinkling sound of boots and spurs on the resounding timber sidewalks.

Bobby parked his pick-up at an acute angle in the wide road; slung it at the building frontage as if he were a trail-weary horseman just finished driving stock and hitting the bars.

Sarah peered through the windscreen at a saloon that wouldn't have looked out of place in nineteenth century Dodge City. Most of the Stetson-hatted, cowboy-booted pedestrians swung in through the paddling doors. Country music escaped through the open sash windows. The place heaved with drinkers and loud voices clucked with laughter.

'This is it!' Bobby announced, trying to share his enthusiasm with Sarah. 'Saturday night is party night at Pippa's Place. Everyone in town'll be here.'

This was Bobby's haunt and he was excited by the prospect of showing it off. Sarah tried to shrink into her seat. She couldn't speak. Lyme Regis hadn't prepared her for this. Nothing in her insular life could help her cope with a brash American bar that thundered with corralled beer-swilling, thigh-slapping, cigarette-drawing occupants.

Bobby opened the truck door and tugged at her hand. Sarah wormed lower in the seat. Bobby, the smile still stuck on his face, pulled harder. 'You all right, girl? You're goin' to love it here. Real Yankee night life.'

Sarah's face was glued with a horror that Bobby mistook for awe. Her eyes were stretched with fright. A cat caught in the lights of a juggernaut. She didn't speak. Couldn't speak.

Bobby managed to unplug her from the seat and stand her on the path. 'I see you're a bit nervy, not knowing anyone and that. Just follow me. Got us a table.' Bobby ensnared her with his own excitement and an arm round her shoulders. Bobby thought the waist too familiar. 'Place has the finest music, ma'am. And folks are real friendly.' He pushed her forward, her unwilling legs sliding on the smooth wood.

Sarah hugged her handbag and seemed to be on skates as Bobby thread her through the other tables and the boisterous drinkers. He dragged out a wooden chair and set her down. A scared sparrow placed on its perch.

The bar clamour carried on without her. Lavish noises and glorious aromas of whiskey and cheap women.

A first drink carefully spiked had Sarah loosen the rigour mortis and place her handbag on the floor beside her. A second got her looking at her surroundings and almost smiling. By the time Bobby had encouraged Sarah to down the third she was successfully transformed.

'What they going to play next? Who's that over there, looking this way at us?' Question after question. No longer the frightened bird. The bravado of alcohol.

Bobby relaxed. His date had melted. She was in the swing now, and from then on he had to deliver the drinks kosher.

'Told you it was a great place, didn't I.' Bobby watched Sarah's silly grin and her swaying shoulders.

'Great. It's great.' Her elbows were on the table, and she was raising her eyebrows to a couple of bearded men on a neighbouring table. 'Let's have another drink.'

Bobby wasn't sure. It looked dangerously like he'd overdone it already. 'You okay, ma'am?'

'Course I am. You get them in and I'll go to the toilet.' Bourbon courage in a faded English frock.

'Bathroom? Sure. It's over there.'

Sarah tilted as she pulled herself up. It took two attempts to get her feet working in unison. She made her way to the toilet, stopping at nearly every table to broadly smile only inches from the occupants' faces.

In the bathroom it was difficult to keep her reflection still enough to refresh the hideous pink lipstick that she had purloined from Stella Roberts' dressing table. An annoyance that she reported to every occasional user of the facility. She smacked her lips and her eyes rolled. She couldn't let go of the washbasin. Finally leaving with her handbag hanging open and her teeth painted Barbie pink.

'You sure you're okay, ma'am? You ain't too steady at the moment.' Bobby stood to guide Sarah the final four yards back to her seat. His companion greeted whoever she bumped into with a steadying hand and a display of cherry pegs with every toothy grin she offered in apology.

Bobby eventually gave in. With Sarah's head ready to crash into the table he knew his evening was over. He pulled her upright from the waist and frogmarched her through taunting onlookers back to the pickup.

Bobby was cursing his tactics as he rounded the front of the vehicle, and even more so when he heard the distinct gush and slap as vomit hit the foot well in front of the passengers seat. He retraced his steps and yanked open the door. Sarah almost fell out. He sat her on the sidewalk while he collected as much sick as he could in a pad of tissue that he grabbed from the glove compartment.

When he plonked her back in the vehicle there was little

sign of Sarah's gagging, but even a heavy spray of de-icing liquid couldn't disguise the pervading stench. Bobby nearly threw up himself as he wrenched at the handbrake and hurried to let the cool evening air rush through the open windows.

Half way back to the cottage Bobby stopped to breath some forest air and empty his bladder. Even the smell of his urine was a relief from the acid air in the truck.

Sarah was stirred by the silence. She awoke to the sound of Bobby pissing. She wondered where she was, and scanned her surroundings. First the ripped roof of the cab, then Bobby's vacated seat and finally the hanging door of the glove compartment in front of her. She felt in the darkness. There was an object that was pushed well down and that had previously been hidden by the paper tissues. Sarah grabbed at the grimy handle and slid it slowly out, grating metal on metal as she withdrew it. A huge revolver.

She didn't know anything about guns. This one was dark metal and heavy for her to hold in one hand. Using both hands she laid it in her lap, where it started to sink between her legs, taking the pale blue cotton material of her dress with it. Sarah had never felt like this before. There was something erotic about this weapon and where it now sat. She stroked the barrel and fingered the chamber, felt the smoothness of the muzzle and the coolness of the metal. Alcohol was still in control, but now it had changed tactics. Sarah remained detached from her sober and dour personality. No longer tormented by nagging guts, but held on the edge of sleep. A hammock of a trance, like one induced by drugs.

A disturbing jolt broke her reverie. Bobby had jumped into the truck without her noticing, and was quick to refresh the air in the cab. He hadn't looked at Sarah, assuming she would still be comatose. He didn't see her fondling his gun, didn't see the tightness of her lips, or hear the low groaning of satisfaction as she repeatedly caressed the weapon along the silkiness of the barrel and down to the fullness of the handle. Her breathing was shallow and her eyes rolled behind closed lids. Even in the mist of her head was a recognition of its deadly authority.

At the cottage Sarah had succumbed to the rocking vehicle and the fantasy of the revolver, and slept. Bobby held the steering wheel with one hand and reached over to wake his date. There was an urgency in his movements. Stationary the truck stunk. In the dim light he didn't spot the gun, which was wedged almost out of sight between Sarah's thighs. Only when she slid out of the passenger's door did the weapon crash to the floor.

'My gun!' Bobby watched the revolver twist to a halt on the rubber mat. 'What's that doing there?' He quizzed some invisible third party.

'Gun?' Sarah's cotton wool voice murmured, hardly audible.

'Yeah, my gun's on the floor of the truck.' He leaned across to pick it up. 'I keep it in the box. Weird it should be out.'

'Gun?' Sarah muttered again. 'Yes, it was in the glove compartment. I just had a look. That all right?'

'Yeah, sure, ma'am. I was just curious. Don't like the thing being out, like.' Bobby was pissed off about it, but wasn't going to air any blame.

'Why do you have a gun?' Sarah wanted to talk about it. Even though her mouth was feeling like she had eaten a tennis ball and her legs were quivering like shaken jelly, she needed to know about the gun.

'Vermin ma'am. I needs it for the vermin.'

'Verming?' Near enough for a drunk. Sarah leaned on the open door, nearly missing her handhold.

'S'right. Squirrels mainly, grey ones. Nuisance round here. Eat the timber off the houses, some do.' Bobby was trying to soften the blow, offer some feeble excuse for his cold-blooded killing.

'Next time you do it. Next time you shoot some verming, can I watch?' Sarah's interest verged on voyeurism. She moved towards Bobby on wobbly legs. There was an eager look in her eyes. Bobby Clayman had a new attraction. Almost like a new man.

Sarah slept until midday. Her head felt twice the size and someone hammered from inside. A coating of white Styrofoam made movements of the tongue feel like manoeuvring a wire brush through her gums. And her guts ached. She thought about the gun, but only when the pain in her body allowed her.

There was a truce of sorts with the kids who were keeping well out of the way. They had learned their lesson, at least for now. Stella was quick to understand the nanny's plight.

'Been through it myself. You're not used to it dear. Bobby shouldn't have let you.' Stella moved about Sarah's body stranded in the kitchen, where she cupped a tumbler of water at the breakfast table. 'You take it easy for the rest of the day. I'll watch the children.'

John Roberts breezed through a couple of times. 'British, can't take their drink. No wonder they lost their empire.' It wasn't clear whether he was attempting humour or not. Sarah wanted to say something about a shit being covered in shit, but she wasn't able to get her tongue round such wit, especially as it was still sugarcoated and the size of a whale.

Bobby phoned to see how Sarah was feeling, but only spoke to Stella. She assured him that Sarah had survived the night, was now feeling very sorry for herself and would make a full recovery. Bobby received a sound admonishment and a lengthy lecture on alcohol abuse.

It was nearly a week before Bobby was round at the house, making repairs to the boathouse. Sarah left the children playing near the wood store and followed the path down to the lake. Her pace was noticeably quicker. A woman with a mission.

'Hi, ma'am.' Bobby yanked at his cap and nodded.

Sarah stood in front of him rocking on the spot, her lips pressed tight.

'You all right now, ma'am?' There was the tone of an apology that was echoed by his eyes.

Sarah affirmed with a gentle nodding.

'That's just fine. I'm glad.' He wasn't going to comment on the disastrous evening. Couldn't say what fun they'd had or what a great time. Anyway she probably couldn't remember anything that had happened.

But she could remember one thing.

'You doing it today?' Her first words. Leaden words from her chest.

'Doin' what, ma'am?'

'Them verming. Are you going to shoot them today?' She could feel the saliva that lubricated the words. Could feel the heavy metal of the revolver on her lap. The tugging of her dress as it slipped into the crevice between her thighs.

'Squirrels like? Well don't rightly know, ma'am. I usually catches them in them cage traps first. Then...' He didn't want to explain this part. 'Then I does it point blank in the woods, like.' There was guilt now. It's what he'd always done. Now it sounded like the Holocaust.

'You caught any yet?' Sarah was insistent.

'Sorry, ma'am.' Bobby tilted his head and shrugged his oxen shoulders. He turned to examine the panel he was fitting. Sarah seemed disappointed. Not at all interested in him. He felt a little hurt.

Sarah sat on the dock watching the convoy voyage of a family of ducks, well no drake of course. Tiny chicks no bigger than hummingbirds. Always one loitering behind; an inquisitive rogue. A pike's dinner.

'You got the gun here? Got it with you?' Sarah followed the ducks being lifted and separated by small swells on the lake. 'Is it here?'

Bobby was mystified by the interest in his grubby old revolver. One that was second hand when his father owned it. No accuracy. Only good for close range euthanasia. 'I got it in the truck.'

'Show me.' Sarah was eager, but embarrassed by her own urgency.

If it was what she wanted he would fetch it. 'Sure.'

Mother duck had found a warm dark boulder and was organising the sleeping arrangements. Ducklings were either hoisted up or made acrobatic attempts to launch themselves using their immature wings. When the mother had them almost smothered in her rich down the prodigal son was still absent; swimming round the sleeping rock looking for excitement or trouble.

'Here.' Bobby handed Sarah the weapon.

It had lost its magic. Nowhere near the exhilaration from the first encounter. The chambers were empty. Not the weight and not the same feeling of power. 'No bullets?' Sarah enquired.

'Guns are dangerous things, ma'am. Shouldn't handle them loaded.' A serious voice. He'd grown up to respect the gun. Too many of his pals had been shot fooling around with guns. 'Certain rules you need to follow.' His dad was speaking now. 'Rule one, never point a gun unless you intend to use it, loaded or unloaded.' He stopped short of giving the whole lesson. Sarah was too concerned with the rifling in the barrel and oblivious to his ramblings.

At every object Sarah pointed the gun. Lining up the sights and aiming. Bang! Bang! she said in her head. Her hand held it awkwardly, loosely. An inexpert and unsteady hand.

'No, ma'am. Like this.' Bobby tugged the pistol from her. 'Yer right handed, okay. So grab the handle like so.' He demonstrated with a firm grip of his right hand and a protruding forefinger aligned alongside the trigger. 'And then cup your right hand with your left, like this.' Bobby proceeded to support his firing hand with the steadying spare hand. The gun was held facing down at the decking, between his legs. 'Now when you are ready to shoot at something you raise the revolver from down here until you have the target in your sights. Straight up. A vertical line.' He was the trainer now. Back at his gun club, on the indoor range. Where he went most weeks with his selection of arms, neatly arrayed in his gun box. 'Never pull the trigger.' Bobby aimed at a nearby tree.

'Squeeze it.' His trigger finger slid inside the guard and squeezed. There was a deafeningly innocuous click.

Sarah's eyes flickered. 'Let me try.'

She grabbed the gun and tried to imitate Bobby's demonstration. Her hands weren't as big and the weapon felt uncomfortably heavy. She swung it up with both hands, several times before she attempted the squeeze. The trigger was surprisingly stiff. With the first click the gun swayed dangerously. She couldn't hold it in line.

'Yer goin' to blow someone's head off if you fire it like that.' Bobby clasped her hands with his. Firm glass-paper hands as big as puppies. From his position behind her he went through the motions again. 'And remember, ma'am, if this thing was loaded yer goin't get some hostile recoil from this beast. Could end up shooting yourself in the foot or something.' Bobby chuckled.

Sarah continued to choose targets as she and Bobby in tandem lined up the gun. He pressed closer. She could feel him resting against her buttocks. It wasn't unpleasant. Click! Click! Click! Almost like a dance as they twirled, aimed and squeezed.

'Think I'd better get to work. And get the gun put back. Don't want Mr. Roberts seeing, an' all.' Bobby pulled away. Neither wanted to stop. Bobby was on the way to an erection and was too polite to stab Sarah with that. Perhaps they could dance again.

'Just one more.' Sarah held the gun solo, crouched slightly, closed an eye, raised the pistol until the ducklings were dead in line and fired. A resounding click! Direct hit. She smiled.

'Thanks ma'am.' Bobby took the gun and headed for his truck.

'Let's do it with bullets next time.' Sarah called after him.

Bobby refrained from reloading the gun whilst still in view, and smuggled it back.

'Yes, bullets. Live ammunition.' Sarah spoke to herself. Every snapping click was turned into an explosion and every shot a bullseye.

Spring nudged its way in. John Roberts, markets closed for the weekend, had plans for a two-day visit to the mountains. Some walking and cycling. It was something he wanted to do with the kids alone. A father's role this outdoor stuff. No matter how much Lucy Marie and Tommy protested, they were off on the expedition with their dad, into the forest and onto the summit. Stella rubbed her hands. Outward-bound activities were not only down her list of favourites, they were off altogether. He could take them. She would attack some shops in a neighbouring town. And the moody English nanny could stay back and sort herself out.

John Roberts had set off early because *that's what you did.* He'd been told, or it was on television. Stella didn't leave long after her husband and children, her only baggage the gold credit card.

Bobby turned up around ten. There was some tree planting he had to finish, close to the house. Sarah watched from the window. She drank tea, her hands encircling a white mug. She watched Bobby working, taking whistling sips of the hot liquid. Huge hands and long arms. Thick trunk legs and firm buttocks. Exciting energy in every heave and thrust. Had he got the gun? Had he got the bullets?

A screech from the scraping screen door announced her approach. Bobby offered a smile as she came as near as she dare. Into deep pits that the mechanical digger had excavated he plunged the saplings, and proceeded to pack the loose soil tightly around the slight stem. A film of sweat stuck to his forehead and his hands were stained by the red soil.

'Got it then?' No greeting. 'Got the gun and some bullets?' Sarah was single-minded.

'What's that, ma'am?' The grumbling engine of the digger drowned her questions.

Sarah climbed closer. 'I asked about the gun. Have you got it?'

'It's in the truck.'

'Bullets?'

'Sure.'

'I'll get it.' Sarah headed for the truck.

'Okay, ma'am.' There was resignation in his voice.

Behind the replenished stock of tissues, deep in the glove compartment where they had first met, was the revolver. As she removed the delicious weapon there was a metallic clunk from inside the compartment. Sarah shoved her hand in again. It was another gun. A revolver, but smaller, lighter than the one she had handled before.

'A .22, ma'am.' Bobby had caught up with Sarah. His voice startled her. 'It's more for a lady. Easier to use. Thought you might prefer it.'

Sarah balanced one on each hand, feeling the difference. The original one was heavier now. Six bullets were in the chamber. And compared with the .22 it was a beast. But you always remember your first love.

'This one.' She handed back the .22. Bobby slipped it into his back pocket. He knew the recoil on his .38 would come as a shock to Sarah and she'd welcome the lightweight weapon.

'Can't fire them round here. Soon as I'm finished I'll take you to a place I know.' He reached to take the gun from Sarah.

'It's all right I'll hold it.' She pulled her hand back and held on firmly.

'Just don't point it my way, ma'am. Or take a peek down the barrel. Keep the safety on.' Bobby was resigned to finishing up quickly. He wasn't sure about Sarah and his gun, and that safety catch was sure temperamental.

Sarah held the gun in her lap. Her grip set secure on the butt and supporting the barrel with the other hand.

Bobby completed the planting of the trees without a lot of care. Not exactly vertical. Good enough. One eye was engaged in observing the antics of the nanny. There were some ludicrously tilting Douglas firs.

'Right, let's go.' Bobby climbed into the cab still covered in soil and the brown debris off the trees. 'Only take us twenty minutes to get there.' He removed the small pistol from his pocket. He didn't want to shoot himself in the arse.

It was a site about a mile off the main road. An old sandpit or quarry by the look of it. A wall of yellow sand was topped by a barricade of forest that almost wrapped round the bowl of the pit. From the amount of smacking undergrowth they had driven through the site hadn't been visited for at least a year.

Sarah emerged from the car with her gun at her side, trailing in her extended hand. The gun she had nursed throughout the journey. *Bonnie* preparing for the bank raid. *Clyde* joined her, the .22 a toy pistol in his large hand.

They walked through the brush in silence. An awful silence, as if they both knew the consequences of this moment.

In the centre of the amphitheatre she raised the revolver from between her legs astride, slightly bent at the knees. Both hands hauling it up in an arc, quivering level at her one open eye.

'Hold on, ma'am.' Bobby's voice betrayed his apprehension. Jittery words. 'A few pointers before we start here.' The sandpit bowl an auditorium with two sparring partners stalled. Each syllable circled the high banking and returned at the tail of the next. An anonymous announcement on a deserted railway station.

Sarah hung the gun, barrel to the ground. Head bent over it. An incongruous image. Dowdy nanny, pale green skirt and high-buttoned blouse, clutching a deadly weapon. Mary Poppins armed and dangerous.

'It's goin' to kick like a horse. An explosion that'll be deafening. No ear protectors here, ma'am.' Bobby coached. 'And don't forget to just squeeze that trigger.'

'What shall I shoot?' A question from her hanging head.

'Don't matter, ma'am. What ever you aim at you'll miss. That beast don't shoot straight. Never has.' Bobby chuckled. A nervous attempt at humour. 'Just shoot at the bank. Can't miss that.'

Picking fingers of her left hand pulled some interloping strands of hair that threatened to obscure her vision. Quickly she brought it back down to cup her right hand that gripped the gun, resting against her skirt. In a smooth curve Sarah brought the weapon level with her squinting eye. The barrel twitched. Her finger slid to the rivet trigger. Sarah squeezed. A vague image of the hammer cocking and then stabbing forward. A flash. Thunderclap boom that bludgeoned her eardrums. Hands barely holding on were thrown back above her head. The gun held limp now, ready to fall.

Bobby grabbed at the revolver before it tumbled and struck her. Numbed by exhilaration, moderated by physical pain, she rocked. Speechless.

'Warned you ma'am.' Bobby steadied her at the waist. 'Told you that gun's a real brute.'

Sarah didn't hear the slug thud into the bank. Only saw the drifting blue smoke and some slumping grit dislodged by the slamming bullet.

It was a good ten minutes before she stopped shaking and her imploding eardrums lost the violence of the pounding throb.

Bobby recognised her recovery. He held up the .22 as soon as she was focussing again. 'Now this little fella would suit you down to the ground, ma'am.' He held it as if it were a delicate morsel. Tantalising. 'Just the one for you.' Bobby was a smarmy salesman. He pushed it into her hands. 'Feel that.'

It had no weight. No substance. A toy. Sarah eyed it with suspicion. An impostor; not the real thing.

'Same action, same rules. But this little lover won't knock you about, ma'am, and he'll shoot straight. Try to hit that wood there.' Eager suggestions. Keep up the interest. Bobby pointed to a snaking root that poked through the sand near to the top of the cliff wall. 'Accurate gun this. A target pistol.'

Sarah hoisted the featherlight firearm from the same stance. Its lack of weight sent it past her aiming eye. She let it fall back, all the way to her trampolining skirt. Up it came again. The sights in line. A compressing squeeze. The merest crack. A cap gun. Barely a nudge for recoil. Sarah saw the bullet hit and a curtain of dust from the ejected sand.

'Missed!' A cry of disappointment that was muffled by the strangled report still held by the entrapping bowl.

'Good effort though.' Bobby approached to take the gun.

But Sarah was already bent over, handgun clasped. A runner on the blocks. She sprang up. Determined for retribution. Crack! Crack! Two shots at the disobedient target. Two resounding smacks as they hit.

'Now, ma'am, don't you get too excited like.' Bobby was dusting off his cap that had fallen as he stumbled in retreat. 'Need some rules round here.'

He couldn't remove the triumphant grin stuck on Sarah's face.

Bobby took charge of the guns as they climbed back into the truck. 'You gotta use these things with some caution.' He was still prattling on after his unceremonious tumble. 'Guns kill. Gotta remember that, ma'am.'

Sarah sat in silence; still reliving the explosion of the gun. The little thing was all right, but she needed to master the maverick. She had the taste.

When Bobby had stopped nagging her about the proper procedures when handling firearms, the truck fell quiet.

Sarah watched out the window. No gun to cuddle. Timber-clad house after timber-clad house. Trees and more trees.

On the outskirts of Sapphire Lake, a small settlement some five miles from the cottage track, impertinent traffic signals halted the pick-up. As if for a ghost car. Nothing crossed. Bobby cursed in a whisper. Sarah stared at a crudely tied poster announcing in a child's hand a GARAGE SALE and giving time and address.

'What's one of those?' Sarah asked aloud. A question not really directed at Bobby. He nevertheless offered an explanation.

'Garage sale, ma'am. People moving or clearing out some things. Selling off stuff they don't need.'

Curiosity prodded. 'Let's take a look.'

'Usually just junk, ma'am. Not much goin' to be there that'll interest you.' Bobby couldn't abide trailing round the garbage people sell at these things.

'Just a look.' A tap on his arm with her nails. Almost a reprimand for Bobby Clayman.

'Okay ma'am.' Easy pickings.

Bobby found the house without much trouble. Once in the road a route marked out by kids' signs led to a hive of activity across the front lawn and up the drive of a neat detached, clinker-built home.

'Trash by the look of it.' Bobby was dismissive, but not totally inaccurate. Old laundry machinery pieces were stark white statues in a haphazard arrangement of knackered sports equipment, children's abused toys and some hideous object d'art. They made a particularly inconspicuous couple. Bobby led, insisting on a fast pace.

'Look at the rubbish. Told you ma'am.' But Bobby was way ahead, clucking to himself.

Sarah was stopped at a deep bin where ice hockey sticks with huge chunks hacked out of them shared with stringless tennis racquets, lurid golf umbrellas and some broken shot guns. There were other inquisitors inspecting the collection, and Sarah pretended to be interested in a battered parasol. Once alone her attention was hastily transferred to the heavy stocks of the old guns, their lumpy triggers and their smooth barrels. Cumbersome weapons. Armaments for gamekeepers back in England or sheriffs in old western movies. She imagined the discharge, the recoil that she now understood, the spread of shot. A scattering of lead pellets. Untidy. Not the neatness of a single bullet hole.

'Pieces of shit, ma'am. Excuse my language.' Bobby had hurried back, flustered. 'Them guns are a danger to anyone using them. More likely kill yourself firing those antiques.'

Bobby tugged encouragingly at Sarah's arm; coaxing her on and hopefully all the way back to the truck. At the front door of the house she paused. A large hand-drawn red arrow, bent and flapping, pointed to the inside. Men's deliberating voices percolated through the half open door. This time she pulled at Bobby's arm and nodded towards the door, where two men were now emerging.

Inside a paunchy middle-aged man in a checked shirt stood behind a dining table covered in an old tartan blanket.

Sarah's eyes widened and she held her breath when she saw his wares.

'Hi, folks!' A sharp and friendly greeting. He was still rearranging the display on the table. 'How's your day going?'

Handguns, at least eight, were set neatly on the blanket. The portly man was laying magazines alongside the appropriate gun and separating detachable chambers from revolvers. 'You looking for a gun? Some real bargains here, folks.'

Bobby spoke to balance the conversation. 'Got some beauties myself.' He picked up an old Colt, snapping it open and spinning the chamber, just to impress the man and display his knowledge of firearms.

Sarah surveyed the array of weapons. Most of them were large handguns, revolvers and semi-automatic pistols. What an arsenal. While Bobby continued boasting about his shooting expertise and listing all his buddies at his gun club, Sarah window-shopped. They were all gorgeous, but there was one that shouted out to her. She could forget the beast. She wouldn't remain faithful in that relationship. Her new love was a polished gunmetal blue Smith and Wesson .38 revolver. Now the other guns disappeared. A mist obscured all except this gun. She only had eyes for him.

The two men quickly exhausted some ridiculous anecdotes and trivia central to handguns. Bobby placed an arm round Sarah's shoulder and headed for the door. Other people were milling around the table and picking up the guns. Sarah dared them to touch hers. Reluctantly she obeyed his urging, but braked hard when they were outside, almost tripping Bobby.

'What's up, ma'am?' He steadied himself on some fencing.

'I want that gun. I really do. You going to get it for me?'

Sarah looked up at him with spaniel eyes, trying to hide a crazed compulsion.

'What gun?' Bobby quizzed. He'd been shooting the breeze with the guy inside. There hadn't been any talk of buying anything.

'The one in the middle with the black handle.' She was almost dribbling. Surely he couldn't have missed it.

'You mean that Smith and Wesson model ten with Uncle Mike's combat grip.' He could have gone on. Four inch barrel, carbon steel, six rounds, .38 special, target trigger, serrated front sight. Bobby knew his guns, but he was uneasy about getting Sarah too deeply involved. Had to cool his enthusiasm. He sensed a sinister change in Sarah since the night at the bar.

'Yes, I think so.' She only knew its looks and the buzz she anticipated from holding it. Her gun. One of her very own. She dismissed some hideous images of herself with that gun, and fearful dark thoughts were pushed away. 'Can we get it?' More pleading eyes.

'If we can move out after that, ma'am.' Bobby was negotiating.

'Yes, of course.' He could have three wishes from the genie if he wanted. It was hers. She could tell.

'I'll knock him down. Get a deal on it. He knows I'm a club member.' Bobby trudged back into the house.

It seemed like an age to Sarah before he returned. In his hand he held a brown paper bag, as if he had just collected a takeaway.

And on the journey home she peeled open the folded top as if she was opening a Christmas present. Slowly and deliberately. The excitement clutching her throat. Inside the bag the gun was heavy on her lap. With a lucky dip hand she fingered the cool metal and the rough grip. Hauled it out by its barrel and set it down on the crumpled paper. Just looking. Just what she wanted. Santa had been good.

'Thanks.' Sarah rarely showed gratitude. Bobby was honoured.

'You happy now, ma'am? That's a powerful gun you got there. We need to go through some of them procedures again. You can't afford to make mistakes with that fella.' Bobby couldn't understand why she wanted the damn gun. He was treading carefully. What was she going to do with it?

'*Yes.*' *Whatever you say Bobby.* Sarah answered without looking up. Her hand was in the bag again, pulling out a cardboard box stuffed with cartridges. Each in its individual section.

'Here we are.' Bobby announced, as they pulled up at the cottage.

Sarah didn't have time to gloat any longer. She stuffed the gun and ammunition back into the bag and said her goodbyes to Bobby. She wouldn't need him anymore. There was a new love to distract her. Courting someone new.

Stella Roberts was back from her shopping expedition and greeted Sarah on the doorstep.

'Ah, you're back Sarah. Had a good time?' She had no idea where the nanny had been, but she was wearing one of her new outfits and needed some compliments.

'Hello Mrs. Roberts.' Sarah tried to skulk past her dapper employer.

'Brought in some dinner?' Stella enquired, looking at the brown bag Sarah was smuggling in.

'No. Bobby bought me a present.' She managed to get past Stella and scuttle off to her room.

As Sarah locked herself in Stella was still lobbing comments. 'That was nice of him.' Lost words like paper pellets tapping at the closed door.

Sarah tipped the gun out of the paper bag onto the bed, where its weight made it sink into the cover. Sarah lay on the bed with it. Curled around the depression in the bedding. Lifting her gun and turning it. Stroking. Her Smith and Wesson .38. After several minutes of toying she grabbed it by the grip. Kneeling on the bed she held it in both hands, lined up the sights and shot nearly every object in the room.

Bang! Bang! Bang! Mental pictures of real targets and real bullets. Bang! Bang! Bang! But when the terrible images came she left the gun on the pillow and proceeded to empty out the shells from their box and examine them. Eventually she opened the revolver's chamber and slid the cartridges in. There was something sensual about the process and their snug fit. The gun, fully loaded, would spend the rest of the night with her.

Lucy Marie and Tommy were back around lunchtime the next day. Earlier than planned. Lucy Marie had not been enamoured at all with the outdoor life, and had complained so much that John Roberts was forced to curtail the mountain hike and the under canvas experience.

'That's it. We head back to England on Wednesday. Spoiled brats sometimes those kids.' John Roberts groaned as he stripped off his khaki outward-bound garb. 'You try to give them a rich experience of this glorious countryside, and what do you get in return. No gratitude at all. None. Tommy wasn't too bad. But Lucy Marie was a pain in the butt.' He explained to Stella, who was prancing about in another new number that she had bought on her shopping spree. 'I don't know what Sarah puts into their heads, but they've lost their spirit of adventure, those two. Must be being English that does it, ha?' He suggested to Stella as his boots thumped to the floor. 'There are things I need to do over there so let's head back. I'll change the tickets tomorrow. Tell our English nanny so she can organise our little darlings ready for the trip.' John Roberts wouldn't forget his aborted adventure very easily.

Stella found Sarah on a bench near the lake. The children were playing in their tree house that Bobby had built. A painstaking effort that had produced a weird mongrel building. A cross between a fort and the one Dorothy flew in *The Wizard of Oz*.

'Can you get the kids' things together between now and Wednesday, Sarah. We're leaving then.'

'What?' It was an involuntary cry of astonishment. 'Going?

On Wednesday?' There was despair in the tone. Sarah was devastated. 'Why?'

'He wants to go. You know how he is. Sorry, I didn't realise you liked it here so much. Oh, of course, Bobby. We'll be back. You can write, and phone him a little if you want. Serious is it?'

Sarah was breathing loudly through her nose, staring at the ground. She hadn't even fired the revolver. Now she had to go. She couldn't take it back to England. She was despairing at the forced separation.

When Stella had walked back to the cottage Sarah's exhalations turned to loud snorts. What could she do? There was no time that day to take the gun out. All she had left was the next day, Tuesday. But where? Where could she shoot it?

Ahead of her the kids scrambled back to the house. Sarah rambled along, deep in thought, picking at her teeth and pulling at her chin.

The opportunity came when, over breakfast, Stella announced that she would take Lucy Marie and Tommy to town. They needed new shoes. She needed one more shopping fix.

John Roberts fled to his office and the latest news of technology companies on the rocks.

Sarah wrapped up the Smith and Wesson and the ammunition in a towel and pushed it into a carrier bag. She crept out of the cottage, off the track and began walking deep into the woods. Little Red Riding Hood with her bag of goodies. Ferns scratched at her ankles and the wet needles of sagging pines brushed her face. She heard the scuttling trails of rodents and the frantic flap of anonymous birds as she ventured into arcane territory. Not that Sarah was at all interested in her surroundings, only enough to ensure she was miles away from civilisation. No compass and an appalling sense of direction swung her round, so that her three-mile hike only took her half a mile from the cottage.

It was here she found a fortress of high boulders and a thick screen of forest, and no sound of life. Damp grass licked her ankles so she stamped down a space where she could stand without the annoying tickle. There must be no distractions. It was good to be alone. No Bobby to nag her. She unwrapped the revolver and laid it on the towel alongside the box of shells. For a short while she just looked at it. The two of them together. Such a beauty. She picked him up with a sigh, spun the chamber and held on tight. Both hands on the grip and barrel pointing down she twisted on the spot. What to shoot first? Through the sights she decided on the thick trunk of a tree some twenty feet away. This time she was ready for the kick. Sarah squeezed. Nowhere near the bronco buck of the beast, but firm and gutsy. And the blast a striking up of the band. Music to her ears. This time she heard the dull thud of the .38 bullet. On target. Sarah raced to the tree and traced the hole with her finger. She could see the crumpled lead buried inside. She fantasised about the damage in a softer material. In flesh?

Sarah waddled back to her firing position and chose other innocent objects. Not all her shots were successful, and one particularly wayward attempt sent her prostrate to the ground as the renegade discharge ricocheted off the smooth surface of the giant rocks. Scorching pings, deceptive and alarming. Only when she heard the offending shell rip into the foliage did she raise her head and gasp.

That was enough. She was ready to pack away. The towel and the rest of the ammunition were stuffed into the bag. She held on to the gun. Carried it, hanging, in her right hand. Ready. Just until she arrived back on the track. It was a good feeling. More than protection. Power. She had always been the freak, always the target. Now she was in charge. It was the nearest thing to personality.

Trees and undergrowth were still wet as she battled through some woven branches and slobbering leaves. Her journey back was quieter, and waltzing round an obstructing boulder she was confronted by an equally puzzled racoon. A toilet brush tail and badger markings. They eyed each other. One nervous, uncertain, some curiosity. The other determining range and allowing for movement. Lifting ever so slowly her hideous firearm. Nocompunction. Slipping finger, symphonic report, tiny slumped body. That calibre shell could smash a lot of skull. What a shot. Her first kill. *Except for Rupert, but that was different.* She quickly binned that thought.

Back at the cottage Stella's car was parked at the door. Boxes and bags were being unloaded. John Roberts was sighing at every trip back to the boot of the vehicle and at the unnecessary expenditure.

'Left anything for others? Sure your card can take this damage? Any of it for the kids?' He grumbled.

Sarah tried to avoid him.

'Now where's our English nanny been?' He confronted her. He was in the mood for that. 'Well?'

She could have done it there and then. The revolver, weighty in the bag, was against her leg. It would be quite easy. Enjoyable.

'My wife's been shopping as you can see. Bought up the whole of town by the look of it.' John Roberts filled his arms with parcels.

'Been walking.' Sarah winced. She hated talking to the rude man.

'Walking? You shouldn't be doing that round here.'

'Why?'

'I'll tell you why.' He was about to preach. 'There are hunters out there, in the woods. And they're real close to the house. Heard them myself this afternoon. Gunfire, a lot of it, about a half-hour ago. Last blast couldn't have been more than a hundred feet away. It's irresponsible to be out there. I know they shouldn't be that close, but I'm not about to go and tell them that. Make sure you don't let the kids go searching those woods.' He started to move with his baggage. Sarah managed to slip upstairs as he struggled into the hallway.

Had she been that close? What if he had investigated?

Somehow she got some pleasure from him hearing her fire. And imagining him bursting in on her in the clearing.

In her room she cleaned up. First the Smith and Wesson. And when he was laid out freshly polished, it was her turn. Not half the attention or satisfaction from that. As she sat drying her hair on the edge of the bed next to the gun, she was faced with the torment of separation. A hiding place? This companion had to stay. But where?

That night she wrapped her weapon in the towel, and using three zip-lock freezer bags that she had purloined from the kitchen ensured that her .38 Smith and Wesson was protected from the harsh extremes of the weather. Finally she laid it in an old sports bag that Stella had left in the basement.

And when they were all in bed, Sarah crept from the house. She waited a few minutes outside in the drive, looking up at the windows to see if anyone had stirred. Assured that they were safe in their beds she grabbed the shovel that was used for snow clearance, and paced out a distance from the corner of the wood store into the forest. There she dug. In the dry, needle-strewn soil below a particularly protective Douglas fir, Sarah interred her gun. A hibernation rather than a burial.

Chapter 6

Life back in England was a chore for John and Stella Roberts and for the children. For Sarah it was heartbreak. She was away from the only thing she had any faith in; her companion. Her power. Here she was just the barely literate, dull nanny, who performed mechanically the set tasks, and played out a bearable association with parents and children.

Bobby hadn't thought twice about the gun. He knew their relationship, such as it was, had cooled. Drudgery of work and limited deductive skills successfully dulled any sense of concern over the Smith and Wesson he had bought Sarah. The gun had gone with her. Back to England.

Horrific accounts of the shootings at Dunblane hadn't registered with Bobby Clayman. There were always shootings somewhere. Severe limitations on the owning of handguns now in force in the UK were unknown. He had seven, or was it eight, weapons. Second nature in his neck of the woods to have guns. It was their right. Written in the constitution, it was.

So Bobby Clayman had no idea that he walked past that revolver every time he was on the Roberts' property, especially close when he was humping or chopping logs. That deadly gun and its deadly future.

'Fucking idiots!' John Roberts was on one. Beaten to the corpse. 'Bastard knew I was in for at least half a million.'

'John, keep it down.' Stella waddled to the door of his office, still clutching the needlepoint she had been picking away at.

'Just lost a few thousand dollars, my dear, because of some arsehole. Keep you in pocket money for a week that.' He had a dig whenever he could at his wife's spending habits.

'Yeah, yeah, yeah, whatever. Missed out on suffocating another innocent, have we?' Stella was equally wounding.

'Cow.' It was low and without too much malice. 'Let's change the subject shall we? Caribbean in ten days. Remember?'

'Yes, I remember. Why?'

'It'll be four weeks we're away. Weren't we going to get someone to help the kids? It's a long time out of even that poxy school.' John Roberts was forgetting his snatched profit.

'Mrs. Gleeson has given me a name. He's a friend of hers. A tutor.'

'A friend of that old bat? Hope he's better than the staff at her dimwit establishment.'

Mrs. Gleeson ran the local pre-prep school much in the same way she had run it for the last thirty years. She hadn't actually understood the National Curriculum. Thought it must mean more new fangled teaching schemes that *The Forests Pre-Preparatory School* wasn't going to get involved in. Little did she realise the power of the new body that was about to send its forces to inspect her Dickensian establishment – the Ofsted hit squad. But for now this dusty academy with its emphasis on the three Rs, its neatly attired Jaspers and Charlottes and the gaggle of gloating mothers encamped at the gate, was an essential landmark in parochial Wentworth.

'Very well qualified. Working for some rich sheiks, Mrs. Gleeson tells me.' Stella nodded her head, but her eyes remained fixed on the needlework on her lap.

'Another fucking limey I've got to use my sterling on. No wonder the pound's so damn strong. How much is this leach goin't cost?'

'He's coming here tomorrow. An interview.' Stella proudly announced.

'What are you goin't be asking him? If he's a fucking academic you won't know what to say. If that bat Gleeson reckons he's the business let's leave it at that.' John Roberts had a point.

'Just wanna see if he's nice. Be good with the children. Fit in with the family. You have to see people and introduce yourself. Can't just get him to turn up in the Caribbean without a proper meeting.'

'So we gotta have him around us all the time? Just like that doughnut of a nanny?' John Roberts huffed and smuggled his jumbled newspaper out of the room, leaving his wife to her stitching.

Martin Preston was in teaching for the money. However ludicrous that sounded. Just turned fifty he had worked in numerous schools in Berkshire and Surrey for over twenty years. Held full time posts where he just went through the motions. His main interest was the lucrative tutoring business that he conducted after the school day and at weekends. He could teach anything, or so he said. What he could do was convince credulous parents that he was the master of whatever they were looking for. A thoroughly decent fellow with a catalogue of qualifications and impeccable knowledge of even the most obscure subjects. Educational equivalent of the notorious car salesman or estate agent.

When Janet Gleeson approached him about Lucy Marie and Tommy Roberts and the prospect of several weeks in the Caribbean, not only did the cash register clang loudly, his sleeveless shirts and mothballed shorts were brought out for an airing.

Smart casual would suit, he thought as he prepared to meet John and Stella Roberts. Americans wouldn't appreciate the reinforced elbows of his corduroy jacket with its row of assorted pens in the breast pocket. They would need something to relate to. Low-key dress that wouldn't be threatening. There was no need to highlight the intellectual differences. Needed to meet them at their level. Like visiting a ranch with your jeans on or an Indian restaurant with your hands in prayer. Part of the smooze.

Martin packed his briefcase with a collection of unrelated

papers and vaguely apposite texts. Some of his scruffy business cards were stuck in a back pocket. His real stuff was his bullshit and that he had on tap. No need for all the props. This couple would be easy meat.

'Have you references?' Stella asked of the rather superior Englishman who sat across from her in the sitting room.

As many as you want, Martin signalled with his wide eyes, trying not to rub his hands. 'Of course. But surely Mrs. Gleeson is reference enough? We have known each other for many years.'

Martin Preston didn't want to be fagged with hunting down some of his satisfied customers. Janet Gleeson only knew him by name, and knew nothing of his expedience, guile and craft.

'I see.' Stella wasn't going to insist. She was flummoxed now. John Roberts was in his office announcing a life sentence to someone at the other end of the phone. Martin could hear him from the front room and wasn't so sure he would be the patsy that this woman was.

'I'll get my husband. He'd like to meet you.' Like hell. John Roberts had better things to do than talk English education with some nancy teacher. 'I'll just see if he's free.' Stella was glad to escape. Martin Preston had her fooled. An accomplished schoolmaster offering to cover every subject on the curriculum and at the highest level. A scholar and a gentleman. Her humble education in a wooden school house in the Appalachians still a monkey on her back.

'John Kendall Roberts,' he barked, almost crushing the teacher's hand. 'Hear you're goin't' be teaching the kids. Good to have you on board.' John Roberts' head shook in a rapid jerking motion. In his left hand he held the cordless phone. Hopefully it would ring and he could escape from this pointless exchange. 'So you've taught many kids. Experienced at the game, eh?' He sounded ridiculous.

'Ah, yes, children. Charming creatures with an enormous energy for learning. Young minds, eager searching and researching. Soaking up knowledge. Delightful students.'

Martin Preston stroked his jacket collar. He was in thespian mode. A ham actor playing to a gullible assembly. 'I have lead them to the treasure trove of wisdom. So many minds shown the jewels of education.'

The phone rang. John Roberts sighed with counterfeit disappointment and shrugged his shoulders as an apology. What the hell was the man rambling on about? Damn English nerd. He turned through the door, the handset clamped to his ear.

'Business. It's all he thinks about.' Stella stepped in to fill the space.

'Tough tycoon, I bet.' Martin smirked. 'Wheeling and dealing. He's a sharp one all right.' He kept up the jollying of his potential employers.

'Suppose I go through our schedule. See if all the dates fit in with your own commitments, Mr. Preston.'

'Such formality, my dear.' Martin was almost oozing with it. 'It's Martin. Do call me Martin.'

'Of course.' Stella's cheeks turned scarlet. 'I'll just get my diary.' She scuttled off, eager to complete the arrangements.

Sarah was at the other end of the house watching the children make a camp out of a travel blanket and some other assorted paraphernalia.

She knew the teacher was in the house. Wasn't too keen on teachers. Her eyes were on the kids, but she was thinking through the four weeks she would have to spend with this teacher fellow. Teachers made you look stupid. And in front of others as well. They had at school, and this one would now. Sarah was certain of that. Certain that she was going to appear a fool to the delight of John and Stella Roberts. There were some things you could get away with when it was just the Americans. A cultural thing. Lost in the translation. But with an English teacher there was going to be trouble. Felt it in her bones, she did.

'Anegada. Have you heard of it?' Stella spoke as she re-entered the room. 'Part of your Virgin Islands. John chose it to keep away from some of the unsavoury characters he had dealings with in New York. Gangster money, is what he said.'

'Gangster money?' quizzed Martin, liking the sound of it.

'Yes, laundered money from the mob. John wanted to keep clear of the US Islands for that reason. You can't be sure, and John insists we think of the children first. Their safety is our utmost concern.' Stella's face was glum. She was serious about that.

'Most interesting.' He rubbed his chin. Pictures of stashed money lighting up some inner screens. 'And most commendable that you have the children's best interests firmly at the top of the list.' Martin Preston didn't mean a word of it. But it was something that Stella liked to hear. He was very aware of that.

'But our island is heaven. Lots of your lot. Brits that is. Lots of them there. A private island. Just a collection of large houses. Beautiful scenery. Deserted beaches.' Stella was flicking through her photo album memory. She was already on holiday.

'I am not familiar with that particular Caribbean island. Of course I have visited many, but Anegada, no.' Martin Preston hadn't been out of Europe, but he wouldn't be caught out. A man like him does his homework at the travel agents. All those brochures and just window-shopping.

'Not many people have. John and I are very lucky. It costs a fortune to buy anything there. And they're fussy who they have purchase property.' It was her only ammunition. The one subject where she could talk down to Martin Preston was money. She could belittle the starchy teacher there.

She was blissfully unaware of the narrowness of the vote that allowed her and her shark of a husband on Anegada. The island was run by The Anegada Company, a collection of old school ties slipping out of the Carlton Club or the like, and it was with reluctance the directors agreed the sale of *Seawind House* to *those ghastly loud Americans*. Old money was draining away in Britain through death duties and the upkeep of stately homes, and there were very few new capitalists seeking the resplendent tropical idyll of Anegada. A few infiltrators from the old colony wouldn't be too dangerous, but they'd need watching. Standards mustn't fall.

'Of course, of course. Absolutely. Mrs. Roberts you are so right.' The bag was getting on Martin's nerves now. 'Your Nirvana in the sun. No more than you deserve.' He'd keep the smarm trickling through. No need to upset anything. This was going to be a doddle.

'I have spoken at length with Mrs. Gleeson and you can be assured your delightful children will receive the finest education, even so far from their school and their peers.' Martin stood and collected his belongings. 'Now if there is nothing else?'

Stella thrust a sheet of paper in his waving hands. 'The schedule. You look through it and let me know if it's okay.' She was pleased he was going. There were doubts bubbling to the surface. Unnecessary and illogical questions about what she was doing. It was uncomfortable and unnerving. Best not to re-examine her motives or their plans. Not now. John would go crazy.

Chapter 7

Eight hours from Gatwick to Antigua, and an hour on an unnervingly fragile light aircraft jerking and bouncing to Anegada was the agenda. Enough to exhaust the most formidable traveller alone, but a journey accompanied by John and Stella Roberts and their demanding kids was to be pure hell.

Martin Preston arrived early at the airport. He was beginning to panic when there was only forty minutes to go before the flight and still no sign of the Roberts family. Fortunately they tumbled into the check-in area just as he was ready to fly out without them.

'Sorry, Mr. Preston.' Stella bustled past his greeting hand. 'John and that damn phone. Couldn't get him off.' Stella spoke into her handbag as she delved for the tickets and passports. 'This always happens. Never wants to get here too early. Just one more deal. Then he gets his claws into something, or someone.' Stella thrust the documents at the airline representative. Boarding passes were shoved back with reciprocated rudeness. Stella was oblivious.

John Roberts wrestled with the luggage while Sarah stood holding the children's hands. Three kids confused by the commotion.

'Hello!' Martin Preston approached the group. 'You must be Lucy Marie.' He bent over and touched her hair. She pulled away. 'And you, fine lad, must be Tommy.' Martin made a fist and, stooping lower, pushed it at Tommy's chin. 'My name is Mr. Preston. I'm sure we are going to get on famously.' Martin was aware that the parents were observing his introduction. Charm oozing in all directions.

When Martin pulled himself upright he came face to face with Sarah. 'And excuse me. Martin Preston is the name. The children's tutor. Who may you be?' A gallant courtier addressing a lady. He had to keep up the oily enchantment.

'Our nanny,' chirped in Tommy.

'Nanny? Wonderful. A real Mary Poppins, what.' The grin of a clown and a weak attempt at humour.

'Sarah's the name. Pleased to meet you.' She hung out a limp hand. For Sarah this was amazing confidence.

'Charmed, Sarah. Didn't realise I would have such pleasant company.' Big hips, matted hair and a face like a kicked-in bucket. A mess. Martin Preston would have been flattering to Godzilla that day.

Stella and John Roberts managed to sit several rows away, strategically separated from their children and domestics. Sarah and Martin Preston sat either side of the children in the central section of the Boeing 747. Sarah controlled Lucy Marie and Tommy with sharp yanks of their clothing and the usual stern look of disapproval. She watched the children's film on a minute screen on the back of the seat in front. Few words were exchanged with the teacher fellow.

Martin Preston sat on his throne. He didn't travel much and was determined to enjoy as much service as possible, even from his economy seat. He didn't bother to use his earphones, but he kept all the trinkets that came in a clear plastic wrap – earplugs, blindfold, miniature toothpaste and disposable brush. A real cheapskate.

At meal times he was at his most bumptious. He laid out meticulously every course that he removed from the blue plastic tray and from under the clear plastic dome.

'What would you like with your meal, sir?' A young stewardess dressed in a crisp white blouse and snug-fitting red skirt enquired.

'Wine I think. Have you a list?' Martin peered at the delightful girl from above his reading glasses.

'List? You have two choices, red or white. Sorry that's all.' She successfully strangled a giggle. There was always one on each flight. Thought that their ticket had bought them five star service, a la carte menu and the finest wines.

'Then it will be your best white, my dear.' Martin tried to make light of his pretension. 'Perhaps you could suggest a good year.' He launched a chuckle around the immediate passengers. Hoping to amuse his fellow travellers.

The stewardess forced two small bottles of the white into his outstretched plump hand, and quickly turned to more affable customers.

Martin shielded the opening of the bottles. Screw tops. He couldn't believe they would package wine like that. The philistines. At his *restaurant table* he wrapped a paper serviette around the tiny bottle to hide a tacky label, and proceeded to act the connoisseur.

Tommy tucked in next to him. Wrestling with cutlery and discharging food and wrappers. Martin looked at his own fare and ahead. Trying not to be distracted by the appalling manners and total disregard of etiquette. Didn't that nanny teach them anything? Martin briefly glimpsed Sarah spooning her dessert. Her utensil held like a hammer and her head dipping down to her dish, as if her nose would collide with the wobbling trifle. A shovelling process; stoking the boiler. No wonder.

Martin dribbled out more wine. It wasn't to his taste. Some sort of aircraft catering blend of Chardonnay grapes and New World Sauvignon. And it was getting warmer by the minute. When he had his pathetic slice of mature cheddar poised next to his wafer-thin water biscuit and his glass raised, Tommy nudged his arm.

'Need the washroom,' Tommy informed him.

'Is it urgent, son?' Martin wanted to stall him.

'Sure is.' Tommy wriggled; his hands clutching at his pants.

Martin began to disassemble his picnic area to make way for the frantic boy. He was just stacking his potted milk and untouched sweet when desperation took hold. Tommy clawed his way out of his seat and squeezed behind the bent form of his tutor, throwing Martin's head forward. By the time the boy had fled down the aisle Martin had broken off the hinged plastic table and thrown the remnants of his meal down his beige trousers. And when Tommy sauntered back Martin was on his feet cursing his pupil, the inadequate space provided on *these planes* and dabbing ineffectively at the stains on his clothes.

Afternoon tea would be better planned. Martin made sure that nanny had tested the waters, so to speak. They were quizzed repeatedly, and Martin added, simply to confuse them, that the place where they had a pee was a lavatory, not a washroom. It was to be a dedicated campaign throughout the session in the Caribbean. The Queen's English had to prevail.

'Battle of Britain by the look of it.' Martin Preston stood on the apron at St. John's airport studying the assorted light aircraft that were in various states of disrepair. 'I'd rather go in a Spitfire; some of these flying machines don't appear that airworthy.'

'No need to worry. Use these regularly. Of course John has done his homework on safety records, pilot experience and maintenance schedules. Won't fly in any old plane. Researches the airlines like he does the companies he buys or sells. Just as ruthless.' Stella nudged her hand luggage, lying on the ground, with her foot.

Sarah gripped the children's hands. It didn't look at all safe to her. But Lucy Marie and Tommy wore delight on their faces. A fairground ride to them.

'Over here.' John Roberts approached, flustered. 'They haven't got the Commander I ordered. We're having to go in the damn Islander. It's a real tub. I'm going to sue them for this. Bring the bags Mr. Preston, can you?'

A pilot in white shirt and black trousers trailed behind him. More like a waiter hailing a customer leaving the restaurant without paying. Only the gold striped epaulettes distinguishing from the chasing server.

In the Islander the journey was fifty-five minutes. Despite John Roberts' protestation the plane was up to the task. A workhorse. No pretence with this aircraft. Inside was like a cigar tube. A bucket that took off and landed in a short distance. Wheels stuck out on thick legs with no retraction. Martin Preston's confidence grew as the flight progressed.

Anegada airport was a shed with flags. Well, the tin roof was decorated with brittle brown palm leaves and the walls faced with split bamboo, but there was no disguising it - it was a shed. A hand-written sign welcomed visitors and an immigration official slept in a cockpit of an office.

'Passports and landing cards.' John Roberts declared. A cheery command now that he was on terra firma.

'Go easy with the bags, Kane.' The butler of *Seawind* had grabbed the luggage and was tipping it into the back of a large pick-up truck. Trying to fill it rather than load it.

'No trouble, sir, no trouble at all.' Kane was oblivious to John Roberts' concern, and repeated one from his limited and random phrase collection that usually satisfied the owner of *Seawind* or the occasional American renters of the property.

'Some valuable stuff in there, so go easy.' John Roberts heard another suitcase crump into the truck.

'Yes. Have it done, boss.' Kane tossed the last case and threw another meaningless utterance.

'A classroom in transit. Steady now.' Martin Preston approached the back of the vehicle to see where his suitcase was buried. 'Educational material in there, my friend.' He gave Kane a generous glare.

The shaven-headed black man opened his eyes wide, exposing more whiteness. Given a boater and striped blazer he could well have been a music hall performer with that face.

Kane rode on the mound of luggage and John Roberts drove. It was the way of things. Unwritten rules in Anegada. England in the nineteenth century. Serving classes knew their place.

Seawind was a palace. Sarah stood at the grand entrance with the kids in tow, unsure whether to cross the threshold into this fairytale castle. Such visions disappeared in dreams or became the grubby sitting room at her mother's house in Lyme Regis.

Through the double doors waltzed a maid dressed to serve. She balanced a tray crowded with glasses of fruit punch and decorated with the blood-red flowers of the Flamboyant tree.

'Welcome to *Seawind*.' A Caribbean lilt and an extravagant smile. She offered the thick drink to all the milling party and the frozen nanny.

Tommy's eager steps dragged Sarah into the house, almost stumbling on the splendour of the interior. 'Going to my room. Tons of stuff to play with in there.' Tommy remembered his Action Men and the last days of his previous visit, the battle that was raging and the daring rescue mission from imprisonment in the shower cubicle.

Lucy Marie slipped into her room and interrupted the last grand ball that she had sumptuously dressed her Barbie for so many months ago. She was cross-legged on the floor in seconds and reacquainting herself with the other players at this royal engagement. In a Disney film all these characters would have had a fantastic romp in the child's absence, but these were stuck rigid, petrified figures excitedly created and discarded by fickle imagination.

'This way. Yours is along, missus.' Kane stood behind Sarah who was still cemented to the spot, taking in her surroundings. Her mouth glued open and her eyelids held ajar.

Kane showed her past interior gardens of waterfalls and lily ponds. Bedrooms were in Bali style. A bazaar of carved wooden furniture and teak bed heads broken by the wafting of pastel drapes.

'Nice.' Sarah spoke the single word.

'Leave your case here, missus.' Kane retreated with a possible bow of the head.

Martin Preston was shown to a room away from the main house. A cottage within the property, but away from the hub. An hibiscus-trimmed sanctuary that he would enjoy. At least while he was well.

A rectangular glass dining table sat sixteen, and allowing room to subtly separate Martin and Sarah from the family core.

'Everyone settled in?' John Roberts enquired as Kane approached with the soup.

A row of nodding heads acknowledged that they were well satisfied.

'Cracking house, don't you think?' He was looking for admiration. Caesar seeking the flattery of lesser mortals.

Martin was only too ready to brown-nose the yank. 'Marvellous hovel, old man.' Martin laughed at his own humour. 'Seriously, you have a magnificent home. Excellent taste and some surprisingly imaginative décor. And the gardens so meticulously manicured. Splendid.'

'A lot of money tied up in this lot.' John Roberts waved his hands around, flat palms to the ceiling. Very Jewish. 'Sacrifices and fine American work ethics built this baby.'

Stella sensed trouble.

'Something you don't find in your country I dare say, Mr. Preston.' John Roberts was heading for one of his Brit-bashing moments.

'Meaning, Mr. Roberts?' Martin enquired.

'No commitment, the British worker. Don't you agree?' John Roberts stabbed the teacher with quizzing eyes and smiled knowingly. 'Hasn't got the drive or the purpose of workers in the United States. Won't see them building houses like this beauty.'

'I don't think it's that black and white.' Martin Preston was going to have to dribble the ball carefully. 'Some lazy types in the UK for sure, but it's regional.' He'd try and blame it on those idle Northerners and Scots.

'It's regional all right. In Europe the workers reckon you owe them a living, and in the States they have to earn a living.' John Roberts almost snarled at the end of his declaration. He picked up a section of red pepper from his salad. 'Sure I've known some lazy bums over there, but the work ethic has a solid foundation.' He jabbed the air with the piece of pepper.

Sarah ate slowly and paid more attention than normal to the children's table manners. She was ducking this one; knew exactly where it was going.

Martin Preston was ready to leave it there. The yank was getting on his high horse for some reason, but personally he wasn't going to upset the apple cart over some misplaced pride in the British worker. This arrogant bastard was paying him top dollar and Martin knew his role only too well.

'Well?' John Roberts wanted to pursue it.

'You are probably better placed to make such a statement. I therefore must bow to your superior knowledge, Mr. Roberts, on this subject.' That would hand him off surely.

But no, the American was still running with the ball. 'Come off it. Don't take an expert to see the difference. You don't stand a chance in hell of getting a skilled worker willing to put in extra hours to meet a deadline, or some middle manager wanting to get his hands dirty when it's shoulders against the wheel. It's not in the blood. An attitude difference. The company means jack shit to the union-based intelligence.'

Sarah tried to duck lower. Looking for an escape. She was afraid John Roberts was going to round on her.

He did. 'What do you think, nanny? You seen this back there in *Rule Britannia* land?' More drink than sense now running the engine.

Sarah shrugged her shoulders. Dumb and uneasy. Lucy Marie and Tommy were shaken alert. Their dad had been rambling as usual, but now he was picking on the old bag of a nanny. They didn't want to miss this.

'Not really. We tries hard. I...I don't think you should say these things. Not right.' Her face screwed up and she bit her lip. It was inarticulate and desperate. The kids fought back booming grins.

Stella was forced to intervene. 'Enough of this. It's been a long day. I suggest some shuteye is called for.' She rose from the table, trying to haul them all with her.

Her husband pulled a disgruntled face. He was having fun.

Nothing like winding up the Brits. He was up first. Off in a huff. A concerted scratching of chair legs on the tiled floor announced the relieved departure of the rest.

Urged towards their bedrooms the children mimicked their nanny's stumbling attempts at defending the British worker. 'Not right', they muttered, stretching the second word in order to replicate the Dorset drawl. Sarah heard them but didn't react. It was stored for later. They wouldn't get away with that.

After a sticky night Stella and John Roberts and the children camped around the pool, frequently fed cold drinks by Kane. Although John Roberts was accompanied everywhere by a plastic bottle of spring water. He was more than aware that he had to rehydrate himself in this climate. Paranoid about it. And whenever he had the opportunity would spread the gospel, reminding Sarah repeatedly about the dangers of dehydration.

'And the sun.' John Roberts knew the dangers here. 'Skin cancer. It's in the family. Make certain the children are covered in this before they do anything during the day.' He held out a plastic bottle displaying a large number thirty. 'They need this on, and one of these.' Exhibit two. He produced a garish sun hat covered in photocopied flowers and with a flap, reminiscent of a French foreign legion kepi. 'And in the pool they keep the hat on and a T-shirt. You can't be too careful.'

Sarah looked at him in disbelief. Even her tick-tock mental processes were alerted. Why have a mansion in the Caribbean when the kids have to don a protective armour against the sun? It's daft, she said to herself.

'You got this straight?' John Roberts was barking now. 'Have I made myself clear? I know what you're thinking. It's only sunshine. You British are stupid. Just walk out in the sun without any sunscreen. Madness. I've seen them on the beaches. British doughnuts. No respect for the ultra violet rays. Killers if the dangers aren't recognised. Well I don't want Tommy and Lucy Marie put in peril. So forget what you have learnt from being British. Do exactly what I tell you. Is that clear?'

How she hated him. How dare he treat her like this. The pig.

Martin Preston had a stay of execution. He would begin teaching the next day. In some ridiculous khaki shorts he wandered about in the garden. Livingstone or Stanley ducking through curtains of vines and palms.

Sarah found some shade reasonably near the family. Stella had half-heartedly given her some time off, but from experience Sarah knew she might very well be called upon to take the reins once the kids became over active, especially in the pool.

Stella wisely arranged staggered sittings for the meals. Martin sat with her and John about an hour after Lucy Marie and Tommy had been fed along with their nanny. Some flimsy excuse was offered to explain the new arrangement, but all of them were well aware it was a diffusion strategy.

John wasn't going to be silenced, but it was long into the evening meal and guards were down. Some glasses of red wine later, he started.

'Sports in America; the real thing. Don't you agree Mr. Preston? You invent it and we perfect it. Same as with industry and technology.' John Roberts was on one. He was pleased with the notion that his country stole ideas and profited from them. It was in line with his own philosophy.

'Which sports are you referring to?' Martin innocently asked. He'd do his best to support Britannica without offending the man who was paying the wages.

'Three that stand out, I would say. Football, baseball and basketball. Won't find a limey team to match the States in these sports.' A sneering grin hung on his face.

If Martin Preston had been a violent man this would have been the time to smack John Roberts in the teeth.

'You are probably right, but I'm equally certain that an American team taking the field to play rugby, rounders or netball would be no match for their British adversaries.' It was as delicate as he could get.

'Nancy sports still played without fire.' John Roberts

relished the challenge from the English teacher. 'Winning. It's not the Brit way, is it? Like the war. We had to come in to win that for you, didn't we? Another story, another evening.' John Roberts would remember to raise the flag some other evening with that account. 'I've seen them. Lucy Marie plays rounders at that stupid school she goes to. Girls' game. Where are the leagues? The professionals? The media coverage? The fans? The passion?' He searched Martin's face for an answer, knowing he was at least five homeruns ahead. Satisfaction a twinkle in his eyes. 'Same with netball. Even Britain has imported the refined version. Not that they can play it very well. Except where they have imported the players as well.' John Roberts was almost salivating.

Martin Preston was nearly forgetting how he needed to lick up to his boss. Even a patient man becomes irritated by a gloating face and absurd rhetoric.

'Rugby. You haven't mentioned that.' Martin was on firmer ground. 'You can't really say there isn't the passion or the courage in that sport.' He wouldn't rub it in.

So the nerdy English teacher wants to contest it does he? John Roberts regrouped. He rubbed his chin, but never took his eyes off the jousting academic.

'Maniacs in mud.' John Roberts' head nodded rhythmically. 'A lot of Celts re-enacting some notorious wrestling battles from their primitive origins. It's not sport. We did it some big favours sculpting our spectacular game of football from that chaos.'

'I think you would have some objections to that sentiment in the valleys of South Wales, the lowlands of Scotland and Saturday afternoon at Harlequins.' Martin chuckled at his own mental picture of touchline support. It was usually muddy and there were some moments of frantic grappling. But there was passion and commitment. There was camaraderie with your team on the field, and with the opposition in the bar afterwards. There wasn't any of the razzmatazz and Disney antics of an American football game. Thank God. Martin wanted to rail about the ridiculous padded uniforms, the helmets, the excessive number of team members, staccato play and sickening hero worship. He, however, was a mere minion who had to be seen to behave like one. An unshackled debate would have the obnoxious American licking his wounds.

'Can't progress. Can always identify a moribund game. And that's what rugby is. Went as far as it could go.' John Roberts had a pre-set course. He wouldn't be trapped. 'Good amateur game that is stuck in its history. As I've said, Mr. Preston, humble beginnings and fervent involvement won't help develop a truly complete sport. In America...' There was almost a chorus, echoing the glorious country, resounding around the dining room. 'In America we know how to take the blueprint and redraw it, take the rough cast and smooth the edges. Cut out the crap and make the contest an entertainment. A game for the people. For families. Old or young. A day out with all the trimmings. Miss it.'

A bloody circus. Obese rednecks cupping dripping burgers, wearing garish clothes and the ubiquitous baseball cap. Martin could only think it. He would choose another tack.

'There are the internationals. Rugby is played by quite a few countries now. I understand that American football is a little restricted in its appeal. In Canada they play a version of it, but generally it has been landlocked in the States. Wouldn't you agree?' It was argument, but neatly disguised as harmless comment.

John Roberts was ready. Adrenaline driven. 'Italy, Romania, Argentina. They're just tiny nations that the British have shown the rudiments of the game and then challenged them. Easy pickings. Sure, we could have introduced our national game to some tin-pot state and then given them a whipping. Hardly the sporting ethics of the Empire.' Satisfaction wrapped up in a broad grin. Knock-down. Eyes beckoning the English teacher to get back up from the canvas.

A fixed fight.

Martin Preston rose from his chair. He would spar but he

had no stomach for a bloody title clash. 'Good night Mr. Roberts. Time for me to retire.'

'Yeah, goodnight.' John Roberts smirked. Teacher had thrown in the towel. Victory. He punched the air as he headed for Stella in the bedroom.

Sarah had more time to herself once the children were receiving an education from Martin Preston. She even ventured poolside when the Roberts weren't there. It wasn't easy for her to feel relaxed even in a one-piece turquoise swimsuit bought in the sale at BHS. She held the towel in strategic areas as she manoeuvred the sun-bed. Her skin was tallow and she knew nothing of bikini-line hair removal. Sarah was an ungainly, blubbery seal trapping a tousled otter with her thighs.

The sun's menace so aptly explained by John Roberts was a mystery to Sarah Bickles. She had come to sit in the sun. Was it so difficult to do? She did possess some plastic sunglasses from Boots and a sun-cream that her sister had used on the beach at Lyme once. It was lumpy now and the bottle farted when squeezed, and didn't deliver easily.

It was bound to happen. John Roberts bushwhacked her at the pool. He paraded around the stranded porpoise, deciding where to begin his sniping. It was beyond his understanding of tact to walk away.

'You know that white reflects the sunlight. Just look at Jerusalem. A city spilling over with vanilla buildings. I need glasses just to look at you.' The same self-satisfied teeth showing. 'British lard.'

Sarah hauled her towel to under her chin. She was slow and never quite in the groove, but she knew she had to be on the defensive. Her employer didn't swap niceties. 'Sorry?'

'You're white Sarah. Blinding me just looking at you. Has that body ever seen the sun before? If ever there was a candidate for skin cancer it is you.' He didn't say ugh! But his eyes did. His protruding tongue echoed the repulsion.

Sarah grabbed her belongings and retreated to her room,

dropping and scooping up much of her impedimenta as she scrambled to escape the onslaught. She wouldn't cry. Vivid in her head was the future. Was, John Roberts at her mercy. You didn't speak disrespectfully to Sarah Bickles. Nanny remembered these things only too well.

John Roberts, self-satisfied with his assassination, skipped back to Stella.

'Too sensitive these Brits. Where's their sense of humour?'

'What have you been saying now? You really are a tease, dear. Let them go. You are milking this a bit too much.' Stella slapped his wrists. A naughty rogue. She had no idea the torture Sarah was putting her husband through, in the dark and vengeful movie-drome that her mind was running.

Martin Preston was finding out what he had let himself in for. Lucy Marie was a spoiled brat who wasn't going to co-operate with her tutor. This was soon evident in the makeshift classroom tucked at the back of the staff quarters. Mrs. Gleeson had spoken of a reluctant pupil, but Martin had dealt with many of those. Lucy Marie wasn't reluctant she was obstructive.

Tommy, however, was an eager student, and bright. Martin Preston wasn't ready for that. A little annoyed. It would mean more preparation. But, then he could claim it was his excellence that brought about Tommy's success. He would have to set up a piece of theatre where he could display, for the Roberts, his outstanding abilities as a teacher of children. The boy would be primed and rehearsed. Yes, that was worth the effort.

Lucy Marie could sit and ignore his instructions if she wanted. Tough shit. He was getting paid. It wasn't his fault the girl didn't want to do any work. Blank face sat in front of the same exercise doing nothing. As long as she wasn't disruptive. He would have to behave schoolmasterly towards her. Keep up the pretence. So that Tommy wouldn't grass him up.

Lucy Marie would use the time to plot some mischief. Nanny was easy meat here. With her parents always nearby, nanny wouldn't dare come down heavy.

Metro, whose real name was Brian McGregor, was a native of nearby Virgin Gorda and had been gardener to Mr. Roberts since he bought his house on the island. With unemployment on Virgin Gorda endemic he was pleased to be in a secure job, even if he despised his boss. There was always the compensation of planting enough marijuana to keep him content, and earn some extra cash catering for visiting tourists a long way from their own supplier.

Metro was shining black fronting a generous smile that ignited his face, from his ivory teeth to his watery eyes. He cut the lawns with a frenzy, cleaned the pool with a song and grovelled much lower than he ever wanted to in front of John Roberts.

Metro loved Lucy Marie and Tommy. He loved all kids. Even the spoilt issues of the arsehole he had to work for. The children found him, gumboots and vest, in the garden digging a ditch at the same frenetic pace he attacked the grass. He would have a made a superb tunneller in a WWII escape plot.

He saw them only when he stopped briefly to wipe the sweat from his eyes. With one step he was out of his hole and hugging the children. They weren't so keen on that aspect of his friendship. A seal covered in slime was how Tommy once described Metro's clammy, oily skin. It wasn't meant to be discourteous.

'Good to see you twos again.' Metro managed. Not a man of many words. His head shook and his grin persisted. 'You's got a nanny and a teach wid yous, Metro sees.' The children understood enough. Both stuck their fingers deep into their mouths, and groaned through puking eyes, to indicate their feelings about the two outriders that their parents had landed them with.

'Yeah, Dragon and Squelch,' blurted Lucy Marie. 'Hate them both.'

Metro's smile turned to amazement. These were figures that children should be looking up to. He had seven children by various ladies from his island. Didn't see much of them, but he would be certain to reprimand any such talk about learned people. Professionals that these two despised openly.

'Now miss, dey can't be dat bad.' He tried to resurrect his trademark – the beaming smile. It was lost on these imps.

'Step back.' A fortunate change of subject. 'Dat will sting yous.' Metro pulled at the children and dragged them four feet from the ditch. 'See 'im?'

'What?' Lucy Marie was annoyed at the rough handling. The man was an employee, a servant. Daddy would have to be told.

'See 'im Tommy?' Metro knew the girl was getting uppity and concentrated on the boy. There was something about boys that Metro could relate to. A strange bonding. Male elder to male heir. Perhaps tribal.

'Didn't see anything.' Tommy was confused.

'Scorpion. Dat was a brown one.' Metro announced as though he was a proud owner. 'Probably come from dat tree. Der dead one.' He loved to show the wonders of nature to the kids. Even the lethal varieties.

'Scorpion? Where?' Lucy Marie forgot the impolite treatment. She moved closer to the pit. A scorpion? How intriguing. Already there was conspiracy afoot.

'Scorpion eh?' Tommy followed his sister closer to the edge.

Metro spun round to take up position at the lip of the ditch. He would see this through as director of the wildlife exhibition. Knew how to handle these creatures. Stories he could tell about dangerous species he'd dealt with as a kid. Uniformed and at attention. Ready to pounce at the entrance to the natural history museum.

'Goes easy. Lets me see if 'e's still here.'

Metro peered at the terracotta mud at the base of his ditch. On a shiny patch where his spade had sliced the damp clay was the creature. It hadn't moved. But now its tail was sprung up and thrust forward. Standing astride.

'Sbeen alerted. 'eard us 'e 'as.' Metro pointed out the

scorpion to the two children who were now holding on tightly to his left arm.

'Where?' There was annoyance in Lucy Marie's voice. As though she had been tricked.

'There! I see it.' Tommy jabbed a finger in the direction of the insect.' See it? Can't you see it, doughnut?' There was nothing better than getting one over on your sister.

Metro held the sides of her head and forced her to look directly at it. He felt her hold on to that position and relaxed his grip.

'Gorgeous.' Her lips curled with a smile. 'I want it.'

'Want it?' Tommy quizzed. 'What for? A pet? You are a crazy, jam-filled doughnut.'

'Gives terrible bite for child.' Metro had his knowing look on. 'You has to go see Doc Lewis if you gets bit from him.'

'Get a box. We can keep him in a box.' Lucy Marie had the imprisonment planned, and more importantly the role the scorpion was going to play in her future holiday entertainment.

'What's he do for food,' Tommy asked. He'd kept other things before. A bird with a broken wing, a mouse, a toad (it could have been a frog, he wasn't sure) and a variety of disgusting slimy things from the garden. All of which had been forgotten a few days later and had to be buried by his mother. 'I'll get dinner for it.' Things were making sense for him now. A game. He was the veterinary surgeon or animal rescue.

'Ants and stuff I expect,' Lucy Marie suggested. Not too interested in its survival. Only its purpose.

'S'right miss. Dem little insects 'e 'as.' Metro was half listening. He was busy deciding how he would transfer the beast to the shoe box he had quickly collected from his room.

Both children were getting braver now, and only a few feet from the scorpion.

Metro had made his decision. Ripped off his tattered vest and threw it over the unsuspecting animal. There was movement from beneath signalling an effort to escape.

Pointless. Metro scooped up vest and contents and dumped it triumphantly in the box. With the lid partially closed he proceeded to pull slowly at the cotton rag until the whole of his garment had been retrieved.

'Dere yous goes.' Lucy Marie was presented with the trophy. She tipped the box to hear the scaly creature scuttle back and forth, unable to hold a grip. A skater out of control on the changing incline.

Metro examined his vest as he pulled it back on. It was still the same grubby torn undergarment. He jumped in the hole and held his spade ready.

Lucy Marie and Tommy moved slowly away. Side by side. Holding the box to their ears between them. Listening to all the fascinating scraping noises their captive beast was making.

John Roberts' decision to take his UK domestic staff for a drink at the only bar on the island was littered with dreadful possibilities. Even a brief visit to the *Dragonfly* to show them the haunt of the island's celebrities was a potential minefield. The owner, who had escaped from Las Vegas only three years earlier, presented a threat on his own. Sam Raymond had *disappeared* on the eve of a dangerous territorial dispute reaching armed conflict. He'd registered ownership of the *Dragonfly* in his second wife's name. Who luckily was just old enough to be eligible for such an honour. He planned to stay invisible on Anegada. Drinking and socialising with John Roberts was going to ensure he was conspicuous from now on.

Sarah and Martin Preston were summoned to rendezvous at seven thirty. *Smart casual* was ordered. Martin spoiled a reasonable pair of chinos and a floral shirt with his old college blazer. A tatty, once navy garment that had lapels the size of A4 paper and so many hanging threads it was almost more at home on Wild Bill Hickcock. Martin had left several buttons of his shirt undone and dragged the collar out to sit on the wings of his jacket. A sprout of grey chest hairs sat nest-like; an absurd centrepiece.

No matter what she chose to wear, Sarah could not have

looked *smart casual*. Drab wasn't ordered but drab is what they got. Pale green hanging off hanging shoulders. Hair carefully matted, and a long and cheerless expression. She didn't want to go out. It was on a flashing neon sign stuck to her frown.

'Let's go.' John and Stella Roberts waltzed through the front entrance. Fred Astaire and Ginger Rogers arriving on set. Martin Preston may have lacked sartorial elegance, but John Roberts epitomised American middle-age bad taste. Checked trousers in some synthetic material, pressed to give a razor crease and to emphasise a slight flare. The turn-ups rotated round his ankles as he walked. Never touching his white socks, and at least two inches clear of his shoes. His translucent polka-dot shirt, baggy and occasionally filling with air, resembled the blouse of a Spanish dancer.

His partner in the Latin American section wore a dress that erupted from her waist in lavish layers and wild petticoats, that with every swirl lifted and dropped in a cascade of colour and the scratching of rough silk. The neckline was sickeningly low and a shoving brassiere produced two vein-ridden globes fighting for dominance as she proceeded. Stella's hair had been permed or heavily set. Tight curls like ladder rungs climbed up either side of her head. Thick eyeliner, reflector lipstick and the pinched nose of a synchronised swimmer.

'Let's party!' It was almost a skip as she left the step. Poor Stella had no idea how ludicrous she looked and sounded. Nothing was less like a group about to rave than the four assembled misfits.

Sam Raymond was glued to one particular barstool - by habit, history or intoxication. It was to the far right as you entered. Where he could reach the telephone and the short-wave radio. Custom for his hillside establishment often came from hapless mariners randomly sailing through the islands. His moods went from politely formal, through indulgent grovelling to inebriated obnoxious, depending on the level of alcohol invading the bloodstream.

'Welcome.' Fortunately early evening and a gracious

greeting. 'John and Stella, and some new faces. Good to have you at the Dragonfly.' Sam's arse slid from the stool but he was carrying too much bulk to stand fully upright. He was held by the supporting seat, dribbling out his salute. 'How the devil are you?' English accent that hadn't been too disfigured by the many years wheeling and dealing in the States.

John Roberts offered his hand. Sam shook it limply. He had his sights on Stella. Despite her ridiculous appearance he was keen to pinch her buttocks. It was an island tradition to kiss on both cheeks, and Sam had perfected, even from his seated position, a method whereby he could fondle the women's arses at the same time he was pecking their faces. Stella got the full Raymond squeeze. One he saved for the fuller bottoms he had to negotiate. She would feel that twinge for the rest of the evening.

Martin and Sarah didn't look particularly game for a laugh. Sam was ready to ignore them.

'Our tutor and our nanny.' Trophies brought up to display. John Roberts ushered Martin and Sarah towards Sam. Inspect the status symbols. Sam held out a flaccid hand, which was grabbed in turn by the two *domestics*.

'How long you down for, John?' Sam took little notice of Martin and Sarah. Brushed them off with a nod. They quickly retreated to find their own corner.

Sam Raymond was ready to unload his library of sick and dirty jokes that everyone on the island despaired at. Standard practice when greeting new arrivals. There was the drone of synchronised low chuckles.

Sarah watched some statue lizard stuck to the wall next to a light. Waiting for a frenetic moth to settle. Patient. Seemingly unmoved by his meal's fickle behaviour. Was the lizard looking at her?

Martin Preston surveyed the bar. A refuge hostelry furnished with items Raymond and his bride, Donna, had brought back from Bali. He was at home. Damaged pride for the moment, but that was a quick healer. Especially with some booze down his throat. A bartender, who introduced himself as Patrick, was alert to the eyes of a thirsty man.

'Drink?' Martin leaned across to ask in a whisper. Sarah's gaze was riveted to the ceiling and the gladiator lizard, motionless. Out of character for Martin Preston to offer so readily. Some motive. Get them in when you are just a couple is a wise move. As the party increases you're in the round with currency. Having entered at the shallow end. He didn't miss a trick.

'A wine.' Sarah would comply as best she could.

'Wine?' Martin's eyebrows shivered. 'Which particular wine would that be?' Sarcasm not well hidden.

'A red one.' Sarah momentarily lowered her eyes. She sensed she was sounding anything but knowledgeable.

Any lecture on the marked difference between the chateaux and estates of south-west France would have taken time. A precious commodity. Martin sensed the Roberts ready to abandon the foundering Sam Raymond, who was swaying precariously and had done the arse-fondling thing. They would want some extraordinary and expensive cocktail. John Roberts was fitting more and more into the market-stall-holder image that Martin's creative mind had originally but only transiently allotted. Add some cheap American loud mouth and he was nearly there.

'Not a bad landlord?' John Roberts spoke to the empty seat that Martin Preston had vacated in his scramble to reach the bar. 'For an Englishman,' he added with a smirk into his cough-retarding hand.

Sarah had given up on the lizard, but kept her gaze swinging around the bar. Stopping at anything and everything. She wouldn't look at her employer.

'Teacher getting the drinks in?' he asked her sweeping head.

Sarah bobbed, her eyes fixed on a terracotta plant pot. A stepping stone of no significance.

'Oh, you are here now. Sorry. Got them in. Thought you were chatting.' Transparent nonsense. Martin thrust the wine into Sarah's hand and thumped down beside her. Close call.

Stella grinned her way across the bar. Patrick followed her Barbara Cartland waddle. He balanced two dubiously tinted Martinis on his crooked arm.

'This is cosy.' She shuffled comfortable. Her dress exploding into a series of crumpled fans as she sat. Rapid hands made urgent attempts to quell the inflating petticoats. A quick reconnoitre to notice who was looking her way. 'A bar in paradise. Wouldn't you agree Mr. Preston?' She panted with the exertion.

'A bar is paradise, Mrs. Roberts.' Martin laughed at his own joke.

There were several other groups in the bar. A French party off a yacht, some Germans who were renting one of the houses and a spattering of homeowners. This last assembly was not a fully formed unit, and each straggling element was huddled in conversation. They hadn't acknowledged John and Stella Roberts when they arrived at the bar or whilst Sam Raymond was entertaining. It was deliberate myopia. Common knowledge amongst the island community that the brash Americans were worth avoiding. But both Stella and John Roberts were ready to exchange a smile with any of them. Their eyes alert for a glimpse of recognition. As if sending out the radio waves of a radar system John Roberts began at an alarming volume.

'Last time we were in here.' A distant ducking of a head indicated the prey had been detected. 'Or was it the time before? Doesn't matter. You couldn't move for celebrities. That's right isn't it, Stella?'

'Sure, John. Bunch of them in here one night, as I recall. There was that guy from that film, with the one from the TV programme. You know.' Poor Stella wanted to help but she was thinking through mud.

'Bruce Williams is who you mean. He was in Sixth Element. Excellent film.' John Roberts was pleased with himself. Oblivious to his own limited knowledge.

Martin Preston flipped a coin in his head. Should he step in and humiliate his employer. It was perhaps a mistake to have looked so pleased when the decision was made. Heads!

'Forgive me, but I'm certain you mean Bruce Willis who was in both Fifth Element and Sixth Sense. I wouldn't share your enthusiasm for either of those films.'

Smug little shit. John Roberts' face said it. 'Sure.' Suitably dismissive. His mission was to impress, so the celebrity tales continued. 'Milling round, swapping stories, no prima donnas, no pretensions. Like a family we were.' John Roberts still studied backs of heads and the phantom faces he tried to reach. They weren't being baited.

Sarah had resorted to watching the floor through the pinkness of her wine. Rose quadrilateral tiles that distorted, broke and stretched with every slow spin of the glass.

'Royalty as well.' Stella directed this towards Sarah. 'Really let their hair down when they get here.'

Sarah looked up and nodded. Hopeful that would keep Stella happy.

'Hangers on. Not proper Royal Family.' John Roberts wanted it known. 'You know. Married into it, or the son of some wacky Viscount. Some chinless wonder with a state apartment and pension.' He searched for a response.

'That's not nice.' Sam Raymond had found a second wind and was stumbling towards the toilets. Outside lavatories that he had amusingly labelled *boys* and *girls.* Such a joker. 'By Royal Appointment I am. I'll be displaying the sign above the entrance. You go steady on running down our ruling family.'

John Roberts grabbed Sam and hauled him to sit and hailed Donna over. Sam's wife, ever alert to a sale, marched Patrick over with her.

'Just telling these people about the raucous times we've had here. It's a happening place all right.' John Roberts needed the company. 'What's it to be Donna? One of those pina coladas that get you going?' There was almost a *nudge, nudge; know what I mean* to follow. 'And for you Sam?'

'Off to the little boy's room.' He bumbled to his feet. 'But, I won't be rude. One of my specials, Patrick.' Code of course. Patrick knew it was just another champagne out of his existing bottle, served in a small goblet that would be charged up to John Roberts as an exotic cocktail.

'We certainly have the top people in here.' Donna began to sell the Dragonfly. Part fable, part anecdotal. 'Can't remember you being at any of the mad bashes, John, but we've had some crazy times.'

Martin Preston didn't care a toss. Different if there were powerful people there. Where he could rub shoulders and network. Scrounge out some work. But to listen about the comings and goings of mildly interesting actors or popular music entertainers was purgatory. And anyway there weren't many drinks being doled out.

Sarah was out of her depths but unscathed. She could be his passport. 'I think we ought to go. Sarah isn't feeling too good, and besides there's only the maid looking after the children. I am a little concerned.' Martin rose and straightened his crumpled blazer. Sarah was relieved but not pleased she was used as an excuse. She knew he would never be aware of the children's needs. Martin Preston suffered the brats for the same reason she did. There was money in the urchins. They both relied on these hostages.

'Wait now, Mr. Preston, you haven't heard this one. Sam, tell him about the Sean Connery episode.' John Roberts guffawed. 'Go on, let's all have a laugh. You've got to hear this.'

Sam had lived off this one for years. Nothing like an old faithful to fall back on. 'Do I have to?' It meant *only too pleased to.*

'There I was, in the bar. On my stool. An ordinary day.'

'Pissed, eh?' Donna chirped in. It was obviously going to be a double act.

'As I was saying, before I was *so* rudely interrupted.' Sam scanned the group with a sickly smile. 'Just at the bar minding my own business.'

'That'll be the first time.' Donna was eager to make it a duo. 'He's the worst, he is. Knows what everyone's up to. A right nosy parker.'

What an intolerable cow! Martin Preston, still stuck in his escape position, was suffering now. Perhaps it wasn't worth the money?

'In comes this chap. Straight off the beach. Sand all over him. Scruffy bugger.' Sam screwed up his nose. 'You know, the type that slips off one of those French yachts. Fuck-all money. Get them popping in occasionally. I can tell you, I'm owed some serious money from those pirates.'

'Keep to the point, honey.' Donna was enjoying orchestrating the story. 'So you're a tight wad. No need to tell everyone.'

'Asks me for credit. Just like that. Red rag to a bull, or what. Comes up to Sam Raymond and has the audacity to want a tab. Saucy blighter. There he is in his swimming shorts, a towel over his shoulder, bits of seaweed in what's left of his hair and there's sand. Probably in his mouth at that.' Sam shook his head. 'And I can see that there are others at the door. Over there.' He pointed to the very spot they stood. 'This guy's family. A motley crew I can tell you.'

'So what did you tell him, Sam?' John Roberts was helping out now.

'I told him, no bloody way. Fuck off. Too many of his type asking for tick.' Sam was getting into the part. Real feelings taking over from the yarn.

'This is the best bit.' Donna was back in the act. 'What happened then?'

'Don't you know me? He says. No I bloody don't I says. Some Jock I reckons by his accent. He swings his head round as if to get help. And sighing. As if it was me that was the waster.'

'What did he say to you?'

'Nothing for a while, and then he says he's an actor and

that surely I recognised him. I said I don't know you from James, fucking, Bond. Then he collapses with laughter. And when he stops tells me he *is* James Bond. Well I'd had enough by then. I tell him not to take the piss, and I get Patrick to help me chuck 007 out.'

'And it was Sean Connery?' Remarkably it was Sarah who spoke. It was the only thing she'd listened to all evening. Liked Sean Connery.

'Yes, it was Sean Connery, who was staying at Atlantic House. The huge one on the hill. And my intelligent husband throws him out of the Dragonfly. What a berk!'

'Looked nothing like James Bond. I've seen the films. Real smoothy in them. Tidy with well-groomed hair and tailored suits. This scruff looked like a beach bum. Bald as a coote. No resemblance at all. But, Christ, soon as I found out I was round there like a shot.' Sam came to his own defence.

'Yeah. Tried to tell him it was all a game. A joke like. Sorry he didn't get it. See the funny side. Gave him a bottle of Dom Perignon.' Donna was enjoying reliving her husband's faux pas.

'You're a character, Sam, right enough. Good tale eh, Mr. Preston?' John Roberts was chewing on his last chuckle.

Martin was moderately entertained. It confirmed what he thought about Sam Raymond. He nodded in agreement. 'Ready now, Sarah?'

She rose. John and Stella Roberts looked over to where the other homeowners had been. They had escaped. A strategic use of Sam Raymond's parable to make good their flight.

'Not much going on tonight. We'll come with you.' John Roberts pulled Stella to her feet. She tried to groom her dress. But when she was upright her arms weren't long enough to tame the wild layers.

No one spoke on the way home. John Roberts had nothing to brag about and the others were ready for bed. Not all of them would have a good night's sleep though.

Sarah relieved the maid who she found fast asleep on a

bench outside the children's rooms. She didn't bother to check on Lucy Marie and Tommy. All was quiet and she wouldn't endanger that.

She wasn't meticulous enough in her habits to notice the difference. Bedclothes had been interfered with, and grubby hands had attempted to tuck in the flapping mosquito netting. But she was aware of the gritty material on her sheet as she slid into bed. Just like soil. It didn't alert her. She fell asleep quickly. A deep and swirling sleep, frighteningly suffocating and numbing.

Sarah never felt the sting. There was just fighting to wake up. Pulling at her heavy body in an attempt to retrieve it from sinking into the depths of the spiralling room. As she flickered in and out of consciousness Sarah only knew she was lying in a soaking bed, and her head was being beaten senseless, from the inside. It was difficult to distinguish between reality and the phantoms born of fever. She fought desperately to stay afloat.

Lucy Marie and Tommy listened from their room. Listened to the moaning. Listened to the thrashing arms that smacked the sodden sheets. Listened to their own hearts thumping in their ears and to each other's quick breathing. Tommy tapped the empty shoebox and looked again for scorpion shit.

Sarah managed to slip out of bed. Sliding off the skidding sheets.

They heard her slump to the floor.

She tried to slither. To reach the door. To keep awake. Her leg was huge; bloated. The skin tight and shiny. Urging to burst. She dragged it. Impedimenta. It was the weight of steel. Was she dying?

On her bed the sheet twitched. Something scratched, also seeking to escape.

Metro found her. An arm hanging out of the barely open door. He had no idea of his complicity.

Dr. Geoff Lewis briefly thought it was a nasty virus or food poisoning, until, on further inspection, he found the puncture in Sarah's leg. He kept her in the clinic building all that day until he had lowered her temperature, and allowed her back to the house in the early evening. She would be treated there. A couple of visits a day for a week should do it.

Stella visited with the children and Martin Preston looked in after classes. John Roberts sent a message with his wife but never ventured near his sick nanny.

Lucy Marie and Tommy had triumphed. It was difficult not to wallow in that victory when they saw their nanny. Sarah was feeling lousy, her swollen leg was throbbing and she looked like a dishevelled witch. But, beyond the pleasantries of Stella Roberts seated close to her bed, Sarah was aware of the self-satisfied glint in the eyes of her charges.

'Apparently it was a nasty little scorpion that did this to you.' Stella tilted her head to demonstrate her compassion. 'Geoff Lewis was quite shocked that one should be in the house. First he's known. Keep themselves to themselves in the bark of dead trees normally.' A consoling smile. 'A bit of hard luck, my dear.'

Sarah tried to raise herself on her elbows. Stella thought she was going to speak. Instead she stared beyond. Narrowing eyes that were aimed at the children.

Stella was impressed that nanny, in her sick bed, should still be concerned about Tommy and Lucy Marie. 'As I was saying, these awful scorpions aren't found near the house, so you should be safe in future. But I think we all will be searching our beds before we go to sleep from now on. And Metro tells me that he was digging a ditch for...Oh, never mind about that.' Suddenly aware. Stella turned to her children. It was too much of a coincidence. They wouldn't, surely? She would check the shoebox that Metro had said it was in. Of course they were scoundrels at times, but not this. Nothing so awful.

Sarah sensed Stella's awkwardness and turned her hooded eyes on her.

'So, let's hope for a quick recovery.' Stella knew when she

was a target. She scooped up the kids and ushered them from the room. A little more brutal than usual.

'It must have escaped.' Tommy was plausible. 'It was our friend.'

'Yes, we're very sad.' Lucy Marie feigned distress, badly.

Stella examined the shoebox once more. 'You shouldn't have brought it in the house, and you should have taped the top down. This is irresponsible of you. I'm assuming, of course, that your little pet is the culprit here. And I would be bitterly disappointed if I thought that you had deliberately placed this creature in your nanny's bed.'

The most innocent of smiles exuded from both moon faces. As angelic as they could manage. As if.

'Get rid of the box.' Stella left them in their room. She wasn't convinced of their integrity.

Martin Preston should have questioned why Lucy Marie was eager to enquire in class the next day, about the toxic nature of scorpion stings. And about what other poisonous critters inhabited the islands. She turned a routine science lesson into research for future terrorist attacks on her nanny. Not that he knew much about the subject, and chose solely to recount an episode when he found himself face to face with a viper on Chobham Common. This soon dampened Lucy Marie's interest and she slipped back into obstructive mode.

After four days Sarah was up and about. She had nothing to do with the children. Stella covered as much as she could stand and shared the rest of Sarah's chores amongst the rest of the staff of the house.

Kane was very attentive. Metro had spoken to him about the brown scorpion and he was intuitive enough to lay the blame squarely on the kids. Not that he would ever suggest such a thing to his employers.

'We're leaving on Friday.' John Roberts declared at breakfast. It was a little earlier than planned. Martin was pleased he was going to get paid for even less work. Sarah was relieved she could get home. She was due some holiday time on their return. Even Lyme Regis would be a haven after the trauma she had been through.

John Roberts would conclude the stay on Anegada as antagonistic as ever. Out of touch with the market where he would normally vent his aggression. And it was the ailing nanny and stereotypical schoolteacher who would remain centre target.

A final meal before the return to London. Kane was magical. His white gloves like a conjuror's whisking dishes away, and filling glasses only seconds earlier at the lips of ambitious drinkers. Almost a celebration of departure. A last supper.

'Here's to Anegada.' It was Martin Preston. Well oiled and letting his hair down. 'And to all the staff at *Seawind.*' He raised his glass where he stood. Waving it towards Kane, and through to the kitchen. It wasn't aimed at the Roberts. The other diners took a while before they were ready to join in.

Kane whispered in Martin's ear as he took his plate. 'T'ank you sir. Most kind.'

'No more than you deserve.' A little loud for the butler. Kane cringed. 'A gentleman's gentleman, that's what you are my friend.' The glass was half raised again. He regretted that. John Roberts was no gentleman.

It took a while for John Roberts to reach equilibrium with the intoxicated schoolteacher. When he was there he was eager to discuss one last niggling aspect of his adopted country.

It started harmlessly enough. 'I suppose when we get back it will be election fever. Well in the States that is. As long as another Democrat doesn't get in I'll be happy.'

Most at the table nodded. It was inconsequential stuff to them. But Martin couldn't resist. 'Strong Republican are we? Right wing man from the Reagan school?' Alcohol bravery from the teacher.

John Roberts relished the challenge. 'Better than being a woman of a Democrat. We need strong government. You won't get that from some girl who wants to pamper to the immigrants and give millions of dollars away in welfare to people who can't get off their asses to do a day's work.'

'I know little of the parties in America.' Martin Preston lied. 'But from what CNN has told me, naïve as I am, the Democratic Party appears to be similar to our Labour Party and the Republican Party on a par with our Conservatives. Is that right?'

'Your Tony Blair is a nancy like Clinton. That's true. Same sorry policies that drain the wealth of the country. Same idealism that stinks.'

'So a Republican President would be the answer? Is that how you see it?' Martin was out to compartmentalise the American's politics.'

'Remember the eighties. Reagan in Washington and Maggie in London. What a pair. What a winning combination. What a stock market.' John Roberts was forever thankful. It was when he really made his money.

'A real capitalist.' Martin spoke to the ceiling.

'Nothing wrong with that schoolteacher. Being a capitalist in America though is the real thing. There's real politics there. None of this monarchy business and a bunch of wimps reacting to Her Majesty's whim. Strength in government. That's what you get from the Presidential system. Real authority.' Confused notions from an inebriate.

'Sounds almost fascist to me.' Martin complained.

'Reflects your understanding. A regime with muscle aiming to help the people is the answer. Too many of these timid administrations that haven't the guts to get anything done.' John Roberts thumped his chest as if he were the man in power, or Tarzan.

Sarah wished she could simply evaporate. Stella was lost. They sought refuge in some futile discussion about the children. Pulling their chairs away from the worsening exchange.

'I do believe you would have voted for Adolf Hitler.' Martin was beginning to forget the money. He knew his wire transfer had gone through, but he was sabotaging future cash from this family. Drunk enough to undermine a sound investment.

'And you for Liberace.' John Roberts smirked. 'Come on man, face the facts. There's a racial time bomb in the UK as there is in the US. If we don't do something now, we're lost. No disrespect to Kane here, but it's no-go for us whites in lots of cities. Don't you agree?'

Martin Preston did not. 'So the United States has the best political system, the best sports and the best workers?'

'Yeah.' John Roberts was a proud American.

'So how come you want to live in Britain?'

'What it doesn't have, that beautiful country of mine, is the best tax system. Democrats out to screw me. Chasing me from my homeland.' He sounded bitter.

'So you are only over the pond...'

'To save money. Too damn right.' John Roberts finished off for him. 'A financial exile. If the Democrats don't learn soon about driving away the entrepreneurs that built America, the country is going to be in the shit.' John Roberts was a hero. In his own money-grabbing way he genuinely thought he was one big fairy godmother to the USA.

Chapter 8

Sarah arrived at her mother's house unannounced. It was the same; only the black water stains on the sandy masonry had reached the front door and more flakes of paintwork were raised on the window ledges. No one had moved out. She waddled down the path. Her case scratched on the ground and alerted someone inside. A seated figure.

'Who's there?' A gravelly female voice. Old and infirm. Agitated and sour.

'Me.' It was enough. No more than that was ever said.

'Sarah?' A confused enquiry.

'Yeah.' Almost a conversation for the Bickles family.

'What you doing here?' The old woman asked of the head only just appearing at the crack of the door. 'Lost that fancy job?' Some bitterness seeping in.

'No. Home. Just for a bit.' Now it really was communication.

'I see.' Resentment in the reply.

Heavy thudding on the stairs heralded Debbie's arrival in the lounge.

'Sarah?'

'Debbie?'

Repeating of names and swapped stares. Not even a touch of hands, let alone the embrace of long-separated sisters.

'She's not well.' Debbie nodded towards her mother.

'What is it?'

'Her joints and stuff.'

'Arthritis is what it is,' Mrs. Bickles announced with a mixture of pride and gravity.

'You here for long?' Debbie needed to know. 'Can you help out? She can't do nothing.'

'Burden am I?' Mother Bickles was touchy.

121

'It ain't that, Mum. You know. Just some time.' Debbie was awkward.

'Got 'erself a man, she 'as.' Mother declared, as if Debbie had some contagious sexual disease. 'No interest in 'er poor Mum. And with you away. Might as well be dead. That's me.' On her throne she wallowed in self-pity.

'I'll get the kettle on.' Debbie retreated to the kitchen.

Sarah tugged her case upstairs. Her mother put her hands up to her face and sniffed.

Other than a couple of cardboard boxes stored there Sarah's room was much like Miss Faversham's. Saved. Stuck in time. Stale and dank. A reminder of a sour childhood and a fermented adolescence. Meagre. Everything about Sarah was meagre.

Debbie squeezed in while Sarah unpacked. 'His name is Roy. Known 'im a couple of months. She don't like it. So long since we had a man about. We don't talk men do we?' Debbie examined her nails. They were red now. Part of the uniform when you're dating.

Sarah didn't care and couldn't think of anything she wanted to know about the subject. She fiddled with some clothes in a drawer.

'Don't s'pose you understand, like. Not into men are you?' It wasn't meant to be hurtful. But it was.

'Had one in America, I did.' A defensive response. Sarah was sorry she said it.

'Christ! Did you?' Debbie was showing some respect. 'Tell me more.'

'Name's Bobby. Bobby Clayman.' It wasn't a lie. She wanted it to sound natural. Sarah pictured him in his truck. His bungling. The night out. There was a smidgen of pride.

'You done it with 'im? This Bobby?' Debbie was very interested.

Sarah simply stared at her. *Done it*. Her sister was getting cheap.

'I 'ave.' Debbie wanted to tell her sister how good it was. A dragging sensation in her gut held her back. She couldn't show off about that.

Debbie gulped and looked at the ceiling. 'Expecting I am.' Debbie had to admit it. Wanted Sarah to know. 'Roy's goin't marry me. 'e said, like.' There was no conviction in her voice. 'Get a place. You know. Live together, like.' She wished.

Her sister doing it? With a man? Sarah cringed and made for the bathroom. Her sister having a baby. She washed herself twice and scrubbed her teeth. But the smell and the nasty taste persisted.

'If we get married you can be bridesmaid. What'd you think, Sarah?' Debbie spoke to the closed bathroom door and the frantic cleaning that she heard.

Sarah didn't speak again that night. Debbie left her sister sitting on her sheet, picking at the scab on her bad leg. Her hand hovering over the light switch. Before she slept Sarah heard her mother in the well of the house. She spoke loudly to herself about all the things she had done for her daughters, and how betrayed she felt. Her being in so much pain, as well. Sarah couldn't adjust the volume and drifted off with the record still playing. Stuck in a groove.

At breakfast her mother was shuffling about the kitchen. Remarkably mobile. They nodded to each other without speaking. Too much had been said the night before. Dishes and cutlery made the only noises until Mrs. Bickles leaned on the draining board with both hands and inhaled deeply.

'You never came back. Never came back after that boy died. Did you?'

Sarah looked hard at her empty cereal dish. Rupert? Why is she on about that?

'Thought you'd see us after all that. Poor little fella dying, an' all.' Mrs. Bickles winced. Scuffing her feet. Just a reminder of the arthritis.

Sarah was trapped. Her legs tingled and her skin perspired.

'Debbie tells me you got a man as well. That right?' Almost a blade on the final words.

Now she really regretted blabbing to her sister. 'No.' Almost a whisper.

'Why'd she tell me that then?'

'Just a man I met when I was away. It ain't anything.'

'Men. I thought what with your father you'd 'ave learnt. You and your sister. Learnt about men.' She pictured their father. 'Users and traitors. That's what men are. 'specially that one. Do nothing but 'urt you. Mark my words. Yeah, mark my words, men aren't worth nothing.' Mrs. Bickles felt for the chair and slumped down. She still had her husband's cheating face stuck in her head.

Sarah watched her mother's shoulders as they jerked with every despairing sigh.

'So. Now you both'll be leaving. Leaving me here with my arthritis. Alone. No one wants me. Wants an old woman. You go with your men. You and your sister. Leave an old woman and her pain.' *Stay and look after me, please.* That's what she was pleading. But it was melancholy ranting that made Sarah cringe and slide away. Out of the kitchen and to her room.

Sarah hid out all day. Debbie came up when she arrived home from work. There were things about Roy she wanted to talk about. But knew from Sarah's icy manner that she had prattled too much about Sarah and the man to her mother. There was an embarrassed exchange that promised to end in protracted silence so Debbie left.

She was digging. In some underworld of dreams she was digging furiously. Spraying out loose and stinging soil. Like a dog recovering a bone. There were people shouting at her. In a ring...Calling names...Chanting. And the more they yelled the more deliriously she dug. But with one wave they retreated. With just one wave of the gunmetal pistol they were on their knees. Begging forgiveness...A split second change...The power of the gun. And the sun shone. And she was some princess. A drawn one from a child's book...Pressing into the side of her mother's head...Making a crimson ring mark at her temple...And an urge to pull (no, squeeze) the trigger...And then pointing at Debbie's newborn baby and an anonymous father...The same red rings as the barrel was thrust and turned...And she spoke invisible dialogue...More words than she had ever used...Telling them who she was...And who they weren't...words that splattered them...Like blood...Silent words...Wounding and maiming words that fired volleys at their dumb carcasses and pleading mouths...

Sarah woke to pee and drink. The scorpion was still biting.

In the fitful sleep that followed until morning she never returned to those phantoms. Disappointing in a way. These were spectres not so appalling.

Stella Roberts phoned the next day to remind Sarah about the schedule for their next two trips. Her impatience to get away from Wentworth motivated by the reprobate behaviour of Lucy Marie and Tommy. Stella wanted her back to the Surrey home as soon as possible, garbling on about the children missing her and what a diligent worker she was. Even Sarah could recognise bullshit.

'My mum is very ill.' A convenient excuse.

More dribbling nonsense from Stella about mothers and their ailments, during which several mentions of *hypochondria and you know what old people are like.*

'And my sister is about to have a baby.' Sarah was finding these conditions useful.

Even more tripe about natural births without too many people interfering, *special times for the mother and father. You can feel left out of this sort of thing.*

Sarah conceded. She would return to work the following Monday. Anyway it wasn't going to be that pleasant at home if her mother continued to forecast doom and her sister prattled on about babies and an absent father named Roy.

Avoiding her sister and her mother was the main occupation for Sarah during the five days she remained on the decaying council estate in Lyme Regis. Debbie tried her best to persuade her to stay and help her cope with their mother. And her mother used every opportunity to play the guilt card.

'You goin't just take off and leave me. Your sister doesn't care. She's got this man, hasn't she? No room for a crippled mother. She's told you about the baby I suppose. It's a disgrace. That's what it is. Thought you were good girls. Thought I'd done enough to warn you off men. Fools, both of you. She'll go when the baby arrives. And I'll be left. Left all alone. Won't last long. Might as well be dead now. Wish I was. No one would care.' The tears rolled down her cheeks. Lava escaping from a crater. Running over the dry crust of previous eruptions. 'Just for a while. Until I'm back on me feet.' Hound dog eyes and a dabbing handkerchief. A huddled figure, hairnet and flowery housecoat, slouched on a kitchen chair. The lingering odour of streaky bacon.

She brought paltry belongings home and would take paltry belongings away again. Sarah didn't own much. Would never own much. There wasn't enough of her to spend money on.

Laid out in her battered case were the pale frocks and the lifeless material of her other assorted scraps that made up her wardrobe. Only the garish turquoise swimming costume shouting out amidst the dreary garments.

Her escape from home was a furtive affair. Sarah took every tread of the stairs with kissing feet, ensuring the harsh material of her case didn't scrape the handrail. No telltale noise to alert the two women with their imploring hands and accusing stares. The unlatching of the front door brought them out. At the end of the hall. Just as Sarah was stooping to lift her case. In a low light, as if at the end of a cave. Betrayed and forlorn.

Damning eyes met. She dropped her case and stood bolt upright? Both her hands were gripped together, the left thumb stuck in the right palm. The right forefinger pointed along an imaginary barrel and then bent crooked around a precarious trigger. No last wishes.

Bang!

Bang!

Sarah almost skipped to the bus stop. There was no one to worry about now.

Chapter 9

'Fall's closing in. Autumn to you. And when winter arrives it's like the Arctic,' Stella explained to Sarah. 'We'll need some of the coats from here, but most of their snow gear is at the cottage. They'll be skiing and skating. And I expect John will take them out on the snowmobiles. He just loves to dash around on those. His toys, that's what those things are. Kid at heart.'

'Right.' Sarah sounded a touch buoyant. If that was possible. 'I'll pack it up right away ma'am.'

'We have several days before we're off, so don't bother to rush it now.' Stella hadn't seen her nanny that keen. 'The kids have school right up to when we go. I have spoken with Mrs. Gleeson and they will need tutoring again while we are away. She isn't able to recommend anyone else except that squirm Preston. John can't stand the man. Won't have him along. Reckons he'll give them lessons. I'll believe that when I see it. Just hope they don't fall further behind. Pity I'm no good in that area.' Stella gritted her teeth and raised her shoulders. She was talking to herself now.

Sarah wasn't that interested. There was some respite, however, if the children were in the classroom, and Martin Preston would have deflected some of the flack from her. Now she'd be the sole British representative. Not much of a team selection.

'At least we won't have him and John detonating at mealtimes, will we?' Stella was still shaking her head as she waddled from the room.

Sarah tried to picture the cottage and the lake, and how it would look in winter.

'Sorry, Sarah, I haven't been thinking straight.' Stella had swept back into the room. 'Your clothes. I should have thought about that.'

My clothes, thought Sarah, what's she going to say about them? She pictured the drab material flattened in her case. Unpacking it meant putting it on show. Better to pull things out when you needed them, than display her ordinary collection.

'You'll need some warm stuff to keep that cold out. I don't expect you have anything suitable.' Stella tried to be as polite as she could about Sarah's wardrobe. She knew only too well what a bad dresser her nanny was. 'How could you, the weather being so different. You wouldn't need such protective clothing here. Look, I have some spare coats, boots etc. It'll fit you I'm sure.'

Sarah had huge feet. She had once tried to step into a pair of Stella's high heels while intruding in her bedroom, and felt like one of the ugly sisters trying on the glass slipper. She couldn't even squeeze into them. Sure a coat might fit; scarves and such accessories, but there was no way that footwear would be provided.

Stella was aware of the problem, and had already solved it. She wouldn't tell Sarah that she was actually destined to slop about in a pair of John Roberts' heavy boots.

Lucy Marie and Tommy weren't fitting in at school. Their spasmodic attendance broke up curriculum continuity and peer group bonding. They were left out of the most conspiratorial break-time gangs, and often the target for some mean bullying by those holding higher positions in the pupil hierarchy. Martin Preston's negligent teaching on Anegada led to huge gaps in their schoolwork and some massive amounts of homework. Not that Mrs. Gleeson informed the Roberts of this discrepancy. A recommendation from *The Forests* must never be thought dubious or lacking professional evaluation. A permit for Martin Preston to escape any comeback from his shoddy teaching.

John Roberts had returned to find the market was sick and

numerous lame companies were taking their last breath on Wall Street. He was in his element. It meant he was imprisoned in his study and well clear of Sarah. He ate irregularly and mostly at times when the family wasn't around. If he did manage to take his meal in the dining room he would invariably have his mobile phone tucked between his shoulder and his ear. His words hurdling mouthfuls of food.

Sarah drove the children to and from school. She hadn't improved much, but at least she was now familiar with the route. Since the episode on Anegada there was a distinct frostiness in the relationship. Icicles rather than just the usual chill.

Lucy Marie was determined to drive Sarah away. Nanny had been there too long and there was no doubting her dislike of this foul woman. The scorpion escapade had gone well, but it hadn't done the trick. The old bag was still here. Tommy kept talking in giggles about the size of nanny's swollen leg and the noises she was making from the next room. It was a hoot. He was impressed by that trick.

In the car returning from school Lucy Marie would sit looking very snooty. Eyes front. Unless tugged at the sleeve by brother Tommy. Tommy spoke, but only to himself. Playing demented games with a couple of toy cars and some assorted bricks of Lego. A language that consisted of exaggerated sounds depicting swishes, swoops and zooms, and the crunching of fatal crashes.

There was just one last chance to get nanny to throw in the towel before they left for a winter break in New Hampshire. Lucy Marie was heedful of any opportunity and would endeavour to increase the effectiveness of this next ploy. Though she put it simpler than that. She wished Tommy was more attentive and coming up with some plans himself. There was only so much deviousness a seven-year-old could manage.

Yet in a way it was Tommy who initiated the prank that would be their last ditch attempt to dislodge the hag of a nanny.

At home in Wentworth it suited both children and their minder to keep to their own territory and in this way they coexisted. Lucy Marie and Tommy studied and played in each other's rooms. Companions. A camaraderie born out of a common enemy.

After gruelling homework Tommy continued sweeping his toy cars around. Following a pattern on the carpet. As if cornering at a racetrack. Lucy Marie refurbished her dolls house. Sedate activities, until the relative calm was broken by a tinny voice giving out the order of cars in a forthcoming race.

'In the red car is Jim Smith, famous driver from the USA, and in the gree...' Tommy's muffled voice announced.

'What are you doing?' his sister demanded, annoyed by the disturbance.

'Announcer at the race, silly.' Tommy explained. Also annoyed. It was a good game and his sister knew he hated having to clarify himself.

'Announcer?'

'Yeah.' Tommy grabbed hold of the small mike. 'And disturbing the whole event, the final championship, is my sister.' His metallic voice clanked out of the tiny speaker by his feet. 'She is being a real girl. What a pain she is.' He was on his feet avoiding Lucy Marie's swinging slap. 'She could never drive a real racing car. Not her.' He danced from side to side to prevent her clutching the loose cable. 'Ha! Ha!' Canned laughter.

Lucy Marie was contemplating getting up from the floor and chasing her infuriating brother. Instead the cogs in her brain started churning; almost audibly. Of course. What a great idea. It would work. She had the blueprint drawn.

'Look, Tommy. Come here.'

'Why? It's a trap. You're going to twist my ear.' He edged nearer as there was no sign of Lucy Marie raising her hand in anger. 'What you going to do?' Closer. Within range. He pushed the mike at her. Where she could snatch it. She ignored his test.

'Sit down. I've got a plan. That thing you were talking through?'

'It's from my old tape deck. That stereo thing Aunt Betty gave me. Now it's my loudspeaker unit for the Grand Prix and Indy series.' Tommy was proud of his improvisation.

'We can use that. Use it to scare the shit out of our nanny. The cow.' Lucy Marie had Halloween eyes. She pulled at the wire and the microphone fell from Tommy's hand.

'How?' As usual Tommy was well behind.

'We fix it up. Hidden somewhere. And you speak. You know, in a funny voice. Scare her.'

'What do I say?' Tommy gave Lucy Marie a wide-eyed stare; buck teeth bared.

'Not sure yet. I'm thinking about that. What do you reckon would frighten the old bag?' Lucy Marie stuck her fist under her chin and tilted her head in thought.

Tommy scrambled off to his bedroom and clambered on to the stool that he used to reach the highest shelf in his wardrobe. He threw down some bundles of paper that hit the floor with a crump in an aurora of dust. Then jumped down alongside them. With the magazines under his arm he slid back into Lucy Marie's room.

'There.' He announced.

'What?' Lucy Marie was still deep in thought.

'Comics. Some real creepy ones that Mom doesn't know I've got. Philip from school gave them to me. A swap for that set of Pokemon cards.' Tommy was the excited one now.

'So?' Lucy Marie wasn't that impressed.

'These are great. Real spooky.' Tommy was a goofy kid. 'If we look through these we might see something to broadcast on my speaker to terrify her. Make old Sarah go weird. Yeah, make her jump. Just like the scorpion.' Tommy would never forget that trick.

'Let's see.' Lucy Marie pulled some issues from the centre of the pile to send the rest toppling. 'Just stupid kids stuff. Not going to scare an adult, is it?'

'Aagh!' Tommy thrust a front page into his sister's face and danced about her. There was a robot as tall as a house on the cover. 'He'd make you poo your pants.'

'Stop it!' Lucy Marie slapped down a copy in front of her as she sat cross-legged on the floor.

Silence for several minutes, as both children hunted for some dreadful script. Lucy Marie reading aloud and Tommy inventing dialogue from some frightening pictures. Swapping chilling lines.

'You are mere earthlings who will perish when we invade.' Tommy did his best to sound like an alien.

'Beg for death quickly Dangerman, or do you wish me to pull you apart myself, bit by bloody bit.' Lucy Marie adopted a sinister voice to deliver the excerpt.

It was a good game, and they forgot their intention for a short while as they bombarded each other with trite phrases and corny repartee. Comics were read, folded and discarded. A carpet of blues and metallic greys. Aliens and cosmic clones speaking in bubbles and suffering or instigating horrible violent abuse.

'I've got it. Here, listen to this!' Lucy Marie was jubilant. She spread out the dog-eared page and straightened her back.

Tommy spun round to take a peek at the picture on the page her finger was resting on.

'You are going to take some lead. A swine like you must be rubbed out. You are in my sights. My finger is on the trigger. Say goodbye, bitch!' Lucy Marie gasped. 'What about that, then?'

It wasn't what Tommy had in mind. 'I thought something like aliens invading or a robot maybe.' Tommy scratched his head. He didn't really know what bitch meant. Some vague idea that it wasn't complimentary, but nowhere near the language he wanted to shout through his microphone.

'She wouldn't understand some of those bits and you can't read it.' Lucy Marie tore the page out and began practising a voice for the delivery.

'She'll know it's you.' Tommy decided, even before the final version was ready

'You have a go then.' Lucy Marie threw the page to him.

Tommy summoned up his most gruesome intonation and roared into the mike, as Lucy Marie helped him with the words.

'That's useless.' She grabbed back the paper. 'Can't hear it all, and you can't disguise your voice either. *Wubbed out.* Obvious it's you. Wub, wub, wub.' Lucy Marie tormented. 'Wubberly words, Tommy.'

'Mom said you weren't to say that. Not my fault.' A tear slid down Tommy's face. He'd tried so hard to get his obstinate mouth round the letter r, but there were always words to trap him. He curled up and twitched as he sobbed.

'Sorry, Tom.' It didn't sound a convincing apology. Sincerity wasn't her strong point. 'We'll get someone else to do it. At school maybe.'

'Mmm.' Tommy whimpered.

'Who do you think?' She tried to get him on track. Involved in the conspiracy.

He lifted his head and wiped his face with his sleeve, smearing some dirt across his red cheeks. 'There's that guy Howard who had the throat operation. Have you heard him talk? Sounds like some sort of freak.' Tommy was well and truly hooked and back with the programme.

'Yeah. Take your tape recorder to school and get him to say it during break. Do that. We'll listen to it tomorrow night.' Lucy Marie was bored with the subject. They had discussed it enough. 'I'm off to bed.'

Tommy scooped up the comics. They had a second life. From rummaging through them he had a fresh taste for aliens and adventures. And back in his room he ploughed through the pile on his bed and didn't fall asleep until well after the rest of the household. Cradling a few and resting his head on the favourites he had sorted out.

'Told him that I'd been asked to audition people for the school play. Had to record all his gang just to get what we wanted?' Tommy explained as he threw his school satchel to the floor and rested the tape recorder on the tallboy.

They listened to the raucous playground scrummage and competitive voices. Trill and immature deliveries of the comic script. And then there was Howard. Deeper. A growl coming from his stomach and echoed through his bloated trachea. Somewhere between Boris Karloff and the Jolly Green Giant.

'Great.' Lucy Marie was impressed.

'Good one, don't you think?' Tommy fished for praise.

'Now all we have to do is fix it up in her room.' Lucy Marie was a step ahead of her brother.

'Going to be tricky.' Tommy was disheartened.

'When she's not in her room we need to hide the speaker.' She continued.

'But where?' Tommy was subdued. Once again the scheme was doomed to failure.

'Not sure, yet. Once we're in there we'll find somewhere. When she goes down to help Mom we'll make our move.' Lucy Marie was feeling the excitement.

Tommy was less enthusiastic.

Sarah's room smelled of Sarah. She had brought with her the odour of her mother's house. It was in her clothes and on her belongings. Measly possessions rich only in dank scent.

Lucy Marie and Tommy had been there a few times before. Waiting at the door. Just peering in really. Now they trod the carpet and pulled at wardrobe doors, slid open drawers and poked at stuff on the bedside cabinet. It was the ogre's lair and their stomach muscles were tense and their bladders precarious.

'On top here.' Tommy whispered, pointing to the dusty top of the wardrobe.

'She'd see it. Remember she's taller than us.' Lucy Marie hissed.

'Under the bed, then.' Tommy suggested unsuccessfully.

'Now this is a different matter.' Lucy Marie held open the lid of a wicker clothesbasket. She breathed in the pong of Sarah's stale garments. 'If there was a way of hiding it at the bottom the sound would come through the small gaps.' Her head was pushed into the basket and pulling at an old blanket at the bottom. 'Yes, under this would do.' She tugged at Tommy's sleeve. 'Look. If we covered it with this. What do you think?'

'Suppose so.' He was losing interest. The reek of musty clothes getting up his nose.

'Get it then. We'll push the wire through here.' Lucy Marie pulled at the basket's woven twigs, splintering at her wrench.

Tommy was unsure of his nanny's movements and was scared their plan would be foiled by her early return. He dashed to his room and hurried back with the tape recorder.

'Leave the play button pushed in and then we can just plug it in from outside when she's asleep.' Lucy Marie was in control. She tucked the lead under the edge of the carpet and then under the door that led to the upstairs landing. Luckily the small continental plug was easy to push between the skirting board and the rolled carpet lip.

'There!' Lucy Marie was pleased with her performance. She clasped her hands and wrung them.

Tommy was relieved and managed a smirk.

The children couldn't wait to get to bed. Not that they were contemplating sleep. That should have been a giveaway. They could hear nanny shuffling around in her room, water running and the occasional cough. Why didn't she settle down and get to bed?

Lucy Marie was woken by a hand on her shoulder. It was Tommy. He had got up to have a pee. Both had dropped off, and now irritated by their lack of alertness. On the landing they wiped the sleep from their eyes and listened at Sarah's door.

Lucy Marie placed praying hands at a tilt to her ear, to indicate nanny was asleep. Tommy nodded his agreement. She picked the plug from where it was lodged in the carpet, and held it to the socket. Her eyes were pulled wide as she searched for Tommy's concurrence to launch the attack.

Sarah slept soundly. The slightest hint of dribble at her lips. Her eyes jerking rapidly beneath the closed lids. A mixture of phantoms and fantasy entertained her slumber. Under the covers a hand quivered and knee trembled. *Out of sucking purple clouds Rupert's waxen body floated towards her stuck in paralysis. His crazy face spitting burning acid drops and whistling motionless wind. Debbie stood at the door. She laughed a sinister cackle as she pulled the baby from between her legs, bloody. Rubber body and screwed eyes. Her mother's voice, stabbing, drilled her head from somewhere in a haze. Calling out her name. A damning chant. Suddenly broken into the devil's mantra.*

'You are going to take some lead. A swine like you must be rubbed out. You are in my sights. My finger is on the trigger. Say goodbye, bitch!'

Sarah grabbed at her gun. But it was heavy and cumbersome. Like wielding a sledgehammer imbedded in tar. No defence. From where she could lift it to she squeezed the trigger. The weapon melted in her hands. She lunged in the direction of the devil...

...and slumped to the floor. Sweating and shaking. From the wicker clothesbasket some playground murmurs were still escaping. Tommy wasn't thorough enough. She plunged into the basket and clawed at the clothes. The tape recorder was still muttering as she held it with both hands. A palaeontologist with his greatest fossil find.

Anger was one of the last emotions to hit. Sarah snapped open her door, traced the electrical lead with her eyes and stormed in on Lucy Marie.

The children had waited for Howard's gruff rendition before scuttling back to their rooms. It was stupid not to have unplugged the machine. It was too late once they were in bed and begging for sleep.

Sarah pulled at Lucy Marie's bedclothes, but the girl held on tight as if she gripped the material in some sort of comatose slumber.

'You done it. Didn't you?' Snapped Sarah.

Lucy Marie groaned. A person being woken. 'What?' She managed a degree of indignation. 'Why are you pulling at me?' Lucy Marie yanked free.

'This! You done this.' Sarah held up the tape recorder, its lead still attached and swinging like a caught snake. 'Done it. Didn't you?' Hissing with steam. A boiler about to explode.

'Done what?' An enquiry tempered by disinterest.

'Trick me you did.' Sarah shook. She felt the heat rising. The tape recorder was heavy. A weapon.

Lucy Marie turned her back and nestled her head into the pillow. She gave a sigh to signify both her desire to get back asleep and hopefully the quick departure of her nanny.

Tommy could hear through the walls the bones of the confrontation and hung on to his duvet as if it were a life raft.

Sarah lifted the tape recorder higher. Sweaty hands slipped on the plastic casing. She was nearly over Lucy Marie's twitching body. The thudding was in Sarah's head. Pounding out her vengeance.

'You shouldn't have done that. Not done that to me.' Almost like a footballer throwing in from the touchline she swung the machine behind her head. Ready for the deadly blow.

'What's going on?' Stella Roberts stood in the doorway. A pink puffball and doily dressing gown. She rubbed her eyes as she spoke. 'Such a lot of noise.' Stella wasn't looking closely.

Nanny stepped back and let the tape recorder fall to her chest where she cradled it. She blew silently through pursed lips.

Lucy Marie sat forward and went through the routine of waking up again.

'It's so late. You woke me and your dad.' Stella mumbled, fighting the irritation of a broken night's sleep.

'Sorry.' Sarah clung on to the recorder. 'I'll get her settled.' She placed the weapon on the floor and fumbled at the bedclothes and puffed the pillow.

'Yes, but do it quietly, please, Sarah.' Stella's voice trailed off as she retreated to her bedroom. It was degrading for the nanny to see her in such subservience. In the morning she might remember to unravel the reasons behind the tape recorder and the unbelievable fuss.

Deep breaths on the edge of her bed helped Sarah push the anger into storage. So much vengeance as cargo. A pressure cooker. *Tommy must have been in on it. She couldn't have done it on her own. Why did they pick on her? Why always the target?* It was an agony she'd think through. Not make hasty decisions. The boy wasn't all bad.

When she slept the spectres returned. Accompanied by new ones who had tormented her in the past. School corridors and recreation grounds on a swaying horizon buffeted by insane light and shade. At the swings and the slides. Hiding in bushes to escape their cruelty. Suffocating on the stabbing words. Wet with despairing tears. Ghosts she couldn't erase from an appalling collage. Jumbled and lacking definition, they played awful games with her mind throughout what remained of the night.

It wasn't mentioned at breakfast, but it stood firmly on the table like a huge block of ice that nobody was prepared to mention. Only the children's yawns and Sarah's metal stare indicators of the previous night's antics.

Look at them. Evil children. Tart mother. Sarah's head was buzzing. Her eyes spoke. *Mocking me still, they are. I know. Not stupid you know.*

Every move at the table was clumsy and awkward. Every noise an apology.

Lucy Marie and Tommy wanted to cheer. Quite a success, except nanny was still there. They waited until school before they really celebrated. Huddled between playground and football pitch. Between the strangled cries of a chasing game and the hailing voices of boys insisting on a pass.

'Standing over me with the machine. Thought she was going to bash me with it.' Lucy Marie babbled excitedly.

'Never saw her.' Tommy explained. A little disappointed he

wasn't confronted. 'Wan like hell when I heard her. It was great.' Always braver after the event.

'Lucky it woke Mom. I'm sure she was going to do something to me. Boy, was she worked up. It certainly did the trick.' Lucy Marie was self-congratulatory. 'Knew it would. Good team, you and me, Tommy.' An unusual compliment for her brother. And an arm placed on his shoulder.

'She's still here. Didn't budge her did it?' Tommy could be a realist at times. Excitement diminished.

'Takes time little fellow.' Motherly. Lucy Marie touched his arm. 'What we must do is watch out. I think our tricks are getting up her nose. She's not saying much, but have you seen the look in her eyes. Got it in for us. Don't trust her.'

Silver rain settled on their navy coats as they crouched down in a comforting huddle between the savage football game and the primeval stalking of the playground pursuers.

Chapter 10

The White Mountains were sugarcoated. Glistening. Winter had New Hampshire at her mercy. Trucks steamed against the crystal forest, and scurrying rednecks stomped along wooden sidewalks beating the snow from their heavy jackets, and confirming to each other that this was the coldest it had ever been.

At the cottage Bobby Clayman had kept things running smoothly, although John Roberts was certain to find something to complain about. A fire was crackling like a distant firework display and there was plenty of fuel. Douglas fir that had died the previous year. Splendid fare for a hungry grate.

John Roberts' Suburban mowed through a layer of light snow as it entered the cottage compound. Bobby had ploughed out the drifts on the road earlier, otherwise even this robust vehicle wouldn't have negotiated the rutted track leading to the isolated property. The vehicle's headlights bounced off thick piles sculpted smooth against the building. A flash of some sparkling airborne flakes caught ignited in the beam.

Lucy Marie and Tommy were woken and hustled through the deep snow, unaware, in that semi-consciousness of broken sleep, of the crisp air and the scent of burning wood. They would be fully awake to the excitement of snow in the morning. Sarah and the Roberts dumped their baggage in the hallway and followed the children to bed.

Lucy Marie and Tommy wouldn't be the only eager risers in the morning. Despite the punishing journey, Sarah would be up with the lark. But before she gave in to her aching eyelids she searched in the darkness for the wood store and the sentinel Douglas fir that stood guard over her gun. Her face smudged against the window in a halo of condensation. The night had invaded too close to the house. All the outbuildings were swamped in an oil-black flood of frozen air.

When Sarah heard the jackhammer echo of the red-plumed woodpecker she cursed herself for sleeping so long. There was already movement in the house. Any sortie into the snow was out of the question. It wasn't the kids. Their doors were shut and there were none of their noises. Stella was downstairs arranging her kitchen and checking expiry dates on food in the fridge. Sarah wouldn't escape her attention. There was work for nanny to do.

Awoken to the pleasures of winter Lucy Marie and Tommy played on their own in the snow, until they came in red-nosed and damp. Once warmed by the fire and over the pains of reheating they spent the rest of the day in the basement. It was their territory and nanny did little besides occasionally put an ear to the door and listen to the progress of their game.

When John Roberts announced that he was going out to check the post box in town Sarah prepared to visit the site of the buried gun. Stella was at her dressing table. Certain to be there for a couple of hours. As expected the only boots that Sarah could get into was a pair of John Roberts', rubber, calf length ones that took forever to lace up. She was sacked up in a ski jacket that Stella used for gardening. A billowing appearance, when topped by a headscarf, reminiscent of a demented bag lady.

Snow near the door came up past her boots and wet the thick tights she wore. It was a struggle to walk. Every step threatening to pull a boot off.

Orientation was difficult. Snow a concealing drape. Ghostly shapes not revealing their real identity. Furniture, dustsheet-covered in an abandoned house. At an open plot Sarah searched for a familiar landmark. She spun slowly. Her trudging boots flattening the snow. She detected the wood store by following a path of disturbed snow where Bobby had stomped backwards and forwards with pine logs for the fire. At the corner of the shed she rested. Her back pressed hard against the crude timber. Somewhere there was a distinctive tree. Guardian Douglas Fir. Pictured in her mind was the pacing up to it with the *corpse* held tightly. Ready for burial. Cruelly every tree was a clone of another. Dressed in diamond-white *her* tree was indistinguishable from the other Klan members clustered beyond the wood store. Her head went months back and paced out the distance across the soft pine needles. Watched the neat pile of soil grow beside the resting place. Nothing clicked. There were no clues now. No chance of an unearthing.

Blank and grave Sarah plodded back to the cottage. She never imagined such disappointment.

John Roberts met her as she was trying to shake off the obstinate boots.

'Just the person!' His face was thunder. 'Are you aware that the kids are destroying the place, Sarah?' He put his face very close to hers. 'I am trying to do some work and all I can hear is the sound of destruction. Why aren't you dealing with it? That is what you're paid for, isn't it?'

A dreadful morning. He'd been beaten to a deal where he would have scooped up telecommunications stock for a song. He was ready to pick on anything and anybody. 'It may be okay in England for kids to run wild, but I need order and those kids need standards to observe.' John Roberts pushed closer. It was hard for him to communicate with his children. To confront them. A big man on the block but often inadequate with his own kids.

Sarah had one boot off with a trailing toe of her tights being dragged around in the wet of melted snow. She was near to overbalancing.

'You have to get this right. You're not the only nanny. Here in the States there are plenty of women who could do this job. And a darn sight more efficiently.' He pulled back and stood hands on hips. 'Do I make myself clear?'

John Roberts had made himself clear. Crystal. Sarah muttered something in agreement as she stumbled off to quell the riot.

He shouldn't have said it. Not my fault, those kids. Blame me. All the time Sarah Bickles gets the finger pointed. Always me. When are they going to leave me alone? Sarah was processing it. Loading more ammunition. It was almost out loud when she reached the warring children. The expression hanging from her face was enough to halt traffic let alone two squabbling kids.

John Roberts had obviously pointed out the failings of their nanny that afternoon to his wife. Stella sought Sarah after the children were sent to bed.

'Children were noisy today I hear. Well, enough to disturb their father. You know what he's like. Fragile soul when he's working.' A gentle introduction. 'A bit of a tiger when there's money concerned.' She nearly said vulture. 'I've noticed that they aren't very warm to you are they, Sarah? What do you think about them?' A sudden departure. 'They're ganging up on you. Giving you a hard time. I've seen that. You know I have difficult times with them. A real handful. If it's getting too bad then perhaps we need to rethink it.' Stella was skirting the subject. 'On both sides it might be beneficial if there was some breathing space. Time to reflect, so to speak.' She was losing Sarah. 'I'm doing this badly. Look Sarah. Maybe you need a rest. I don't think you are coping as well as you should.' She watched Sarah's face become rigid. 'Not that it's your fault. It's just one of those things.' A weak attempt at saving grace. Stella touched her lips nervously. 'You run along and sleep on it. We'll talk in the morning.' Stella signed off with a sickly smile.

It was time for nanny to go. She had lost it all right. A fresh face. Someone to stimulate and amuse those horrors. Stella knew her own limitations as a mother. Once the nanny was in the same boat changes had to take place.

Sarah lurched from the chair that she had been grasping in a death grip. Swimming inside her head was a whirlpool of confusion. She fell into her room and lunged at the bed. Under the duvet she buried her head. Hiding from brutal words. Discarded. Thrown away. A disposable item. Garbage. Treated like waste. Sarah rarely cried. This was an exception. Tears for herself. Sad, ridiculed and unwanted.

Someone had to pay. Sarah wasn't going to accept this unhappiness without attributing responsibility. Deep in her quilt cocoon she was picturing it clearly. The red haze was forming images of those at fault for her despair. The children. That girl. Made her look bad.

Sarah didn't have the intelligence or the initiative to retaliate on the same terms. Reaction would be no masquerade. Pure vengeance. It was her way.

Heavy snow throughout the night added to her misery, but did nothing to alter her resolve. A fitful sleep punctuated by gross shadows and grotesque demons.

Morning brought scimitar shards of sunlight slicing the dismal bedroom. Sarah's eyes were painful. Cold water scooped onto her face brought some relief, but the agony was deeper than this.

Tactfully the Roberts had taken Lucy Marie and Tommy to town early. To avoid a difficult breakfast. The children weren't slow to pick up the atmosphere. Aware that they were near to victory.

It was a mechanical agenda for Sarah. Heavy clothing, anything, thrown on. Puffy layers added without thought. Bustled down the stairs, scrambling for the clumsy boots.

A new camouflage of snow obscured the landmarks. At the wood store, insulated by a sandwich of snow, she gritted her teeth and shook her face with short twitching movements. Searching for her bearings. The shovel of burial held ready for exhumation. Thirty paces. She had reminded herself every day she was apart from the gun. There was no distinguishing the firs dripping with snow. Icing sugar cake decorations. Branches sagging under the weight. Hanging, despairing arms.

Cold, like probing fingers invaded layer after layer of her clothing, threatening to occupy. Sarah gambled. One looming trunk that seemed possible. One, two... Pacing through treacle. Clinging snow ready to rip off the squidging boots at every step. Eighteen. Not enough. She stood almost thigh-high. A sinking person in quicksand. Loose snow flicked off her desperate head as her periscope eyes sought the fir just twelve paces further. A likely candidate to her right. Sloppy, inaccurate strides. Almost hurdling the drifted banks.

Under the protective boughs the snow barely ankle deep, that could be pushed aside with the merest sweep of the foot. Sarah bent down to feel the pine needles uncovered and now mixed in a porridge of snow. Green and brown, like spices in an exotic dish. And below, the steel-hard soil she scratched at with her nails. Sarah tested the first few inches with the tip of the shovel. Only powdery traces. She rested her slack boot on the shoulder of the implement and put all her weight into the attempt. Some success. Two or three inches that she levered out. A neat triangle of crumbly earth. It spurred her on. Within minutes Sarah had reached beyond the frozen layer and was removing worthwhile amounts of khaki soil.

At the time of internment she hadn't gone too deep. About what she was looking at. A shallow trench. Disappointment abruptly chilled her hands and crept up her lower back. Enemies insignificant during the chase. Another site. Sarah stared back at the wood store. Took a new bearing and cleared the light snow from a new spot. She banged her numbing hands on her hips and began again.

Not a bullseye. An outer ring. Good enough. In the looser loam the shovel scraped the very last tooth of the zip of the sports bag. A corner exposed, which she tugged at. Hopeful. It didn't budge. Sarah needed to dig all around the half-frozen bag and push the blade underneath to prise it from the clinging soil.

Her frozen hands couldn't carry the trophy. There was no need to tidy up, pat the infill or scatter cones. Sarah tucked the bag under her arm, ignored the shovel and left the grave open.

Back through the dragging snow. Hard against her ribs. The

gun. She could feel the bulk of the chamber and the slenderness of the barrel. Sarah nudged it closer and clung on. As if carrying a child to safety in a storm.

Many layers were simply thrown off in the hallway and the boots kicked against the wall. Stella would have had a fit to see such disregard for the décor.

Sarah huffed and puffed to bring back feeling in her hands. Ran hot water on them and groaned at the pain that brought. Aimed the hairdryer. They were only half way defrosted when she jerked at the zip. Some response. An obstinate fastener. Sarah was ready to slice the bag open if necessary. Two more tugs and there was no need for a caesarean. She dipped in her tingling fingers. The zip-lock bags were not sealed. Rubber fasteners don't obey instructions at those temperatures. Only a damp towel away. A lucky dip where there was only one prize. She withdrew the Smith and Wesson revolver. Condensation clung to the cold metal. Not the handsome weapon that had been buried. Sarah stroked it dry with a hand towel from the bathroom. Which she repeated until the blue steel was warm enough not to develop another coating.

And then she opened and closed the cartridge chamber, pulled back the hammer and fired with repeated clicks the tantalising trigger. Oiled and de-soiled. Preened and cleaned.

Finally she slid into every waiting orifice the brass-coated, phallic bullets. And never let him out of her sight. She rested on the bed with him. Now she was warm and he was too.

Broken from her reverie by the sharp clacks of the Suburban's doors.

Chapter 11

Sarah slipped and stumbled through a staccato sleep, with regular inspection of the pillowed pistol. Knowing what daylight meant. Something incredibly exact about what she was doing. Washing and dressing automatic. Every movement precise and calculated. Every small noise heightened. A rustle, the clatter of Canada geese taking to the air. The click of a door catch, the loud report of the riveter's gun.

Sarah left her room with her companion by her side. Hanging. Arm full stretch. At each step she felt the weight slap her thigh and drag on her full skirt. Her grip was vice-like. But only a light finger tickled the trigger. Even the chill air didn't prompt her to wear gloves.

Nobody was up. They slept in on their last morning. There was no dreaming of dying in that drifting dawn napping. John Roberts was lusting after sickly firms whose stock had plummeted in some Dickensian city where dollar bills fell as confetti. Stella shopped in a heavenly mall with a flunky who balanced her pink-boxed bargains at her heels. Lucy Marie was Alice in a maze confronting an assortment of vivid but ludicrous characters. Tommy was a comic hero winning wars and racing huge trucks with giant wheels.

A coat against the cold. Loose and ugly boots. She wouldn't look like a killer.

She wouldn't go far. To the wood store. Wait near there. Where she could see the house. The first lights switched on. Knew where they were.

There was tension in their stirring. No one had seen nanny after their return the previous evening. Passing her room they imagined her misery inside.

'Probably sulking I should think,' Stella said softly to her husband struggling with his socks in their dressing room.

'Yuh.' It was agreement without the interest.

Sarah saw the light. Knew what they would be doing.

Lucy Marie and Tommy met early. Nanny was going. It was great. Now to plan for freedom. Tommy took a remote control car into his sister's room. She sat in bed combing the hair of three Barbie dolls. Ken had fallen to the floor; face in the carpet. All dolls a sparkle in their eyes.

Breakfast was apologetic sounds of crockery and cutlery. Unspoken acknowledgements. Stella turned every few seconds to watch the doorway. To greet nanny with a *never mind* smile. She picked at her food. A nervous sparrow at the bird table.

Nanny never showed.

Sarah retraced her deep foot holes in the snow. Another circumnavigation of the wood store. A drill. Focussed the mind. She stayed alert.

John Roberts did all his dirty work over the phone. A vulture at arm's length. Someone else used for the close quarter final throes and to pick at the entrails. Cleaner that way. No use shit flying. When it came to firing domestics he had no stomach for the small print. He made an excuse to leave the house while he thought nanny was sulking in her room. Before there was a scene.

'Just going to check on the Goldstein's boathouse. Sure that's against the byelaws.' John Roberts pulled on his heavy coat. It sounded a valid excursion. He was always trying to catch his neighbours out. Grass them up to the Lake Association.

Stella tutted at his motives. Wished he wasn't such an asshole. She never said goodbye.

Sarah saw him leave the house. Rounded shoulders and a cloud of breath. Thudding steps to release clinging snow. She watched his progress through an avenue of white birch that led to the adjacent property. Heard his thick cough. Heard his arrogant voice in her head. She checked on her fingers. They were cold, but not frozen. He would have to return the same way. Interwoven bushes cloaked in crusted snow would hide her until he came back.

Stella busied herself in the kitchen. When nanny came down it wouldn't be as if she was waiting for her. Anyway she needed to play the real mum now.

Lucy Marie and Tommy grabbed a lightning breakfast and returned to the safety of their rooms. They would play subdued, intense games until nanny was gone. She was a weird one and there was no knowing what she might do.

John Roberts was brought to an abrupt halt as he pushed through into the small clearing where the blueberries flourished in summer.

Nanny stood in his way.

His mouth started to speak. Silent rounded vowels. No actual sound.

One moment nanny was just a drab obstacle in his path. An awkward situation. Then she was bent at the knees. Two fists on the Smith and Wesson.

His open mouth and bulging eyes saw the gun. He made a desperate dive. A high bound. Too far away.

Sarah fired. A crisp snap, like breaking dead wood.

There was no spurt of blood. Only the thump of the bullet burying itself in his ribcage. His body slumped to the soft floor well short of her.

John Roberts' mouth was still open. His hands felt for the hole in his chest. He spoke more invisible words. A child's bewilderment.

A second bullet smacked into the side of his face and lodged in his brain. Ridiculous contortions in death.

Sarah gasped. As satisfying as stain removal. In the silence of the clearing the smell of fireworks.

Loud explosions nearby. It didn't register in the kitchen.

Nanny gambolled back over ridges of snow.

Stella dried a saucepan lid with a check teacloth.

Nanny burst through the screen door. The revolver chiming on the metal frame.

Stella looked up. Half a smile turned to a taut mask of terror when the barrel was levelled. Pleading eyes.

Less than two metres from her face. Point blank. Good acoustics in that kitchen. An explosion rather than gunshot. A massive wound fringed with dark grey powder. Much more blood.

Stella's head, what was left of it, cracked like an eggshell as it smashed into the tiled floor. A crimson soup spread from where her right nostril had been. Gathering speed with an escarpment leading edge and smooth surface tension.

My resignation, Mrs. Roberts. Sarah couldn't suppress her satisfaction.

Upstairs Tommy had found Lucy Marie and a corner to huddle in. Questioning eyes but no words. Faces of fear.

Footsteps on the stairs. Scuffing paces. Audible breathing.

Tommy clung on to his sister. His eyes dribbling. Her lips quivering.

Nanny pushed the door with the barrel of the gun. It swung to conceal them in their corner.

They saw only her clown's boots. Heard her pulling open doors and drawers.

Tommy's blubbing turned her around.

She prodded the air with the revolver and beckoned them to their feet. Both children snatched up a comfort toy. Tommy clutched a yellow Chevrolet truck. Lucy Marie cradled *Florida Barbie*. Orphans padding through the doorway, obeying the directions of the flicking barrel. Children tumbling from freight wagons at Belsen.

No one spoke. The silence of terror.

Past the kitchen where their mother swam in her own blood. Front crawl. Face to the side. But not for breathing.

Sarah pulled them beyond Stella's leaking body. Urgent thrusts with the muzzle.

Near to the front door nanny pulled open the broom cupboard. Full of cleaning paraphernalia and smelling of furniture polish. Again she motioned with the handgun. She wanted Tommy inside. It would be difficult to execute him. Needed time with that one.

Please don't! No! Not in there. It was sculpted on his face and in the radar from his eyes. He hated the dark and cramped spaces.

Nanny yanked at his sleeve.

Tommy held on to his sister and a wood moulding. Dug in with his nails.

Nanny had the strength that comes with commitment. She plucked him from his handholds and brusquely heaved him into the pokey cupboard. Pails clattered and brush handles clicked as his small feet clattered amongst the debris. He fell. Sprawled across the plastic dustpans.

Sarah secured the door. Momentarily carrying the gun under her arm to use both hands.

Tommy yelled. A snorting cry that bubbled through snot and dribble. Some tribal noise. An incoherent mix of dread and despair.

Instinct ejected Lucy Marie out of the front door. Scrambling in panic to flee. Windmill arms and twirling legs. Anywhere. Someone? Futile aspirations.

Nanny clomped along in pursuit. Gaining from the outset.

Lucy Marie found her father. She scratched at his back to wake him. Tears came off at tangents from her reddened cheeks and landed on his back. He was no help.

Nanny's burping boots expelled whooshing air with every galloping stride.

Lucy Marie heard her closing approach. Onwards, with Barbie held like a relay baton. Rapid arms and frenetic legs.

A film played her escape in slow-motion. Fleeing in a dream, where your body won't respond to the urgent messages from the brain. As if someone had cut the connection. Separate entities.

Nanny was on fast-forward. Maniac speed. Slashing through the air. Flapping coat and squelching boots.

Nanny nearly overran Lucy Marie. The boots were

ineffective brakes; swinging round as she grabbed the girl's coat to halt further progress beyond her prey. Lucy Marie's puffing face stared up at Sarah's determined countenance. A child beyond speech. Her eyes had surrendered.

Hooking her fingers under the collar of the girl's anorak, nanny dragged her catch back to where the lawn of the cottage met the crust of the frozen lake. Tugging the trophy along. Her small feet often missing a step or sliding when her slack legs buckled, and she was pulled, skidding across the mud-stained snow.

Sarah stopped. Twisted Lucy Marie around and cupped her slender neck. Nanny's two thumbs located the protrusion, brittle and proud.

Nanny squeezed. Pressing out the last sigh from Lucy Marie's darkening lips. Eyes in a whirlpool. Drowning. Nanny wasn't letting go.

Lowered the limp body into the rippling pool, created around the boathouse by the *bubbler* that Bobby Clayman had installed to protect the building from expanding ice. Lucy Marie sank into the dark water. But not for long. An infuriating reappearance.

By the time Sarah had made certain the bull-headed girl was gone for good, she was cold. The numbness of her upper limbs annoyed her. There was Tommy to deal with.

In the kitchen where Stella Roberts' blood was pooling at the skirting boards and disappearing under the base units, she slumped against the wall. Dipped her shoes into a deep puddle of blood to cover the splatters. Telltale speckles that come from the first spurts of an inflicted wound.

It was easier to talk to her now. Sarah told the smashed face and flattening cheeks how all this was her fault. *Wasn't right to treat her like what they had. Been the same all her life. People talking down. Walking all over her.* Let Mrs. Roberts know that she had feelings too. Told her that she shouldn't have brought this on. Shouldn't have pushed her. *I comes back with that tightness in me head, I do. Do stuff I shouldn't.*

By the time Sarah had blamed the slaughter on the way she had been treated by the whole family, her heavy skirt, trailed on the floor, was damming the mercury-smooth liquid. Soaking the back with a crescent of gluey fluid. Crimson black.

It dripped treacle blobs as she collected the Smith & Wesson from the shelf. And smeared her legs with a much brighter hue when she walked. Walked towards the painted door. The door behind which Tommy was incarcerated. Sniffling and trembling.

This wasn't the same. Poor Tommy. She surprised herself.

Nanny retreated from Tommy's tidal bleeding. Small steps. Eyes never leaving the encroaching pool. Backing out of the front door. It swung back and shivered shut, cutting off the carnage.

Sarah sat on the step. Until the air blew bitter and the sky graphite sombre.

She was bounced upright by the clack of a car door. An alarm call. Her eyes stretched wide to clear the floaters in her vision.

Who was there? Her head shook. Panic breathlessness. Pinching stomach.

Footsteps heading away from the house. A mumbled song. Bobby Clayman.

Sarah scooped up the gun. Left her own smearing of blood by the door. On the white paint of the porch upright. Fled like a Bosnian Muslim ducking Serb sniper fire. Crouched, scampering. Into the brush. Smacking foliage. Deeper, towards concealing trunks and curtains of snow.

She'd tired of killing. Bobby wouldn't go into the house. Wouldn't see anything at the boathouse. Lucy Marie wouldn't bob back to the surface. Would she? What clues had she left? Was there a trail? She was thinking rationally, if erratically.

Bobby loaded up some logs in his thick forearms and headed towards the house. He piled them up near to the door to the sitting room. Nowhere near the sprawled body of Stella, or the seeping broom cupboard. There was the deer-feeder to fill and to check on the backup generator down at the dock. Only a quick call. No major jobs to attend to.

Sarah could hear his unhurried movements and his matter-of-fact humming. Perhaps he would go without noticing anything. Not even come across John Roberts only yards away, kissing the forest floor. But then, this was difficult, what if he went away without him seeing her? How would she explain that? Maybe she should show herself. An only survivor of some murderous villain. Escaping into the woods after this fiend had butchered her employers and their beautiful children. Such terrible sights. Skittled by fear. Sarah was straining hard to make it credible. As she juggled with tidal notions she scratched at her ankles with sharp pieces of bark and tore at threads on her skirt. She scrambled around for a small twig. Thin but strong. Into the barrel of the gun she shoved it. Seen that on TV. Thrust the weapon into banks of snow and wiped it on uncovered leaves and pine needles, rubbed along her clothing and dug it into a porridge of mud.

Bobby was down at the water. Near the boathouse. Treading on the snow flattened by nanny's squelching boots and Lucy Marie's limp body. His noises were muffled. Well out of sight of her hide in the forest. She pulled herself upright and stepped gingerly towards the gravel drive and Bobby's pick-up.

Something heavy in her swaying pendulum coat. She held the pocket steady and dived in. The wet hair of *Florida Barbie*. She had forgotten that witness.

At the passenger's door of the battered truck she eased it open. Dropped the gun into the glove compartment. Heard it slide through some paper and clang against the old Webley deep in the well. A much better plan was being hatched. And around the back of the pick-up, in the cavernous trailer, between sopping logs she slid Barbie. Her blond hair swallowed up in the darkness. Much like a girl's body sliding into the blackness of a freezing lake.

Sarah made herself into a rocking, sobbing ball. Next to the raised decking. Bobby would have to see her as he returned to his truck. She increased the volume when she saw he was carrying the bag of feed, chin in the air. Dangerously indifferent to the plight she had feigned.

'Whoa, what's this?' Bobby lowered the sack. 'What's the problem, ma'am?'

He pulled Sarah upright with strong arms. Stroked her shoulders, but went no further. Touched her hair to make her look at him. He saw the bloodstains, but they weren't blood, couldn't be blood. Some berry. A spillage in the kitchen.

Sarah inhaled her snot. Heavy intakes that rattled and snorted.

'Gotta tell me. Gotta speak up, Sarah.' He was uncomfortable using her name. 'Come on, there's something serious, ain't there?'

She jabbed out a finger. Pointing to where Bobby would find his employer. Where he could pull at his shoulder and tip him over. And gaze at his dead face. Stand above the crumpled body. Examine from that distant the holes in John Roberts. Disbelief.

'Who done this?' Bobby quizzed at close quarters. 'Killed him out there?' His head shook. It was difficult for him to assimilate. Although at the back of his head there were enemies he knew he could name.

Sarah waved her head from side to side. Her crooked finger motioned towards the house. In the direction of the kitchen.

Bobby chewed at his bottom lip. It was dawning on him that this nightmare wasn't confined to the broken body in the woods.

She hadn't been a bad looking woman. Handsome was what he thought would be the best description of Stella Roberts. But, on the floor was a creature. A bundle of flesh. Nothing like a human. Mangled and disfigured. He trod between the skin-topped pools of blood on tiptoe. Almost ballet. Stella's face was glued to the tiles. He wouldn't try to lift it. Afraid that more of her collapsed face would fall away.

Outside, bitterly cold, Sarah listened in her huddled pose for the silence of discovery. Waited for the slow return of Bobby Clayman. Deliberate paces. Not able to take all of it in. Too much of a puzzle for a plain old caretaker.

After several minutes standing over the nanny. 'And them kids?' Naked eyes. Laser beams. 'What about the little kids? What's happened to them?' Bobby pulled at Sarah's tottering shoulder. An insistent yanking. This was critical information.

She gazed straight through his questioning face. Easy to read.

'No. No. Not them little ones. Who would have done this to those innocent children?' His touch became more like clawing. 'Where? Where are they?'

She knew perfectly well where Lucy Marie was dragging weed, but could only imagine wee Tommy spread out amidst the fallen brooms and leaking over upturned buckets. 'In the house.' Weak words that sent Bobby running back to search the rooms.

His foot slipped on the tacky floor of the hallway. He poked his finger into the holes ripped open in the white-painted door. One ear pressed against the splintered wood was all he could manage. He wouldn't open it up. Both kids had been slaughtered in there. That was clear. He'd let others discover their bodies. Enough carnage for one day. And with kids it was different. Too painful.

'Who? Who done this?' Bobby bent over Sarah. It wasn't the first time he had asked.

She didn't reply. And certainly not with *it was me*.

As he dialled 911 with trembling fingers Sarah was piecing together a story. An ambush.

'Yes...at Camp Falcon. Buttress Headland. There's been...a...killing. It's awful. Those poor kids.' He paused, time to drag in some air. 'Clayman, Bobby Clayman. Caretaker. No I'm not related. Just work here. Look hurry can you. No. A doctor's no good. Too late. Far too late.' Bobby threw down the phone without signing off. He crouched down to Sarah's level and tried to encourage her, with hands at her shoulders, to wait in the car.

The house was out of bounds. A mausoleum.

Chapter 12

They all clutched polystyrene cups full of foul coffee. Men with protruding stomachs and ugly women who should have been traffic wardens. Steaming breath and serious faces. No small talk about the Raiders' chances in the Super Bowl here. Police cars and ambulances parked at ridiculous angles. Discarded where they had swung in. Forever the cavalry. Far too many. There were desk candidates looking to be heroes. Out of Concord and Hampton.

Fruitful activity was confined to few places. Taped-off areas where bodies lay in congealed blood or where they had spilled, along with a circus of cleaning implements, from a cupboard. And posse after posse scouring the other rooms and the nearby forest. And in two warm police cars, gentle questions were being asked of Bobby Clayman and Sarah Bickles, separately. Emerging, discrepant accounts that were waving huge warning flags.

'You say you arrived at around quarter after twelve and things seemed ordinary?' Detective Chuck Nolan reiterated Bobby's recollection.

'Yeah. Just getting on with my chores. Didn't know anything was wrong. Didn't know what was inside. And him lying out there.' Bobby's eyes flickered nervously. Head nodding towards the forest clearing where John Roberts lay disarmed, stiff.

'When did you realise there was a problem?' Nolan quizzed.

'When I seen her. Crouched down. Trembling. Pointing to where Mr. Roberts were lying. Covered in blood.' Bobby's voice faded a little. 'Didn't know that's what it was first off.'

'So, you went and found Mr. Roberts in the woods?'

'Yeah.'

'What did you do then?' It was just cursive questioning. He'd have to get it in detail later, at the precinct.

'Sarah pointed...'

A rapping on the car window interrupted Bobby's reply.

'What is it?' Chuck was annoyed. This was crucial stuff.

'No sign of the girl, sir.' A uniformed officer apologetically informed the detective.

'Shit!' Chuck Nolan wasn't happy. 'Keep going. Let's hope she got away or was out. Get the Lieutenant to ask the nanny if the girl was at a friend's, or if she knows what happened to her.'

'Girl?' Bobby turned, his forehead creased. 'Weren't she in the cupboard? I thought she was in there.'

Nolan gripped his arm. 'Only the one. The boy. That was all we found.'

'God.' Bobby hissed through his nose. 'God, I hope the sweetie made it.'

Three cars back in the higgledy-piggledy line of police vehicles, Sarah was whispering bare details to Lieutenant Dick Kaltenbach, provisionally in charge of the investigation.

'Now you ain't saying much, ma'am. What did you see? Weren't you in the house with them?'

'I didn't see nothing. Found 'em. Hid as far as I could. Didn't come out until he arrived.' Sarah waggled a finger in no particular direction.

A rap on the window. The young officer on his errand.

'What? Get out of here.' Dick was sensing something. 'Not now.'

'Sorry sir, only Detective Nolan wants to know if the nanny knew of the whereabouts of the girl.'

'Not found her yet?'

'No.' A regretful wave of the head.

'Hear that? Did the girl escape or was she out some place?' Dick inquired. Less interested than he was in the eventual answer to his previous question.

'Don't know. She were in when I left for me walk. And

when I got back there weren't anyone...alive.'

'Keep it up, son.' Kaltenbach confirmed to the frozen face of the state trooper. 'She's got to be out there.' It was a patronising and expeditious dismissal.

He turned quickly to Sarah. 'Who arrived? You said earlier that someone arrived. Who?' Kaltenbach leaned forward to hear this answer.

'Him. Bobby Clayman.'

The Lieutenant rested back in his seat, and gave the woman officer sitting alongside Sarah a knowing series of short, sharp nods.

'So, Sarah.' He was keen to explore this line. 'The caretaker, Mr. Clayman, Bobby, wasn't here when you returned from your walk? No one here or sign of anyone?'

'I hid in the woods. When Bobby turned up, I were hiding. Wasn't going to get me. Whoever done it.' Awkward answers. Losing the sequence.

Dick Kaltenbach missed it. He was clinging on to his hunch on this one. 'Excuse me, Sarah. Carol, get one of the lads to get some more tea for her. I won't be a minute.' Dick Kaltenbach squeezed out of the vehicle.

He grabbed the nearest police officer. 'Make sure Chuck keeps that caretaker busy. I don't want him leaving here on any account.' An urgent tone that the policeman recognised.

'Sorry, Sarah, you can imagine all we have to do. Three members of a family slaughtered. Nasty business.' Squirming back in. In more than one way.

'So, you return from your walk, and what do you find?'

Sarah was ready. 'The terrible scene what's here. Couldn't believe they was dead.'

'Give me a little more detail, please, Sarah.'

'First I finds Mrs. Roberts, like. On the floor. Not moving. Blood and stuff. In the kitchen.'

'Anything else?'

'The old cleaning store. Where I keeps my clean cloths. Polishes and sweepers. Blood pouring out. Tommy were in there.' She could only imagine the pale body of the little boy slumped amidst the buckets and the mops.

'Yes?' Dick had her opening up.

'Goes looking for her, the girl, as she's not with the others. Reckon she's gone with him, Mr. Roberts. Across the lake or the like.'

Dick Kaltenbach was finding it hard to grasp some of the subtleties of the Dorset dialect. 'And then did you find Mr. Roberts?'

'Yeah. He was in the woods. On the ground.' She remembered the thunder of those first shots and the satisfaction of seeing his desperate and futile gestures.

'Did you touch anything?'

'No.' No, she didn't want anything to do with them then. As long as they was dead.

'What did you do next?'

'I goes back to the house. Sits there looking at Mrs. Roberts. On the floor. Dead.' Sarah wanted to smile at the thought of her employer's impotency. Nicely done. One shot through her nagging face.

'You okay?' Dick was puzzled by the dream-like expression stuck on Sarah's face.

'Yes. Was awful.' She was lying convincingly enough.

'If I can just hurry this along a bit.' Dick Kaltenbach wanted to get past the mundane. Not that the massacre of a whole family was an ordinary event, even in New Hampshire.

'After a while I sits outside. Confused like. Trying to piece it together. Who killed 'em? Why? Then I 'eard the car. Thought it were 'im back. To do me in. Ran. Ran to the woods.'

'But it was only the caretaker, Mr. Clayman. Wasn't it?'

'Not sure then. Weren't taking chances, was I?'

'Why did you think it was a man who had killed the family?' Dick was following his nose.

'Dunno, 'spose it had to be.'

'Yes.' Dick nodded. He was still thinking. 'And you eventually came out of hiding when you realised it was Mr.

Clayman?'

'Yeah. He were down by the boathouse. I crept out and waited 'til he came back.' Shrewd ploy if she intended it.

Chuck Nolan's car was steaming up. He rubbed his chin. Not certain about the direction. 'Mr. Clayman, Bobby, after you discovered Mr. Roberts' body you went into the house, yes?'

'That's about it. Sarah was in shock, but she was pointing to the house. Not speaking. Crouched so low. So scared. I went flying in. Didn't think he might still be in there. Found Mrs. Roberts. Fuck me! Never seen anything like that. Nearly threw up. Sorry...about the language.' Bobby's head seemed elastic. Swinging it and sighing to himself.

'No matter.' It was police practice to use coarse vocabulary more than just frequently. In fact if you didn't you'd attract suspicion.

'You saw the blood in the hall, seeping from the store cupboard, yes?'

Bobby nodded. Solemn eyes.

'You didn't open it up. Why?'

'Kids...didn't want to see that. What a bastard. Why take out the kids? No, I couldn't open that door.'

'Kids? We haven't found out what has happened to the girl, er...Lucy Marie.' Chuck checked his notes. Not yet familiar with the name.

'Know what I mean? Thought she were in there with the boy.' Uncomfortably defensive.

Chuck Nolan noticed. 'And next?'

'On the phone to you lot. As quick as I could. It ain't no ordinary police problem, and it ain't no problem I could deal with.'

Sarah chewed her thumb. A matador. Cape ready. Every question a charging bull.

'When you first arrived at the house? After the walk wasn't it? Did you see anything that might lead us to the killer? Dick Kaltenbach persevered.

'Like what?' Sarah retorted.

'Indication of a car being here. Some tracks. Anything. To be honest, Sarah, at this time in the investigation we are happy just to grab at straws. Maybe one will prove significant.'

'There's always tracks. Mr. Roberts' car and Bobby's truck.'

Lieutenant Kaltenbach was embarrassingly aware that he was relying a great deal on her now. His convoy of gung-ho police officers had chewed up any evidence of an alien vehicle. 'What about smells? Something strange? Anything out of place? Foreign to the normal?'

'No.'

The door of the police car swung open. A middle-aged woman in a white suit and wearing rubber gloves stood there.

'Need her clothes.' Only faintly apologetic.

'Forensic.' Dick announced to Sarah. 'Sorry about this.'

My clothes, thought Sarah. What's on them? What they going to find? She had watched programmes on television where they did all kinds of tests, and even minute bits led to the culprit. Clever sods those scientists. She started to worry.

'It's all right, ma'am, they'll give you some stuff to wear. Not very flattering. Overalls I expect.' Friendly approach.

Bobby was already discarding his clothing. They didn't give him a reason. It was a nuisance. A blue boiler suit with POLICE printed on the back was hung over a chair and a young policeman waited with an open polythene bag, and some security tags that would seal the contents until it was opened for examination in the laboratory.

'Don't know why they want me to do this,' he grumbled to the officer. 'Don't think I did it do they?' A prophetic question.

Sarah watched him climb out of the wagon. They exchanged the briefest of glances. Her chaperone carried the same evidence bag and standard security seals.

Chuck Nolan met Dick Kaltenbach at the boot of his car. Getting some air, and his boots. Fieldwork. Time to compare notes.

'If you say baffling I'll knee you,' Dick Kaltenbach announced. 'What did you get out of the caretaker?'

'Not sure on this one. He seems to be playing it straight, and there ain't no form. Done a check through the precinct. Upset and mystified by it as far as I can ascertain. What the nanny have to say?'

'She's giving me some concern over this Bobby boy. I need to find the truck tracks that we haven't screwed up on. And look for others. No one's getting here with a shooter on foot and trying to escape. It's not making much sense at the moment.'

'Motive?' Chuck inquired.

'Fuck knows.' Dick Kaltenbach scratched his head. 'We are going to need to examine all the backgrounds. No one wipes out kids without reason. This is some kind of weird fucker or a contract from the city.'

'This guy Roberts, apparently he was in the finance business. A broker, dealer or something to do with stocks. Could be he had enemies on Wall Street. Easily done when you are making decisions. Going to be a few casualties, I reckon.' Chuck wasn't really sure about the world of high finance, but he wasn't far off the mark. There were many business fatalities in New York who owed John Roberts one.

'Maybe.' Dick Kaltenbach had another agenda. 'The house was never locked so no need to look for a forced entry, but forensic need to examine every square inch for foreign debris that an intruder inconspicuously leaves behind.' He liked sounding like a Lieutenant should. 'We'll go through the gardens next to the house, look at snow disturbance and generally nose about. God, I wish we hadn't arrived like the D-Day landing. Anyone who's been in that house or environs get their shoes logged with forensic. I trust everyone's been fingerprinted. Our dabs are all over the place.'

'Yes sir.' Chuck Nolan had his pen and pad ready. He was prone to forgetting some of the detail.

'I want to look round that boathouse as well. The nanny says that Bobby Clayman was in that area when she emerged from her hiding place. Just my nose again.' Dick Kaltenbach was notorious for sniffing out important clues and coming up trumps from one of his hunches.

'Excuse me, Dick.' Forensic pathologist Simon Marston interrupted the briefing. 'We've done everything here. Can we take them away?'

'Photographs, soil tests, measurements? All that as well?'

'Of course, you distrusting bastard.'

'Just checking.' Dick had worked many times with Dr. Simon Marston, knew he was thorough, but couldn't help the wind up.'

'Yeah, yeah. I'll bag them up then.'

Chuck had images of kitchen zip-lock bags. It was too impersonal.

'You do that.' He didn't want to dwell on his own haunting perception. 'Chuck, let's go before we lose the light.' Dick had his hunting boots on.

The two policemen ducked and crawled through the entwining dead twigs and leafless boughs of vegetation growing close to the house. Stopping to look at depressions in the snow or tickling what might be fibres or dusts, with the end of a ballpoint pen.

'Kills the fucking back.' Chuck stretched upright and clutched the small of his back. 'And it's freezing.'

'It's the job, Chuck. Always been unpleasant in more ways than one. Gotta do it. It's the badge.' Forever phlegmatic. Somewhat pompous.

'Looks clean to me.' Chuck was still straightening himself. 'I'll just give the windowsills the once over and meet you at the back of the house.' If you like it so much you do the bending, he thought. 'Okay?'

'Yeah.' Kaltenbach was well aware of his partner's intentions.

When Chuck arrived at the rear of the building Dick Kaltenbach wasn't there. He was about to retrace his route when he was hailed from down near the lake.

'Chuck, over here.'

Chuck skipped towards the voice, clutching the bottom of his flapping jacket to stop it swishing about as he went.

Dick Kaltenbach was crouching over a watery patch of snow. His nose only inches from the slush.

'Found something, Lieutenant?' Chuck enquired, not wanting to jeopardise his back by joining him on the ground.

Fortunately Kaltenbach stood up. 'In this spot.' He waved his hands above an area almost circular and about seven feet in diameter. 'There's been some activity. Melted snow and dirt from the woods. Looks like something has been dragged here.' He gestured at a smoothing of the sugary snow. 'There are a few prints.' He pointed to the marks made by large boots with a distinctive tread. 'May only be from the family or one of those two.' A wagging finger indicated the police vehicles where Bobby and Sarah sat, separately. 'But it's worth a try. I'll just pop up and get forensic to target this area next.' Dick disappeared with brisk leaps towards the mobile laboratory that sat on what was the lawn.

Chuck poked around in the boathouse and watched the spluttering *bubbler* stirring up the water around it. Nothing seemed out of the ordinary. Bobby kept it tidy. Summer play and boating stuff neatly stacked in cedar lockers. Autumn fishing equipment in regimental racks. Ropes curled and flooring swept. Chuck walked out of the back of the boathouse and along the lake shore until he came to thick ice. Tentatively he placed his mudded shoe on the surface. It slid a little. Steadying himself with his hands on the bank, he stood on the frozen lake. With shuffling steps he made his way around the edge of the open water until he was opposite the lakeside entrance to the boathouse. He hadn't noticed it from the shore or from looking out of the boathouse. Someone, or more than one, had been out on the ice. There was no vertical edge to the snow as had been the case elsewhere along the border between open water and solid ice. It was glassy, almost polished.

Where nanny had fought to thrust the reluctant body of Lucy Marie, again and again. Where she had knelt watching the child's protracted progress to a grave below the ice. Deep into the Bovril water.

And in places no snow remained. Removed from the ice surface altogether. Depressions marked where footprints had once been. Now just hollows in the thawing snow coating. Traces of forest litter nestling in shallow pools of water. Intuition jabbed him in the ribs. A prodding, urging finger.

'What are you doing?' Dick Kaltenbach stood over his partner, who was clearing great swathes of snow with his arcing arm. Snow soaking into the trousers of his neat Italian suit.

'Don't disturb that spot, Lieutenant.' Chuck raised his sweaty head. 'Sure there's been something happening round here.' He drew out a rectangle in the snow where he wanted his superior not to venture.

'What d'ya reckon?' Dick was interested, if a little baffled.

'Maybe the other kid. The girl. Don't know why, but I've a strong feeling for this.' He went back down on his knees and cleared more snow.

'What ya hoping to find there?'

'Just need to look. See if I can see anything pinned below the ice.'

'You won't see nothing there, Chuck.' Dick huffed. 'Ice'll be too thick. Wasting your time. Ain't like glass.'

'Need to have one look see.' By now he was peering only inches from the surface. As if at Seaworld, peeking through cloudy water at a killer whale. He'd forgotten about his sore back.

Dick lit a Marlboro Light and watched the antics of Chuck Nolan with a degree of mirth. By the time he had finished his cigarette he was ready to get back to the house.

'Come on. You ain't found nothing.'

'A little longer. I'm sure there's a dark patch just here.' Chuck pointed it out to his Lieutenant.

'Looks all the same to me. Different ice thickness that's all. Water can seem like all sorts of things when you sees it through that. God, it's like looking through porridge. Come on, call it a day.'

'Look, Lieutenant, I'd be happier if we got the divers just to take a look. It's only here. Not in deep water. Right near the boathouse. Give me a break on this one,' pleaded Chuck.

'If this is a fuck up, Chuck, I'm not taking the blame. Right? And it's only to stop you grovelling round there on the fucking ice. You're soaking.'

'Thanks.' Chuck shivered, but managed a smile.

Dick Kaltenbach manoeuvred about to achieve a satisfactory reception on his cell phone. From his conversation it was obvious that there was a great deal of reluctance on behalf of the New Hampshire Troopers Dive Team, stationed at Portsmouth, to venture out that afternoon. And in particular to imperil their lives searching in the murky water under six inches of ice. They didn't elaborate, but it would be written on their faces as they prepared to descend, that pulling kids from such a grave was one of the most heart-aching experiences.

Chuck and Dick left them to it. Neither wanted to be there if there was either success or failure.

Dick Kaltenbach's tossed his boots. They crashed into the boot of his car. He was glad to squeeze into his trusty police shoes. Chuck didn't have the luxury. He would stay damp for a long time.

'Get some coffee. You need it and I'll die without it.' Dick ushered Chuck towards the mobile canteen that was the meeting point for all sections of this investigation.

'We wrapping this up, Lieutenant? We're losing the light.'

Both men held their mugs like sacred chalices. Steam from their breath mixing with clouds spreading from their drinks.

'Reckon so.' Dick studied his coffee. Another Marlboro. Deeply inhaled. 'Get some overnight accommodation for the nanny and Bobby Clayman. We'll get the statements tomorrow.'

Chuck nodded. His teeth were chattering despite the hot drink.

'And get that rust-bucket truck of his taken down to the precinct. You'll need to cover the plates. There are news hounds swarming around. Camped out at the end of the road. Yeah, and you better give it the once over. Need the tyre treads taken. If only to eliminate him.' Dick rubbed his chin. Had he forgotten anything? 'And...what's wrong with you?' Chuck's jaw had dropped and he was almost dribbling.

A wet hand grasped Dick's shoulder. A powerful grip. Holding him to the spot. He struggled to turn.

Chuck had seen the diver hurrying up the slope from the boathouse. Shining black. A stag beetle. Ripping off his hood. A cascade of lake water caught in the sun's dying glimmer. Seen the blatant message on his face. A memory he wouldn't erase without time or alcohol.

Chapter 13

Four bodies lay in Tipper Lake mortuary. Clothes, grime, blackened blood; dripping, strangled with weed. Stuck rigid in death. As found. A family gathering.

'What have we got Chuck?' Dick Kaltenbach knew. It was a fucking nightmare.

'Lieutenant, we have four fatalities, adult male and female, juvenile male and female, three with bullet wounds and one *cause of death to be determined*.'

'Yeah, okay, but what will that be?' Dick was aware of the routine and the protocol, but someone in the Coroner's office was well conscious of the cause of death.

'Looks like strangulation from the marks on the girl's neck.'

'Not drowning?'

'No. Doc's first exam goes with her being dead before hitting the water.' Chuck tried to block out the image of Lucy Marie's swollen face. 'Lungs will tell us.'

'Carry on.' Dick didn't want to dwell. His stomach turned easily.

'Two witnesses to the post homicide scene. Caretaker Bobby Clayman and nanny Sarah Bickles. No evidence of forced entry. Area in vicinity of killings combed. No possibles discovered. No unidentified tracks discovered as yet. Awaiting forensic reports on sites external and internal. Prints being processed. No motive. Money and jewellery appears intact. Background on family still underway. Main residence in England. English nanny. Left States to avoid filing return. No known threats.' Chuck was getting breathless. 'Need anything else?'

'Lots of things worrying about this. Lots.' Dick showed his teeth. 'Three shot, one strangled. Why? No sign of an intruder.

Are we missing something? All the fucking family? Who kills the whole fucking family?' He shook his head. 'I'm not happy.'

'I've got Bobby Clayman and the nanny coming in later this morning. Put them up at the *Quality* on Main. Should have had a decent rest there. Though it may have been difficult to sleep.'

'Good, Chuck. Maybe we've overlooked the obvious. It needs running through afresh. Coffee?'

'You know me. Always need the coffee.' Chuck tucked away his pad and followed Dick Kaltenbach out of the office.

'Starbucks. I'm not having that shit from the Sergeant's machine.' Dick pulled Chuck through the front door and across the yard, and headed for the nearby coffee shop.

'And we've got to go over that heap of shit.' Dick nodded as they passed Bobby's truck impounded alongside sick patrol cars.

'Forgot about that wreck. See to it when I get back.' Pandora's Box would wait for a cup of Colombian dark roast.

Sarah was out of overalls and wearing clothes from a collection kept at the station for such events. Witnesses, offenders, suspects were all vacuumed and examined under a microscope nowadays. Forensic science had risen out of the dark ages. Sadly she wore a far more fetching outfit than she had ever owned. Colours that did enough to improve her usual dowdy appearance.

'I'm aware this is asking a lot, Sarah.' A policewoman lead her by the elbow. 'There are no close relatives we can call upon. It will only take a few minutes. Yes, it will be a devastating sight. I always tell people to think about them when they were alive. On a bright sunny day. Keep that thought strong and don't take in what they are like at this present moment. Make it brief, dear.'

They stopped outside rubber double doors, scored and marked by a succession of trolleys. Trolleys laden with the dead. Rammed. Without any concern for the passengers' comfort. Baggage.

'When I see you nod your head we'll move on. Is that

clear?' The policewoman was used to prompting a response. Dealing with shock. A mistaken assumption with Sarah Bickles.

'You okay, dear?'

'Yeah.' Sarah wasn't that pleased about having to fuss like this.

No sheets. No tags hanging from toes. John and Stella Roberts filled their trolleys. The kids looked lost. Such shrunken bodies on massive padded carts. Less blood. Most of that had been spilled on the forest floor, under the kitchen cabinets or out of the narrow clearance beneath the broom store door.

Sarah's eyes darted along the line of her victims. She was a little concerned they were receiving such notoriety. But, what trophies. What a day's shooting. Almost a smirk on her face.

She sauntered up to the crumpled body of John Roberts. Half an eye was open. One of the eyes that saw the final deed. Saw her killing him. Was it still there? Lodged in some dying memory chip? Perhaps someday they'll be able to reach into the storage inside your head. Attach some wires and it all plays back on a screen. Solve some murders then. Not this one though. Sarah swallowed to hold back a smile heading for her eyes.

It would have been nice just to stay there and revel in his uselessness. Stand over her prize. Pine needles stuck to his shirt, and his arms still lunging. Groping for air. It was all relived.

She nodded for the policewoman.

Stella was a mess. A bullet smacking into the right place produces such a satisfying result. Her face was collapsed. Almost a pancake on the white sheet. Seeping charcoal blood. Like an out-of-date piece of meat. Every insult and criticism glued to the morgue's crisp cotton sheet. Struck dumb.

Sarah nodded again. Fighting back the beam of satisfaction.

Lucy Marie was a different colour. The colour of death but

much blacker around the eyes. A panda mask. And a pale yellow skin. Like you get surrounding a bruise. Pink anorak tucked under her chin, dirtier now, and a shoe missing

No satisfied grin or dismissive cock of the head. No trouble, no more. *Nanny told you who was boss. You believe her now, don't you?* Sarah stared at the child's face and dared it to move.

Fearing the onrush of tears the policewoman tugged gently at Sarah's sleeve. 'Come now, don't upset yourself, dear.'

No chance!

Sarah was gloating. A fulfilment that she couldn't divulge. A crisp nod and they moved on.

Sarah didn't want to look at Tommy. Last she had seen of him was the pleading eyes from a shadow fixed in the bowels of the cupboard. A cornered rodent.

'Nearly over,' urged the policewoman.

Tommy was her only victim. An innocent bystander. A soft spot for the boy. Even monsters have feelings.

He hadn't started off with much blood. A spindly creature. Nothing of him. But wiry strength and a sense of fun. Had reminded Sarah of the illustrations on the cover of a *Just William* book she had once seen in the library when she was at school.

Frozen white. Chalk skin caked in the black tar of his own blood that he had collapsed into. Laid out without a thought. Twisted and contorted. An impossible arrangement of limbs. She wanted to untie him. Assemble him straight. Wasn't right for him to be deformed like that. Even in death.

And his smile had been stolen and replaced with a haunting visor. A devil face. Sunken sooted eyes and ivory cheeks. As if polished or stretched. Tight skin ready to crack. That of an Egyptian mummy just unwrapped.

Again the soft murmur and the tugging hand. 'Don't dwell, dear. Don't you distress yourself.' Sarah resisted for a few seconds and was then pulled clear of the crispen bundle.

Strange emotions. She hadn't wanted to kill the mite. But it had to be the whole package. No loose ends. How she regretted little Tommy's demise.

'All done?' Dick Kaltenbach was refreshed. A bolt of caffeine does wonders. 'She manage it okay?' He asked, pulling the policewoman aside, leaving Sarah to slump in a chair outside the mortuary viewing room.

Her turn to nod. 'No bad moments, thank goodness.' She sidled off. A well earned rosemary tea for her.

Chuck Nolan pulled on gossamer thin rubber gloves. The texture of condoms. It was probably an unnecessary caution. The truck had been manhandled by an army of greenhorns and this was only routine stuff. He too was invigorated by the coffee and felt better playing by the rules.

He had to yank the driver's door. It ground open. Metal against grit and timber debris that Bobby had deposited over several years. In New Hampshire you kept your engine finely tuned, changed tyres for the season, brakes effective. But you didn't do no sissy thing like clean your cab or empty your trailer.

Plastic water bottles down the back of the seat, gum wrappers and grime on the floor, receipts and other sliding sheets on the dashboard. Smeared stains across all surfaces. A filthy cubicle. Chuck was glad of the gloves.

He peered under the seat. More discarded paper and indeterminate matter. Chuck pulled a face. A parcel shelf sagged and carried rusted tools and a vest Bobby had shoved there last summer. Chuck noted these things. Only the glove compartment to unlatch.

Lucky dip. Newspapers, curled magazine with girls in thongs shoving their asses in your face, and two guns. Chuck shuffled the papers straight and laid them together on the seat. It was too dark to make out the arsenal. He withdrew the handguns one at a time. A brute of a pistol, some forty years old. He held it by the barrel and hung it above his head. Viewing it from every angle. He laid it on the paper. Nothing unusual for a caretaker in the White Mountains to carry a gun.

Never knew when you'd hit a deer on the road. Need to put them down.

Then he pulled out the plum. Even now it was sticky. Chuck smelled it as he saw it. Telltale streaks. Black cherry blood. He breathed heavily through his nose. Smith and Wesson .38 model ten with Uncle Mike's combat grip. Chuck knew his guns. He sniffed at the chamber. Knew when it had been fired. Knew what he had found. Knew the consequences. Knew his man.

Dick Kaltenbach was just inside his office when Chuck Nolan burst in.

'Steady on, Chuck.' Dick steadied himself against the desk. 'Nearly had me over.'

Chuck hung the Smith and Wesson in front of the Lieutenant's nose. Smiled. Glowing with self satisfaction. Got him. The look of the scavenger-hunt winner.

'Fuck me! Where'd that come from?' Dick blinked and refocused. 'Where?'

'Bobby's shit-wagon truck.' More than a hint of triumph.

'Stick it in this.' Dick held up a clear plastic evidence bag. 'Slowly.' He made Chuck twist it in all directions as he lowered it in. Every smudge and every trail of blood he followed. And even when it was in the bag he continued to examine the grubby weapon.

'Where is he?' Chuck enquired.

'Still at the Quality, last I heard.' Dick responded. 'I'll get him in pronto.' There was gravity in his voice now. A killer close. Kid killer. As foul as a cop killer. 'Have you been through the rest of the truck?'

'Came with this soon as I found it. There's another gun. An old Webley. Don't think it's been used. An antique. There's only the trailer to go through. Stuffed with lumber. Shouldn't think it's important.'

'Might be. A thorough search, Chuck, you never know.' Dick pulled at his lower lip in thought. 'He must have known we'd find it. I hope he hasn't tried to do a runner.'

Chuck grabbed at the intercom. 'Sergeant. You've got Bobby Clayman under close supervision, haven't you?'

'Tony's down at the Quality with him. Playing chequers last I heard.' Sergeant Jamie Phillips was quick to reply.

'Get two guys down there to bring him over here. Don't panic him, but he needs watching closely. May not be just a witness. If you get my meaning.'

'Sure thing, Chuck.' The portly sergeant pounced on two officers perched near his coffee machine.

'Any hint when you were with him? Seem nervous to you? Gun in the truck only feet away. Must be a cool customer.' Dick pondered.

'We're making one big assumption here, Lieutenant. Until we get forensic diving into that bag, we ain't going to know for certain our caretaker ain't been assisting local game with euthanasia. Know how it looks but let's not jump the gun, so to speak.' Chuck was unusually cautious.

'You're right, Chuck. But I've got twenty bucks that says that revolver's stinking of the Roberts' blood.'

'Just touching the handbrake, Lieutenant. My twenty's with you. That's the murder weapon all right. Sure as the Pope's Catholic.'

'If we've got ourselves a real suspect here then we need to tighten up. Our enquiries need to lean that way.' Dick was making a mental list. 'Tracks, Chuck. I need to know there were no other vehicles. English nanny must've got to know this guy. Must know the history. Any disputes. You know the score. I'm searching for the motive. An employee doesn't murder the golden goose without good reason. And he needs a fucking good reason to slay those kids.' Dick had Bobby Clayman in his sights. It was a heartless massacre. The pictures were still wallpaper in his head. Here was the perpetrator. He had to hang on to a semblance of serenity. Innocent until proved guilty. By the book. It would be hard being a policeman.

Bobby lumbered into Dick Kaltenbach's office heavily escorted by two glum-faced cops. He didn't consider why he was afforded such excessive security.

'Ah, Mr. Clayman. A good night I hope. The hotel comfortable?' Difficult pleasantries for the policeman.

'Yeah. Okay.' Bobby wasn't feeling like exchanging trivia.

'We need to go through a few things with you. Officer Nolan will be here shortly and we are going to tape the proceedings. It's procedure. You understand.' Dick hunted through the Venetian blind, pulling the slats into a triangle, to spot Chuck.

Chuck came sprinting from the far side of the open-plan general office, clutching a new prize. Side-stepping desks and secretaries. His tie flew behind him. Beaming with delight.

Bobby Clayman sat with his head bent, studying the grain of the desk. Chuck could see his hunched back. Could also see his boss pulling at the blind. His last paces were slow and deliberate. He approached the window where Dick gazed. A glare of annoyance at his partner's antics. With both hands he held up a small, clear-polythene evidence bag inches from the Lieutenant's eyes.

Florida Barbie's smirking face met Dick Kaltenbach's. Her straggly hair and smudged swimwear would have disappointed Ken, but how can one look one's best when you've been wedged between filthy damp logs.

Chuck shook the bag slightly to settle some of the moisture. He pouted his lips and cocked his head. A dog bringing back the stick. What a good boy.

'Where'd you get that?' Dick had darted out of his office and grabbed the bag.

'In the trailer. Down at the bottom. Under those logs and shit.' There was no removing Chuck's satisfied grin.

'Forensic will need that quick. Get it down there, Chuck.' Dick squeezed Chuck Nolan's shoulder. 'Well done.'

'Leave it to me.' Chuck wanted the boffins in Forensic to know what a great detective he was.

'No.' Dick hauled him back. 'A better idea. Take this along to the nanny. See if she recognises it. I've a hunch it's the girl's.

And if I'm right I'll need it back here. I'll throw it in this guy's face.' Dick gestured with his thumb to where Bobby sat arched over the table. 'Could be just the thing to knock him off balance.'

'Coffee, Mr. Clayman?' Dick would bide his time until his partner returned. 'Slightly better than they dish up at the Quality. But only just.' Even a plastic smile for the cameras. Some background questions about the Clayman family and the White Mountain National Park would pass the time.

Chuck found Sarah still sat on the chair in the corridor outside the morgue. He encouraged her into an office nearby.

'Sarah, this is not part of your statement proper, but we have in our possession what we believe to be important evidence in this case.' Chuck rushed through the usual settling spiel. Not the standard period to make a witness feel at ease. He knew Dick Kaltenbach well. Patience was not one of his virtues. 'I want you to take a look at something and tell me what you know about it.' He wasn't going to lead her.

Sarah was jittery. What was it? Was it a trick? Did they suspect her?

Chuck pulled out the polythene bag. Barbie had slipped to the bottom. In water. Drowned. Plastic arms reaching up to the zip-lock. Stuck there pleading for mercy.

The only witness. Dumb toy. Sarah knew where Barbie had been. What Barbie had seen. But better than that, she knew the story to tell. And the doll could never contradict her.

'Well?' Chuck watched the nanny's eyes as they flicked through the last stages of Lucy Marie's disappearance. 'Do you recognise it?'

Sarah nodded an affirmative. 'It were hers. The girl's.' *It were in my pocket until I put it in Bobby's truck.* Sarah thought through the truth. It helped with the lies.

'When did you last see it?' Chuck trod carefully.

Sarah rubbed her chin. 'She were playing with it that morning. At breakfast.'

'Are you certain? It was this one, right?'

177

'One with the swimsuit. Had to take it from her. Put it in me pocket until she'd eaten. Know what kids are?' Even Sarah was aware that Barbie dolls moulted. Wouldn't catch Sarah Bickles out with that one.

'So, the last you saw of this doll it was in the hands of Lucy Marie Roberts?' Chuck wanted it cut and dry.

'Yeah.' Sarah appreciated the significance. Knew Bobby's head was on the block. Air whistled slowly from her nose. She was breathing easier.

Chuck slammed some coffee on the table for her and hurried back to the Lieutenant's office.

'Ah, Detective Nolan's here. We can start. Sorry to have kept you waiting, Mr. Clayman.' Dick was quick to acknowledge a discreet nod from Chuck that confirmed the status of the new evidence.

'I have arranged for the duty lawyer to join us. Best you have some representation during these sessions. Sure you understand, Bobby. Steve Reynolds; sound guy.' Dick stacked some papers and ushered a spider of a man wearing an ill-fitting suit into the room. He simply nodded and pulled up a chair. Comforting to have a police stooge to satisfy a criminal's rights.

Dick ran through what Bobby had told Chuck the previous day, and asked him to confirm that it was an accurate account of what had happened. Bobby was pleased to agree the details. Cold run before the waters were tested. Bobby thought he was going home.

'You get on with Mr. Roberts, Bobby?'

'He could be a moany cuss some of the time, but it were fairly friendly like. Bit me tongue a few times.' Bobby smiled at the memory of John Roberts haranguing him for not getting the boats out before October and leaving the woodstore messy. Trivial stuff that meant nothing.

'He mean to you? Tear you off? In front of the kids? That sort of thing?' Dick searched.

'Naw. Nothing like that. Why you asking me this?' Bobby

was smelling a rat.

Dick sucked back. Pushed his face nearer to Bobby's. 'I'm not convinced, Bobby Clayman, that you're telling me the whole truth.'

'Well I am,' Bobby snapped.

The weasel lawyer looked up, but stayed silent. He knew the routine. Knew not to interfere.

'Detective Nolan here has been over your truck. Going through the cab and the trailer.' He watched for a reaction. Disappointingly there was just a shrug of the shoulders. 'Seen everything in there, Bobby, everything.' Still no sign.

'So?' Bobby was stoic to the last.

'So,' demanded Dick, 'what was the blood-stained pistol doing in your glove compartment?'

Bobby smiled. 'Pistol? Blood-stains?' Bobby screwed up his eyes. 'Good move. Expect me to fall for that one?' A nervous laugh escaped unconsciously.

'Forensic have it right now. Testing the blood and checking to see if it is the murder weapon.' Harsh words. No longer the chummy police lieutenant. 'You better smarten up Mr. Clayman, because the shit has hit the fan, and you are not only getting covered by the spray, you are up to your neck in it.'

Bobby gulped. He could read *serious* written on both police officers' faces. He gushed, 'Only gun I carries in my truck is an old Webley that I uses on the squirrels. Is that what you're on about? Ain't been used on no humans.' Big eyes questioned. Confusion mixed with concern.

Dick and Chuck exchanged glances. Knowing looks that signalled new tactics. Clayman hadn't been thrown by the finding of the weapon.

'Gun used on this family is a thirty-eight, Bobby. And what we found in your pick-up is a Smith & Wesson .38, Bobby. You getting where we are coming from? You had a Smith & Wesson .38, and the whole fucking family were shot with a gun like this.' Chuck forgot that Lucy Marie had drowned or whatever. 'No one else there to do these killings, Bobby. Just you and the thirty-eight. Makes sense, seeing as this gun was found in your vehicle, that you done it. Right?'

Bobby cringed at the tirade. 'I ain't done no harm to them people. Come on, this ain't no police state. You're barking up the wrong tree if you think I done it.' Bobby searched their eyes for a sign.

Reynolds extended a hand to touch his client's shoulder.

Dick Kaltenbach pulled out the zip-lock bag where *Florida Barbie* was in the sauna. The bag dripped with condensation. And Barbie had fallen down. She slept at the bottom of the bag. Stiff legs and arms that were still raised as if she was catching a ball on a beach.

'And this, Mr. Clayman?'

Bobby looked at the bag and shrugged his shoulders. 'What? A doll, so what?' His face creased and shook at any suggestion they were about to make.

'A Barbie doll, Mr. Clayman.' Dick circled Bobby. 'Seen it before?'

'Probably. Kids have them.' This was getting unreal. Guns, Barbie dolls. Bobby was feeling dizzy.

'Did the girl have one like this? Little Lucy Marie, that we dragged from the frozen lake. Ghost grey she was. Just a little girl who should have been playing with her toys. Stone dead. Lying under a sheet in the morgue.' Dick wanted the killer. Bad.

Bobby's shoulders jerked. His head tilted and fell to his chest. 'Yeah, she had them dolls.'

'Have this one did she?' Dick stabbed.

'Dunno if that were one. Could be.' Bobby shook his head to clear the fuzz. Blinked to throw off the nightmare. 'You ain't serious. I ain't no kid killer. Been in some fights and things in my time, but never pointed no gun at anyone. Except for vermin.'

'Perhaps that's how you saw the family. Vermin that needed exterminating. Is that how it was, Bobby? Roberts cross you? Have it in for you? Nasty bit of work was he? Rubbed him out so the anger could go away? Then had to tidy up by wiping out the witnesses?' Chuck threw illegal punches to the body. Prided himself on making them crack.

Tears. Bobby couldn't hold back. Cracked his head down on the table and groaned. 'It ain't nothing like that. Ain't killed no one.'

Dick still swung the polythene bag. Barbie swung too. He lowered his head to get closer to the stooped figure of Bobby. In for the kill. 'Why was this little charmer hiding in the back of your truck, Bobby? Been playing with it yourself? Or did you have the girl in there? Like young girls do you, Bobby? Was that it?'

His chair smashed against the partition wall as he exploded from it. Ejection. Bobby grabbed at Dick Kaltenbach. Caught him by the shirt at first and hauled him nearer. Then managed a firm grip on his throat. Rage drove him to smack the lieutenant's head against the glass door of the office. Blood spat from a wound inflicted on impact. He pulled the half-conscious officer towards him, ready to force Dick's skull right through the glass on the second attempt.

With a sharp rap at the base of Bobby's skull with the butt of his police pistol, Chuck efficiently prevented further damage to his partner's head and perhaps serious injury.

Dick struggled away from Bobby's fallen body, giving it a satisfying kick in the ribs as he passed. 'Fucker,' he managed as he stepped behind his desk.

'You okay?' Chuck enquired as he knelt down to examine his handiwork.

'Been better. Thanks. Bastard was going to kill me.' Dick panted out his gratitude. Dabbed his bleeding head with a handkerchief he kept in his pocket but seldom used. Barely a button remained on his shirt and his tie was hung over his shoulder. He held on to the back of his chair, breathing deliberately to control his tremor

'Come and get this fucking Clayman shit, Sergeant.' Chuck was on the phone to the custodial officer. 'Lock him up and throw away the fucking key. Oh, and for your own sake you'd better get the MO to take a look at him. He's fallen over and banged his head.'

At the other end of the line Sergeant Robins nodded with knowing eyes. He recognised Chuck Nolan's craft. Wasn't the first time he'd cleaned up after the unconventional interrogation techniques of the young detective.

Bobby Clayman's world was collapsing. Not that it had been an enviable world anyway. *No killer. Why ain't nobody listening?* His head thumped from the crack to his skull and his brain was resting in porridge. He sat on the bench bed in the clinically grey cell trying to piece it together. *Where'd it gone wrong? Gun in the truck? Doll?* Them saying things that made him fly off the handle. Perhaps, if he slept it all might go away. But he would find night just as deadly as day and there would be no one to take the monsters away.

In Sarah's 'prison' the television chatted nonsense and flickered colours on the wall. Just another of those cheap, chintzy hotel rooms. So many chains in the US. Cheap buildings and trashy furniture delivered with a cardboard smile.

Sarah sat on the edge of one of the two queen-size beds, one knee bent, other leg to the floor. She had her own pictures to flick through. A collage of horror. Nothing was real. *Had she really killed all the family? What now? Another fine mess she'd got herself into.*

Warm phlegm rose from her throat. Enough to chew. So far she was out of the woods. Bobby Clayman was suspected. Had to be. They were sure to have found the gun by now. If things went according to her impromptu plan she'd run clear on this too. A hastily contrived scheme, that was now faultlessly playing out. She was unaware how much Bobby Clayman was now contributing to his own downfall.

Chapter 14

Dick Kaltenbach had scabs on his scratched neck, and it was only the previous night that the heavy clot had fallen away on his pillow from his head wound. The attack had done nothing for Bobby Clayman's chances of a fair investigation. And the papers sitting in a folder on his desk, awaiting Dick's perusal, were going to ensure the caretaker stood less than an earthly chance of even being listened to.

'How's the head?' Chuck slipped into the office behind Dick Kaltenbach. 'Pretty sore still, I expect.'

Dick's eyes were glazed. There was a noose on the table. Neatly packaged in a beige folder. The executioner's axe. Dick's smile widened. He salivated. Engrossed. Bobby Clayman was nailed. Not just the simple caretaker now. His assailant. More reason to send him down.

'That what I think it is?' Chuck asked, trying to peer over Dick's shoulder, at the beige folder.

'Hm.' No distraction. His hand waved behind him to whisk away the disturbance. 'Hold on, Chuck.'

Chuck parked himself against the doorframe. Waiting for the Lieutenant to respond.

'Got him!' Dick Kaltenbach held his back as he pulled away from the desk and straightened himself. 'Got the bastard.' Satisfaction hung on his face. Smirking lips.

Chuck's eyes lit up. 'Forensic reports? Is that it?'

'Sure is.' Dick slapped the folder with his free hand. 'In here is all we need to lock that killer away. He fucking slaughtered that whole family. There's no reason to doubt it. Looks a neater package than I expected.'

Chuck tugged the reports from his partner's hand, and hunted through the papers. Occasionally he let out contented sighs, and turned to smile at Dick who was an avid spectator. It was just as enjoyable to watch Chuck Nolan marinate in the juicy evidence as it had been to read the condemning reports himself.

'Yeah. Speaks for itself. Can't believe we wrapped it up so quick.' Chuck shook his head.

'Not over yet. Need the fucker to announce it. Tell us he done it and why. Neater that way. Sews it up without the doubts.'

'Want him in now?'

'A few minutes. It ain't that it's a jigsaw, but I want to play about with this a bit. Catch him off guard. Ain't so simple, Chuck.' A serious voice. Dick knew the ropes. Knew how to close the body bag. No loose ends.

Like a hooded man on his way to the gallows. Head bent. Stained-blue prison denim. No chains, but handcuffed securely. A bulky trooper thrusting him forward. Bobby Clayman scuttled in.

'Down there, Dave.' Dick indicated the lone chair in the centre of the room. He didn't look at Bobby as the caretaker was thrown into his seat. Word was around already that he'd attacked a lieutenant. Worse, he was a child killer. Evidence was stacked up. No question on this one. Rough treatment wherever he went at this precinct.

Bobby kept his head down. Steve Reynolds followed in. A timid girl.

The two officers prowled around their prey. Lion detectives of the New Hampshire Police Department. Homicide. Ready to pounce. Prodding their quarry with their eyes.

'How you feeling now, Bobby?' Dick didn't wait for an answer. 'Got off to a bad start last time you were in here. That's behind us.' Dick Kaltenbach tapped Bobby's shoulder gently.

It wasn't behind him. A wretched monster that had been conveniently shoved in a room and locked away. It would appear with horrifying regularity for some time yet. Such was shock.

'Chuck, if you could read Mr. Clayman his rights, there. A formality for this interview, as Mr. Reynolds will confirm. 'Dick gestured to the delicate lawyer.

Chuck flipped open his service pad with a whip of the hand. Bobby heard a voice. Metallic and distant. The standard caution. From any police series he'd seen on television. Nothing was real.

'Now we have a small problem, Bobby.' Dick stalked his desk. 'You see.' He was hanging on to the opening. 'You see, you've told us what happened out there at the Roberts' place. And it don't quite fit with what we've got here in the department.'

Bobby only lifted his eyes.

'You can understand the dilemma?' A rhetorical question. 'One that I hope we can sort out between us. Clear up the inconsistencies, you understand.' Dick managed a manufactured smile.

Chuck and Steve Reynolds were pensive. Audience to the thespian Lieutenant. A masterly performance. Dave Gardener, state trooper, a rock at Bobby's shoulder.

'I've got this report, Bobby, from the boffins down in the basement, telling me...let's see. Telling me that they've been through all these complicated tests on that thirty-eight. You know the type of thing. With them microscopes and chemicals. Beyond me all that.' Humouring the man. 'Telling me that the blood on that gun...' Dick closed in on Bobby. '...comes from that shocking wound to Stella Roberts' face. Same blood that was spilled all over that kitchen floor. And ballistics confirm that the bullet that ripped off her nose and lodged in her brain came from that same weapon.' Dick shook his head slowly. Reliving the scene for Bobby's benefit.

He waited for some response. Bobby didn't move.

'Now, where the problem lies, Bobby, is here. This gun, covered in the blood of Mrs. Roberts, was found in your truck.' The words were slow and deliberate. 'Your truck.' A pause. 'And you've been telling us that that ain't your gun.'

'Ain't my fucking gun!' Bobby blurted. Almost spitting from his dry mouth. Lips cracking.

Chuck sat up abruptly. Dave Gardner stepped forward to tower over his prisoner.

The chink Dick had been waiting for. 'I see, Bobby. The thirty-eight ain't yours?' An apparently sincere enquiry.

'No. It ain't.' His lips stung with the salt from his sweat. 'You gotta believe me. It ain't mine. Never seen it before.' But he had. It wasn't coming back to him right now. Bobby sat with his handcuffed wrists on his lap. A begging pose.

'So, this is what we have.' A new tack. 'The gun is obviously the murder weapon, it's covered with the blood of one of the victims and it's found in your truck.' Dick lowered his face as near as he dare to Bobby's. 'And you're trying to tell me, Bobby Clayman, that you know nothing about all this? Bullshit!'

Dick stalked round the office. 'It's all fucking lies. Ain't that right, Bobby?'

Dave Gardner held Bobby's shoulders down. Firm and debilitating. There was little resistance. Bobby was spent. Steve Reynolds took notes, but no part.

'Your gun. In your truck. Yes.' Dick Kaltenbach circumnavigated Bobby's stooped figure. 'Wiped your dabs off. Cute that. But it ain't getting you off the hook. No way.'

Dick returned to his desk and read his next line. 'Down by the boathouse, Bobby. You were down there, right?'

Bobby shook his head from side to side. Minimal movement.

'That's where you were all right. The nanny said she heard you down there.'

Bobby stirred. Nanny? She'd know he weren't the one. Know he didn't kill no-one. A lifeline. He didn't realise how precarious that could be.

'Footprints confirmed by the lab. You were there all right.' Dick patrolled again. 'Just where the little girl was drowned.'

Chuck coughed. He waved one of the documents from Dick's desk. Dick approached and took it. Irked by the interruption mid flow. He studied the paper in the centre of the room.

'My apologies, Mr. Clayman. It would appear that the little girl didn't drown. No, she was fucking throttled there by the dock! Then pushed out under the ice. That was a nice thing to do. Don't you agree?'

Bobby shivered visibly and tears ran through the dirt on his face.

Dick was ready to lay it on real thick. He clutched the folder like a prosecution lawyer. 'And we found that the only tracks left on the Roberts' property, other than those left by us and the Roberts' Suburban, were ones made by your rust-bucket truck. Strange that, wouldn't you agree, Mr. Clayman?'

Bobby didn't move.

'Can't imagine a killer reaching that property without transport, can you? Certainly didn't want to hitch a lift out of there, did he?' Dick closed in on Bobby again. 'Did he?'

'One last thing in this list of troublesome areas, Bobby Clayman.' Dick perched on the lip of his desk. 'The doll. Our little survivor. Been in the lake she had.' Dick scanned the sheet in the folder. 'They can tell, those eggheads. Real wizards.'

Bobby gazed up. A lull in the bombardment.

'Blond hair. Sexy swimsuit. Silent witness.' Dick strode across the room. 'In the lab they found that same blond hair in the strangled child's pocket. In the back of your pick-up as well. We found her there, remember?' Dick was winding it up. 'Remember that. Bobby? In the timber in the back of your pick-up.'

'You can see my dilemma, Bobby. And I'm sure you don't want to spend time here unnecessarily, do you?' Dick skirted. 'Peaceful and tidy, that's how I like it.'

Time to consider. That's how Dick Kaltenbach saw it. If there was this weight of evidence against him he was sure to capitulate. He engaged Chuck in some trivial conversation at his desk as he waited for Bobby to blurt out his confession. Chuck was prompted to be prepared for Bobby's outburst of regret and mitigation. His notepad at the ready.

'I think Mr. Reynolds here will tell you, Bobby, that the cards are pretty much stacked against you. Ain't that right Mr. Reynolds?' Chuck took over. 'Now the sensible option is to tell how it was. You had your reasons. Any man would have reacted same as you. I'm sure.'

Bobby stared at his lawyer. Searching eyes looking for an escape, looking for guidance. Steve Reynolds scribbled more notes and offered only a doleful countenance.

'It's over, Bobby.' Dick was back to sum up. 'You're impaled, my friend. Your only avenue is to come clean. It can only help your cause. Blood, ballistics, footprints, tyre tread and Barbie hair. No one's lying. It's all scientific. All kosher. An impossible escape. Tunnel all you want. You're nailed.' Dick stacked his papers and arranged his pens.

Bobby didn't move. Couldn't believe the conspiracy. Shook his head from the inside and stretched his lips. A cringing motion. He tried to speak. Exaggerated movements of the mouth. Chewing air. A man plummeting from a building, grabbing at nothing and cycling legs gyrating in thin air. No purchase.

'This doesn't have to be painful. Experience tells me that sharing that load is an awfully powerful comfort. Keeping it churning inside you can gnaw at your guts and drill your brain.' Dick Kaltenbach took a traditional path. He hoped, a path to a quick conviction. A drawn out trial would be a fucking nuisance. And he was pissed off being nice to this guy.

Chuck's turn. 'Can send you crazy holding out. Seen it many times. Go mad internalising all you've been through.' Made Bobby sound like a victim. 'Suffocates you in the end. Choke on trying to keep it from exploding out, like poisonous vomit.' Chuck was close to Bobby. Talking low. Encouraging. A brother.

'You can help Mr. Reynolds here. He's goin' to have a tough time if he has to go into court and try and explain all of this.' He motioned towards the forensic file. 'And it'll look bad for you if you go in there shouting innocence and they find you guilty as hell. Wasted time for a lot of people. Sentencing bound to be more severe. On the other hand judge'll look kindly, I'm sure, on a man who has admitted his guilt, comes to the court cap in hand, assisting the authorities in every way. Then they'll listen to the mitigating circumstances. You can tell 'em what drove you to it. Better to have an audience than a lynching party.' Chuck winked out of sight. 'Take it from me. Useless to fight this one, Bobby. Keep your head up. Show them some spunk.'

Steve Reynolds whispered in his client's ear. Chuck and Dick kept their distance. He offered weak words supporting an expedient conclusion, but insisting, that should his client maintain his innocence, he would naturally be assisting in his corner.

'I didn't kill them people. I didn't.' Steve Reynolds was covered by the spray of stale saliva. Bobby suddenly awoken. 'I told you. Why ain't anybody believing me? Not my gun. Doll I ain't seen before. It's all fucking stupid.' His head was up now and shaking wildly from side to side. Dave Gardner alert at his elbow.

Dick and Chuck eyed each other, and closed in. 'Better stick him back in the slammer to dwell on it.' Dick suggested in a cornered conversation with Chuck.

'Yeah. He ain't goin't start singing yet.'

'Look, Bobby, best thing is you go back and think over what we've said. You'll see it's best course for you. Take your time.' Dick dared to touch his shoulder and smile as broad as he could manage. 'Dave, see Mr. Clayman back to his cell.'

Both watched Bobby led away along the corridor. Breathing through their teeth.

'Your reading?' Dick asked Chuck.

'I'm not as happy as I should be,' Chuck explained. 'He's got it all stacked against him, yet he ain't acting like I expected. Something missing here. Can't put my finger on it, but I ain't as pleased as it reads. What about you?'

'He did it all right. This is the key to his cage for life.' Dick patted the beige folder tenderly. 'He'll crack. Just needs time. Let him sleep on it. We'll have him in tomorrow. Nurture it for a day or two. Reynolds will comply.'

'See you in the morning.' Chuck pulled on his jacket.

'Oh, Chuck. There's a few points I want to cover with that English dame. The nanny. Get her along here tomorrow. Okay?'

Chapter 15

Sarah was hailed from her musty room at the Quality Inn. Protective hands. A woman officer to guide her and speak reassuringly. Collectors' items, witnesses. Placate and indulge.

'Course, didn't see him there until after the event. Didn't see him kill the whole fucking family. Can we use her?' Chuck doubted Sarah's relevance.

'I want to see if we can get something concrete on the relationship he had with John Roberts. I'm missing a motive. Uneasy about that. That and the dabs. Surely we've got him in the house?' Dick checked paperwork scattered on his desk.

'Yeah. At the boatyard, in the house and at locations outside. But they tie in with his account. And the nanny's version. Nothing on the gun or the doll, or the cupboard where the boy was hit.' Chuck threw down the reports.

'Let's have her in.' Dick ordered, unsure of his strategy.

Sarah was escorted from the corridor. Humble and apologetic in her carriage. A victim.

'Take a seat, er, Sarah.' Chuck was unfamiliar. 'Not the most comfortable, but Precinct doesn't get the funding.' An attempt at humour.

'Hopefully we won't need to see you much more, Sarah. This has been a shocking business and I'm sure your world has been thrown askew by the devastating loss.' Dick adjusted his half glasses. He needed them for close work if the light wasn't good. Middle age was snagging him gradually.

Sarah sat, knees together, handbag at her side. A withdrawn spinster.

'Bobby Clayman's been charged with the four murders. You've heard that?' Dick enquired.

Sarah nodded to acknowledge the good news. But offered

painful eyes.

'Bobby ever make threats? Tell you he was angry with the family? With Mr. Roberts in particular?'

'No.' Wide eyes questioning the reason for Dick's query. Not the definite *no* of denial, more a *no* in the guise of *maybe*. Sarah knew she mustn't stifle suspicion altogether in that direction.

'Ever see them arguing or having a difference of opinion about something?' Dick was clutching at ectoplasm. Chasing shadows.

'No.' Sarah saw more was needed. She added, 'No, nothing.' Devious to the last. Getting Bobby suspected of this foul crime was part of her hastily scrambled manoeuvres. Being a reliable witness was to be avoided at all costs.

'We got so much on this guy, Sarah. There's got to be a motive. Unless he's a fu... damn nutcase.' Chuck controlled his language, just. Not in front of this innocent old-maid.

'Mr. Roberts shouted at anybody a lot. It was his way.' Sparkling rhetoric for Sarah. 'Meant nothing by it, I dare say.'

'So, Sarah, there has been no specific incident, that you can recall where Mr. Roberts may have offended or castigated this man.' Dick was quick to simplify the language. 'Told him off? Angered Bobby at any time?'

'No, sir. Not that I can remember. Sorry and all.' Sarah offered spaniel eyes. Fingers crossed out of sight.

Dick hunted through some loose leaves. 'I've got it here somewhere. Yes. Here it is. The day the family died. You arrived back at the house from your walk to find the grim scenes, and during this horrific time Mr. Clayman turns up, as if to carry out his duties. Did you feel he was acting normally or was there a certain purpose about this particular visit? Arriving to organise some cover-up of his dreadful act?'

'I was scared. He came as usual. Always did that day.' Sarah stretched her neck towards Dick Kaltenbach. 'Hid in the woods till I were sure it were safe. Recognised his truck.' She strained to say more but couldn't think of anything.

Dick hauled Chuck to one side. 'This is going nowhere, fast. What's your feeling?'

'This dame ain't going to help the cause. Not going to send him down on these crumbs,' Chuck decided.

'Certainly hasn't much to say. I'm not sure there's any value in her testimony if she gets on the stand. Any jury here's going to lose the plot listening to her.' Dick was ready to dismiss Sarah's input.

The two policemen were completely blinkered. Hounds high on the scent. Bobby Clayman had slain the Roberts family. That was certain. They'd have shouted 'fool' and more to anyone suggesting that this mouse of a nanny only feet from them was really the vicious assassin.

'Might need her for some background. Fill in some of the gaps. These guys travelled a lot. Kept themselves well isolated. That camp was furthest in from the highway, tucked away past the lake headland. You never know, once we delve into this fella's past, things could spill out that she can help us with.' Dick had concluded. 'Can't see why we're keeping her here.'

Chuck nodded agreement. 'Yep. Can't see no reason. She's been through enough.'

'Sarah.' Dick turned abruptly. She had picked up the gist of the conversation. She wasn't that daft. Doleful eyes. A lost child. 'Looks like you can head out of here. We don't have any reason to keep you hanging about.' He held out a hand to help her from the chair, as if coaxing up an invalid. 'We will need you to sign some forms. It's a formality. Requiring you to come back should we need you.' Dick directed her to the door. Passing the baton to an officer to complete the paperwork. 'And you take some time out.' Sarah was already in the corridor. Being ushered along. 'Been through an appalling experience. You see someone back in England if you get any nightmares. Good luck.' Dick's words floated after her. An insincere afterthought dissipating in the bare arcade. Words. Just words bouncing off the back of the fleeing butcher. Escape almost complete.

Deliberation time back in Dick's office. 'Word from the cells is that our boy's not talking. Reynolds has been down several times to see if he can scribble out a confession and so far Clayman's stayed dumb.' Chuck winced. 'Thought he'd cry out in the night and want to spill it. Known that happen. In the dark they see their phantoms. Haunting places those dungeons when you've got the ghosts tapping on your shoulder and the guilt drilling your skull.'

'Nice imagery, Chuck. Now let us get down there and squeeze him some more. If he don't squeal quick, we are going to go full distance with this.' Dick grabbed his jacket and goaded Chuck forward.

Cell nineteen. Near to the end of a morbid row of grey-painted metal bars. A bank vault or some religious inner sanctum. Stench of a urinal mixed with a sweet suet odour. Distinctive.

Bobby Clayman was kept away from transient offenders and habitual drunks, cooling off or sobering up in pools of vomit. These were housed in the cells next to the duty officer's room. Often nursed or coerced through their quarantine. Loud criminals with lots to say or shout about. Not worth prosecuting. But they knew he was there, Bobby. Knew the *fucker* who had killed children was in the bowels of the station. Tucked away. Unclean. He'd have heard them if his senses weren't paralysed. Heard them call his name and make grotesque threats.

Dick and Chuck left their guns outside. Dave Gardner took them through the hyena barrage offered by the occupants of the first three cells. No respect on either side. Dave kicked viciously at a leg stretched out from the bars to intercept the Lieutenant's stride. 'Broke it I hope,' Dave commented as he opened another gate leading to the heart of the underground catacomb.

Bobby wasn't clinging to the bars, searching the approach to his cell. Not clambering to see who was there; what word they brought. No. Bobby was sat where they had left him.

Dick and Chuck stood at the open door. Dave Gardner had turned the key without any reaction from the inmate. Bobby was a grey man now. A shadow. As if someone had stolen the real Bobby Clayman and just left his imprint. Hollow sockets edged in black. Sharpened cheekbones. He rocked. Like an ape in a sixties experiment on behaviourism. One of those black and white recordings. No surrogate mother here. Not a steady rhythmic movement. Rapid and destructive.

'Bobby?' Dick spoke to the jerking body. 'Bobby Clayman.'

'Won't get no sense, Lieutenant. Been like this last couple of days.' Dave advised.

'Not said anything?' enquired Chuck.

'No, sir. He's been a rag doll just tottering on the edge of the bed. Been shitting himself and pissing all over the bedding. We're not bothering to change that now.' Dave shrugged.

'Yeah, that's obvious.' Dick held his nose and blew from puffed cheeks.

'Bobby, can you hear me?' Chuck crouched down to intercept Bobby's forward sway. 'Detective Nolan and Lieutenant Kaltenbach here. Like to continue out discussion.'

Bobby's wide eyes aimed as he lurched and withdrew. No alteration of pace or regularity.

'Reynolds been down today?' Dick enquired.

'Every day. Down here earlier. Just the same. No reaction. Like talking to a robot. One that's switched off or stuck in destruction mode.' Dave held on to a chuckle. 'He can't get a word out of his client, let alone sense.'

'Is he in the building, Dave?' Dick asked.

'Yeah. He's acting for some psycho who turned his parents' home to chippings with a Samurai sword. He's in cell five with him now.'

'Dave, get him down here now, will you. I need to brief him on this.' A hint of resignation in Dick's voice.

Steve Reynolds arrived with his tie askew. A school prefect being hauled before the headmaster for an indiscretion.

'Thanks for the time, Steve. Won't keep you too long. I

expect you have more than a handful down there.' Dick pointed along the tunnel. 'Only, it seems we have a real problem with this guy. Don't you agree?'

Steve Reynolds swallowed. 'Yeah, you're right.' His head shook up and down and his eyes agreed.

'You're going to have to do your best here, with this jerk. He ain't answering shit, and I ain't hanging around to give him the chance.' Dick hurled stinging words. 'I know the fucking arsehole did it. Murdered that whole fucking family. I want him down forever. You understanding me?'

Steve Reynolds almost took a step back. Managing a further nod of agreement.

'A bit of advice. Remember it well. Won't say it again. You'll need to go for a whacko plea to get this past me 'cause I ain't moving on a murder one.'

Bobby rocked some more. Chuck threw a congratulatory glance towards Dick. Steve Reynolds back pedalled almost bowing as he left.

Dribble glistened on Bobby Clayman's lip. A dark yellow stain marked the path of previous saliva flows. Flaking crust now. Frightened eyes. Like a man watching his own death. Getting smaller by the day; his hunched body lolling in the speckled shafts of sunlight. Lasers in his cell.

Chuck and Dick were gone. It wouldn't be worth returning. Steve Reynolds would. Spend hours watching his client locked in some inescapable torment. Talk to himself, and hope that Bobby would eject out of his personal prison and answer lucidly. Steve was an optimist.

'We'll need Doc Prentice, Dave.' Steve Reynolds informed the jailer as he left towards evening. 'I've lost him. He's real sick now. Only saviour for him is a psychiatrist.'

Sarah liked the window seat. But not the fat man who sat beside her. She'd put up with him and his chubby arms. All the time the plane remained on the ground she imagined a squad car screaming across the tarmac and burly policemen hauling her from her seat. She didn't feel like a murderess. It really hadn't been her fault. Finding a comfortable position was difficult. Squirming beyond her neighbour's encroaching thighs and surveying all the vehicles toiling around the plane. It happens. She'd seen it somewhere. Where the villain thinks he's got away, only to be apprehended at the last minute. She was sure that was in a film.

As the aircraft sprinted down the runway, straining to lift its bulk into the air, nanny was perched on the front of her seat. Restraining seatbelt. Clutching at the harsh material. Rocking gently. And quite uncharacteristic, a smile.

Bobby also smiled. A jackal smile from haunting eyes. Maybe a snarl. Tottering perch. Embraced by his own arms. Straitjacket oblivion.

Chapter 16

Detective Constable George Rundle, retired. That's how he liked it. Working life with the force was over. Done his stint. From the beat in the Smoke to CID down in idyllic Dorset. But he couldn't shake off the appearance. A sleeveless jumper, or was it a tank top, in navy blue, light blue shirt, grey slacks and Police Federation tie. George was still signing in. Could easily be mistaken for a man heading for the office. Wore his uniform all day, everyday. Organised a devoted wife, Deirdre, and followed a meticulous routine.

It was ten in the morning so Deirdre knew where he would be. The worn leather armchair in the lounge, or was it the sitting room. His armchair. Territory that all his family and good friends observed.

'Coffee, dear.' An exchange of smiles.

George from over the top of his paper and Deirdre escaping through the door to the hallway.

He had another forty minutes before it was time to venture into the garden. It was part of the retirement package. It's what you did.

The Telegraph hadn't many captivating stories on the front page. In reality George did not much care for the reporting style in recent editions. But he would never desert his Daily Telegraph, his heavy broadsheet. Status. Part of his personality, part of the Force, part of his politics.

Bank interest rates, relatively relevant. Footballers in trouble at a night club, or wanting more lucrative contracts. When he played for the Met Police team way back in the fifties there weren't the prima donnas there are now, no sir.

Animal Rights groups were still sending out parcel bombs that ripped the occasional limb off some unsuspecting secretary or mail clerk. There were some brief headlines listed to entice readers to undertake a visit further into the paper to find more fulfilling reports on Palestinian violence, crime figures in New York City, Gay outing and a planned state visit by King Fahd of Saudi Arabia.

George whistled through his teeth as he turned pages to reach the inside. Here the reports were a little more salacious. Contemporary trials of provincial politicians on fraud charges or clergy who couldn't keep their hands off the altar boys. George skipped the more sensational reports and concentrated on ones where he knew the lawyers by reputation and where he could use his deductive skills, make his decision on the guilt of the accused. There were some cases he had followed over the last few days and proceeded to update himself and mutter opinions. Views that only the curled cat heard from the busy brain of the armchair detective.

By the time George was struggling with the sails of the centre pages Deirdre was back in the room, dusting. He could never manage to keep his Telegraph under control, and ended up wrestling it into a badly folded sandwich of askew sheets. The sports pages would be savoured last. City and Finance, tedious. At the top of his pad of contorted paper was the International News section. Usually he skimmed this. Too much on the 'Stan' countries that had dropped out of the Soviet Union, or were being clung on to by the new Russian Government, mainly for their oil reserves. And ferry disasters in the Philippines or Indian sub-continent, held little interest for him, however tragic.

Deirdre was alerted by her husband's change of practice. A serious matter. It was well past the time he donned his gumboots and strode into the garden. She dusted closer, peering over his shoulder. Most unusual.

'Something the matter, George?' she enquired lifting the mantelpiece clock and flicking at its base.

'Hm, no. Fine.' George Rundle shrugged off his wife's query.

Amidst the general tripe, appearing under a sub-title of *US*

Today was a headline that had ambushed ex DC Rundle.

Family Slaying – Suspect Held.

It was just his cup of tea. Two adults and two children murdered at their isolated lakeside cottage in New Hampshire. Three shot and one strangled. Absorbing stuff. Caretaker questioned and charged. George read the account meticulously. Something a little more glamorous about American crime. Perhaps it was the television shows. His investigations seemed so tired and obsolescent. No dapper suits and screaming squad cars.

It was in the last paragraph. He read it three times. Bells rang but he hadn't placed it yet. There was an English nanny working for the family. She'd discovered their bodies. Sarah Bickles.

'Bickles? Bickles?' George repeated.

Deirdre, who hadn't gone far, dusted her way back into the sitting room. 'What did you say, George?'

'Bickles. Where do I know that name?' It was half in answer and half a question for himself.

'Sure I don't know.' Deirdre carried on at pace past her husband to the chair he was about to vacate. She arranged the scatter cushion and plumped up the seat.

'Get me some scissors, Pet,' George requested, still playing back the name in his head. 'I need to cut this out.' He waved the jumbled sheets above his head.

George had edged the lawn and pruned some roses before he reached his eureka. 'Got it!' He danced back to the kitchen where Deirdre was preparing lunch.

'Boots, George!' Deirdre kept an immaculate house.

'Sorry, love.' George plodded into the kitchen trailing mud. 'Where's that cutting?'

'On the side, with your stuff.' George was allocated what Deirdre termed his scruffy area where she deposited his bits and pieces.

'It was the Rupert Bassnett case. I'm sure the nanny there was a Sarah Bickles. Absolutely certain.'

'Whatever you say, George.' Deirdre was somewhat concerned about her husband's continuing strange behaviour. But took little notice of the content of his ramblings.

George perched on a kitchen stool and read through the report once more. Yes, he was almost certain that was the name of the nanny he had interviewed over the death of young Rupert Bassnett. But he had to be sure. He was a detective and there was a procedure to follow.

George's first port of call was Patel's Newsagent. Some of the other 'heavies' would surely have reports. Even a tabloid or two might pick up a sensational story like a family massacre.

Mr. Patel valued George's custom, but he was somewhat disconcerted that Mr. Rundle was opening up his neatly folded broadsheets, laying them over his ice cream refrigerator in the centre of the shop and leaving them in bundles that were too dilapidated for sale. It wasn't a library and he wasn't a charity. And it didn't look as though the man was going to buy one.

'Yes, good.' George muttered when he saw that The Times had the story covered. 'Hm, damn it.' He wasn't so impressed when The Guardian only used an inch of column space for its report, and didn't even mention the nanny. Typical of a left wing rag. He'd buy The Times despite only needing the one article. The Daily Mail had picked up on the English nanny aspect, mainly because it had dealt with the Louise Woodward case in depth only recently. George would have to fork out on that also.

Mr. Patel was a little happier when he saw there was a sale. And he was prepared to tidy up the dead albatross newspapers that George had left fluttering their feathers every time the shop door tinkled open.

Now George had the three newspaper cuttings on the kitchen counter. He poured over them clutching his turquoise highlight pen. Every now and then dragging it along a relevant part of a report. George was a man who, from experience, questioned coincidence. On too many occasions coincidence had read habitual or modus operandi. Although, he was still unsure where this was all leading. Following his nose. And George Rundle had one of the finest noses in CID. The garden would have to wait that morning.

'Hello, Harry? George here. Yeah, fine. She's fine too. It's looking great. Out there every day.' George was on the blower to Harry Fielding, a sergeant at George's old nick. He was parrying the usual questions aimed at recently retired officers. 'Look, Harry. Everything's going well this end. Need a favour. One of my cases. Can I pop down to look at the file? Thanks. See you around three this afternoon.' George had the scent. A hound on the trail.

Harry Fielding was a plump man, red cheeks and an infectious chuckle. Your typical station bobby. They must cater for the portly policeman at the Police tailors. Although well overweight his uniform fitted him dutifully. Every bulge accommodated by the blue serge material.

'Not really the practice, George,' Harry informed him with a chortle on his arrival. 'Inspector wouldn't be pleased. Procedure and all that, eh?'

'Trust me. Something really bugging. Can't get it off my mind. Appreciate it.' Being in the same Lodge had its advantages. Despite never finding Freemasonry up his street, George had persisted so as not to feel an outsider. It was rife in the force.

Harry unlocked the basement door. Files fitted to the ceiling. Only Harry could negotiate his way through them. It was a jungle or a maze to the rest of the coppers. One day Harry wouldn't be around and then the whole of the East Dorset force would grind to a halt.

Harry threaded his way through shafts of sunlight peppered with drifting specks. Natural light from high skylight windows.

'File number?' Harry asked.

George gripped his bottom lip with his teeth. 'Sorry, Harry.'

'You're all the bloody same. Make hard work of it you do. Name of deceased?'

'Rupert Bassnett.'

'Oh, the young kid that drowned in the bath?' Harry recalled them all. 'Sir Peter's lad.'

'That's it.'

Harry headed down an aisle and grabbed a set of ladders. He tripped up the steps. Agile for a heavy man. A shower of dust exploded as he tugged the manila file from high on the shelf.

'Here, George. This is your baby.' Harry handed the file to George and descended. Not so sprightly on the way down.

George wiped the face of the folder to read the details on the front cover. Harry was good. It was his case. Number GR34266. He'd opened and closed this one. Knew it well. Everything had been concluded satisfactorily, except for the loss of such a young life. Now it was being reopened. Unofficial like. He was going to have to read most of it at the station. Harry would stop at having police property removed from the premises. Some photocopies of relevant pieces, that's about all he'd get away with.

There was a desk that Harry managed to swing for him and a reasonable supply of tea and stale biscuits. Just like the old days at the nick. He rummaged through his own words. Good notes and reliable avenues pursued. He'd done it by the book. Policing at its best. Young Rupert Bassnett had died from drowning. Lungs full of water. Most likely struck his head on the proud taps and become unconscious. A dangerous thing in a bath. Cut and dried. Foul play ruled out. A tragic accident. Another case closed. George had interviewed all concerned. Forensic had made their deliberations. Neatly packaged and filed away.

But now. Here was George Rundle cutting at the strings that held that package together. Deliberately pulling out securely documented material. Exhuming the corpse and hacking into the rotting flesh of this 'misadventure'.

'You don't want to play with them ghosts, George.' Harry brought another cuppa and grinned at his friend. 'Best left to lie undisturbed. Always brings trouble. Mark my words.'

George smiled back. But he was on a mission. You don't leave your garden and the bliss of retirement if there isn't anything stirring. And George was stirred. Every and any mention of the nanny, Sarah Bickles, he set aside. The small pile of mainly notebook sheets that Harry was asked to copy.

It was late when George arrived home. He'd missed tea and supper was ruined. He smelled it from the front door. Deirdre had been keeping it warm. On a higher gas than usual. So he could sniff the aroma as he entered. Be entertained by that. It was a shepherd's pie past its *eat by* time.

She wasn't going to say anything. Just sit in the lounge (or was it the sitting room), crochet and make out that there was nothing out of the ordinary. But curiosity prodded too often. She had to ask.

'Where *have* you been, George?' Just as an aside. Never taking her eyes off her needle.

'Research, dear.' George strode into the kitchen, seeking his supper. Following the heavy waft. Only to find the cremated pie. He couldn't eat cinders. The fridge provided some mature cheddar and he grabbed a handful of broken water biscuits. There was no point raising the matter of the burnt offering in the oven. Silent acknowledgement.

Back in the lounge he snuffled his food like a badger. Sunk back in his chair. Watching Deirdre stitch and sniff.

'An old case that I needed to look through. Harry let me have the file.' Deirdre stitched on and sniffed higher. A haughty air. 'And what with that report in the newspaper. Couldn't leave it alone. Needed following up, that.'

'You're out of the force now, George. It's just you and me at home. I put up with the lonely times. The nights when you never came back to bed. Long hours and dreadful phone calls in the middle of the night. All for the sake of your ever-so-important position as an officer of the law. But now you are plain Mr. Rundle, and if you didn't know it I am Mrs. Rundle, your wife. Don't I deserve this time with you?'

George cowered. 'Sorry, love. Instinct. A hound with the scent.' He offered the Rundle smile. George knew about making peace.

'Well, what did you find out, Sherlock?' A snooty enquiry. But Deirdre was melting. She was a glutton for a good story. Loved some intrigue.

'Not sure yet, love. Needs some probing. But if it's what I fear it is I'm not certain I can leave it alone. Wouldn't be right. Some victims right close here and some a good distance away, that could be relying on me.' George crunched at his biscuits. His head still nodding from his last words. Self-elected. Equaliser.

Newspaper reports tend to be selective in what material they use. Depends a lot on the readership demographics and the column space allocated by the editor. George wasn't satisfied with his cuttings. He wanted more detail. Wanted the nitty-gritty, ins and outs. Fussy bugger who wouldn't be content with what some newspaperman decided he should be fed. His appetite was far more voracious. Where to go for his feast was his next objective.

George's garden fell victim again. All the next morning he sat at the dining room table. Basildon Bond writing pad and his reliable fountain pen. Old school was George. It was a general letter that he would send to all the editors of the national press in the States and local New Hampshire papers. Plus he would send a missive to the detectives in charge. They hadn't been named but he would just direct it to the authorities in New Hampshire. From a fellow policeman, well ex-detective, who had closely followed the case. He wouldn't let on the real reason for his enquiries.

Most of the table was decorated by snowballs. Screwed up paper that wasn't quite right, or where the fountain pen had dolloped a puddle of ink exactly when he'd got it just so. Two hours later and there was half a page staring back at him. A neat hand but little substance. He'd walk in the garden with his coffee. Some fresh air. Think it through.

No peace there. The kid next door was kicking a football at his fence and shouting out soccer gibberish. George was getting old. Mr. Plod emerged. Strode up and shoved his head over to challenge the anti-social behaviour. Have fun but respect the wishes of others. And his wish was to be able to run this letter past himself. Sculpt out some relevant phrases. It was tricky; these were Americans he was dealing with.

'Jamie.' He beckoned the gangling boy over. 'Do us a favour and keep the noise down.' A policeman's nod of the head and a wink. 'Can't you go up the common and thrash about there. No one to upset. Much more space.'

'Sorry Mr. Rundle.' Jamie approached. Chin on chest and eyes levelled. What a moaning bastard that copper was, he thought. His face didn't betray him. 'Been stuck in with homework. Some heavy shit, I mean, stuff for physics. Does my head in. Just needed a break.'

'Know the feeling, son. Got my own homework to sort out. And that's not going well.'

'Homework, Mr. Rundle? You've got homework?'

'Not like yours, Jamie. Policeman's business. International enquiries.' George made it sound grand.

'Wow!' Jamie wagged his head. 'Now that's wicked.'

'Could well be,' George acknowledged, not really in tune with teenage vernacular.

'Murder or terrorism?' Jamie was hooked.

'Can't say at the moment. Understand?' A knowing expression displayed by his mouth. George enjoyed being important.

Jamie was still salivating. 'Boy, I wish my dad was a detective.'

'Not all fun you know. Paperwork. That's the curse, Jamie.' George realised he was playing it a bit too James Bond. 'I'm in there.' He pointed through his French windows to the snowdrift table and his A5 pad. 'Contacting the States. Communication. Exchanging information and ideas.' Now it was some sort of science.

'Database access?' Jamie chirped, eyes lit with eagerness.

'What?' George was thrown.

'Over the Internet. Case detail retrieval. Mind-blowing stuff, Mr. Rundle.' Jamie was puffing with excitement.

George trod carefully. You don't expose your ignorance to a spotty fifteen-year-old. 'You understand all this then, Jamie?'

'Well, yes. But not anything like you. That's heavy matter, man.' Jamie scratched at his recently shaved head. 'Instant isn't it? Just like it's in your house. Libraries of the stuff. Awesome.'

George was on stepping stones. 'So, you are familiar with what can be achieved using computers to untangle the complexities of crimes, young man?'

'No expert, like yourself, Mr. Rundle. But I do pride myself with being able to surf that Net with *a certain skill.*' Jamie sucked his lips and polished his tee-shirt with his knuckles. A generous smile.

'Well, Mr. Boffin.' There was an audible ping and a light flashed in George's head. A plan was emerging. Policeman's craft. 'Here's a test for someone with a certain skill. How do you think a detective could read all the information ever published about a crime?'

'Won't catch me out, Mr. Rundle. We all know how to access newspaper articles on the Web. Good try.' Jamie had picked up his football and was holding it like a goalkeeper ready to punt it up field.

'Good lad. Glad you are on top of the subject. No moss on you.' George bumbled. 'Truth is I'm having some problems with my computer.' Now it was downright lies. 'Playing up it is.'

Jamie came closer to the fence. 'Internet provider letting you down. Who's your ISP? Dial-up or Broadband?'

'Er.' George was definitely up the creek and definitely without a paddle. 'Who's yours?' Clever quick thinking. He gritted his teeth.

'*Netkonect.* Had some hiccups but no real failures. Must be a bummer. Still you've probably access to some other hardware. Must be some sophisticated PCs at the Yard.' Same generous smile. 'Personal computers not police constables.' Jamie added, a little embarrassed by his joke.

George was straining for the words. And the excuses. This was no dumb lad. 'International, as I said. Hush-hush business. Interpol and all that.' He raised one eyebrow. A stupid face.

'I see.' Jamie was young. Momentarily gullible.

'Perhaps you would like to help the Force. Just on this occasion, Jamie. Nobody else need know. An assignment. I can swing it.' George's grin was glued on.

'Me? Man, that would be great.' Jamie's eyes were ablaze. 'Sure. I mean I wouldn't breathe a word.' He made a cross with his finger across his chest. Initiation to the Famous Five. 'Crumbs.'

'Your mum and dad in?'

'Only my sister and her friend. They're watching telly.' Jamie explained, trying to dismiss their presence.

'Best, for security, if you pack up the computer gubbins and bring it over.' George was speaking lower now. Very conspiratorial. It was how it was done.

Jamie didn't like the idea of transporting all that equipment next door. Especially as he had it all set up neatly in his bedroom. His command module. It would be a real pain. But, he did have to remember how unique this opportunity was. In a flash he had kicked the football into the vegetable patch and was bounding into the house to disconnect the cables.

George held the door as Jamie squeezed through with the first piece of the puzzle; a grimy, beige monitor. Wires trailed and George trundled after the boy's leaping path up the stairs, scooping up the spaghetti leads.

'In there Jamie. Where the door's open.' The detective spoke through puffs of breath. 'On the table I've cleared.' Even for his short stay there had to be order. Deirdre would be most concerned if there was a mess.

Jamie made five trips to ensure he had all he needed. He had thought he would be able to use some of George's peripherals, but there was no sign of any software let alone hardware. Even the extension lead that had lived under his desk for years needed to be dusted off for the move.

Unfamiliar territory and some hastily and insecurely connected plugs delayed progress. Jamie beavered away until he was ready to navigate. The pest from next door was impressing George. A transformation.

'All set, Mr. Rundle.' Jamie turned from *Houston Control* and beamed. 'Where are we going?'

'Er...going? Yes, of course.' It took time for George to slide into the vernacular. 'American newspapers. National and regional. New Hampshire to be exact.' An element of control now.

'When we arrive at these papers what especially is our interest?' Jamie knew how to reach his target without unnecessary navigation.

'A most diabolical crime, Jamie. Whole family slaughtered. Name of Roberts. There's been a lot about it.'

'I'm accessing the press facility based in Boston. We can comb through all the national newspaper sites from there, and also delve into the provincial press. It's real easy to find things. User friendly.' Jamie plucked at his keyboard, and jerked the mouse.

'Need you to keep this safe. No mentioning the details, even to your parents.' George watched over Jamie's shoulder and spoke to the screen. He revelled in the drama.

'Twenty three hits.' Jamie turned to George. 'Not bad, eh?'

George wasn't too sure what a hit was, but the boy sounded excited so it boded well. 'Good.'

'Print them out, shall I?' Jamie quizzed. 'You aren't going to read them on the screen, are you?'

'Yes. Thank you, Jamie. That'll be fine.'

'Some good stuff here by the looks of it.' Jamie read as much as he could as the numerous articles zipped from the printer or flickered urgently on the monitor. 'Is there any aspect to be highlighted? We can zoom in on that if you want.'

George tugged on his chin. 'Put this name in, if you can. Sarah Bickles. Yes, see if it picks up the name. Sarah Bickles.'

He was half talking to himself, and running the name out loud to see if it brought back memories or sparked initiatives.

'Sarah Bickles?' Jamie was more than curious. 'Why Sarah Bickles?'

'Told you it was a delicate department matter. Now forget I even said that. This is under wraps. You've been told.' George put on his stern voice and pushed out his chin.

The whirring finally rested. A clacking noise that had been driving George mad. The tray was full of swaying sheets spat out by the latest inkjet printer.

'There we are, Mr. Rundle. Best results. No mean effort, eh?' Jamie sat, hands on thighs, feeling like a hero. 'Need me anymore? Any unsolved murders?' Jamie's bravado was mixed with seeping humour.

'You're a good lad, Jamie. You've done well. I'm most appreciative. And...so is the Force. I'll inform them of your assistance.' George conjured up some more lies.

'I'll pack this lot away. Get it back home then.' Jamie felt slightly used. 'That's if you don't need me?' A last appeal for further involvement.

'You get along. Need any help? Sterling effort, lad.' George patted his back as he stood up. Pulled at some plugs once he had seen the picture fade and the buzzing killed. He carried the trailing wires and held a light box or two. No heaving bulky items. Well, his back being what it was, you couldn't really expect him to lug that lot.

It was a small mountain of paper. Avid reading for that night and all the next day. Jamie had done well. George had a wad of A4 sheets to pore over. From the first gruesome discovery to the arrest of the perpetrator. And in there, kindly referred to as a victim herself, was the frightened and timid English nanny, Sarah Bickles. Only a bit player in the family massacre, once the attention was focused on the evil caretaker. Sources ranged from the much-respected *New York Times* to the *White Mountains Gazette*. There was even some Canadian coverage in the *Globe and Mail*, a Toronto based broadsheet.

Chapter 17

There was nowhere else for Sarah to go. She slid anonymously back to Lyme. To the ugly estate and the dingy house. Unsure what the media coverage had been in Britain. She didn't need to worry. Even such hideous crimes committed abroad lost their despicable labels, and most of the outcry fell into the Ocean. Another planet away. And the individuals tied up in the drama, unknown actors with easily forgotten identities.

Suitcase at the gate. A replay. She detected no movement from inside, but her imagination had her mother shuffling from kitchen to television, a mug of tea held pathetically. A groan with every step. Across the grimy carpet. A walking dead person.

A shadow stirred. Even through the yellowing net curtains someone could be seen against the light of the patio doors that led to the back garden. Bulky swaying movements. Her mother? Yet not the same dragging gait. More a fat pantomime character, waddling.

Sarah's first step into the hallway revealed the identity of the portly silhouette. Debbie. The weight hadn't shifted after the birth of the baby, Victoria. Wrestler's arms and barrel legs striped with purple veins. Frightening deterioration.

'Home, again?' More an accusation than a greeting.

'Yeah.' A defiant reply. The jousting had begun.

'Mum's not here.' An achievement to be announced. Debbie spoke with pride.

'Where's she?' Sarah was sure she had died. It would be a relief.

'Put her in a home. Senile she was. Struggled to get about. Yeah, I had to do it.' Debbie was spitting blame. 'With the kid. It weren't safe her being around. She'd lost it.'

'Home?' Sarah pondered aloud. It was as good as dead. She tugged her suitcase upstairs. Debbie lumbered to the bottom of the staircase to watch Sarah's progress.

Vicky, as the baby was already known, hollered every few hours. Debbie thumped around the house clutching bottles and other baby paraphernalia. Sarah didn't rush to see her niece, but drank the sweet aromas that wafted from the nursery. Intoxicating scents that she inhaled deeply.

Both sisters prowled. Different agendas. Debbie broke an uneasy truce.

'Follows you don't it? Death.' She had cornered Sarah outside the bathroom. 'First it were the boy, now a whole fucking family. What is it about you, Sarah?'

Sarah swayed and held onto the door frame. 'What d'you mean?'

'Boy Rupert died when you looked after him, and now both the children and their parents are murdered when you're there in America. Read it all in the papers.' Debbie was proud she had done her homework.

'So? Don't mean nothing.' Sarah pushed past her sister.

'Strange ain't it?' Debbie wasn't dropping it. 'Two jobs and deaths in both.'

'Happens. Ain't my fault.' Sarah turned from her bedroom door. 'Why, you thinking something?' She squeezed her eyes and aimed them at Debbie.

'Just curious.' She showed the makings of a knowing grin.

'Thought you were moving out.' Retaliation. 'Thought that bloke, Roy, was taking you away from all this. Setting up home. Getting married.' A volley from the trench.

Debbie rocked. Roy had fucked off. Hadn't even wanted to see the kid. A deserted mother. Unmarried. Single parent. So many labels. She fled in tears. Vicky screamed for a nappy change.

The battles continued. War wasn't over. Both armies regrouped. Debbie determined to get the matter off her chest.

Sarah, scouting for some breakfast the next morning, found

a newspaper article, the one from the Mail, Sellotaped to the fridge door. Her finger followed the lines as she read of the deaths in New Hampshire, of Bobby Clayman's arrest and an account of her grim discovery. Detached somehow. Not what she had done. Almost fiction.

'That's him, ain't it?' Debbie spied over her left shoulder. An awkward bundle in a washed-out housecoat. 'That's the bloke you told me about last time you was home.'

Sarah didn't look round. Caught in the middle of reading the story she held her finger at the last word read. 'So?'

'Why'd he want to kill all them people? Maniac or something?' Debbie wasn't leaving it. 'It don't seem right somehow.'

'But he didn't kill me, did he? Your Roy is wanted for murder. You seen how you look, Debbie?' Sarah had never been so lucid. Almost erudite. Brutal words, a shower of rocks. Debbie cowered from the onslaught.

Chapter 18

Bobby Clayman had been transferred to a prison in upper New York State. Not far from Lake Placid. An Olympic resort, and tourist town summer and winter, boasting celebrity visits during both seasons.

His mental condition was unchanged. A shadow of the affable caretaker bustling about the Roberts' camp, hauling boats and heaving lumber. A few friends and relatives had travelled to visit him incarcerated. None had managed to reach him. An impenetrable shell.

Chuck Nolan and his partner Lieutenant Dick Kaltenbach had moved on. Pressing cases. A few homicides and armed robberies. Local hoodlums that were easy to process.

'Clayman's in court in three weeks according to the DA.' Dick announced to Chuck. 'What's your thinking on our position.'

'Dead man rocking.' Chuck was dismissive. 'He ain't going nowhere and he ain't fit to get his due, unfortunately. A bastard like that needs to know he's suffering. Defeats the object if he's in cloud cuckoo land.'

'Reckon he's genuine? Experts we've had in do.' Dick enquired.

'Yeah. Gone too long for anything else. The arsehole's gone crazy. Perhaps he always was.' Chuck conceded.

'Well, just in case, we've been contacted by some guy up country. Reckons he can identify the murder weapon and the fella that bought it. A garage sale. Quite definite by all accounts.'

'Bit late on the scene ain't he.' Chuck acknowledged. 'This case is months old.'

'Not a registered firearm, plus he didn't know the details.

Can't say we were extravagant with the publicity once we had our man, can we?' Dick decided.

'Best see the man. Any witness is a good one I always say.' Chuck had been short of some essential ones in the past.

'I'll get him in on Friday. I'm with you on this one. Probability is that we won't need him but you've got to cover your back. That's one thing I've learnt in this job.'

Chuck nodded. Wise move.

Blutto careered in early on Friday morning. His belly nearly dislodging the pot of pens on Dick's desk.

'Daryl Crocker.' He offered his hand to the two detectives.

'Lieutenant Kaltenbach and Officer Nolan.' Dick reciprocated. 'Take a seat and we'll go through the procedure.'

Daryl dropped into the chair. Springs in the legs sent it oscillating for a while. He wriggled to centre his weight. He'd dealt with inconsiderate furniture before. An audible expulsion of air, like a tyre puncture. Carting that bulk up the stairs was exercise he usually avoided. He stank. Not easily discernible. Diesel oil mixed with farmyard, Dick decided.

'Good of you to come forward, Mr. Crocker.' Chuck welcomed the gross man. 'Seems you reckon you can help us in this case.' Chuck kept his distance. Daryl was unwholesome. The breath of a smoker and a beard that could easily have been inhabited.

'When I sees that them kids are killed, right shakes me up.' Daryl rotated his greasy baseball cap which he had removed on entering and which he held against his chest. Fingers like rolls of linoleum. 'Got kids of my own. Four. You don't go killing little kids, no sir.' He swung a rag to dab saliva that was sticking to the stray stalks of his moustache.

Dick stepped back. Debris fell from the filthy red handkerchief. Hopefully it was just wood chipping, Dick thought.

'Mr. Crocker, Daryl. Can you tell us how you can help in this matter.' Chuck was sure Daryl was going to be superfluous. They'd got their man, and he was certain Daryl Crocker was going to stretch this interview out. Lamenting the death of the children was just the beginning of his digression.

'Don't make much money out there. Country folk, me and the wife. Need to rake in those extra bucks. Sell off some of the clutter.'

'Yeah, we understand. No trouble from us if there's been a bit of, let's say, irregular dealing.' Chuck winked. Cosmetic gestures. Christ! I wish he'd get on with it, he thought.

'So we have these garage sales every now and then. Stick up some signs locally and folks turn up. Get a good bunch of people usually.' Daryl smiled. Enjoyed making money from his junk.

Dick and Chuck nodded. Urging him on with broad grins of acknowledgement.

'Well, several months back, Holly, my wife, says I got to get rid of my handguns. Never like me having them. And there being lots of accidents and kids picking them up. You know. So at that sale I displays them indoors. Not open like. Just so the adults can take a peek.'

'And you reckon one of these guns was the murder weapon in this case?' Chuck couldn't contain himself.

'I do, sir. I seen the photo of the man you've got, and I seen the description of the revolver he used. Brought it all back. Can picture him now. Bought it from me at that sale he did. No mistake. I never forget a face.'

Chuck wished he had a dollar for every time he'd heard that.

Daryl slurped. His mouth was dripping again. Out came the disgusting red rag. 'My favourite, that gun. Shot straight. Soft kick. Accurate weapon.' He sucked on his lips. Realised how accurate and how deadly it had been.

Chuck pulled open a drawer near his knee. A dark handgun sat in a plastic bag. Tags, like moths, were attached to the bag and the trigger guard.

'That's my baby. Smith and Wesson model 10, .38 special, four-inch barrel, single and double action, smooth target trigger, fine carbon steel, a stunning blue. Know it anywhere.' Even through the translucent plastic Daryl recognised his revolver. Almost excited to see it again.

Chuck looked at Dick. A knowing exchange. No doubt about Daryl's knowledge of firearms and his familiarity with this revolver.

'Daryl, tell us what happened on the day you sold this gun.' Dick was more enthusiastic about this witness now.

'It was late afternoon. Hadn't had any sales. Some window shopping but no takers. Arranging the display when this guy and his woman come into the room.'

'How come you remember it so well?' Chuck needed reassurance.

'The guy starts on about his guns, handling the Colt if I recollect right. How he has a grand collection, knows all these friends at the gun club and asks if I'm a buddy of some of these people. Lots of stuff about ranges and firearm performance. Sweet talk him a bit. Needed a sale.'

'And then?' Chuck interjected, impatient.

'Him and the lady leave.'

'So he didn't buy the gun?' Chuck jumped in.

'Not then. He comes back on his own a few minutes later and says he'll take the thirty-eight. Packs it up and shoves in some ammo. Then he's gone.'

'Had he shown an interest in that gun? Slipped back in when his companion wasn't aware?' Dick queried.

'Don't remember him really looking at the display. She were. He was just being the big guy. Knew it all. So he thought.' Daryl didn't like fellows who reckoned they were experts.

'But he was quite definite in what he wanted when he returned?' Dick added.

'Yeah. In a hurry. Huffing and twitching. Wanted it packaged up real quick.' Daryl recalled Bobby's urgency.

'Who was the woman?' Chuck's question was casually asked. He had no idea of its significance.

'Never took much notice, sorry. She weren't a stunner. I can tell you that. Never forget a pretty face or a good body.' Daryl slobbered. Out came the stained handkerchief. He mopped up.

Dick and Chuck had heard enough. Daryl was a filthy specimen but a good witness.

'Thanks, Daryl. You have been a great help. A keen eye and a fine memory. Appreciate it.' Dick stood and encouraged Daryl to lift himself from the seat. 'We'll have this all typed up for you to sign. It may mean attending court just to repeat this, but we're hopeful we can prosecute this case without calling on you and causing you any inconvenience.'

'Ain't no bother for me, sir. I'll be willing to put this animal away. You just give me the call. Only doing my duty to see the bastard pay.' Daryl squeezed out of the chair. It vibrated as he was unplugged.

Chapter 19

Steve Reynolds' office was mahogany and white. Deep brown furniture and towers of paper. Bundled documents that would some day be filed. String bound and tilting. Under desks and on precipitous shelves. Stories of languid defences and ill-conceived motions.

He had been a spirited young lawyer destined for a fortune in private practice. Inexplicably he was now marooned at a provincial precinct as the nanny attorney. Ready to protect the rights of even the most violent or most inebriated client where the State required. Trouble was, it was a sound indication of his ineffectual technique that he performed so miserably as the defender of those without hope. A status they would continue to enjoy despite his apparent intervention.

There was no intention of being a hero. No sudden awakening and wielding the sword of justice. Just something he felt. In his stomach more than his heart. Bobby Clayman was no killer. A no-frills guy, not a bright button, overawed by police vindictiveness. Overpowered by some convenient evidence. A man lost. Only seen it once before. Mental breakdown. Complete shutdown of the system. Bobby's mind had circled the wagons. No penetration.

Dick Kaltenbach had called. A trial date was being set. Police investigation complete. Daryl Crocker's statement released. Steve had cringed when he read through it. Damning testament.

As often as he could Steve Reynolds drove over to the prison in New York State. There was little change, and he wished he hadn't bothered. Bobby Clayman dribbled and rocked as he had done for weeks. They'd got him in diapers and were feeding him intravenously. He hadn't spoken and was unlikely to.

Doctor Samuel Greenberg was the recognised authority on insanity pleas. A lawyer and a qualified psychiatrist he had found a profitable niche in the system. Anyone caught red-handed or facing an insurmountable wall of hostile evidence had one option. That was to call Sam Greenberg. Steve Reynolds had eagerly made that call. No matter how much he wanted to be Bobby Clayman's Perry Mason he stood more chance defending the local statue of George Washington.

Greenberg met Steve at the prison gates. A sharply dressed, petite man. New York suits. Slim, bespectacled, quick-witted and overtly Jewish.

Steve Reynolds felt underdressed. His tailor specialised in bulky materials, called them rustic, appropriate for New England weather, his shirt wasn't pressed and he'd already tugged his tie from his collar on the drive to Lake Placid.

'Sam Greenberg.' He announced himself several feet from the oncoming New Hampshire lawyer. Short legs made him scurry like an eager rodent. 'You must be Steve Reynolds.'

Coming to an abrupt halt their extended hands met. Sam Greenberg shook firmly. Steve Reynolds offered a wet fish. Handshakes are moderately good thermometers of confidence or bravado.

'Morning Mr. Greenberg.' Steve found it difficult not to be subservient, despite his physical superiority.

'Sam. Just Sam.' Greenberg patted Steve's shoulder. 'We don't need formality here.'

'Fine.' Steve was not exactly comfortable with Greenberg's pally approach.

'I've been through all the details that you sent me.' Sam Greenberg pulled a folder from his buckskin briefcase. 'Tragic business. Merciless executions. Those poor kids.' It was difficult to tell whether Greenberg really cared. 'They'll want to bury this guy. Can't see them accepting an easy surrender. Public will want blood. See that the devil's punished. No one's going to want such a vile being enjoying a sourjourn in a leading psychiatric hospital, where he can't be jail raped or beaten senseless.' Sam's eyes smiled and his eyebrows twitched.

'Yeah. Poor bastard hasn't got a lot going for him.' Steve's glum look betrayed some strong emotions.

'Don't get personal, Steve. I learned a lot carving my name in this profession, and fundamental to doing a good job is not to get involved.'

'You seen those panthers and pumas in the city zoo. The ones that sleep in the stinking straw?' Steve began. 'Well, some have just given up. And some have had the wild kicked out of them. Seems their stripes or their spots fade when there's no need for camouflage. And all the elegance they had as creatures on the plain is gone. Scrawny cats that plod from one end of their cage to the other. A constant journey. That's their savannah grassland.' Steve Reynolds had never been so articulate. Sam Greenberg fumbled with his case. It wasn't often he was lost for words.

Steve continued. 'Bobby's a simple guy who's been bludgeoned unconscious by what's happened to him. I'm not sure whether he did kill those folks. The truth's trapped inside him. In his cage. Comatose in his stinking straw.'

Steve was still bemoaning his client's fate when they reached the prison entrance.

Regulations adhered to, which involved Sam Greenberg having to strip off most of his clothes, they were escorted through to the hospital wing of the prison.

Corridors stank of disinfectant. High ceilings with brutal acoustics. Sauntering white-coated staff. Sinister, strong-arm male nurses recruited from the forces, eyes following you, shaven heads still. An edible silence. Drug induced.

Bobby Clayman's room was naked. High barred windows riven by steel sunlight. Biblical shafts impaling the floor. He'd shrunk. His head a peanut on a croissant body. Propped up in bed. Open-backed gown. Nursing a kidney bowl. Black eyes abandoned. Empty tunnels seeing nothing. Shackled to the iron-framed bed. Needless precautions.

'Bobby, this is Mr. Greenberg, who has come to see you. He needs to assess your condition.' Steve knew they were wasted words. It was procedure. 'Your trial will be coming up shortly and a lot depends on how well you are. Mr. Greenberg can help us to determine this, and to advise on how to proceed. Do you understand?'

No recognition. Bobby's glazed eyes were fixed on a point near his own feet sticking up under the bedspread. They didn't flicker.

Sam Greenberg shook his head slowly. 'Mr. Clayman, Bobby. Your lawyer, Mr. Reynolds here, is doing a fine job for you. Has your real interests at heart.' Sam felt slightly silly. As if in a film shoot. Talking to a camera team instead of the person in the scene. 'I need to ask you some questions and talk to your doctors. Do you agree to this?' A look of exasperation.

Every question floated and stalled. Bouncing off the jerking head of Bobby Clayman. No one was at home. Sam Greenberg stuffed his papers back into his briefcase and sighed. 'Shame.' He bathed in the sun's rays. 'Man's dead. Maybe in there he's cocooned and treading water, but I doubt it. Never seen one so firmly entrenched.'

'Good day, gentlemen.' Sam's ruminating was cut short by the appearance of a tall, balding man, strikingly upright and clinical. The high, round collar of his crisp white jacket more reminiscent of a dentist than a doctor. 'Wingate Freeman, gentlemen. Head of this unit.'

'Ah, Doctor Freeman. Steve Reynolds.' Steve jumped to his feet. 'And this is Sam Greenberg.' Sam strode forward.

'Bobby Clayman.' Wingate Freeman shook his head. 'Sad.' He looked across at the pathetic figure stuck in his bed.

'As you are probably aware, Dr. Wingate.' Sam waded in. 'We have a trial facing us, and we are looking to confirm the status of our client and how we plead his case. You can help us here, I'm sure. First, give us your diagnosis and prognosis.'

'Well it's not good for your client, as we can see. The man's wasting away. He's very sick.'

'Sick with what?' Sam wanted to get to the point quickly.

'I've taken a personal interest in this case. Bobby has enjoyed almost a celebrity status here. Not that he would know that. So he's a special person to us. Frankly, we haven't ever been faced with a patient offering absolutely no communication whatsoever. Worse than a zombie.' Wingate Freeman managed a crooked smile. 'Clinically we have had to approach Bobby from a different angle. It's been more like detective work. We have visited some of his family and neighbours, seen the case notes that Officer Nolan and Lieutenant Kaltenbach have provided. Heard tapes of interviews and talked with his guards. A truly exhausting yet absorbing case.'

'And?' Sam Greenberg had little patience with the doctor's story.

'Your client, in my opinion, is a victim of trauma. Violent and miserable shock. And you don't get anything more traumatic than being charged with quadruple homicide.'

'You mean this condition hasn't been the instigator of a dreadful deed, but is a result of the crime? It's not a problem that poor Bobby had previous to the killings?' Steve spoke with alarm.

Wingate Freeman straightened his jacket. 'No. In my view. From the history and the events following his detention I'm convinced this boy has been subjected to post calamity trauma and an enormous assault on his belief system. He's shut down. Only seen evidence of this twice before, but I can recognise the facets.'

The two lawyers homed in on each other. Fearful eyes. Freeman had delivered a dilemma.

'What we have, Steve, is a fucking catastrophe.' Greenberg was pissed off. 'If he'd gone crazy and killed the fucking family and was still as fucking mad we would be able to plead insanity. But now the quack reckons he's only gone deranged because someone thinks he's done it. So, how do we go to court and say Bobby Clayman's innocent, but your honour, we can't prove it because all those naughty police officers blamed him and sent him raving? He can't tell you jack shit, as he's completely senseless. We'll look as fucking idiotic as he does!' Greenberg held his chin with one finger. 'What does help us, on the other hand, is that we could play for time here. An incompetence motion would put this on hold.' Greenberg's eyes lit. His mind was whirring. Clicking away like an abacus solving a tantalising mathematical problem.

Steve Reynolds was still uneasy. He turned to the doctor. 'You're saying, sir, that you have found no evidence of my client being in an unstable condition that might have prompted this act of violence on the Roberts' family? And that, in your professional judgement, it has been the investigation and the subsequent accusation that has thrown my client into the realms of insanity?'

'Succinctly put, dear fellow. Yes. Bobby Clayman has no history of paranoia or schizophrenia, or the symptoms, prior to this terrible crime. He didn't exhibit behaviour that would indicate mental instability, and in contrast demonstrated reasonable patterns of activity. I could never testify that Bobby Clayman was insane at the time of the crime. However, I can be quite categorical in my diagnosis of his deterioration that was initiated by the accusations made against him.'

'Thank you, Dr. Freeman. I will arrange for you to make a witness statement.' Steve Reynolds was trying to tidy this up.

'Bottom line, Dr. Freeman. You can testify in court that Bobby Clayman isn't fit to plea when we go to trial, can't you?' Greenberg needed this assurance.

'Certainly. Most certainly.' Wingate Freeman emphasised his reply.

'We need to talk.' Sam Greenberg scooped up some papers and made ready to go.

'Definitely.' Steve Reynolds replied. Cringing at the thought of his next move.

Chapter 20

'So you think you're going all that way to America on your own, on some sort of wild goose chase?' Deirdre blew out some air. She stood in the doorway watching her husband fold his shirts.

'Not like that. Give them to me.' She snatched the shirts from George. He had hoped she would. He couldn't abide packing. Deirdre always did it when they went away in the summer.

'Won't be for long, dear.' George encouraged.

'Hmm.' Deirdre had the shirts spread open on the bed, and was laying in some tissue. An expert at keeping her ironing intact. 'All those bits of paper. You haven't left them alone for days. And getting young Jamie involved. I don't know what's got into you. I really don't. Haven't touched the garden. I suppose you expect me to get out there. You being away.' Deirdre paused. She realised she was nagging.

'If I'm right then it's worth all this.' George was thinking aloud. 'If we can prevent an injustice it's going to be justification enough.'

'There you go. On your white charger. Saving the world. George Rundle hero of the Universe.' Now Deirdre was poking fun.

George trudged downstairs. He had all his papers laid out on the dining-room table. No precision when it came to clothes, but the master of organisation when dealing with the necessary documents.

Passport that he had only used on his one visit to Spain, tickets that he'd bought at the travel agents in the high street with his building society cheque, currency ordered from Barclays and other assorted pieces, including his driving licence and travel insurance. All to be packed into the leather shoulder bag that Deirdre had haggled for at the street market in Benidorm. A bit feminine but practical.

Like a boy going to school. Deirdre saw him off. Just a peck of a kiss. George tramped down the path to the waiting minicab, scuffing his suitcase on the path as he went. Hardly the intrepid detective.

Even in the taxi he hauled out his sandwich of paper. Still hunting through the fluorescent-green highlighted articles. A bloodhound's persistence. Sarah Bickles appeared in numerous reports of the family massacre, but Bobby Clayman was the central character. Especially once the incriminating evidence had been discovered. Sensationalism demanded that the horrific scenes at the lakeside camp were at the core of most reporting. Gore sold copies. Photographs were prolific. Body bags; small ones for the children. Loaded into ambulances. Police divers around the boathouse. Idyllic views of the lake and the Roberts' home. Maps too; of the camp showing the location of corpses. Police spokespersons (George hated the word) were quoted as they updated the newsmen throughout the investigation, but following Bobby Clayman's arraignment Dick Kaltenbach had led the press conferences.

Heathrow, Terminal 3. George was the lost boy. Clutching his Virgin Atlantic ticket. Return to Boston. Guided by a most attractive ground stewardess he was soon checked in and through the departure portal. The first passenger at Gate 21. Time to pick through the package of papers. He read from a copy of his letter to Lieutenant Kaltenbach. Just a policeman's interest. He would be in the area and would appreciate talking about those aspects of the case that the Lieutenant was able to discuss. In the pursuance of his duty he had encountered one of the players. No more information than that. Hoped he could perhaps assist, if only on the periphery, as a fellow detective with relevant knowledge.

A window seat. Deirdre chose that when they flew to Alicante. Now he could watch the Thames change from a serpent to a worm and the reservoirs around Staines become hand mirrors. Only when his view was replaced by a carpet of cloud and sizzling sun stung his eyes, did George take notice of activities in the fuselage. Not even the safety drill performed so expertly by the cabin staff distracted the ogling detective.

Now he was ready to be pampered. Every meal or juice in a plastic cup was greeted eagerly. His neighbour, a large black woman, didn't acknowledge his cheery *hello* and only grunted when he needed to dislodge her to reach the lavatory. It didn't matter. There were more papers to sift through. He was going a long way. Must be sure of his purpose, certain of his thesis. While the groaning woman whistled in her sleep, George unfolded the photocopies that Harry Fielding had carefully provided. A wink and a cuppa. Good friend, Harry.

'Dick!' Chuck waved an envelope at his partner. 'Someone writing to you from England.' He slapped the letter on Dick's desk.

'At least I know it's not from the IRS,' Dick joked, as he waddled across the room, Starbucks coffee and bagel carefully balanced.

George Rundle's meticulous hand and Queen Elizabeth looked up at him. 'Who's been sending me mail from England?' Dick thought aloud. 'Can't be a distant relation, all my ancestors were Krauts.'

'Probably goin't make you one of them knights. Sir Dick. Can see it now.' Chuck giggled at his own quip.

Dick tore open the neatly sealed envelope. Five accurately folded sheets. Ten minutes of silence save for the scratching of paper as he laid them out, like tents on his desk. Separate leaves of A5 Basildon Bond writing paper.

'Sure got your tongue.' Chuck was unsettled by the unusual quiet.

'Yeah. Need to take all this in.' He wasn't sure of the significance. Annoyed by the interruption.

Chuck waited. He recognised Dick's complete distraction. Curious to know the contents of the letter.

'There you go. From across the pond Sherlock Holmes wants to help us solve crime.' Dick smirked.

'What?' Chuck was bitten.

'Some English gumshoe reckons he can assist us with the Bobby Clayman case, important evidence, knowledge of one of the people involved. All fucking cloak and dagger stuff.' Dick guffawed. He tossed the letter over to his partner.

'Coming here. Holidaying locally. Very convenient.' Chuck contributed. 'What d'you think he's offering that's so important?'

'Says he knows someone concerned with the case. I reckon he has something on the father, John Roberts. Lived in England didn't they? Probably some tax stuff or other inconsequential matter. Not sure they realise over there what a real mass killing is all about. Anyway the sleuth from Scotland Yard is calling in on us. We are being treated to a special visit.' Dick bowed. 'Honoured I'm sure.' He wasn't taking George's interference seriously.

Chuck searched through his post. 'Trial date's through for Clayman,' he announced. It didn't hold as much importance now. He left the notice to one side and filtered through the rest, chair tilted and feet on desk. Usual game of screwing up the junk and playing basketball with the waste bin.

'When?' Dick asked from behind his letter from England that he was reading again.

Chuck grabbed the note and struggled with the maths. 'Ten days.'

'Steve Reynolds is coming in this morning, and I'm seeing the DA at two.' Dick flicked through his diary. 'Should have the Clayman case sorted out this week. Not that it's the result I was hoping for.' A heavy sigh. 'No, not at all satisfactory. Uneasy feeling about the whole thing.'

'How are we playing this?' Chuck enquired.

'Can't be anything else. Clayman's a vegetable. Just need to come up with a package that we can all agree on. Negotiation. That's what it all comes down to, Chuck. Like haggling over the price.'

'Price to pay for slaughtering a whole family. Difficult one to assess.' Chuck was cynical and also angry. It stuck to his voice.

'Bothers me too. Can't say I'm going to exorcise any of those ghosts. When it's kids you need closure. If that psycho is getting cotton-wool treatment at some lunatic asylum then I ain't happy. But what can I do?' Dick strummed the table with his fingers.

'Clayman's past help. All the reports I've had say he's wasting away. Looks like one of them nuggets I get in my cereal bowl each morning. Reckon he'd break like a potato chip if you bent him. Brittle as candy.' Chuck was lining up further analogies.

'We ain't topped anyone in this State for over sixty years.' Dick was talking serious. 'But here's a fucking bastard that should be executed, and what do we have to do? Talk about his mental stability. Death penalty, my ass! You've got to drop one of our guys, slit the throat of someone you're raping or be a hired gun to get topped in this State. Fucking stupid. If we were in Florida they'd revel in it. Lethal injection, firing squad. No problem.' Dick grappled with one of the lower drawers in his desk. There was a packet of Marlboro Lights there somewhere. He needed one now. Sure, he'd packed up but there were times when only a smoke would do.

Steve Reynolds rapped at the door. He could see Dick Kaltenbach was pacing the room and dragging on a cigarette. Recognised the tension and felt the electric atmosphere.

Chuck hailed him in. Dick dropped to his chair and stabbed his butt into a saucer ashtray.

'Can come back if you wish.' Still apologetic. 'If there's a better time.'

'Sit down, Steve. Just the usual frustrations of the job.' Dick waved him into a chair.

Both sides pulled out files and arranged paperwork. It was part of the window dressing.

'You get the notification this morning?' Chuck enquired.

'Yes. Ten days to prepare. Not a lot of time.' Steve observed.

'Come on, Steve. We all know there ain't no need to prepare much for this case. You can't hide the state of your client from us. He's fucked.' Chuck forever down to earth.

Steve knew only too well his client's state of health, but he needed to tread a lot more carefully than they expected. 'He's ill. Very ill.'

Dick stood up. 'How ill?' He looked to the ceiling. 'That's what we have to decide, isn't it, Steve?'

Steve Reynolds nodded. He wasn't showing his hand yet.

It was up to Dick Kaltenbach to start the bidding. 'Guilty, while the balance of his mind was disturbed, or I'll take insanity with some reservations.' A long look at Steve Reynolds. As if offering a second hand car for sale, at a bargain price.

'No. Nowhere near.' Steve was playing as if he had a full house. He was lucky to have card high.

'Look Steve, I could send the Pope down with the evidence I've got.' Dick was doubling the stake.

'What have you got?' Calling his bluff. A poker face.

Dick glanced over to Chuck. Nervous eyes. 'You expecting me to give you all the details?'

'You've got to divulge on what you base your case. A little more information won't be too revealing will it?'

'Shit, Steve. This one's a certainty and you know it.' Chuck burst out.

Dick carried on. 'Murder weapon found in his truck, girl's doll in the back and at the scene. Tyre marks and footprints. And the nail in Bobby Clayman's coffin.' Dick was going to enjoy this. 'We now have the guy who sold him the Smith & Wesson, and who has identified him. Good enough?' Smug looks all round.

Steve recognised a wall when he smashed into it. This new

witness could sink his case. He hadn't got a winning hand at all. Where did they get this witness from? Baffling.

'What are you looking for?' Dick was dealing now. Looking to increase the stakes.

'Incompetent to proceed. Judges discretion for treatment.' Steve mumbled. He wasn't so sure of his ground.

'He did it Steve. I want that decided so I can put this to bed. I won't rest if we need to keep this open until he is ever fit enough to answer these charges, and then it will still be a foregone conclusion.'

'No need to tell you this, but I will. You've been open. Doc at the prison reckons our Bobby has ended up in this state, not because he's mad, but that it's due to trauma manifested by the accusation.' Steve had a sound hand and laid it on the table. 'You have to remember, an insanity plea relates to a defendant's state of mind at the time of the offence.' Perhaps Steve had better cards than he thought.

'Bullshit!' Chuck wasn't impressed. 'Fucking psychiatrists will try anything to help this arsehole squirm out of paying the price. Think of the Roberts family. Think of them kids. You been to the morgue and looked in the fridge? Tiny bodies riddled with bullets or throttled and dumped in the lake. He's a monster. You can't dig an escape tunnel for a fucking bastard like that.' Chuck stood and ranted.

'We all know that judges side with an expert's conclusions.' Steve hammered home his advantage. 'Can give you the precedent if you wish?' Almost gloating now. Steve Reynolds was definitely calling their bluff.

'You being a cantankerous bastard for the fun of it, Steve?' Chuck enquired.

'Nope. But I could be. I ain't so sure Bobby Clayman killed those people. Well certainly not as sure as you.'

'Okay, mister smart-arse, let's have it.' Dick was not amused.

'Bakersfield, California, 22nd November 2000. Levon Bryan Weston. Declared mentally incompetent by the judge, with a condition he be returned to court when the hospital concluded he had regained mental fitness. Poor bastard was afraid of buttons on people's clothes. Bobby is a lot worse than that.'

'You'll have to leave it with me. I'm seeing the DA after lunch. I'll see to it that he knows your position. No doubt he'll contact you and arrange a conference.' Dick stacked his papers and left the office. He was pissed off. Left Steve Reynolds to clear away his own documents.

George Rundle nudged open the heavy glass doors of the Concord police headquarters early the next morning. He'd slept well at Day's Inn, phoned Deirdre who was having lunch and tried to eat as much of his American breakfast as he could. It was the maple syrup on his fried potatoes he couldn't stomach. Not quite the seasoned traveller.

'Sir?' A sergeant on the desk confronted the timid intruder.

'Lieutenant Kaltenbach. I was hoping to see the Lieutenant.' George was trying to take in his surroundings. Nothing at all like his old nick.

'And you are, sir?'

'Oh. George Rundle. Ex-detective Rundle.'

'Not from round these parts, Mr. Rundle. Detect an unfamiliar accent.' Sergeant Milpaski smiled.

Accent? George was taken aback. He hadn't got an accent. This was the guy with the accent. What on earth had they done to the English language? 'England.'

'Thought so. Not been there myself but the wife's family come from over there. Scotland. McGregors. Way back like.' Milpaski was eager to shoot the breeze with the limey.

'I did write to Lieutenant Kaltenbach to tell him I was in the area.' George reminded the sergeant of his quest.

'Yeah. Sure. I'll just buzz him.' Milpaski wouldn't be allowed to go further. There was all the Polish history to explore. He'd have to trap the guy on the way out.

George held his raincoat over one arm and carried a slim

case under the other. He strolled around the waiting room looking out at the squad cars and listening to the conversations of officers changing shifts. Watched their sidearms as they sauntered by. All part of the uniform. He'd never been close to guns. Turned down handgun training when they were recruiting for armed response units back in Britain. Deadly weapons weren't part of George's concept of the Force. Alien to his approach. More *Dixon of Dock Green* was George Rundle.

'Sherlock Holmes downstairs.' Chuck announced. Sergeant Milpaski has him cornered.

'Maybe that'll save us.' Dick joked.

'Come on, Dick, you go and rescue the poor man. Milpaski will be torturing him with his Polish ancestry and all that shit.' Chuck knew the sergeant too well.

'Mr. Rundle? Dick Kaltenbach.' Dick approached the ferreting Englishman from behind, just as he was reading up on effective household security devices available in New Hampshire. A Concord supplier was advertising. He offered an extended hand and a welcoming smile.

'Pleased to meet you, Lieutenant.' George reciprocated with a generous grin.

'Dick will do. No formalities. Ain't Scotland Yard.' Dick thought it was a good joke.

Not one that George appreciated, although he did recognise an honest greeting. 'Fine. It's George then.'

'This way George. Let's go to my office and have that chat you wanted.'

Tea in hand, George sat in the same chair that Bobby Clayman had thrown against the wall during his attack on Dick Kaltenbach.

'George Rundle, Chuck.' Chuck juggled past with coffee and a doughnut. He could only offer a hand once his snack had landed on the desk.

'Chuck Nolan. Pleased to meet you George.' He suppressed an urge to laugh at the demure Englishman. Not the impressive detective he had imagined.

'What can I do for you, George?' Dick nestled down to listen. Ready to be less than interested in what the reserved Englishman was going to say.

'Well, I haven't long retired from the Force. Been in it a long time. Done my time on the beat. Ended up as a detective with CID down in Dorset.'

Dick's first instinct seemed to be correct.

'It was during my time working in serious crime in the county that I was called in to investigate the death of a young boy. The son of a local dignitary, Sir Peter Bassnett.' This was George without his notebook. But it was typical plod. 'He'd died in the bath. Drowned. From all the evidence we concluded the poor lad had struck his head on the rather solid brass taps and sunk unconscious under the water. A tragic accident.'

Dick and Chuck listened carefully. It was just like the start of a Hercule Poirot investigation. Very Agatha Christie.

'Forensic were happy with the verdict and there were no suspicious aspects to the case. We filed it away without thinking twice about more sinister implications.' George's face was now glum.

Dick was puzzled. He had thought the visiting Englishman had information about the Roberts family. 'Where's this going? Ain't heard anything yet that concerns us here.' Dick enquired without wishing to appear rude.

'Just coming to that.' George took a deep breath. 'Rupert, the boy who drowned, had a nanny. A woman by the name of Sarah Bickles.' He searched their faces for a response.

Chuck nodded his head slowly. 'Yeah?'

'Same Sarah Bickles that was nanny to the Roberts children.'

'Is this relevant?' Dick was curious, but a little disappointed at the news.

'I read about the terrible murders here and saw that the same woman was involved so I did some investigating. Looked up all the papers in the Rupert Bassnett death, and studied as much as I could of your case.'

'You think there's a connection?' Chuck was more than just interested now.

'When I re-read the notes and replayed the Bassnett case, placing Sarah Bickles in the hot seat, I concluded we had probably been hasty in our assumption that his death was an accident.' George rubbed his chin. He was still walking on eggshells. 'Especially taking into account her proximity to the macabre scenes here.'

'Let me get this right.' Dick rose in his chair. 'You telling me you think this nanny had something to do with the death of that boy, and that she's responsible for the deaths here? No way. We've got the killer. Watertight evidence.'

'So that woman goes gunning down the kids in her charge in cold blood? And their parents? No fucking way. Excuse the language.' Chuck's head was now swinging wildly from side to side. This English detective was some joke. He hadn't meant to swear in front of the guy but it came exploding out. Ejected in disbelief.

'Bruises on the boy's arms weren't really satisfactorily explained. She was supposed be bathing Rupert, yet she said she went out and came back to find him unconscious. Made out she attempted artificial respiration.' George was eager for some sign of interest in his theory. The American detectives only threw daggers with their eyes.

'This all you've got? It don't budge one inch the pile of evidence we've got to show that our man pulled that trigger, that he butchered the whole frigging family.' Chuck was adamant.

Dick was somewhat more sensitive to the Englishman's concern. 'Understand where you are coming from, George. But to think that this woman, a humble, unpretentious person from my recollections, has deliberately got herself a gun and learned how to use it and taken innocent lives for no reason, is too far-fetched. There's no proof. I think you have got a red herring here, George. Sorry to say.'

'Way I read it, but tell me if I'm wrong, because I'm relying on newspaper reports, is that our nanny finds the family dead. Been out for a walk, she says. And it's not until later that your man, the caretaker, arrives. Drives all that way, down four miles of unmade road. To perform casual jobs around the property? Returns to the scene of his diabolical crime?' George was reading his lines well.

'Trying to make it look normal. Didn't want to arouse suspicion.' Chuck waded in.

'What, with the murder weapon still in his vehicle? Covered in the blood of his victim. That's a bit stupid isn't it?' George added.

Dick's tail was up. 'Man's crazy. Did some crazy things.'

'You interviewed him at the scene didn't you? You sure he was mad at that time?' George was getting under the skin.

'Insanity ain't like that. Not always at the surface. Just bubbles up. Many lunatics around that appear okay one minute and then the next they're absolutely raving. Adolf Hitler probably seemed a regular guy at times.' Chuck was mending the breaches.

'Prints on the weapon? On the doll?'

'No.' Chuck snapped. It wasn't something he readily admitted.

'So our vicious killer leaves Stella Roberts' blood smeared all over his gun, but does not leave a single print?' George had hit on more than he expected. He couldn't believe his luck.

'Given a motive you look for the crime. Given the crime you must have a motive. Part of my training.' More than a thorn in the side now. 'What was the motive that pushed this caretaker over the top? Made him annihilate the whole Roberts family?' George was launching stinging questions.

Dick and Chuck exchanged urgent glances. The modest English detective was not as harmless as they had imagined.

'Probably something to do with the property or his employment. Maybe Roberts fired him that day. Sent him over the edge. Just don't know. If he were a fragile guy who lived close to breaking, it could easily happen. And we know he's well beyond the precipice now. Brittle as rock candy. There's a motive, and we'll track it down.' Dick made a strenuous effort to dispel the doubts.

'And Sarah Bickle's motive?' Chuck joined his partner at the barricade. 'What would have driven the nanny to slaughter the kids, and the goose that laid the golden eggs?'

'Thought you might ask.' George flicked through his notes. 'Way I see it, is she's unstable. Flips when she's cornered. Maybe holds on to some resentment that explodes with a fury. Changes her character. Becomes capable of anything. Murder.'

'Not such solid ground now, George?' Chuck was pleased they were shoving from their side.

'Of course she hasn't been a suspect. No one has had a chance to quiz her. You'd be amazed at the response an interview will produce once you have a schedule.' George gave a knowing look. Almost a wink.

'Look, George.' Dick Kaltenbach had listened enough. 'You've given us stuff to think about. Appreciate it. We've got a lot more to do here. Sure was a pleasure having this talk.' Dick stood and encouraged George to do the same. 'If you're still in the area perhaps you should have a look in at the hearing. We have a date next week for Bobby Clayman's plea. Just a block away at the courthouse. Welcome to come along.' Dick expected that George would be well on his way home by then. Not a genuine invitation.

Reluctantly George scooped up all his papers and his raincoat. They hadn't really accommodated his theory. Didn't want to be turned. He wasn't going to save Bobby Clayman. 'I might take you up on that.' A brisk shaking of hands and he was gone.

Chuck wiped the back his hand across his brow to signify his relief. Dick sank back in his chair and sighed deeply.

'What d'you make of that?' Dick asked.

'Well meaning guy. Don't change a lot does it?'

'Nope.'

Sergeant Milpaski greeted George at the front desk. 'Good meeting?'

George shook his head to show his dispondency.

'It's the Clayman case, ain't it?' There wasn't much Milpaski didn't know. Kept his ear to the ground.

'Yes.'

'You had a word with his lawyer? Might help.' Milpaski enjoyed stirring it. And Chuck Nolan was too impudent by half and often impolite about his Polish background.

'Steve Reynolds. Nice guy. Here.'

Milpaski handed George a card. There was always a penniless drunk who needed Steve's assistance. He kept a stock in his desk.

Chapter 21

He had such high hopes. Pie in the sky hopes. George sat down to dinner at Day's Inn. He would phone Deirdre in the morning. It was too late now. The face of a loser who had wagered his last pound on a lame nag.

Hadn't really the appetite but needed to get out of his room and be with people. Peripheral people. Hear them talk. Detached conversations that he could melt into or shut out at will. He had no desire to share a discussion. But it was too lonely in his claustrophobic quarters at the end of the carpet corridor.

He'd ordered the Caesar salad and some pork dish. He knew it would be a huge helping. Mountains were being dished up. Waitresses needed strong arms for some of the meals being hauled past. At the table alone he poked into his pockets. Something to do with his hands. Tinkling change and fingering papers. He plucked out the business card that Sergeant Milpaski had slid him at police headquarters.

Steve Reynolds, Attorney-at-Law, 16a Crystal Chambers, Mount Pinnot Road, Concord, New Hampshire, 456342.

George sat it on the table by the side of his plate when the salad arrived. Sprinkles of the hard cheese spilled onto it as he ate. It's worth a try, he thought. If going to the cowboys was a failure then he might as well try the indians. Another avenue. There was no dislodging the gut feeling he had over Sarah Bickles' involvement. Approaching Bobby Clayman's defence lawyer would be his next move. That was decided.

George felt a lot better and polished off the giant helping of Cajun pork and roasted vegetables that was unloaded on his table.

An afternoon promenade. Walk off the monstrous meal.

George grabbed a street map of the city at the front desk and planned a route that took in Mount Pinnot Road. Quite a hike when he used the scale to calculate it. About four miles. Hardly the constitutional he had conceived. It was early and the evening fair. Time to think and plenty to see. Deirdre would have approved.

Mount Pinnot Road was a wide thoroughfare with herringbone parking. On the ground level a mixture of dubious stores and quasi-industrial premises. Crystal Chambers was difficult to find. George stalked along the raised walkway overhung by balustrade balconies of the upstairs of the buildings. It was detective work. Down every alley between the shops he peeked. Fortunately success came from an informer. A black man filling a garbage dumpster pointed at the flaking paint on the side of a clapper-board store. Embarrassingly, as George had surveyed that backstreet already. Steve Reynolds' office was on the first floor. Reached by a warped wooden staircase.

It was five to eight when he stood outside the glass door. Someone was inside. Voices in discussion. Calm tones as if a testament was being taken. George strutted about, gazing across Mount Pinnot Road and down onto the heads of strollers. Late shoppers and ostracised smokers.

The judder of a sticking door kicked free swung him around. Brunette hair disappeared down the steps he had climbed. At the entrance a wiry figure stood examining the middle-aged man loitering on his landing.

'Can I help?' Steve Reynolds squinted in the failing light.

'Mr. Reynolds?'

'Yes.'

'George Rundle.' A step forward and a firm handshake.

'Englishman?' Steve enquired picking up on the accent astutely.

'Ex-detective Rundle to be exact. From across the Pond.' George used the term as if it were part of his repertoire. 'Like to have a word with you. Concerns one of the cases you're dealing with.'

Steve was intrigued. 'Which case would that be?'

'Bobby Clayman.'

Steve Reynolds was taken aback. This was the case. The only case for him at that moment. All other minor defence work was definitely backseat. 'Come in.' A weak yet inquisitive voice.

Inside was the office of a nineteenth century Wild West advocate. Smell and all. Dusty, leather-bound books, spindle mahogany chairs and a raft of a desk that had once boasted a fine red hide inlay, that was now in tatters and repaired with sticky tape. A rug on bare undulating floorboards. Yellowed walls and low hanging, low wattage lighting. Striking tilting white piles of case notes.

George made a drunken entrance. Every step across the uneven floor throwing him off balance. 'Atmosphere.' George sniffed audibly. 'Feel the presence of justice in here.' It was a stupid thing to say. He was uncomfortable and it helped.

'Bobby Clayman? What do you know about him?' Steve was focused.

'Not too much. But I have read the reports of the case.' George was tempted to tell the story and display the newspaper cuttings. 'And I have had discussions with the two detectives handling the case.'

'Dick Kaltenbach and Chuck Nolan?' Steve was puzzled.

'I wrote to Lieutenant Kaltanbach from England. Felt sure I could help in this case.' George was confusing the attorney.

'Help? From England?' Steve queried. 'How did you think you could help?'

'I worked on a case some months back, before I retired. There was a connection that I felt so strongly about, that I was determined to raise this with the detectives, and perhaps prevent a miscarriage of justice.'

Steve was all ears now. 'You mean the information you were offering was so relevant it could have thrown some light on the perpetrator of this crime?'

'I believed so.'

'Someone other than my client?' Excitement in his voice.

'Most definitely. But I must add that I failed miserably to convince the police officers.'

'No surprise there. Tell me more. Look, a better idea. I'll stick some coffee on and we'll get down to some serious talking. I'm beginning to think my prayers have been answered and you truly are the Messiah.' Steve didn't mean to be irreligious, but a weight was being lifted from his shoulders. His first break.

'Tea, if you don't mind.' George asked apologetically.

'Tea it is.' Steve stepped out back to a small kitchen and boiled water. A new spring in his step.

'Tell me about this case in England.' They were both now sitting comfortably nursing their mugs. 'A lawyer needs it chronological.'

George explained about the death of Rupert and his subsequent investigation. Steve, like Chuck and Dick, was puzzled at first. Couldn't match it to the killings at Gull Point. He feared a waste of time. Perhaps the personable Englishman was just some crazy guy. Then the spark. Ignition. We had lift off.

'Sarah Bickles? The nanny. Roberts' nanny. Same woman?'

'Exactly.' Some pride in George's acknowledgement. 'I missed it I'm sure. She probably had something to do with the poor boy's death. That's something I'll have to examine more closely when I return, but for now the urgency is to see that your client doesn't get the blame for this tragedy.'

'It's a little beyond belief.' Steve scratched at a thin patch of hair on his head, dislodging a scattering of dandruff flakes. 'It would take some proving. It answers some questions but poses others.' He thought through some of the sticky areas. If only Bobby Clayman hadn't degenerated so.

'I tried to shoot down some of their notions at Police Headquarters but they've got him lassoed for this one. They're not listening. I've seen it before. Once there is a prime suspect all the other possibles get shoved out the circle. Impervious to even the most convincing evidence.' George was lecturing.

'Look, I've got to trust you here, George. But there's new evidence that isn't very favourable to us. Anything I mention I'm sure will not go any further.' He questioned George with his eyes.

George responded with a firm nod of the head and a crisp reply. 'Safe as houses. Can count on me.' He was pleased someone was at last listening. It wasn't a waste of a transatlantic flight.

'Dick Kaltenbach has a witness to Bobby Clayman buying the murder weapon.' Steve Reynolds declared.

'Ouch! That's not good.' George was the master of the understatement.

'Fortunately we have time. When I attend the hearing next week I will be asking the court to declare that Bobby Clayman is not competent to be tried. That will send him to a secure hospital until he is found fit to plead. Dick Kaltenbach will be pissed, but it will allow us the opportunity to look into some of the more damning evidence.'

'Too convenient some of it. The gun in the truck is a joke.' George was doing his best to be positive. 'If you want me to let you have some of my thoughts I'll be glad to jot them down for you.' George offered.

'I'd welcome that.'

'Good.' George was glad to be doing something useful at last.

'I'm going to have to disassemble my strategy. All I had was a plan to save Bobby from a trial. Now, I think I can work to get him acquitted. I hope this isn't a pipedream.' Bounce in his step and purpose in his voice. 'The nanny? I will need more than just your theory here, George. Not that I'm deriding all your hard work.'

Both men stood and stretched.

'Do you take a drink, George?'

'Quite partial, though some of this American lager is bit like gnat's piss.' George smiled.

'But it's cold. Not like some of that British ale.' Steve reciprocated. 'Come on.' He grabbed George round the shoulder. 'Let's hit the bar. It's only a block away.'

Steve Reynolds was revitalised. That evening he never let go of his new British friend. 'You really are the Messiah.' Late in the evening. The beer doing most of the talking.

Chapter 22

The garden at 23, Camille Gardens was looking tired. Weeds were reeking revenge and the lawn was in need of its short back and sides. Deirdre Rundle was embarrassed. Neighbours were peeking at the disgraceful state of patio flowers, and definitely gossiping. She'd seen them when she peeped from behind the net curtains. Just enough to catch them at the fence cupping their hands, as if to stop the poison words reaching her as they prattled.

Her husband had disappeared on some whim. Thousands of miles. And left her to cope with the social consequences of failing to keep up with the Joneses. If he phoned today she would give him a piece of her mind. Demand he returned and restored some dignity. What on earth can he be up to now? He was only meant to go for a couple of days.

George Rundle was a busy man. Most of his day was spent bent over a writing pad. The history of the Rupert Bassnett case and some ideas for Steve Reynolds to consider. He hadn't phoned Deirdre for three days. Become something of a crusader. This one was not thinking of getting home from the Holy War just yet.

On the morning of the hearing, in front of Judge Thomas Ludwig, battle lines were drawn, and each camp mustering its troops. Steve Reynolds had three gallant men ready to engage. Dick Kaltenbach and Chuck Nolan preparing to floor him with a volley of evidence, and the potato sack, Daryl Crocker.

Dick and Chuck were a little taken aback when they saw that the diffident Englishman was part of the defence team. Quizzing exchange of startled looks by the two policemen. A dangerous development.

'What's Sherlock Holmes doing here?' Chuck asked.

'Dunno. Not happy about it.' Dick replied. 'Where did he get hold of Steve Reynolds from?'

'They're going to use the nanny as a decoy here, Dick. No other reason for the Scotland Yard sleuth to be still hanging around.' Chuck mumbled as they shuffled into court.

Bobby Clayman was conspicuous by his absence. They were there to talk about him but not to him. Like not having the body present at a wake.

Mark Richards, District Attorney, addressed the court first. He outlined the mental state of the accused and went into graphic details about the deaths of the Roberts family. It was a grievous crime that no sane person could have committed. Heinous behaviour that indicated the state of mind of the killer at the time of his offence. Surely Bobby Clayman was mad when he perpetrated this monstrous act. That he did it was not in question. A mountain of evidence that would be produced showed beyond any reasonable doubt that Bobby Clayman was the murderer.

Mark Richards knew how to tread the boards. Knew his audience and his officials. Played to their weaknesses and their prejudices. Emotive tones that laid the blame for this foul deed squarely on the shoulders of a murderous caretaker. A contemptible maniac.

'It is essential that we do not try this case in rehearsal. The prosecution arguments will only be needed if it is deemed necessary to proceed. You are asking, Mr. Richards, for this court to declare the accused insane at the time of the killings?' Judge Ludwig looked over his reading spectacles and back down at his notes. 'Mr. Reynolds, if you would like to address the court.'

Steve had never witnessed such an arena. He had always been small town and small crime. Suddenly thrown into big time drama. His stomach was gripped by a fierce vice. Stage-fright. A theatre with an audience listening to every word. Waiting for every mistake. No prompting. Small public gallery and two benches of reporters. What had he got to offer? To save this fiend? Their lips spoke with him. A faltering but not failing start.

'Bobby...Bobby Clayman is not mad. While we talk so glibly about this man he rocks himself, oblivious, in a prison hospital. A good man. An ordinary man. You or me.' Good start. Steve was prepared. 'In his present mental state he is not in a position to defend himself. To tell you how it was. Perfectly lucid when he was interviewed at the site of the killings. Understandably upset and baffled. Lieutenant Kaltenbach can vouch for that. Yes, this ordinary man was perfectly sane when that family was killed. He didn't kill them. That's for sure. But when the police arrested him for the crime he slipped from disbelief to dismay and from dismay to deranged. Dr. Wingate Freeman, his prison doctor, can testify that Bobby Clayman was sent into his demented state by the sheer horror of being sought for this atrocity.' Steve paused to see how they were reacting.

'Bobby Clayman is not competent to plead. Not competent to plead.' Steve spoke to both ends of the courtroom. To the learned faces on the stage a sharp retort, and slowly to the stretching heads of the spectators. 'Bobby Clayman doesn't know his name. Doesn't recognise his family. Doesn't utter a word. He has been driven into a tight cocoon of despair. His sanctuary. Hiding from those dreadful allegations.

'Bobby Clayman must be awarded the opportunity to defend himself when he is fit to do so. When he is recovered from this hideous illness, then you can throw all this damning evidence at him. If it is so conclusive now, it will be then.' Steve watched those concerned take notes, and the twitching heads of those exchanging gabbling rhetoric.

'The Roberts family died in horrific circumstances. The killer must pay. Of that there is no question. But don't let us find a convenient culprit. The willing dummy. And for our peace of mind load him with the blame. There must be a trial. Ensure it's a fair trial.'

Steve could feel Judge Ludwig's impatience and scanned

his notes for some final comments. 'There is another suspect in this case.' Steve blurted.

Judge Ludwig's eyes opened. A fixed stare. Chuck and Dick chewed their teeth and sucked hard on their lips.

'There is a strong argument for the investigation of a further candidate. And this is what we trust will be done by the police between now and any postponed hearing. Reasonable suspicion has been levelled against another person. International co-operation has exploded the police notion. We have a witness from England. From the police force over there. Who can supply good reason for this new route.

'The court must also consider that the District Attorney will be unable to suggest a substantial motive for Mr. Clayman committing this crime. And will only be offering the court evidence laid down like a paper chase. A trail left by a killer enticing the police to catch him. In fact, a nonsense.

'Bobby Clayman should be heard. Should be asked all these questions. No matter what your position there is only value in hearing this man speak.'

Steve scuffed his feet and flicked at his papers. 'Let us hear from Bobby Clayman. I ask the court to declare Bobby Clayman incompetent to proceed, and leave any decision on his future fitness to face trial to the judge's discretion.' Steve sank down onto the wooden chair.

Judge Thomas Ludwig scratched at the hair in his ears that irritated him when he was in thought. Nothing was easy. Where were the black and white cases when he could hammer his gavel and make a simple decision? A final bid at the auction. A done deal. Summary justice seen to be handed out.

'Dr. Freeman, please take the stand.' Judge Ludwig waved an arm. The court usher, a uniformed officer, urged the doctor towards the lectern.

'I'm minded to conclude this matter as swiftly as possible. Folks around here tend to be uneasy when brutal murders like this go unsolved.' He spoke to his desk. Raised high above lesser mortals. 'Don't help no one to have a crazed killer

lurking abouts without no solution. You agree Dr. Freeman?'
Judge Ludwig came from an old New Hampshire family. Not
gentry. Lumbermen. Straightforward folk that spoke their
minds and wouldn't look kindly on people who didn't fear
their God and respect their laws.

'Always a reassuring thing to bring about the drawing of
the curtain, see the actors finish their lines and let the people
leave the theatre knowing the play is over and all's well with
the world.' Wingate Freeman had an eloquence that Judge
Ludwig could empathise with.

'But you're going to tell me different aren't you Doctor?'

'Can't say I am going to give you that happy ending.'

Judge Ludwig screwed up his face. His head shook. 'DA
ain't offering us an expert here to contradict your testimony.
Ain't that right Mr. Richards?'

Mark Richards nodded in agreement. He knew that Wingate
Freeman held all the cards. There was no psychiatrist in New
England who could dispute his finding. And he'd searched
desperately for one.

'Seems you are being given your head. So you tell me. Is
Bobby Clayman able to recognise this court and its authority?'

'No, your honour.'

'Is he going to get better and be able to come here and
answer these charges some time in the future?'

'Can't say for certain. It is possible.'

'Likely, Doctor?'

'Possible is all I can give you.' A reluctant tilt of the head.
Wingate Freeman would have loved to announce that it was
dead certain Bobby Clayman would be springing into court to
clear himself. Refreshed and looking for justice. Cavalier
bravado. A hero's entrance.

'You saying it would be unwise for this court to yield to the
prosecution, and hear the evidence that they wish to condemn
Bobby Clayman with? Conclude with an insanity verdict? You
telling me we ain't going to get closure here, Dr. Freeman?'

'Ignore my prognosis at your peril, would not be too strong

a message, your honour.'

'We'll take a recess for half an hour. I need to read up on a few cases and get me some coffee. You good people take the break and I'll see you recharged.' Judge Thomas Ludwig scooped up his beetle-black gown and hobbled out. A vulture on the ground. Lumbering passage to his chambers.

When he returned Judge Ludwig growled at the usher and barked at his clerk. Not a happy man. He cursed the documents on his desk and pushed them aside as if they were tainted or huge household bills he was reluctant to pay.

Steve Reynolds was jittery. He was trying to read Ludwig's body language. Chuck and Dick's interpretations were ominous.

'Responsibility.' Judge Ludwig sniffed aloud. 'Responsibility to the victims, to the community and to the accused.' He paused to wrestle with a gut feeling. 'A very heavy load. Administer it as best I can. The law that is. Have to bite my tongue sometimes up here. It's a lonely place. Too easy to be shot down.' He was struggling. A tussle between his decision he was about to announce and the decision he wished he could make. Rambling.

Necks strained and leaned forward. Frozen silence of anticipation.

'I have decided that Bobby Clayman is unaware of the nature and potential consequences of the charges against him and that he is incapable of properly assisting his attorney. For that he is declared incompetent at this time to proceed.' Judge Ludwig sucked his teeth. He had no taste for his own words. 'He will be taken to the secure hospital facility at Portsmouth and subjected to proactive treatment. A report on his condition will be sent to my office every month. I will monitor his progress, or lack of it, religiously. This was a dastardly crime and it will be my duty to track it until closure. For everyone's sake I will shut the door on this one.' Ludwig stood and gathered his belongings.

The assembly rose out of courtesy. Twittering exchanges.

Bees in swarm.

'Fuck it!' Chuck whispered his annoyance into Dick's ear.

'Shit. This means we've got to keep it open and watch that arsehole's every move.' Not such a subdued voice. Dick Kaltenbach wanted more people to realise the department's frustration with this ruling.

Steve Reynolds occupied the winner's enclosure. An acknowledgment to Wingate Freeman. A job well done. And an outstretched hand offered to his new friend from England. A huge smile. George Rundle was tickled pink.

Chapter 23

Deirdre wore her sour face. George had taken retirement to be at home with her. And here he was gallivanting half way round the world. Who did he think he was? The garden was a mess. The gardener an absentee. Like having a wayward relative. A prodigal son. She would never live this down.

George had expected her to greet him at the airport, but she was making a statement by staying indoors and being busy with her customary activities. He should know that his absence wasn't going to upset her routine.

She was polishing the dining table when he clicked open the front door. A rich aroma of beeswax clinging in the air. George left his suitcase in the hall and headed for the back of the house.

Deirdre heard him coming and hummed defiantly as she buffed in circles the mahogany table.

'Home dear.' A voice heavily laden with apology. 'You okay?' He stood away. Trying to feel the mood. Body language bristly and hostile.

'Okay? Huh.' Deirdre rubbed harder. The same spot. It didn't matter. 'Expect me to be all right. Stuck here.' Almost a tear.

George stepped nearer and extended a hand. On her shoulder and round her back. Deirdre pulled away momentarily. George hauled her back. Wrapping her up. A furling motion that tugged her into his embrace.

'Missed you dear,' he whispered. 'Sorry I've been so long.' George had her. What a charmer.

Deirdre spluttered. Warm teardrops on her cheeks. He tasted the salt. Her words mumbled and tender. The dam broken. George felt the plumpness of her body through the thin cotton dress.

'What kept you? Leaving me like that. Mrs. Jenkins thought you were dead or had left me. Not fair, George, not fair at all.' Tea cups tinkled. Kettle boiling. Deirdre spoke through the preparation. You settled your differences and made peace over a cup of tea in Camille Gardens.

A piece of digestive biscuit stuck to George's lip as he began. He played with his empty cup. 'As I told you on the phone, things didn't go well with the detectives over there. They had their man.'

Deirdre sat watching her husband. An encouraging smile. All animosity forgotten. It would be a whole morning of debriefing before jet lag caught up with the globe-trotting detective and Deirdre turned down the bed for him.

George Rundle slept for twelve hours. In the end Deirdre had to wake him as she kept seeing Mrs. Jenkins looking up from her garden at the drawn curtains. There would be talk at the Friendship Club and she was quite tired of the tales circulating already.

'So, do they think this Sarah Bickles killed all those people?' Deirdre had questions to ask. And after George had finished the hearty brunch that she had conjured up she plonked herself down next to him. 'Did you convince them?'

'They've got the wrong man. I'm certain. He's a mental wreck at the moment, and that gives us some time to do some work here and over there.' George explained as he wiped the smeared yolk with a remnant crust.

'Work here?' Deirdre quizzed. 'Does this mean you're still going on?'

'Just some investigations. Nothing much.' He realised Deirdre's concern.

'The garden, George. Don't leave me with that garden. It's a shameful mess.' She stood and collected up the plates. Stacking them noisily. 'Mrs. Jenkins has already blamed us for the ivy that's creeping onto her vegetable patch.'

'I'll be out there immediately.' George spoke with purpose. But he planned to spend the day only doing some cosmetic pruning and edging. 'Sort that out in no time.' Reassuring tones to put Deirdre at ease. How could he focus on the garden when there was a killer loose that he needed to trap. A bloodhound with the scent.

At lunch he started. In the police notes he had an address for Sarah Bickles. Whilst Deirdre was cutting bread he dialled Directory Enquiries. Only two Bickles in the Lyme Regis area. No problem so far. He'd wait to make the important call. There was a lot to prepare. Not a simple enquiry.

16, Church Cliff Avenue, Lyme Regis. Still three women. A new hierarchy. Sarah, Debbie and baby Vicky. The house a time bomb.

Incessant rain during a bleak spring. Cliffs undercut by the rampant ocean. Spongy precipices mobilised by a saturated water table. Slumped on the beaches. Soil scree. Brown deltas on the marble pebbles. The town forever puddled and grey. Sheltering tourists swapping a drenched industrial street for a doppelganger, fronted by shops selling sticks of seaside rock and saucy postcards. Fish and chips. A film in the evening. Plastic raincoats, buckets and spades. Hapless British holidays.

A cream telephone hung on the wall of the kitchen. Bruised black smudges and some sickly dried-brown stain. Its bell was cracked and the ring more a rattling fire alarm.

'She's not here.' Debbie was surprised to find someone inquiring after her sister.

'When are you expecting her back?' George's voice was jovial yet polite. An innocent query. No need to alert anyone.

'Dunno. Never says where she's going.' Why should she bother with the call? Sarah had been a right bitch since she'd returned.

George didn't want to leave his number. 'I'll call again. Can you suggest a good time?'

'Evening. Cow never goes out then.' Debbie slammed the phone down. Vicky dribbled on Debbie's shoulder as she carried the baby to the lounge. A lobsterpot playpen to keep her out of her mother's hair for a few minutes.

George would phone back. In a way he was relieved Sarah hadn't been in. He really wasn't prepared enough to confront his adversary. It had seemed a simple task, but accusing someone of such a hideous crime wasn't like trying to sell a product over the phone. You didn't risk all manner of legal backlashes by claiming they had slaughtered a whole family. A plan needed to be worked out. Perhaps a decoy motive. But she would know him. He couldn't change that. He was the policeman who interviewed her after Rupert's death. He was in charge of the investigation. It needed an approach that was low key. Just as a matter of interest. Invent some new aspect in that case. A harmless diversion that wouldn't trigger panic, or alert her to his real mission.

Tugging at the dandelions that had infested his cabbage patch he was running through ideas. You could really unjumble mental stuff when you were being physical in your gumboots. Yanking out roots and filling the wheelbarrow.

Lady Penelope Bassnett had instituted a small charity that helped bereaved parents. Not that she was really involved. She fed in the money and gave out awards annually. Somehow it helped her cope with the loss of Rupert. George didn't like the idea of deception but in desperate times, desperate measures were called for. He'd speak to Sarah Bickles. Reassure her by stating he was now retired, but that he was active in the administration of the Lady Bassnett charity. *Touching You*, or something like that. He would have to confirm the name before he phoned. As Rupert's nanny he would contact her to see if she was interested in a part time involvement. Plan a rendezvous. Take it from there. Perhaps let it slip that there were some concerns over the boy's death. Nothing to do with him. A possibility that the file would be reopened. Gauge her reaction. Promise to keep her informed of all developments even though he was not now in the force. It would be a fishing expedition. Just needed the right bait.

It was amazing what a bit of gardening did for the mind. George was proud of his plan.

And when he phoned that evening he spoke to Sarah Bickles.

'George Rundle. Do you remember? We met during the investigation into the tragic accident at Ruckley Manor?'

Alarm bells. Policeman phoning? Sarah's brow creased and her eyes flickered.

'Only I'm not a copper now.' George chuckled. 'Charity work and gardening.' Keep her at ease. 'Sorry for the intrusion. It's just a courtesy call.' Almost a double-glazing salesman now.

Sarah grunted down the phone. It wasn't a problem. George had succeeded in lowering her guard. But she hadn't any time to help with no charity. Didn't want to be involved. She handed off every attempt by George to corner her.

'Look.' One final attempt. 'I'm in the area. Just up from Lyme Regis tomorrow. I could call in and show you some of the work we are doing.'

'Why?' Sarah wasn't taking the suggestion well. Weren't going to meet him. Bloody pest.

'I'm sure Lady Bassnett would like me to demonstrate what a benefit the charity has been...a comfort.' George was inventing as he went. Talking in air. He'd lost her. Not even on the hook. Wrong bait.

A crisp exchange of goodbyes. Maybe good riddance. George fumed. Not like him to blow it.

Deirdre ground her teeth and gasped a lot. Amusing at first but then annoying. Perhaps she always had. But George wasn't sleeping well that night and he had time to take notice. And when he did slide into fitful sleep he had wild dreams about Bobby Clayman and Steve Reynolds. Possibly it was guilt. He was supposed to be making headway with the suspect but could only boast dead ends so far.

The traffic had started percolating through Camille Gardens and the dawn chorus in full voice by the time he had come up with the next master plan.

It took another day to make the garden look respectable enough for Deirdre to venture out and cock a snoop at Mrs. Jenkins, as she peered through her net curtains. A further day to collect the things that he needed. On the third day he ventured forth.

George parked in the town centre. Well it was his car. But he looked very different. Then, when you are undercover there aren't any rules. And George was deep undercover.

He found Church Cliff Avenue without too much trouble. A young woman in the high street was eager to assist a gentleman of great age who was seeking the house of a relative. She was somewhat concerned that a man walking with such difficulty would reach the house in question. He assured her he could. And as soon as she had disappeared into a shop he carried the stick he had held to support himself, and despite the full-length greatcoat scurried off towards Church Cliff Avenue.

Somewhere between the appearance of a spy and a pervert. George sauntered up the road scanning the chrome numbers that were still attached. Sixteen was one that retained its identity. A mucky building. Stained walls and blistered paintwork. Strong vertical lines either side of the terrace home highlighting the greater care over maintenance by the neighbours since the purchase of their properties. Their masonry bright and clean. The dingy exterior of number sixteen given even more shadow. Like the grubby kid in a line up.

Lurking would be difficult. Numerous excursions back and forth similarly conspicuous. George found a bench about sixty yards from the house. If she left and came towards him, going down to the town he could pick up her trail, no problem. Turning the other way he would be hard pressed to catch up and keep up. Patience would be his greatest asset. He had spent many hours on his own during surveillance sessions whilst in the Force.

He wasn't close enough to detect movement in the house and had made the assumption that everyone was indoors, whoever they were. George was not aware of the number of residents. He hadn't bothered to check the electoral roll. It wouldn't have been much help.

After about two hours there was activity outside the front door. A large girl wrestling and cursing. Debbie was struggling out with Vicky in a pushchair. George was alerted and decided to shuffle towards the house. Just in case it was Sarah and she turned away from the town and his interception.

Debbie was heading his way, and passed George halfway down Church Cliff Avenue. Oblivious to the old man. George nodded a greeting, as an elderly gentleman would. Debbie was bent over Vicky, tucking her embroidered quilt around her neck against the cold wind. George scanned as much of the face as he could. He didn't recognise her. And surely Sarah Bickles didn't have a baby or was looking after one. He decided this wasn't his murderess. So he didn't turn and follow Debbie. Continued on his way to the house, passing it at a snail pace. Every window scrutinised. No sign of life. At a reasonable distance past he changed direction and retraced his steps. Again he studied the house. Stooping to tie a lace or adjust a turn-up. Just a minute more. It was enough. A figure moved upstairs. The sharp bark of a cough. A bite. Now to get her hooked.

Could be she wouldn't move from the house. George's bladder sent him scuttling into the bushes. He panicked. An enlarged prostate meant he spent too long getting the flow going. He imagined his quarry leaving the house while he struggled to shake off the last drips of his stream. In his rush to scramble out of the undergrowth he forgot to zip up his trousers.

This drew attention to the old man stuck on the bench. A new identity. Mothers guiding children quickly past and middle-aged women touching their mouths in disgust.

Sarah left the house. Furtive escape through the merest crack of the door. An old grey coat down to her calves, flat black shoes. She followed her sister's route. George, fly gaping, leapt in pursuit as she passed him. Sudden action. Nearly caught on the hop. Her stride brisk. He was quick to lose the stick and loosen his long coat. Occasionally flipped out the back by the on-shore breeze it became a cloak. Batman in chase or Musketeer hounding a scoundrel.

She wanted as much anonymity. Stopping at the occasional shop window. George at a neighbouring display. His open fly shouting from the reflection. A yanking hand too visible to the assistant inside.

Several false alarms before Sarah's entrance through the sticking door rung the bell of a small teahouse near the seafront. George's chance. He examined a faded menu in the window and peeked into the dim interior. A lace curtain on a pole covered half the shop front, but he could see most of the tables. Only three or four people inside. Sarah had sat in a corner. A second tinkle announced his entrance. He took a seat near his prey after first confirming with the girl at the counter that it offered waitress service.

Sarah's face was expressionless. He recognised the blank look. Saw her differently now. Not the meek nanny whose charge had just died in the bath. A dreadful accident. Blaming herself for not offering greater vigilance.

He held a grudge. She had deceived him at the time. Of that he was certain.

Sarah felt his stare. Why was the old fellow looking at her? She felt uncomfortable. Twitchy. Thinking about leaving.

George sensed she was alerted and made his move. He hauled himself up and waddled over to Sarah's table.

Her eyes signalled alarm. He was coming towards her. Discomfort turned quickly to panic. She dropped her head and examined the tablecloth, picking at a thread.

'Excuse me. It's Sarah Bickles isn't it?' George pulled off his hat and exposed his slicked black, but thinning hair. Not such an old man after all. 'George Rundle. We spoke on the phone.' A winning smile. 'Didn't mean to trouble you. Surprising coincidence coming across you like this.'

Sarah swayed in her chair. Leaning way back as if blown by a powerful wind. Thinking about an escape. She gulped audibly and her eyelids trembled.

George knew he had to work to keep her seated. 'Sorry to startle you. Recognised...the face. Thought I'd say hello. Let me get you something.' He hailed a young girl chewing at her nails. 'I understand the food here is surprisingly good. Do you come here regularly?' Enough of a bombardment to hold on to her. Shell shock.

'You from the charity business?' She shuffled back into position and smoothed her skirt. 'Told you, weren't interested.' A sullen voice.

'Not out to force you. Do-gooders not up your street, eh?' This was a tough nut to crack. 'Lady Bassnett's doing a good job though.' He cringed inwardly at his own deceitful words. 'Empathy. She misses that little soul so much. Now she can share her ability to cope with his death and find strength from despair.' Almost a preacher. 'Still, if you have no intention of lending a hand I'm not here to twist your arm.' Understanding smile and resigned lips. 'What with the new developments I suppose it is a bit insensitive to ask.' Bombshell neatly dropped.

Sarah's eyes opened wide and watched an imaginary exchange of tennis shots. 'New developments.' Broad Dorset. 'What new developments?'

'I was at the station not so long ago. The new Inspector, by the name of Griffiths met me in the corridor. Informed me that he was reopening the Rupert Bassnett case. Don't know any more than that. If I hear anything further I will let you know, of course. Maybe they'll contact you direct.'

Sarah felt perspiration soak her collar and her stomach clench tight. 'Why'd they contact me? It were finished long ago. Can't see the point.'

'Shouldn't think you have anything to worry about. Do you?' Tea and Danish pastries arrived. Sarah rocked as the girl laid them out. Holding on to her reply. But they spoke with their eyes. Sarah could see beyond an ex-policeman administering a charity. George saw the frightened eyes of a mouse cornered.

'Like what?' Sarah blurted.

'Well, you told us everything at the time didn't you? If you've been truthful there's nothing that concerns you. It's all a pretty harmless exercise I'm sure.' George forced a smile. A nervy smile of triumph rather than one of anxiety.

'Yeah.'

'That's fine. What I'll do, Sarah, is to find out the exact nature of this matter and telephone the details to you.' George needed to keep the dialogue open. Keep her sweet and not break the line now she had taken the bait. 'Good grub this.' George munched at his cake, and spoke with a hail of crumbs. He would spend the rest of the time talking trivia and let Sarah dwell on the significance of questioning a *death by misadventure* decision.

At the window an observer was loitering. As if unsure of entering, or balancing their menu choice with the money in their pocket. George recognised her portly frame and the greasy hair. The girl who had come out of number sixteen Church Cliff Avenue, steering a child along. Debbie wasn't interested in the brown-edged menu with its biro alterations. She had spied her sister in conference with a man. She needed to stick her nose on the glass window to get a good look. There was no subtlety. Vicky was complaining in the pushchair. Between the occasional rocking of the buggy and a sharp word to her daughter, Debbie managed to catch more than a glimpse of what was going on.

'What's she want?' Sarah caught sight of her sister stuck to the window. One eye positioned at a gap in the curtain and her nose flattened on the pane.

'Who is it?' George didn't like pieces missing from his jigsaw.

'Sister.' Sarah pushed her plate away and stood up. 'I'm off.'

Debbie saw her stand and hurried up the street. Vicky hanging on. Pushchair wheels clacking on the cobbles. She needed to be well clear when Sarah left the café.

George drove home with his costume on the back seat. He was proud of the disguise. Though somewhat less certain about the progress made with his killer nanny. He would phone Sarah Bickles in a couple of days and elaborate on the new developments in the Bassnett case. Fabrication wasn't his best skill but he'd try and make it seem authentic. *Important developments that could include her being interviewed again. Injuries sustained now reveal a degree of external force being used during the inflicting of the wounds to the boy's head. He could help her side-step any new accusations.* Get her to rely on him. A necessary lifeline.

Three days of keeping Deirdre happy. More garden titivation and some chores in the house. Deirdre was aware that he was still working on his murdering nanny theory, but they barely discussed it. Taboo, after the long absence it had caused when he disappeared to the United States.

'Hello, Sarah. It's George Rundle. I said I'd call.' He had got through to Sarah straight away. She was taking calls first since the meeting in the tea shop.

'Yeah?' She pressed the receiver flat to her ear. Vicky was bawling upstairs and her hearing less than sharp.

'We need to meet.' Perhaps too blunt.

'Why?' A warning siren sounded in her head.

'I don't want to discuss it over the phone. I've had experience of surveillance and tapping procedures. It's not a good idea for me to let you have the information on this line.' George cringed. Invention was off the leash.

'Where?' It didn't take much to fool Sarah.

George hadn't thought about location. 'Er...same place?' A hurried suggestion.

'No.' She imagined her sister spying on another meeting. 'There's a coffee shop near the front. By the arcade. *Ronnies.*'

'Okay. I'll find it. Say three in the afternoon.'

'Yeah.' Sarah rang off. Straight to the toilet. Always worked that way with her. When she was anxious her waterworks were triggered.

Ronnies was a dive. Formica tables and plastic bottles. Lingering odour of fatty burger meat and fried onions. Ron cooked and served. Putrid apron and the occasional fag. Plump and jolly. Foul jokes and a spitting laugh. A grease joint that hauled in the punters during the rainy summer days. An unkind ambush for families with disgruntled kids.

George arrived first. He found a corner table and took some coffee. Safest bet. Only one other customer. A dishevelled guy looking for his future in a lukewarm cup of tea. No threat. George was casing the place.

Sarah arrived after a couple of minutes and strode over to the table, where George was having second thoughts about finishing his coffee.

'Tea or coffee?' George rose and made the offer. Only too ready to abandon his own.

'Tea.' An abrupt order devoid of niceties. 'So what's the information?' Sarah wanted this dealt with pronto.

'Take it easy.' George had to get this right. 'Griffiths has been told to undertake a review of the case. Came from above. Some anonymous Chief Super. I have spoken to him about my role in the original enquiry, and I will be seeing him again. I'm surprised he hasn't seen you before now.'

'What they looking for?' Sarah screwed up her face.

'Seems there has been some new development that stems from another case.'

'Another case? What other case?' She was distinctly uncomfortable.

'Well.' George wanted to drop the bombshell then and there, but he held out a little longer. It might bring the result he was hoping for. 'I'm not in a position to know all the details. Wish I was. But this other case must have been related and extremely serious. Although Griffiths' deputy, a young officer name of Peacock, did let it slip that it wasn't a crime on his patch.' George watched for a reaction.

Pewter eyes. Vice-like grip on the cup. 'What's that mean?'

She cocked her ear. Tugging on the line.

'Somewhere else. Not sure where. Another county possibly.' George spoke slowly to observe her response. Vague geography to entice her to suggest locations.

Sarah was wary. 'Don't seem right.' Her mouth strained to pinpoint it for him. But she wasn't dumb enough to indicate the site of her despicable deed. The cottage by the lake. Forest, mountain and snow. A clear picture.

'Peacock did drop another clue. Something about *bloody foreign* methods.' Innocent eyes and a pretend sip of the cold coffee. 'So there's a good chance this earthmoving event took place in another country.' George shook his head. Not really interested. Of no consequence. Skilful decoy.

Sarah slumped inside. Urgent ticking eyes. 'What country?' She blurted.

It was enough. 'America.' George suddenly alert and focussed. 'America, Sarah.' He leant back on his chair, sucked in his lips and nodded knowingly. A very different person.

A face caught in the millisecond of a camera flash. Eyes ignited. Mouth frozen open. Sarah's head buzzed with fizzing wires, erratic connections. She battled to fit the threads. As if falling through a trap door. She flicked at a hair on her coat. Felt his triumph bearing down on her dejection.

'You worked for the Roberts. Went with them to the States. All the family were murdered there. You supposedly found them dead. The caretaker was blamed.' George stung her with a synopsis. Half out his seat, hands on the table. Leaning towards her. 'So you know this other case very well, don't you Sarah? Don't you?' His eyes weren't leaving the target.

The door of the café swung open. A midland family escaping the sweeping rain. Bedraggled parents and scruffy kids. In for a strong tea. Plastic macks shaken and baseball caps slapped across knees. A generally aimed *God it's murder out thar'* to the sparsely populated tables.

'What you up to?' Sarah quizzed from squeezed eyes. 'What's your game?'

Two angry cats hissing at each other. Claws stretched. Teeth bared.

'Sarah Bickles, it's time you came clean. Killed the boy. Killed the family in America. Killing an innocent man. That's the truth of it. Isn't it?' George wasn't playing games. Not at all. Though he was a lot braver on the outside. Inside he was jelly.

Sarah didn't respond. It was a trap, and her mind stormed round the cage she had fallen into. Banging the sides and clutching the ensnaring bars.

'You going to see Bobby Clayman blamed for this crime? Going to condemn him to a life incarcerated for something he didn't do?' George spoke low and close to Sarah's immobile head.

'Didn't do it. Not me.' A feeble attempt to appeal to her captor. A plea of innocence. She could quickly see his incredulous sneer. 'Weren't me.' Just dribbling out denial. Not a chance of convincing her jailer.

The scruffy kids were out of their seats and rolling a drink can along the floor. Their parents, oblivious to the noise, dragged at the last few millimetres of their dog-ends.

Sarah could feel his breath now. 'Just a coincidence. Is that it? These deaths? Your presence?' Yellow teeth and flicking tongue. 'I'm not a fool. And I'm not ready to allow an innocent man to be convicted of this dreadful crime. Your dreadful crime. I won't give up. You won't shake me off.' George's hot breath. Foul with coffee odour.

'What can you do?' Sarah snarled back. 'You ain't a policeman now, are you?'

The lone man had outstayed his welcome. Ousted by Ron's scowl he slid out the door. Feet clapping the wet pavement. Head swinging left and right. Where to go next? Another refuge.

Neither combatants noticed.

'They ain't reviewing no case. You made that up. This is all your doing. No one thinking it were me 'cept you. That's it, ain't it?' Sarah was spunky now.

George was thrown momentarily. Hadn't expected her to retaliate.

Both pulled back and sat square in their chairs as Ron circled the table and reached for the cups. Almost as full as when they left his counter. Cold now. Brown trickle stains on the white stoneware.

'I'm off. Ain't waiting round here.' Sarah stood as Ron retreated with a low growl. *There weren't anything wrong with his beverages. Bloody cheek.*

The Coke can had been squashed on the floor and the stubs were in the ashtray. Parents and children dragged themselves to their feet. They approached the door as a pack. Just as Sarah was tugging it open. George scuttling behind to catch up was held back by the jam. When he got outside, and circumvented the scrum that was marooned by indecision, Sarah was hurrying away with a spirited stride.

Gardening was no workout, not that he had done much of that recently. He could hear his wheezing breath and feel the thumping in his chest. Sarah wasn't making ground despite his frequent rests. But she was out of the town and on a path leading up to the war memorial when his galloping gait took him within earshot.

'What d'yer want?' Sarah turned to confront her pursuer. She was top dog now. Only some crummy ex-policeman who was working on a hunch. Pestering her. Trying to make a name for himself. Cheap trickster. 'Get lost!'

George held his ground. An arm's length away. 'What you don't know is that I've been there.' He swallowed as he caught his breath. 'Been to America. Got back just days ago.'

'Eh?' Sarah blurted.

'Yes, I went to New Hampshire. Concord Police Headquarters.' He nodded, pouted his lips and held on to a triumphal grin. 'Where you were. Where Bobby Clayman has been charged with your crime.'

Sarah breathed in short bursts. Rain fell in waves. She only watched his words and the purpose on his face. An ugly old man dragging her down. Pulling at her as if in a dream when you try to run but are held by a phantom hand.

'Lieutenant Kaltenbach and Officer Nolan. Remember them, Sarah? They would be pleased to see you again.' He felt safe with that. A lie or two here wasn't going to matter. 'Thought you'd got away with it, didn't you?'

Cornered again. Her head sizzled. A time bomb.

'Met up with Bobby's lawyer. Name of Steve Reynolds. Working hard to see justice done. Not going to let his client go down for this. No way.' George could see his punches hitting the target. Squirming with each blow. 'They're going to be calling on you. Extradition and all that. You can't escape.'

Sarah's head was a fuse lit and fizzing. Sparks flying from the spitting incendiary. Breathing frenetically through her teeth.

'Give yourself up. Tell them what made you do it. You probably had good reason.' George puffed. A hint of sarcasm.

Sarah moved away. Turned from the grassy bank where they had halted and headed for a small copse of trees on an incline. George scampered after her. He wasn't fully recovered from the original pursuit but he wasn't letting her escape his barrage.

Unfamiliar territory. George was on a wooded hill. Terrain slippery but unremarkable. Sarah knew it better. The copse had been a substantial coppice on the approach to the cliff top coastal footpath. A popular route for walking boots and khaki rucksacks, and those with camera necklaces.

She stopped at the top. At a patch of scrubby trees. The wind sang with a rush through the scanty branches. Salt spray whipped from the thrashing Channel.

George panted. Wet through. Too old to be chasing. 'Let's go. I'll take you to the station.' Check mate. No escape. Deep breaths.

Flicking brushwood tickled his coat. He was poised above her. King of the castle.

Ignition. Sarah placed two lizard hands on his chest. Dug in her toes. A mighty heave. George was pushed into the thin foliage. Stinging twigs whipped his face. A senseless and futile act. To end up in a bush?

She knew the topography well. This sparse line of trees was all that was left of the luxuriant coppice. Cliff line recession that winter had been most marked at this point. Beyond the fragile barrier was a vertical drop to the wave-cut platform of solid chalk. Over a hundred feet.

George sensed the void and clutched at the skinny branches. Like grasping crane flies. Scratching nails dug at the unstable cliff edge. Dislodging dirt and giving no hold. Jerking limbs made useless swimming gestures. He bounced off some ledges and broke his neck on the rocks below. A tailor's dummy being dumped in a garbage pit.

Sarah ran her hands through her flattened hair, made brushing movements down the front of her coat and turned for home. An adjustment of dress. A trifle dealt with.

Chapter 24

'Suicide?' Harry Fielding pulled a face. 'George Rundle wasn't a guy who'd top himself.'

'Well that's the way it looks. What would he be doing at the top of a cliff in the pouring rain? Sightseeing?' Inspector Trainter enquired as he donned his cap. 'WPC Wilmot is round there at the moment and I should make an appearance. George being in the force all that time.' It was an inconvenience and Trainter didn't have much time for a man who threw himself off a cliff for no reason.

'If I can get cover can I ride along with you, Inspector? Like to express my condolences to his missus.' A genuine request. Harry liked George. Mates for a long time.

'How's she taking it?' WPC Wilmot answered the door and Trainter whispered his enquiry. Didn't like it when there was a lot of emotion about.

'Can't tell. Staring out at the garden, not saying much.' Wilmot shrugged.

Deirdre was sitting at the dining room table when Trainter, closely shadowed by Harry Fielding, crept into the room. More like dubious intruders than representatives of a police force.

'Left me with the garden, again.' Deirdre kept her eyes on the lawn. 'Mrs. Jenkins is going to have a field day.' She shook her head, but didn't turn to greet her visitors.

Harry Fielding approached the back of her chair and touched her shoulder. 'Loved his garden, I bet.'

'No. I'm sure he hated it. Went out there every day, but it was just routine. Didn't really love it.' Deirdre twisted in her chair and offered a smile of resignation. 'Had all the gear. Spent many hours in that damn shed. I expect he was reading half the time, or studying his papers on those murders. Going to miss him.'

Trainter's ears pricked. 'Murders? What murders?'

Deirdre was startled by the second voice. She hadn't realised the Inspector was standing near the door clutching his cap against his chest. 'Harry knows. Been his obsession for weeks. Took him to America.'

Trainter looked quizzically at his Sergeant.

'George was the investigating officer in the Rupert Bassnett enquiry. When he read about a mass murder in the States he reckoned there was a link. Seems the nanny worked for both families. Too much of a coincidence to this sleuth. In his blood, being a copper.' Harry smiled at Deirdre.

Trainter was intrigued. 'So George was doing his own detective work?'

'Yes. He just couldn't get out of the habit. I'm sure he would have been suspecting the neighbours of drug smuggling eventually.' Deirdre pictured her husband hunting through reams of paper at the table she now sat at.

'What was he doing in Lyme Regis?' Trainter asked. He wanted to go further. *Why would your husband throw himself off the cliff?* He resisted.

'He didn't jump. George wouldn't have done that.' Deirdre had pleading eyes.

Harry bent down to her level. 'Slipped, you reckon? Out for a walk? It was a terrible night.' Harry was trying hard. Anything to protect Deirdre.

'Went to see her. The nanny. Bloodhound on the trail. That was my George.' Deirdre sighed. It seemed the grass in the back garden was growing as she watched it. Blade after blade spreading and sprouting. Determined to ruin the manicured lawn. 'Now he's left me with the garden. Why did he do that?' Her lip quivered and she sobbed. A screeching lament that WPC Wilmot countered with a cup of tea from an outstretched hand. Harry gripped her shoulder. Inspector Trainter stood glum and silent.

'Went down to Lyme to see this woman, you say?' Trainter

waited until Deirdre was taking sips from the cup and she'd wiped the tears with a tissue.

'Sara Pickles, or something like that. Didn't listen to what he said all of the time.' Deirdre was apologetic.

'Sarah Bickles.' Harry corrected as kindly as he could.

Trainter jotted the name down in his notebook. Wouldn't ask anymore questions. Even an insensitive police inspector realised the protocol.

An uneasy truce existed at 16, Church Cliff Avenue. Debbie hated her sister being there. She was odd, even frightening. If it were just her and Vicky then things would be better. A family sort of.

Sarah had a separate agenda and hardly spoke. Each girl making their bedroom their living area. The lounge downstairs an empty tomb. Haunted by their mother's ghost. One bathroom. Neutral territory where Sarah smelled the powders and the creams and bathed in the sumptuous scents of the baby.

Debbie sat at the kitchen table poring over the newspaper. Vicky struggling with a feeding bottle like a swaying caber. Bib askew in a highchair. Sarah on her bed listening for them to leave. Counting the people she had killed.

'That's him.' Debbie told the echoing kitchen and her baby daughter. 'Seen him with her.' She smoothed the large sheet of the *Dorset Clarion*. 'He were older. But that's the bloke.' Debbie pointed to each letter as she read the bold type of the headline.

Vicky dropped the bottle she had been juggling and gave her mother a lopsided, enquiring look. Alerted by Debbie's sudden movement and her urgent examination of the newspaper.

'Christ!' Debbie frantically read on. Her finger still leading. 'Shit.' Sweat beads sprang up on her forehead. Vicky sensed the agitation and made the initial sounds that forecast a bout of tears. When Debbie had read the article three times she sat up straight, wiped away the perspiration that had dripped into her eyes and down her cheeks and pulled the bawling child from its chair. 'Jesus Christ!'

With the baby firmly held she looked directly above her, as if having the ability to see right through the ceiling and into Sarah's room. Her imagination went berserk. Vicky felt her mother's grip tighten with every vivid creation.

As quick as she could she dressed the reluctant child and threw on an old jacket. In the rush to leave the house the pushchair collided with the panel of the front door. A loud clack that alerted Sarah on her bed. She slid into her slippers and faced the mirror. Her turn in the kitchen, now the bitch and her nipper had gone.

Like the galley of the *Mary Celeste*. Vicky's bottle where it had rolled. Crusts from Debbie's toast. New moons edged with Marmite on the crumby plate. Half a cup of coffee with the red crescent of lipstick stuck on the side. Tap dripping into a full washing-up bowl stuffed with dirty dishes. Newspaper spread wide across the whole table. She'd dump her sister's shit on the draining board. Her table now.

George Rundle grinned up at her. One of him taken while still in the force. Sarah backed away. A good pace. From where she stood she could read the headline. *Tragedy at Steeple Cliffs*. George still smiled from the open sheet as she sidled up to the flapping page. Sarah read like her sister. Forefinger stabbing each word. Almost as a blind person tracing Braille.

She had only seen him disappear through the curtain of kindling and hear the heavy thuds of his descent. A clean disposal. Like the engulfing drapes of a stage, or those shielding the coffin slid through for cremation. Now she had the result neatly accounted and his stupid picture that wouldn't stop smirking.

Sarah was content with the tragic accident theme running through the article, and an interview with the town's civil engineer talking about the state of the cliff line and the danger of further coastal erosion. There was some suggestion that it was strange for someone to be lurking around that spot on such a dreadful day, but no insinuation that he had been pushed. That George Rundle, respected ex-policeman, had been senselessly murdered.

Sarah folded up the paper and pressed it flat. It troubled her that Debbie had been reading the story. Had left the paper open at that page. Left him staring up at her. Did she plan it? Was it an accusation? Her sister had seen him at the café when she was spying on her. Did she suspect? She'd rushed off with the baby and hadn't cleared away. Normally she'd at least put the stuff in the sink.

A bowl of cereal and then getting dressed. All the time churning it over. If Debbie did have a suspicion then what would she do? Had Debbie gone to tell someone? Maybe to the police? Was that too far-fetched? Nagging notions and fanciful fears drove Sarah out of the house in pursuit of her sister.

Debbie wasn't totally sure why she had fled the house so urgently. She rocked Vicky to sleep in the buggy as she sat on the park bench near the town centre. So a bloke that she has seen with her sister falls off a cliff? What's the big deal? Mountain out of a molehill. Yet...yet, could be more sinister than that. Could be that her sister, who has links with several untimely deaths is very much involved with this mysterious demise. Maybe killed him? Her sister a murderer? No, that would be ridiculous. Or would it? Debbie's head was porridge.

Sarah spotted her sister. Tartan buggies with broken hoods weren't common, and her sister's bulk in an old brown jacket not difficult to miss. An abandoned sack of spuds.

Sarah stood over her slumped sister. Looking down on the parting in her dark hair. A few grey ones appearing, that she noticed for the first time.

Debbie jumped when she saw Sarah hovering over her. 'What you doing?'

Sarah stared into her plump face. A stupid face. She screwed her eyes. Accusing eyes.

'What d'yer want here?' Debbie started to rise and push

down on her disobedient skirt. A billowing piece of material that threatened to fill with air. 'You following me?'

'What you doing with the paper?' Sarah snapped.

'What paper?' Debbie replied indignantly.

'Newspaper. In the kitchen. You were reading it.'

'So?' Debbie wasn't going to be bullied.

'That page you were on, about the accident at the cliffs?' Sarah prodded. 'Why d'yer leave it open there?'

'No reason. What you worried about?' Debbie fought back.

Sarah ran her finger along a seam on the baby's pushchair and gave a half smile to Vicky who was squashed in the corner.

'Saw that bloke. You know I did, don't you?' Debbie challenged.

'Who?'

'One in the paper. Saw you with him at the café.'

'So?' Sarah tugged back the damaged hood, exposing the roundness of her niece's face.

'Strange he ends up dead at the foot of the cliff.' Debbie cocked her head and pulled the buggy towards her. An attempt to retrieve her daughter from the attentions of her sister. 'He was a policeman. Was a detective they said. You've had some run-ins with them. The police. Haven't you?'

'You suggesting something?' Sarah snatched at the buggy to regain possession.

'Maybe. Seems quite a coincidence. Bit 'larming I reckon.' Debbie tugged at the pushchair seat. It didn't budge. Sarah had it firmly gripped. Debbie sensed danger. 'Might let the coppers know.' A further yank at the chair. Sarah held on tighter.

'Police?' Sarah slipped her hands into the buggy and lifted Vicky out. The pushchair sped away as Debbie continued to tug. An empty victory.

Debbie held out her arms. Her eyes demanded her daughter back. Desperate eyes filled with anxiety.

Sarah raised Vicky up with both hands. High in the air as if lifted in triumph. Her face towards her mother.

'No!' Debbie blurted.

'No, what?' Sarah lowered Vicky into her arms and cradled her. Rocking her gently and looking into her blue eyes.

'Don't hurt her.' Debbie edged towards her sister.

'Hurt little Vicky? Never hurt the sweet girl.' She tickled the child's chin with her finger. 'Such a delicate doll.'

'Give her here.' Debbie pleaded.

'Now. What were we talking about?' Sarah swung Vicky as she spoke. 'About you going to the police. Tell them about the man who fell off the cliff, weren't you?' She held the baby out. Tempting Debbie to grab for her. Teasing.

Debbie made a lunge and held on to her daughter. Limpet hands around her legs. Grappling motions. She met Sarah's face. Only inches apart. Snarling gladiators. Debbie gulped. Her sister's visage a deadly warning. Almost spitting her vicious threat.

Sarah released her hold on the baby, letting her slide away into her sister's trembling embrace. Lips slapping on the baby's cheek. Almost smothering Vicky in the protective cocoon of her flabby arms.

Debbie wouldn't put the baby down. Never let go. Out of the park at a scuttle, hauling the buggy, bouncing behind her. Driven by a terrible fear.

Chapter 25

Deirdre had sent note-lets from her flower box set. To those who weren't close enough to attend the funeral or might have missed the press coverage of the *tragic accident* or the *misadventure* verdict. Thoughtfully concluded by the coroner to waylay rumours of suicide. Harry Fielding had his doubts about both theories and even Trainter was uneasy on this occasion, but he wasn't about to stir things up. The station was busy enough and he had a gut feeling this could be messy.

Deirdre had sorted through George's address book to find old friends and colleagues, those that had retired to the coast and abroad. His most recent pile of paper concerned his obsession with the nanny in the Bassnett case and his lengthy stay in the States.

Steve Reynolds' business card had fallen to the floor as she hunted through all the notes. A brief message to inform him of the sad loss of a loving husband. She was unsure of how well this lawyer had known George so kept it concise.

'Shit!' They heard his cry on the sidewalk below and even across Mount Pinnot Road. It was a sultry day in Concord, New Hampshire and those offices without air conditioning had their windows wide open. 'This is tragic.' Steve was less explosive now. 'Poor guy, poor guy.' Conscious of his mercenary considerations.

His secretary was quick to investigate. Steve Reynolds rarely shouted. This was a distress signal.

'Just when we were making progress. Just when I could see us turning this around.' She stood at the door and listened, her eyes expressing sympathy for her boss. She had read the note-let from Deirdre before Steve had arrived in the office, and she knew he was due to make his weekly visit to Bobby Clayman that morning.

Wingate Freeman had been instrumental in getting Bobby the very best treatment available within a system sorely short of expertise and funds. He spent a lot of time at the Portsmouth secure hospital unit. Somehow responsible. A crazy dedication to bring Bobby Clayman back.

Whenever Steve Reynolds was visiting his client Wingate would invariably be present. That morning he had a surprise for the lawyer.

'Morning.' Steve greeted the doctor. No enthusiasm. Transparent dejection.

'Morning to you.' Wingate Frowned. 'Got out of bed the wrong side?'

'Sorry. Some bad news. It's got me down,' Steve mumbled.

Wingate Freeman waited, hands on hips. 'Well?' The collar of his white jacket forcing the creases of a slight double chin. 'You going to let me in on this disastrous news?'

'Sure.' Steve puffed out air. 'It's George, George Rundle. He's dead.' Steve sighed.

'Dead? That's awful. Heart?'

'No. Fell off a cliff apparently.' Steve splayed his hands. 'What a ridiculous way to go.'

'How does this leave things?' Wingate was getting fretful.

'He was tracking down the nanny. It was our lifeline. George was certain she was involved. If he had managed to secure something concrete there was more than just hope for Bobby.'

'We're not looking at another homicide are we?' queried Wingate anxiously.

'You suggesting George was rumbled. Got too close. Done him in?' Steve saw some prospect in that theory. Not that he wasn't truly devastated by George's sudden demise. 'I'll get on to the police across the pond. See if they suspect foul play. Could be his death was his final act of detection.'

'Now let's go and see Bobby.' Wingate was pushy, and for good reason.

'How is he?' Steve asked as they waited at a security gate before being let into the corridor off which Bobby Clayman had his room.

'Wait and see. Not such a bad day after all.' Wingate winked.

A fat, bearded, male nurse patrolled the long passage. Light green uniform displaying his name, an awful mugshot and some certification for the institution. At his hip a collection of keys. A nod from Wingate and the paunchy man unwound the lock on the steel door.

Bobby Clayman was seated. An obelisk in the corner of a sparse beige room. He didn't stir when the door opened. One small window gave some natural light and this was supplemented by two harsh fluorescent tubes stuck to the ceiling. Bobby looked out onto a courtyard garden. As if he had been placed in position. A sentinel.

Progress had been slow but Bobby was certainly on the mend physically. Over the last few days Wingate Freeman had succeeded in communicating with his patient. A major breakthrough that he was about to demonstrate to the lawyer.

'How are you Bobby?' Said as he took off his jacket. Habitual. Bobby Clayman had gained weight, upright and mobile but there was no expectation of an answer to his enquiry. Steve manoeuvred around the chair to see his face.

Wingate watched. A tingling excitement. As a young boy would awaiting the first movement of his Christmas robot.

'Yes!' Steve Reynolds exclaimed.

Instead of the blank stare that he had expected Steve Reynolds was greeted by the early development of a smile.

'It's great.' Steve turned to Wingate. 'Absolutely wonderful.' He couldn't take his eyes off the curling lips and bright pupils of his client.

'Knew you'd be impressed.' Wingate could barely hide his pride.

Bobby Clayman stood. Not so bent now. He kept a firm hold on the smile. Had his own pride in that.

'There's more.' Wingate puffed up like a haughty fowl. Chest out and chin high.

Steve Reynolds sat down. Ready to be entertained.

Wingate waved a hand through the air, hailing Bobby to approach.

Bobby walked tentatively. Many months fixed embryonic. Huddled and rocking. Stuck in the raven depths of precarious sanity. Now, with each stuttering step a fresh adventure.

'Good day, Mr. Reynolds.' As if from a script and unpractised. Slow words, hiding the rehearsal. Words he had said aloud when alone. His words. He could understand the beauty of these utterances.

'Wow!' Steve Reynolds was flabbergasted. 'When did this happen?'

'We've been building up to this. Speech therapist was seconded from the Military Hospital in Maine. She has worked on badly affected soldiers from the Gulf War. A wizard. She's certainly made the breakthrough we've been hoping for.' Wingate was sharing the medals. A team effort.

'You know what this means, don't you?' Steve Reynolds suddenly felt flat.

Wingate and Bobby studied his troubled face and creased brow. Thrown by fresh anxiety.

'We're going to get that trial date in the near future. Kaltenbach will get Bobby in that courtroom quicker than you can say District Attorney.'

'What's so bad about that?' Wingate enquired. A little disconcerted by the lawyer's loss of faith.

Bobby dropped the smile. His eyes narrowing.

'With George Rundle's death much of our case is riddled with holes. I wouldn't be happy going into battle with the ammunition I've got at the moment.' Steve talked only to Wingate. No matter how improved Bobby Clayman was he wasn't in a position to understand the complexities of his own defence.

'Ouch!' Steve turned abruptly. Bobby was tightly gripping

his upper arm. Quizzing the lawyer with his face. He hadn't learnt enough of the script to speak unaided. But the pleats of skin formed at the bridge of his nose and his exposed teeth pleaded for more.

'Look, Bobby, a lot has been going on while you have been er...unwell.' Steve couldn't have been more awkward. 'There's a lot to fill you in on.'

Bobby nodded. An intensity held by his eyes.

'There was this English guy over from the UK. Gave us a new lead.'

Bobby nodded rapidly. He knew that bit. In his marooned state of suspended motion and apparent communication blackout he had heard. While they spoke around him. Over him. In conference corners of the room where he was just a statue incommunicado, he had listened.

'You aware of this?' Steve questioned his client.

Further nodding and grappling fingers moving back and forth calling for more information. Updating.

'Afraid he's dead.' Steve huffed. 'Fell off a cliff over there in England. Sorry.'

Bobby screwed up his face. His mouth straining to wrap around a bag load of words stuck in his head.

'Reckon you know why he came over and his theory regarding the children's nanny?'

'Bitch.' Soft at first. Bobby held on to that one word. 'Bitch.' He repeated it. Getting clearer each time. 'Bitch, bitch, bitch.'

'Don't think we aren't giving this our best shot, Bobby. George was instrumental in offering fresh ideas, and most significant of all, a suspect.' Steve placed a hand on Bobby's shoulder. A further reassurance. 'We're fighting this all the way. Remember that. Now you are on the mend we stand a real chance of beating this rap.'

Bobby looked at Wingate for confirmation. He returned a smile and a gentle nod of encouragement.

Bobby had no more to say and Steve Reynolds packed up and left. A happier man on his return journey. Bobby Clayman was making the progress that was essential, and hopefully he would be able to ask some of the burning questions very soon.

Wingate Freeman was on the phone two days before Steve's next visit to the secure unit.

'Chirping away like a bird,' Wingate was pleased to announce. 'Ever since you left. I'd like to think it's all my good work, but he's been making a tremendous effort to stretch his vocabulary. Vowel sounds in the mirror. Caught him practising this morning. Determined I'd call it.'

Steve took his secretary, Barbara Perkins, with him. Even a statement might be possible.

Bobby was eager to test his language skills. His greeting was slow and deliberate, and accompanied by a warm grin. Steve Reynolds watched the perilous performance as if he viewed a tightrope walker, anticipating a fall at any moment. Steve slapped his hands together. Mock applause. 'Do you feel like talking some more?'

'Let's do it.' An almost cocky retort. 'I'm ready.' Bobby sat at the table and patted the seat alongside him to encourage Steve to sit.

'Barbara's going to take notes. You okay with that?' Barbara Perkins flipped open her pad as Steve pulled up another chair.

For half an hour Steve went through the open and shut case that Dick Kaltenbach was satisfied would put Bobby away for good. Hammered home those parts that were particularly incriminating.

'Need you to go over the events of that day. You say you arrived at the camp that afternoon. What was your reason for visiting the Roberts' place?'

'Often called in to do the chores. Take in some logs and check on the generator.' Methodical words. Economic delivery. But Bobby was concentrating on the accuracy.

'See anyone when you arrived?'

'No. Wasn't until I was coming back from the boathouse that I seen her. Her.' Bobby was chewing on the word.

'Huddled. Sort of crouching she were. Blood all over her.'

'Think carefully now Bobby.' Steve alerted Barbara with a waving hand. 'The blood. Describe where it was on her and the patterns it made.'

Bobby screwed up his face. 'Patterns?'

'Sorry. What I'm getting at is, were there any areas on her clothing where it was spotted? Think carefully.'

Bobby strained to recall the moment. Focus in on the scene. Playing his video back. He gritted his teeth and creased his eyes. 'There were patches. Like maps. All over. Maybe there were spots on the front. I didn't really study her clothes that closely. Sorry.' Bobby threw out his arms. Resignation.

'We'll get the forensic analysis. Don't you worry yourself.' Steve touched Bobby's shoulder. Disappointment well hidden. 'How did she seem? What did she say to you?' Quickly on. Couldn't let Bobby dwell on it.

'Upset I s'pose. Didn't speak. Pointed to where they all were. Thought she was crazy. Distressed like.' Bobby was annoyed he wasn't being very helpful. And his throat was hurting a little.

No headway. Steve went through his list. Underscoring with his pen. 'Coffee I think. Thanks, Barbara.'

Bobby let the liquid pass slowly down. Almost gargling as it went. Steve Reynolds and Barbara sipped at the plastic cups. Pecking the rounded edge. Nothing said.

'If we're thinking that this woman did do it, then let's try and work out how she set you up.' Steve studied a sheet on the table. This is supposed to be your gun. How did she get the weapon in your truck?'

'Always unlocked. When I was down at the boathouse. No problem.' Bobby was subdued. Not a difficult mission.

'Where'd she get this gun from, anyway?' Steve blurted. 'Yeah, why would she have one?' How stupid. He hadn't been attentive enough. 'Dick Kaltenbach reckons he's got you buying the gun. A witness to prove it.'

Bobby's eyes widened. He jumped upright. 'What an idiot.'

Steve watched his client suddenly energised. As if jolted

awake from a deep sleep.

'What type of gun? It must be. That's it. Of course.' Bobby was losing them.

Barbara scribed furiously.

'Steady down, Bobby.' Steve held up a quelling hand. 'Let's take this a stride at a time. Barbara, can you find that forensic firearms report. Now, Bobby, what's struck a chord here?'

'I got her a pistol. Bought it myself.' His head shook. 'Taught her to shoot, and got her a handgun from a garage sale out on the way to the lake.'

'So you did buy the gun?'

'Yeah. But for her. Smith and Wesson .38. Model 10. Uncle Mike's combat grip.' Bobby knew it well.

'Six rounds, carbon steel, four inch barrel.' Barbara had found the forensic report and read the rest of the description out aloud. Jubilant that there was a breakthrough.

'You bought a gun for her? Why?' Steve was thrown.

'Gave her lessons. With an old Webley I kept in the truck. She wanted that gun. Didn't know for what. Bought her the gun that killed 'em all.' Bobby's pain was in his face.

'Let's hope we can convince a jury of that.' Steve showed his annoyance. It was a stupid thing to do, and it would be difficult to prove ownership.

'Thought she'd taken it away. Back to England. Never reckoned on it still being here.' Bobby was still bemoaning the purchase. Muttering to himself.

'So she had this gun for some time. A chance to learn how to use it effectively. Planning this slaying.' Steve was thinking aloud. He rested back in his chair. 'I think I've got enough to go back to Kaltenbach. Check this through with me. I'd welcome some feedback. George Rundle, bless his soul, is possibly murdered whilst investigating our suspect. She is the owner of the murder weapon. She is at the house or nearby when the murders take place. And I'm sure there's forensic evidence somewhere if they were to re-examine the handgun and her clothing. We're closing in on her.'

Bobby nodded his agreement. Barbara was impressed, but felt merely a bystander.

'Time is short. When Judge Ludwig gets the latest on Bobby's condition he's going to set a date for the trial. I can't pretend that my client is incompetent now.' He smiled at Bobby. Pride in his recovery but fearful of the implications.

'Latest assessment is week after next. We are going to have to move quickly.' Steve stacked his papers and cleared the table.

Bobby slumped into his one easy chair. He was exhausted and his throat stung from the smarting words.

Steve Reynolds managed to get an appointment with Dick Kaltenbach as early as the following morning.

'Steve. Good to see you.' The lieutenant wandered round his office carrying flapping files. 'Things good?'

'Fine.' Steve invariably replied that way, despite life being hell at times.

'What's up?' Chuck bundled in. Jacket on his arm and shirt collar loosened.

An uneasy camaraderie.

'How's that fruitcake of yours?' Chuck enquired as he slumped into his seat. Fragile joviality.

'Bobby?'

'Yeah. The maniac Clayman.' Harsh and not so friendly. 'Not you Steve. You know how I feel about that guy.' Chuck's version of an apology.

'He's still pretty sore about the whole thing.' Dick added.

'Just the reason I'm here.' Steve hauled out a folder spilling paper.

'Going to take long?' Dick asked. 'We're a bit tight on time.'

'It's important, Dick. But I don't want to cram it in between other business. Need your full attention on this.'

Chuck was curious. 'You got intentions of getting another delay?'

'No.' Steve was countering. 'I'll be the first to admit Bobby Clayman has turned the corner. He's ready for trial.'

'Great!' Chuck beamed.

'However, may I spoil the party?' Steve adopted his very serious face.

'What you getting at?' Dick was alerted. 'You here to rescue that killer? We ain't listening if this is some plea to prevent justice for that family.'

'Think on this, Dick. Not so hasty. What if I have some more information? Evidence that Bobby Clayman didn't kill the Roberts family. We go to court. I successfully beat the rap for my client. That's it. Can't try him again. Perhaps he did do it, but your rashness screws things up. This big hurry to get him in court. That allows him to escape justice.'

'What you got?' Chuck didn't like the tone, or direction.

'Let's all settle down. I'll tell you as much as I can. Tricky business divulging defence strategy, but if I can convince you it could save both sides from untold dilemma.' Steve waved his hands to demonstrate calm.

'We're listening. You've got a mountain to climb here.' Dick Kaltenbach rested his chin in the palm of his hand.

'You remember our friend from England, George Rundle?' Nods all round. 'Dead!' Steve decided on an explosive start.

Chuck half out of his seat. 'Sherlock? How'd that happen?' He was genuinely upset. The English ex-detective had a certain charm. An honest little guy on a plausible crusade.

'Out stalking our nanny. Died on that errand. Found at the bottom of a cliff.' Steve wanted them to draw conclusions.

'You still flogging that dead horse?' Chuck wasn't impressed.

'So you see nothing sinister in his death? He's on the trail of a suspect he believes is responsible for five killings and ends up dead himself?' Steve appealed to a cop's natural suspicion.

Unmoved. Glum faces of disinterest from Chuck and Dick. Bobby's guilt too deep-seated.

'The Smith and Wesson.' Steve battled on. An actor dying

on stage. 'Bobby bought the gun. He's told me.' Shock tactics.

Sparkling eyes from the detectives, exchanging victory smiles.

'There you go.' Dick Kaltenbach expressed the joint satisfaction. 'From the horse's mouth.'

Steve prepared to trample on their smugness. 'He bought it for her.' Steve paused. 'He bought the thirty-eight for Sarah Bickles. It was her that selected the firearm at the garage sale. Asked him to buy it for her. Bobby Clayman taught her how to use a gun. In that much he is guilty. But he had no idea what she had planned. He was not party to that gruesome deed.'

'You're clutching at some real long straws here, Steve.' Dick Kaltenbach fidgeted at his desk.

'Look again at the gun. Maybe you missed something. You're still holding the clothes they wore at the scene aren't you?'

'Yeah.' Chuck confirmed but without enthusiasm.

'Are there spotted areas? Splattered blood erupting from gunshot wounds? The first puncture spitting out those tell-tale patterns. Bobby's working clothes and Sarah Bickle's spinsterly attire. You sure you've checked?' Steve was almost begging now. Desperate ideas. 'Prints? No prints on that weapon? On the doll? Come off it.' Steve's eyes pulled open. Bold orbs sitting in deep sockets. A mixture of despair and disgust.

Chuck fiddled with his pen. Cartwheels. Until it cluttered onto the desk. Dick blew air out of his nose and frowned. Neither looked at the fizzing lawyer.

'Isn't anyone listening?' Steve snatched up his papers and carried them askew from Lieutenant Kaltenbach's office.

'Hey, Steve!' Dick called after him. Steve Reynolds was gone. Clattering down the stairs and stomping out onto the pavement below.

'Not a happy man.' Chuck filled a cup from the water dispenser. 'No, sir, our lawyer's pissed off with us two, to be sure.' Pride and resignation in his voice.

'Annoying horsefly. Why don't he leave this alone?' Dick looked at his desk top. 'We've done the work. One of the most compelling cases we've had. Agreed?' He turned to Chuck, still sucking at his plastic cup.

'Definitely.' Chuck examined the dribble left in the thin container and squashed it with one squeeze. 'Trouble is, that them horseflies got one hell of a bite. Keeps on biting you until you can rip 'em off. Steve is going to be nipping at our ankles unless we can smother the scent.'

'Chase about until he disappears up his own ass, as far as I'm concerned.' Dick grabbed his jacket off the back of his chair. 'Coffee?'

'Sure.' Chuck was at his shoulder in a flash. Just what he needed.

The two police officers perched on the kerb. Not talking. Both processing what Steve Reynolds had said. Outwardly dismissive, but in some small and irritating compartment both scratching about. Unhappy with their doubts. Bobby Clayman signed, sealed and delivered. But what was driving Steve Reynolds? Why the energy spent on a dead man? What about George Rundle? Why had he died? Why had this ex-policeman come all the way across the Pond to point the finger away from their prime suspect?

The traffic cleared. They walked on and into the small coffee house. Nutmeg whiffs and pungent, freshly ground Columbian. Intoxicating aromas.

'No wonder there's a crime wave.' Mark Richards' head popped between them. Bared teeth and manic snigger. An arm around each officer's shoulder. 'Shouldn't you two be hunting felons?'

'What's the use when you lawyers send 'em back on the streets with a candy in their hands?' Chuck responded. 'Need to shoot a few more in the line of duty. That'll keep costs down and clean up the neighbourhood.' Chuck offered something between a smirk and a grimace as he carried the steaming cups to Dick, now seated by a window.

Mark Richards followed, thinking of a quip to continue the banter. 'Give us some reliable evidence and we're home and dry. Prosecuting some of these assholes is a nightmare when we're scraping around with a heap of circumstantial shit and no concrete forensic.' Less kidding now. Mark Richards shook in some sugar. 'Take this Clayman case.'

'What?' Dick turned sharply from scrutinising the street. A raw nerve. 'Clayman? You got problems there?' Hunting eyes aimed under hooded lids. 'Don't let the department start kicking away trestles. We've just had Steve Reynolds giving us shit back there.' Dick waved an arm towards police headquarters towering above the coffee house.

'Take it easy, Dick, watertight it just ain't.' Mark slid his coffee cup across the table and skipped around in pursuit to take a seat opposite the Lieutenant. 'Looked a peach at the start, but this baby is leaking. Tiny cracks at the moment, but I'm ready for a major breach.'

'What's this shit, Mark?' Chuck interjected. 'The department turning against us, or something? We agreed Clayman was guilty. Cut and dried. No question.' Chuck leaned hard on his elbow. Strained brow and an inquisitive pinching of the nose.

'Steady on. No one's doubting your prowess as sleuths.' Mark snapped a smile. The two detectives were drilling him with their eyes. 'Motive? Heard of it? Nothing established. No reason for this guy to mow down the whole family. You know this. Neither of you has come up with a motive that I can hook a jury with.'

'Red-handed. Clayman covered in blood at the scene, Clayman had the gun, Clayman had the girl's doll. No one else could have butchered those kids.' Chuck screwed up his face. Same record playing. Even he could hear it.

'Forensic evidence? I can hear Judge Bernstein now. *You expecting this defendant to be sacrificed without a trace of forensic evidence? Is the District Attorney insulting our intelligence?*' A weak attempt to impersonate Bernstein's authoritarian voice. 'I'm going into battle unarmed and naked.' Mark Richards was doing a great demolition job.

Dick was unsettled and trying to erase a vivid picture in his mind of the bare-assed DA confronting the court. 'Why the change of mind? You're raising stuff that you were living with before. Steve Reynolds up your ass or something?'

'We ain't residing in a protective bubble, boys. Word gets to us through some dubious filtering process, but we get to know. Too many voices shouting out about the nanny. I ain't comfortable with this game hanging around. Begins to smell right quick if it ain't cooked real soon.' Mark Richards wasn't a native of New Hampshire, and when he got serious the Alabama twang and country metaphors percolated through.

'Red herrings and you know it. We've got the killer. Why is everyone making this difficult? It ain't a problem. We've sent people down on a lot less.' Chuck saw it as betrayal.

'Yeah, and they've come bounding back to haunt us. Want me to give you the sums. False imprisonment ain't cheap. We're paying through the nose for stitching up these so-called *certainties*.' Mark Richards knew he wasn't making much ground. He'd be the first to lift his cup and drink. Even Dick's nutty Colombian sat cooling on the table. 'Give it one more careful survey. Look in all the grimy corners and if it's as immovable as you reckon I'll proceed. But, for all our sakes explore all those areas that are worrying me. We don't want egg on our faces. I ain't going to be the fucking laughing stock of the New Hampshire judicial system.' Mark Richards wasn't prepared to be stonewalled again. He jumped up and fled. A colleague at the counter. Enough of an excuse.

Chuck breathed on the window and wrote *shit* in the condensation and then quickly rubbed it away. Dick drank now. Spluttering at the taste of lukewarm coffee. A groaning silence.

'One more inquest or they won't leave us alone.' Dick pushed his half-empty cup as far away as he could. 'A fine-tooth comb and that's it. Nothing missed. Then we pass it over. Pissed, right pissed I am.' Dick brushed the creases from his suit and headed for the door.

Chuck hissed his annoyance and followed. Kicking as many chair legs as he could as he bustled down the aisle of tables.

Chapter 26

'Everything else on hold.' Dick raised his hands in a gesture of resignation. 'Let's have all the Clayman shit out on my desk. Every scrap. If there's a piece of this jigsaw missing I'm going to find it.' All other papers and distractions were shifted. Piled high and transferred to Chuck's miscellaneous tray.

Chuck didn't speak. Slamming filing cabinet drawers spoke for him. Heavy files crashed down on Dick's desk and Chuck stood over them. Arms folded. Grim faced.

'Lunch?' Dick enquired at nearly one thirty. 'I'm done. List here of what I need.' He handed Chuck a grubby sheet of paper. 'You want to add anything?'

'Nah,' Chuck growled; little interest in Dick's memo and no appetite for this inquisition. 'Lunch suits me.'

'Read the damn thing, man. You expect me to face them on my own. A team aren't we?'

Chuck begrudgingly ran down the schedule with his forefinger. It was a precise itinerary. All clothing had to be inspected by Forensics again, with special emphasis on blood staining. Smith and Wesson and ammunition meticulously examined. Daryl Crocker hauled in for further interrogation. Contact made with cops in the UK to get a full report on the death of George Rundle.

'How about David Copperfield giving a hand? Clayman needs a magician to get him off this.' Chuck cynically added. 'Get it rolling after that lunch you promised.' Chuck was at the door. Jacket gripped in his right hand. 'It's the only thing I can stomach right now.'

Neither detective had an interest in the crimes committed that week, or the unsolved ones that gathered dust on their desks.

Trainter's fax came first. Confidential, a personal view. Daryl Crocker was able to get in to the office the following Monday. Heading to town for a property auction. He'd look in then. Hoped it wouldn't take long. Forensic notified the *officers concerned* that all rigorous tests had been concluded on the clothing and the firearm and a report was on its way. Ms Lesley Rawlins was available to explain and expand on their findings.

Dick waited until it was all there. No mistakes. A holistic approach. Forget the loose ends. He wasn't going to invite any further doubt.

'We'll go through this together. Sieve it between us. I'm not seeing Richards without us having agreed on this.' Dick instructed his junior. 'Open mind. Know it's difficult but they're baying for blood and I don't intend to be the quarry again.' Adamant about it. 'Crocker this afternoon at two and then this lot.' Dick waved his hands over the papers in front of him.

Chuck nodded. However half-hearted he felt he owed it to his boss to obey this request.

'What's new?' Daryl Crocker sidled in, slammed down in a revolving chair. Sent it spinning momentarily. You couldn't control momentum like that. Comically he faced the opposing wall by the time he had completed his greeting. 'Thought you guys had wrapped this all up.' Kicking himself back in position. 'How's it I can help again? Thought I'd told you officers the matter of it already.'

'Mr. Crocker, Daryl, good to see you. Thanks for coming in. Won't take up too much of your time.' Plastic pleasantries. Dick sat behind his desk. Official business now. Nothing disputable.

'You were good enough to tell us about the purchase of the Smith and Wesson revolver.' Chuck wandered past Daryl, file open, as if reading a sermon.

'Yeah?' Quizzing gaze from Daryl. Eyes following Chuck moving across the office.

'And you added at the time that our suspect was accompanied by a woman.' Chuck reminded him.

'True. Was some lady with him. Quiet type. Interested in

the weapons.'

'How interested?' Dick was drawn in.

Daryl shrugged his shoulders. 'Surveying 'em like. You know how women are. Just like they're shopping for panties.'

'Panties?' Dick recoiled. 'Buying a gun is the same as a purchase from the lingerie shop? You sure about that?'

'Know what I mean. Intense like. Sweeping eyes. Not looking up. Want to choose quick so men about don't look. Don't imagine them wearing them. It's a woman's thing.' Daryl wished he hadn't used that analogy.

'This her?' Chuck dangled a languid photograph of Sarah in Daryl's face. It was an enlargement of her passport picture. The only one the department had. An embarrassment.

Daryl held it out. Attempting to find focus. Screwing up his eyes and jutting his chin. His teeth showed on one side of his face. 'Difficult to be hundred percent, it being so grained. Near enough though. Reckon that were the lady.'

'She speak. He say her name or anything?' Chuck needed one hundred and one percent.

Daryl handed the photograph back with one last glance at the sullen maiden. 'Can't say she did or didn't. Can't say he did or didn't. Long way back ain't it? Might have done, but I can't remember. No, mind ain't that sharp.'

Blunt as my police stick, thought Dick. 'If we were to have her here. Lined up with some others; similar types. Hair, height, build 'bout the same. Pick her out d'yer think?'

'Yeah. Do that, officer, no problem there.' Daryl's bravado built on unstable ground. A gesture to recoup some prestige.

'Be in touch, Mr. Crocker.' Dick offered a hand. 'Thanks for your help,' uttered as a goodbye. *Thanks a fucking lot* written on his face.

Dick turned from the door. 'About as helpful as spit in a drought, Chuck. No progress so far.'

'Expecting it?' Chuck grinned knowingly. 'Dead end this one. Told you all along.'

Dick glared.

'Okay, okay. I'm treating it serious, Lieutenant. Can't help the voice in here.' Chuck tapped his temple. 'Like a recording. *Bobby Clayman did it.* Telling me all the time.'

'This will disarm the executioner in your head, Chuck.' Dick pulled copies of Trainter's fax. 'Read bits just to see its worth. Makes better reading than the prattle of that doughnut.' Dick pointed in the direction Daryl Crocker had disappeared.

The office fell silent as the two men pored over the three-page facsimile that had arrived from Dorset, England.

George Rundle was a fine officer, a loving and faithful husband... Trainter rambled at first, outlining George's career in the force ...*tragic death at the cliff in Lyme Regis...* Newspaper stuff that Chuck skated over ...*manpower shortage in the Force...difficult times...perhaps not enough pressure from us at the time...* Excuses. Saving his arse ...*however, the coroner's verdict I am uncomfortable with. Without criticising his findings I am concerned about some aspects of George's death. Confidentially, which I trust you will respect, I am unhappy that a man of his experience would be close to a notoriously dangerous cliff edge, would be out in appalling weather conditions at that time of night and I find no reason for believing he would deliberately throw himself off that cliff.*

I understand he had taken on a crusade that centred on a man, incarcerated in your neck of the woods, that he believed, based on an old case he was assigned to here, was unjustly imprisoned and accused of a heinous crime... Trainter was meandering a bit. Chuck and Dick were getting edgy ...*a suspect living here was being observed. Unofficially, of course. It would appear that Rundle was most likely to have been staking out his suspect who lived quite near to this location. I must urge further caution with my gut feeling that I now divulge...* Trainter exorcising a ghost. Purging himself of a deep guilt...*it would have been very easy, given the conditions, for a person of George's age to have been assisted off that precipice. Violence could have been done to this man. I haven't got a suspicious death on my files, but I have got that on my conscience.*

I wish you luck in your enquiries, and should your findings throw some light on the demise of a valiant ex-policeman I would appreciate your assistance in bringing this to the attention of authorities in this country.

Should you require any further details or help with this matter do not hesitate to call me at the number shown.

John Trainter had concluded with his name, rank and the CBE he had just received, but not yet collected.

'Poor bastard. Liked that little fella.' Chuck muttered as he laid down the paper. 'Don't mean a thing though.' He was quick to repair any damage to his credibility. 'Could have been anything, anyone.'

'But, ties in with what he came here for. Remember him trying to reason with us. Plausible man. No fool. Reasonable motive and one hell of a journey just to state his case. And this guy's fax backs up what Steve Reynolds was barking on about in here.' Dick Kaltenbach felt the sand shifting under his feet and rawness in his stomach. 'Told you this weren't buried, Chuck. Can of worms if I ain't mistaken.'

'Me, I've got my scales out. And so far Bobby Clayman's tray is full of rocks and this guy has only placed a feather on the other tray. Hasn't moved an inch. Stuck down there. Weighted down. And I don't see someone delivering a pile of stones to displace the evidence we got. No, sir, they're just scratching the surface on this. Maybe they'll disturb some soil but they ain't about to walk in with the boulders our prime suspect needs to overturn what we've got.' Chuck displayed a self-satisfied visage. Immovable. Undaunted.

'What if forensic come up with some contradictory evidence, Chuck? What if they point us in a new direction? You goin't' stay entrenched, or you able to pluck yourself out of those concrete boots.' Dick was melting. Uneasy now.

'We agreed we had him, didn't we? Can't see much that's changed that. Am I missing something?' Chuck pleaded.

'Not saying it ain't him, am I? Just got to be open-minded. Can't shut off. Probing and digging to the last. Okay?' Dick caught a nod of approval from his diffident partner. 'That dyke Rawlins from Forensics will be here in an hour. We'll know after her report.'

Dick was re-examining the Trainter fax and Chuck was typing up Daryl's spiel when Lesley Rawlins entered. She strode in as if she was not intending to stop. Going straight through the office. That was the nature of her stride. Brakes went on in the centre of the floor space. She twisted around to face the detectives.

'Got it all here,' Lesley Rawlins announced. Tipping up her head with exaggerated aloofness. A purposeful woman dressed in a grey suit that fitted tightly at her heavy hips and buttoned under huge breasts. Flat shoes reminiscent of Chuck's Dr. Marten's and thick tights accentuating muscular calves. Little make-up and hair scragged back. 'Some interesting work in this investigation. Hope you are ready for some intriguing results.' The hint of a smile as she dropped into an empty chair.

Like waiting for exam results at school. Dick and Chuck watched Lesley open the beige folder. Squinting to see if they could identify some of the content.

There were inner files. Separate enquiries. Lesley withdrew a slim one.

'Firearms discharge residue, FDR, has been inconclusive.' Lesley stopped to clear her throat. She needed to throw away the less convincing forensic evidence. 'We found all the necessary deposits of lead, barium and antimony on the clothes.'

'Whose clothes?' Chuck enquired. Hoping to promote his cause.

'Both sets.' Lesley stabbed back. 'Both Clayman's and the nanny's clothes were covered, to varying degrees.'

Chuck settled back down.

'Contamination occurs. FDR finds its way onto many surfaces and objects. Clothes can come into contact with these. Not only the firer of the gun picks up these traces. The victim gets more than their fair share, especially at close range.' Some horrific bullet wounds that Lesley had studied first hand came to mind as she spoke. Disfigured corpses that had *eaten* shotguns to cure depression. Skulls in fragments.

'Clayman uses firearms almost daily in his job and the nanny was touching everything in the house. No swabs were taken at the time. There's no value in pursuing that line.' Lesley wanted to move on to more lucrative areas. And Chuck and Dick were keen to duck less than meticulous measures at the crime scene.

Lesley pulled out a thicker folder. Bulging with neatly separated papers. Now she could show them.

'Blood.' A smile on her lips as the word almost dripped from her mouth. 'Blood. A family's blood. All bled save the girl. Shot. Close range. It helps.' Matter of fact. Staccato voice. 'Background splatter as well as blood spots of significant players. All makes a pattern. A complete pattern. Neatly in place. Jigsaw. Nothing better than a complete jigsaw. The whole picture. It's the only way. Get incensed if I get to the end and there's a piece missing. I like a puzzle, but only if I solve it. When that solitary shitty piece has been gobbled by the vacuum cleaner or driven down the side of an armchair, I erupt. Can't abide disorder or discord. Parcelled up; organised and packaged. That's the way.'

'Is that what we've got Ms Rawlins?' Dick nervously quizzed.

'Lesley's the name. No need to offer some counterfeit politeness. Not one of your dumb blondes.' Lesley Rawlins had her own campaign. 'And yes, you have got just that neat package. No mean achievement by the department, I can assure you.'

'Okay ma'am. Perhaps we can get going.' Chuck wasn't taken with the hostile woman.

'As I was saying.' Even more severity. 'Blood distribution patterns is my, our, speciality. And you are most fortunate to be one of the first teams to benefit from new research in this field. Fantastic opportunities.'

'Can we get the results, Lesley?' Dick cringed. Her name seemed to scrape across his tongue.

'Just getting there. Patience please. These are detailed investigations. We don't have the luxury of a smoking gun you know.' Lesley held up a sheet that seemed to resemble a piece of the Turin Shroud or an enlargement of a bludgeoned amoeba. 'This is a single blood spot, taken from Bobby Clayman's trousers. There were others. Finer ones on his shirt cuffs and even his socks. Stella Roberts' blood. Notice the shape of the bloodstain. Not concentric. All the stains reflect the same pattern. Dimension and shape differ within an acceptable range. You can detect a globe at the north of the stain as well as the heavy spreading to the south. A halo has formed around the globular shape.'

Dick and Chuck leaned forward in their seats, trying to make out the detail that Lesley Rawlins was explaining. Screwing up their eyes and stretching their necks.

'So, what can we gather from this? I'm afraid I see a tie-dye tee shirt and not much else.' Dick admitted.

'What you see is a bloodstain caused by a spattering of viscous blood hitting the material at an angle of fifty-eight degrees from the horizontal. Rising from the floor. Most likely from treading in a shallow pool of thickening fluid. Thrown up by the foot.' Lesley's eyes opened wide, examining the faces of the two detectives. A perky smile starting at the corner of her mouth.

'And the others?' Dick urgently enquired.

'As I said, all very similar.'

Chuck was puzzled. He hadn't read the significance yet.

Lesley Rawlins held out a further sample. The white rabbit plucked from the conjuror's tophat. A delicious smile of satisfaction. Both detectives found it not dissimilar to the first. Another squashed invertebrate. Another religious relic.

'This one?' Dick asked feebly, the significance dawning.

'No well-formed globe. Usually obliterated by the sinking blood. Congealing together. Becoming as one. All evidence of that first projectile buried beneath the soaking liquor. Longer, trailing bloodstains caused by thinner, liquid blood spurting at speed, fresh from a new wound. Downward or at least level. The result of the material being hit most probably at the time of the infliction of the injury.'

'Murderer's? Got him. You're saying this stain was most likely formed at the time of the shooting? A stain suffered by the killer at the time of his crime?' Chuck was getting excited.

'Yes.' Lesley confirmed.

'See. Told you.' Chuck turned to Dick, beaming.

'Not so neat is it Lesley?' Dick breathed out heavily. 'Not so neat at all.'

'What d'yer mean?' Chuck was baffled by the reaction.

'Tell him.' Dick ordered.

'This stain was one we examined on the skirt. The nanny's skirt. Not Bobby Clayman's clothing.' Satisfaction clearly intoned.

'You telling me this isn't a stain on Bobby Clayman's clothes. It's blood from the nanny's skirt?' Chuck sank along with his voice. Disappearing into his chair, clutching just a whisper. 'Shit.'

A hollow room now. Presided over by the gloating moon face of Lesley Rawlins. 'And there's more.' She was loving this.

'More?' Dick exasperated. 'You've just shot us in the kneecaps and now you've got the gun at our heads, ma'am.'

'Afraid so.' Lesley pulled a further file from the stack.

Chuck moaned from his seat and shuffled round. Dick sighed and sat ready.

'Been looking at the photographs taken at the time. Interesting interiors in that kitchen.' Lesley pulled out the snaps as if they were of her and her partner at their summer retreat in Maine. 'Look.'

Both men edged back to where Lesley had laid them out on the desk. About twelve pictures of the Amana fridge.

'Got one.' Chuck mumbled. 'Look like adverts for the damn appliance to me.' He was still sore.

'Well?' Lesley knew they were oblivious to the importance. 'Any ideas?'

Dick shrugged his shoulders and shook his head.

'If you look closely at the enlargements; the ones at that end, Officer Nolan.' Lesley waved a hand to encourage him to study them in detail.

Dick moved alongside and strained his eyes, the same as his partner.

'Can you observe the shape made out by the ring of perimeter blood spots?' Lesley guided. Her finger tracing along some invisible line around the door of the fridge.

'Where?' Dick screwed up his eyes again and pulled away from the photo. Reading glasses would be one of his next buys.

Lesley pointed again. 'It silhouettes the outline of the killer in my opinion. Not every contour, but enough to determine height and build, and possibly clothing. We have studied these boundary stains for several days and run some intriguing tests. Drawn some uncomfortable conclusions for you two I'm afraid.' Lesley displayed something approaching pity. 'A good nine inches shorter than Bobby Clayman and ...' Lesley paused to swallow an inappropriate laugh. '...and wearing a dress or skirt.'

'How'd you know that?' Chuck was quick to put a stop to the rot.

'Pattern of the blood spattering. Level border to the stains at around two feet from floor height. You get more of a letter A shape when the perpetrator's wearing pants. And if you take this dress.' Lesley held out a photograph of Sarah's dress laid flat on a laboratory bench. 'You'll find that allowing for body fill and creasing you can come up with a near perfect match by putting a digital map of the blood spots here with those here.' She lifted the photo of the fridge door.' Lesley looked at the glum faces. 'Well that's what my computer tells me, and that's what the computer at MIT confirms. We aren't going alone with this. I am not shoving unsubstantiated shit your way. This has been a thorough job by our department supported by some very well qualified institutions.' Lesley gathered up the photographs as she spoke.

Only resigned faces. Defeated, limp body movements slumped in their chairs.

'And, sorry I forgot this bit. As if you needed it.' Lesley looked at her victims. 'Blood viscosity levels demonstrate emphatically that Bobby Clayman was only stained by old, thickening, darkened blood. Blood that had been out of a body for hours, that he had slapped up with his heavy steps through the house. He was never splattered from the raw wounds of his prey.' She knew the damage she had done. A grain of pity. 'I suppose I've stirred this lot up for you two. Not deliberate. No hard feelings I hope.' Lesley Rawlins gathered up all her papers without straightening them. A fan of sheets clutched for a brisk escape. Leaving Chuck and Dick to lick their wounds.

Chapter 27

'If either of the bastards gloats I'll explode.' Chuck cleared the desks and pushed up enough chairs.

'Wouldn't you? Not many police officers caught in the middle. Having both prosecution and defence lawyers squashing them in. Bound to be self-satisfied aren't they. Going to be revelling in it without a doubt.' Dick was nearer surrender.

'Yeah. But you know how we'd packaged this one up. Never known a case that fitted together so sweetly. Couldn't see any problems. No loose ends. Tight and secure.' Almost a whimper. Chuck was finding it hard to give in.

'Steve Reynolds and Mark will be here in about ten, so let's not give them the pleasure of seeing us on our knees. Professionals, that's what we are, Chuck, fucking professionals. So we are going to behave like fucking professionals. Got it?' Dick thumped his desk so that his pen jar rattled. Last remnants of frustration hammered shut.

'How we handling this?' Chuck was showing some interest again.

'In what way?' Dick quizzed.

'Well, we going along with whatever they suggest, nice and cosy like. Tame monkeys catching bananas for the crowd.'

'There's no way we can prevent Steve from getting Clayman released.'

'And the charges?' Chuck was finding some rhythm.

'We'll be asked. And we'll drop 'em.' Dick snapped concisely.

'Leave nothing on the books? Wipe it all out?'

'Yeah.' Dick sighed.

'I'd like to keep a hold on him, somehow. Just to keep him

in the corral if we draw blanks elsewhere. What if our investigations turn nothing up? What if it's all fucked up over there? Can't get her extradited? If it falls flat, dragging, no conclusion? We got to crucify someone. Folks round here need a hanging. Someone to vent their anger at. A public execution so to speak. Does 'em good.' Chuck couldn't let go, even if was just his fingertips clutching at crumbling remains.

'Bobby Clayman goes free. There's no doubt. I ain't risking any more holding on. Whether it's threats from Steve Reynolds about his client's civil rights or Mark Richards whingeing on about the financial consequences to the department. It's a fresh investigation, Chuck. Forget Mr. Clayman. Forget how guilty he was. 'Cos he ain't now. No, sir. We've got us a transatlantic case to start inquiring into. A clean sheet that we aren't going to soil this time.' Dick was getting the energy for it now.

'Am I intruding?' Mark Richards held onto the doorjamb, beaming.

'No. Come in.' Dick responded with his own version of a smile.

Steve Reynolds followed Mark into the office. No sign of satisfaction. Matter of fact and ready to roll. Both lawyers sat together. For once sharing the same campaign. Fighting under the same flag.

Once the leather briefcases had been opened and files laid down they looked at each other, tight-lipped and expectant eyes.

Dick broke in. 'You both seen the papers I sent? Obviously.' Rhetorical. 'Can't say it pleases me...us...to have to admit some mistakes here. Isn't easy, as you can guess to know we've been barking up the wrong tree.'

'Barking? Officer Nolan here has been howling to the moon. Never seen a man who was so sure he'd backed the favourite horse.' Steve Reynolds was stabbing back. He'd spent too long trying to convince Chuck Nolan to let him off too lightly.

'Okay. Recriminations over? I haven't asked you here for a

celebration. We don't have the stomach for a party and there's a crime to be solved. Let's not forget the gravity of this matter. Two kids slain along with their parents. Mustn't lose sight of that. This is serious business and I mean to reach the bottom of it.' Dick was blowing away the ashes of his sense of humour. Guarding his back. He knew the shit that could be flying. 'Mark, next move with regards to Clayman?'

'We go back to Judge Bernstein. But, do we go for a quick not guilty verdict with no evidence offered or are you of the mind to withdraw the charges. Either way we're open to wrongful arrest and all the other crap that Steve here wants to throw our way.' Mark's quizzing eyes invited suggestions.

'I know Chuck'll want to keep Bobby Clayman in the wings. Don't want to put your eggs in one basket. If we don't get ourselves a bird to skin from across there in the UK, he'll want to cook some home-grown meat. Hedging your bets, that's the phrase I believe.' Dick nearly stumbled on his metaphors. 'So I reckon we'll not go ahead with no prosecution at this time, don't want to jeopardise our chance in the future.'

'So I can tell Bobby he's a free man?' Steve enquired.

'As free as he'll ever be, 'til we round up our killer.' Chuck's voice sour and embittered.

'Want you to apologise to the man. To Bobby Clayman. The department ain't getting a lot of pleasure from persecuting the wrong man. Say it's a personal apology from me.' Dick looked across at his colleague. 'And from Officer Nolan.'

Chuck's eyebrows rose and his eyes sharpened. Dagger sharp.

'Decent of you Dick.' Steve Reynolds was taken aback. 'You sure of that?'

'And you bring him along to see me in the next few days. Up here.'

Steve smelled a rat. 'Why is that?'

'Tell him myself, and other matters.'

'What matters?' It was a putrid rat and the stench freely emitting.

'It's a new investigation, Steve, got to ask more questions. Need answers. He's the only witness. Was there when our prime suspect was still at the scene of the crime. An important guy is Bobby Clayman. Crucial to this case. In fact I've got a proposal for him. Could help us out in a big way. Might like to throw some stones himself.' Dick wasn't giving too much away.

'Important guy? Throwing stones? What you up to, Kaltenbach?' Steve was deeply suspicious.

'If it is as we have been led to believe and Sarah Bickles, the nanny, perpetrated this crime...' Dick displayed a stone expression. '...then it was she who left the murder weapon in Bobby Clayman's truck. It was most likely her that planted the doll. She led us to him. She stitched this guy up and was happy to see him go down for it.'

All three onlookers nodded agreement but didn't speak. They watched for Dick's mouth to continue.

'Surely Bobby would welcome the chance to see justice done. Not exactly revenge but a close enough relative.'

'What you got in mind?' Steve needed something concrete.

'Edgy aren't we. No tricks. Bobby Clayman is going to be giving evidence more than likely. I need to take a new statement. What we've got now we ain't about to use. You can understand that, can't you Steve?' Dick patted Steve Reynolds' back. A fatherly gesture. 'If there's nothing else, Steve, I'll start disassembling what we were lining up and clear the decks for this fresh investigation.'

Steve and Mark rose, stuffed away folders and pocketed pens. Chuck stretched and waited to see the lawyers off.

'Don't need me any more do you Dick?' Mark adjusted his tie and smoothed creases from his trousers. 'I'll shoot off with Steve. Let me know what you have in mind. Need to plan out the future of this case.'

Dick caught hold of Mark's sleeve as he followed Steve Reynolds out the door. 'Just some advice on procedure, Mark, if you could spare a minute. See you soon, Steve.' Dick stood between them. His way of separating the two men.

'Procedure?' Mark Richards screwed up his face. Curious and baffled. 'What's this all about?'

'Didn't want to spill the beans right away. Not too sure of the ground being secure enough.' Dick was mumbling.

'Come on. What is it?'

'I've spoken to an Inspector Trainter. Cop in the UK. Trying to get more information on this woman. Making some enquiries myself. Ground work before we get this rolling.' Dick was clarifying.

'First I've heard.' Chuck sounded put out by the Lieutenant's gumption. 'Partners aren't we?'

'You weren't in the mood for it. Left you to fizzle a bit, before you would be any use pursuing someone else for what you've always thought of as Bobby Clayman's crime.' Near enough to an apology.

'Understandable.' Mark agreed.

'Suppose so.' Chuck wasn't so convinced.

'Well, this Trainter guy is quite happy for us to go over there and try and talk to Sarah Bickles.' Dick put an arm round Chuck's shoulder to show his inclusion. 'No promises on more than that. We need an extradition order to go further, and there ain't a lot of chance of that without a leakproof case. We need to work fast. Too much time been wasted already.' Dick gave a knowing but gentle squeeze to his partner's bicep.

'No problem from the Department as far as I can see, Dick.' Mark assured. 'As long as all the formalities are dealt with.'

'Haven't been totally open with this yet, Mark.' Dick looked at his shoes. 'There's one more thing we should look at.'

'Thought it was too good to be true. What you got up your sleeve, Kaltenbach? You shyster.'

'Ghosts.' Dick clipped.

'Ghosts?' Mark and Chuck in unison.

'Yes, ghosts. Person that's hiding something like this. Knowing that they've perpetrated a terrible crime. They're watching their backs and clutching a rabbit's foot. Because the one thing that's still following them and slicing them down the spine is their conscience. Phantoms creeping into their dreams, and their waking hours as well. Not ever leaving them. Spirits that are knocking on their skulls at all times. Never going to let them forget. Never allowing them any freedom. It's a prison or an asylum. Held there by these ghouls that remind them every day of their dreadful deed.' Dick licked away saliva that sat on his lips.

'Easy, Dick.' Chuck was concerned.

'Yes?' Mark more mundane. Oblivious to the near rantings.

'We have the ghost. And if anything is going to ambush our killer it's that walking spectre. Sarah Bickles has her ghost firmly in the cupboard with the skeleton. Neatly housed in a mental institution awaiting trial for this crime. Nothing going to blow every fuse like seeing this apparition standing before her. She'll surely scream a confession just to purge this demon.'

'What you getting at Dick?' Mark was confused.

'We take Bobby with us.' Dick rested there. Waiting for a reaction.

'Take him with us? To where? Over there to England?' Chuck's eyes protruded as he tried to grasp the notion.

'You want to take Bobby Clayman over to the UK and confront the nanny? That's crazy.' Mark's head quivered. 'Excuse me, Ms Bickles, can I introduce the man you tried to have lynched for the gruesome murders you committed. Come off it, Dick. Can just picture it.'

'Nothing crazy about it. If you've framed someone. Seen them disintegrate and incarcerated. Felt safe. Left the guilt nailed to this wreck. You'd be blown apart if he arrived, preferably on a misty night, on your doorstep. Think about it. Sure I've seen a film with this scene in.'

'It's crazy.' Chuck was mortified.

'Look, Chuck, we deal with two matters at once. You still have Bobby Clayman in your gun sights. We take him with us and keep an eye on him. Watch his reactions when he sees the nanny. Perhaps, if we've been right all along, we get front seats at confession time. Make or break at the rendezvous. What d'you say?'

A shrug of the shoulders. White flag. It was as near to defeat that Chuck would offer.

Bobby Clayman remembered the office. Remembered too well the men who manned it.

'Mr. Clayman, Bobby.' Dick tried both labels to find which one he felt better with. 'Good of you to come in.'

'You summoned the man, Dick.' Steve Reynolds was uncomfortable. Justifiably wary of an ambush.

Bobby walked gingerly around the furniture, touching pieces as he went, as if to detect the chair he had hurled those months before. A symbol of his descent into madness. He chose one to stand behind. Fingering its coarse fabric.

Chuck trailed him with his eyes. All predator. He was unhappy that he handled the chair. A weapon. As before. He'd keep a tight rein on Bobby Clayman. He wished Dick had allowed him to keep his shoulder holster on. *Make him feel at ease. No unnerving the guy. We're on the same side now.* Chuck couldn't help what his guts were telling him.

'You're kidding!' Steve fell back into his chair with an audible thump. 'Take Bobby over there? Why on earth?'

Bobby circumnavigated his seat and sat like a boy at his grandmother's for tea. Knees up and elbows in. They were talking about him.

Dick was putting his cards down. The whole pack. 'Can't force him.'

'Good. He won't go.' Steve was adamant.

'Might not make sense at the moment, but give it some time.' Dick knew his strategy well. 'Bobby will benefit. You wait and see.'

'You just want the man to point his finger and scare the shit out of the woman. That's your plan. Shock tactics. A walk-on monster to frighten the socks off her.'

'Can't say that's not part of the scheme, but it's more than just that. If we can nail her quick, and squeeze a confession out of the bitch, Bobby here, is well and truly over the canyon. Safe ground.' Dick explained.

'And what does that mean?' Steve quizzed.

'If we don't have any success in England, and we come back empty handed, you can bet folks round here are goin't' harbour some real doubts about this Bobby Clayman fella.' Dick swung round to focus on Chuck and Bobby. 'If we ain't removed this blemish the stain's goin't' be indelible.'

'Yeah.' Chuck's only offering.

'But if we succeed, and the nanny returns bleating, it'll be a hero's welcome for Mr. Clayman. A wronged man. A courageous son of America. The opportunities endless.' Dick was creaming it. Even Chuck cringed.

Steve Reynolds swung round to face his client. 'Well, Bobby? What do you make of this?'

'Not sure.' Indecision, but a confident voice.

Chuck and Dick exchanged glances. Surprised by the rehabilitation of the man.

'I think it's dangerous, and I'm against you being used as bait. Lieutenant Kaltenbach argues that there are benefits. I find them difficult to weigh against the harm that could come of such an exploit. We can see you're stable now. There's no good reason to risk that and push you back over the edge.' Steve would let Bobby decide.

Bobby already had. An appearance of confusion, but deep-seated and vividly etched, a desire to face Sarah Bickles. Was he the only one who could recall the mischievous, giggling children? The only person to imagine Lucy Marie and little Tommy slaughtered by that woman. Bobby Clayman still smelled the blood that ran from the cupboard where Tommy's body lay slumped across the brooms and mops. Still saw the plastic mask and black lips of Lucy Marie as she was fished from the lake.

'Well?' Steve broke Bobby's reverie.

'I'll go.'

Chapter 28

'You'll need to be firm with this one.' Margaret Moncton chuckled as she watched her three year old swagger past with an armful of dolls and a battered pushchair. 'Grace,' she announced.

Sarah watched the waddling curves of Grace's chubby legs and the swing of the crisp cotton pleats of her dress. The faintest whiff of talcum powder and the padding of slippered feet. It was the part she couldn't resist. It would be better this time. Wouldn't happen again. A smile at the corner of her mouth. Nothing to go wrong with such a gorgeous child.

'There are two others. Lilly, the oldest, and the baby of course, Laurel.' Margaret added.

Two more? Three of them? Sarah hadn't handled that many before.

'Come through. Take a seat. Good journey?' Margaret showed the latest applicant for the job into the large sitting room that she was still persuading her husband, Richard, to call the drawing room. A dowdy woman of indeterminate age who had answered the advertisement in the local paper.

'Not bad.' Sarah replied in a croaky voice. She didn't talk much these days. Didn't even speak to Debbie when their paths crossed in the house. Grunts from bowed heads. Born of fear and mistrust.

'I've taken the liberty to write it all down. It saves me going through it all every time.' Margaret handed the drab woman an A4 sheet. 'Duties, hours, pay etc. It's all there.' She encouraged Sarah to read with a wave of her hand.

Hours, routine, accommodation, appointments, food allergies, bedtimes, contact numbers and salary. Sarah skated through it. There were some long words that she couldn't read and some she wouldn't read.

Margaret Moncton watched this latest applicant pore over the job description and allied information. This one was older. Something she favoured. She'd experienced two young nannies and it hadn't worked out. Her husband, Jack, preferred to have girls in the house. Nothing dubious, but Margaret thought it better to keep the scenery sterile. A serious woman who had been working abroad, poor dress sense and awful hair. But you didn't judge a nanny by those yardsticks. Perhaps a dour and uncomplicated woman would be best for the girls.

'Yes.' Sarah announced with a nod of the head. Enough reading done.

'You've handled children of this age before?' Margaret felt awkward questioning, and didn't really know the sort of thing to ask. Certainly not about the untimely deaths of Sarah's previous charges. Hopefully well hidden from her prospective employer.

'Yes.' Dorset twang pronounced in this response. 'Handled them all.' Sarah fought to dislodge a disturbing image of Lucy Marie's ballooning anorak and her white face disappearing in the icy water. 'Yes. No problem.' She kept talking until the mirage had gone. Sarah Bickles could deal with them all right.

'References?' Margaret bumbled. 'You haven't included them.' Margaret stuffed her hand into the unnecessarily large, brown envelope that contained Sarah's letter of application.

'Yes, see, being overseas and that. You can try if I gives you the details.' Almost convincing.

'I see.' Margaret wasn't happy. Then again, what would a woman of this age be hiding? Nothing serious.

More struggling questions regarding health concerns, bedtime stories and bath time preferences. A clumsy pause where Margaret Moncton read through Sarah's brief letter yet again and studied her own A4 details, and Sarah, head lolling. Resembling a retarded person.

'I'll be in touch. Thanks for coming.' It was no good, she couldn't think of anything else. But she would of course have numerous things to ask once the woman had gone.

'Right.' Sarah picked up her coat and handbag and wandered to the door. 'Right, you'll be in touch, then?' It was easier to repeat what others said than arrange words herself.

Debbie scooped up Vicky when she heard the key scratching at the lock. A well rehearsed manoeuvre. They had been playing downstairs in a communal or no-go area of the miserable house. Almost a kindergarten feel with the toys and crayons, bright colours and nursery rhyme tapes. She would clear these up when the coast was clear, and her demented sister was safely holed up in her room. For now she would rock Vicky gently on the bed. Both listening to the movements in the house. Tracing Sarah's journey out there, beyond their barricade.

Roy hadn't come up with any money and Debbie was sharing the prison with her crazy sister. She'd tried at the council offices, but there weren't any flats. Huge waiting list. But the apartheid was intolerable. She had to get out somehow. Failing that, her sister leaving would be the next best thing. And there was some encouraging evidence that the harpy was considering fleeing the nest.

It wasn't so stupid. Checking her sister's room now and again. You never knew. Never knew whether there was anything to do with the family slaughtered in America, or the policeman falling from the cliff. Never knew if her sister had something planned for her and Vicky. In the room there would be a clue. Weapon or something. Best to keep guard. Be alert.

They were on the floor. Magazines. Ones that advertised jobs in big houses and for rich families. Newspapers opened at the advertisements for housekeepers and to look after children. Underlined in pencil. A scruffy mark. Living-in jobs. Taking her away.

It wasn't easy wishing her to go. Sending her to blight some other poor souls. Maybe suffering at the hands of a person who could well be a psychotic killer for all she knew. Allowing it. Not attempting to alert anyone. Selfish but necessary. Sarah scared her rigid. It was for Vicky's sake.

Sarah had her own needs. Needed to escape again. The skeletons were rattling. Too much time to replay it. It hadn't been really necessary. She'd been driven to it. Not her way at all. Time to start with a clean sheet. Family that appreciated her. No more than that. That would dislodge the demons and dispel the ghosts.

Chapter 29

Recovering had been a slow and methodical process for Bobby Clayman. Walking pigeon step. No extravagant moves. Safe distances and ample time approaching corners. Wingate Freeman had plotted the course and calculated the pace. Bobby had a swaying rope bridge to cross, over a yawning crevasse. At times it felt like walking the plank. But it worked.

So packing his suitcase for the trip to England was another task that had to be approached with the same dedication and precision. Nothing elaborate. Accurate planning. Spread across his bed were the items deemed necessary. Frugal possessions. He would only take those essential to the trip and these he had mentally catalogued. Most from his new wardrobe, post hospital. A few strategic items intact; remnants from boisterous days and old habits. Pride in his placement and arrangement. Almost feminine.

Contrasting greatly with the packing habits of Chuck Nolan, who threw unpressed items from long range, devoid of procedure or ceremony. Then he'd be pleased to hear his method so described. Manly trait to be sure. Quantity rather than quality was his motto. A toilet bag full of foul deodorants and colognes, toothbrush with bristles like a yard broom, toothpaste tube rolled at the end like stored turf and a collection of blunt razors.

Yet, from the outside, as they stood by their luggage at the American Airlines desk, there was little evidence of the conflicting techniques. Unless you were observant enough to detect the small protrusion of candy-striped boxer shorts caught in the hinge of Chuck's wheeled baggage.

They didn't speak. Bobby to avoid complications, and Chuck still dragging around his own ball and chain. Dick

Kaltenbach, when he arrived, would negotiate an understanding between the two men.

'Sorry I'm late.' Dick spoke to both of them. A blanket apology. 'Been on to Trainter. Last minute stuff. You carrying your piece, Chuck?'

'Yeah.'

'Leave it at security. We ain't going to get them in. Not worth the hassle trying to change minds over there.'

'Feel naked without it. Specially on police business.' Chuck hauled out his shoulder holster, swaying heavy with the weight of the revolver. 'You sure we ain't goin't find ourselves needing these?'

'Come on, Chuck. Just a woman we're looking to question.' Dick mocked.

'Yeah, but if she's the one that did the killing who knows what she's cooking up for us.' Chuck glanced at Bobby out of the corner of his eye. Checking the reaction.

Bobby didn't flinch. Focussed. Uncomplicated. He hadn't the stomach or intention to join in the banter.

London, Heathrow. An ants' nest of scrambling travellers. Bobby kept close to Dick. In the absence of Steve Reynolds this was the nearest to a stabilising presence. Chuck Nolan was distant, quietly threatening. Unsettling. Bobby craved order and guidance.

Trainter dressed in his ceremonial uniform. Meeting an important delegation from the United States. It would be treated as an exchange of information. An invitation kindly extended from the Dorset Police to a similarly regional force from the State of New Hampshire, New England. Trainter hadn't publicised his fax to Dick Kaltenbach or approached the subject of a joint investigation to be conducted alongside American colleagues. In particular there was no formal recognition of the presence of Bobby Clayman, previously the prime suspect for a heartless slaying of a whole family.

One last inspection of the blade-sharp creases in his trousers and a gentle polish of his beaming toecaps. A manufactured smile that he held on to until the visitors had left the taxi and were in the hotel lobby.

'Welcome.' Trainter offered a plastic hand. 'Lieutenant Kaltenbach, I presume.' Could have been Stanley greeting Livingstone in the heart of Africa.

'Good to be here.' Dick Kaltenbach stretched to reach it. Like shaking soggy Dover sole.

Chuck followed suit. 'Chuck Nolan. Good to meet you.'

Bobby, like the shy son in a family group, waited for a nod from Dick before giving up his hand to the grinning policeman. He didn't announce his name. Trainter's sinking jaw was enough to realise he'd been recognised.

'Good journey?' More pleasantries as Inspector Trainter tagged along to reception. 'Modest lodge. Not much to offer in these parts. Tourist accommodation. Don't cater for business people and professionals. Comfortable. That's the British terminology.' Trainter was apologetic to an embarrassing degree. The hotel was tired. Like every dingy hotel stepping down to the sea in any coastal resort it satisfied a clientele escaping from inner city dereliction. That was about it. Basic rooms filled with second-hand furniture and dreary drapes. A basin stuck on the wall in the bedroom and a brown-stained bath next to the badly-flushing WC in a draughty bathroom. 'En suite facilities in every room.' Trainter continued.

'The flight was good. Food was a puzzle. Some lasagne that resembled modelling clay. In consistency and taste,' Dick joked. 'Taxi ride a little nerve racking. Your roads. Narrower than my drive at home. And some idiot drivers. They training Formula One protegés round here?' Dick's referral to the boy racers they encountered down some of the Dorset lanes.

'Wrong side of the highway. You Brits have got to get with the rest of Europe. It's a crazy feeling seeing traffic charging down a sidewalk-sized street, opposite direction,' Chuck added.

Bobby said nothing. He surveyed the houses he could make out from the windows in the lobby and imagined the one that Sarah lived in. Pictured her face. Saw her killing the Roberts' kids.

'I'll let you settle in. Pick you up in a squad car in the morning. We'll talk then. Plan our move.' Trainter saluted. Almost clicked his heels. Crisp movement to the hard black brim of his cap. Instinct when in uniform.

Dick and Chuck fought to contain the mirth. *Clockwork clown* was Chuck's impression.

'Seen something like it in a war film. Stuck in time or retro?' Chuck viewed his room with some humour from the door.

'A certain Old World charm all right. The flavour of Dickens maybe? What is that smell?' Dick's face folded into a grimace. He had never encountered the dankness of British seaside lodgings.

Bobby entered his room. No attention to surroundings. Could have been a Travel Lodge for all he was aware. He unpacked as he had packed. With the care and precision of a surgeon. Every item accounted for and stored in the appropriate space. Each being a special belonging. Each with a definite purpose. He handled them with respect and satisfaction. Recuperation had been a methodical process and measured in stages. Like walking up stairs. He was safe with that. Wingate Freeman had made each flight an extensive landing; secure and offering breathing space. So every action followed this pattern. He would never fall down stairs again.

Only Chuck and Dick ventured to the bar that evening. A brief encounter with warm beer, that on the top of tiredness sent them early to bed.

'How do you want to play this?' Trainter spoke from behind his unnecessarily large oak desk. It filled the small office, foundered in the centre, like Noah's Ark in a duck pond.

'You certain of her whereabouts, Inspector?' Dick enquired. He could still taste the beer from the previous evening. Yeast on the tongue and a curdling in his gut. Threatening to erupt.

'Had someone keep an eye on the place. Surveillance, Lieutenant.' More than just smugness. Trainter had something to prove. Nothing better than a British bobby, and no better bobby than Colin Trainer. Trainer emphasised the *f* sound in Lieutenant, just to let these yanks know how to pronounce the Queen's English. 'Surveillance of the highest standard.' Well, a constable on his bike keeping a watch on occasions. 'She's there all right. Another woman in the house. Think it's her sister. And a baby. Just the three of them.'

'If it's okay with you I'd like to send Bobby in ahead,' Dick suggested. 'Rattle the bitch. See if we get a reaction.'

'Not sure him going alone is within guidelines. I'll have to check that one out. Not that he's got any authority. Isn't a member of the Force.' Trainer stumbled. He wasn't one to be caught out on procedure. 'As it is we have to accompany you, as police officers out of your jurisdiction. Him going in alone would have the Chief Constable up in arms, I'm sure.'

'Not alone. Just let him lead. We can be in the background initially.' Dick's plan would be to stay out of sight. Let Sarah feel threatened. Just her and the man she had framed. 'Face to face. Then we roll along. Hopefully pick up the pieces. Breaks down. Tells us everything.' Dick was fantasising. 'If only.'

'We haven't come all this way just to have a pleasant conversation. It would be a waste of all our time if this falls flat and we go home empty handed.' Chuck was impatient. 'Surely Dick's plan would abide by your rules?'

From behind his bulky desk Trainer was higher than the surrounding bodies. A judge overlooking his court. 'Mm, might be okay. If we keep to the book as best we can.' The stirring of flexibility from the Inspector. 'So we go in. If there's no capitulation someone has to ask some questions. That has to be me.' Trainer knew his role here. 'I can assume you have these with you, Lieutenant?'

'Engraved on my badge,' Dick confidently acknowledged. He reached into his case and handed a slim red file to Trainer.

'We'll have to bring her back to the station and get her solicitor in here. That's certain. I don't want any bungling when it's our arses at stake. I have my own line of enquiry, of course.' Trainer spoke excellent police jargon. And always accompanied by a satisfied grin.

'You mean Sherlock?' Chuck alerted.

'Sherlock?' Trainter was oblivious to the nickname.

'He means the guy who came all that way to see us. George Rundle. Nice guy.' Dick assisted.

'Yes, George Rundle. Fine officer. Tragic death. Need to tackle that. Won't mention the original case that George was involved with, but it's on file and I'll use it if need be.' Trainter softened his voice. Some guilt there.

'Good man. Very good man.' Heads turned. Bobby had spoken. He had blended in with the room. Become a piece of furniture or an ornament. 'He shouldn't have died. No.' He spoke to himself. Facing a window. Gentle tones but heavy with emotion. An unsettling voice.

Trainter motioned his head in agreement and searched the faces of Dick and Chuck for their reaction. Startled by the man speaking. Thrown by the intensity of the utterance.

'What I do need to know is crucial to this matter, Inspector. Are you going to pursue a case against this woman if you get a confession or enough evidence to prosecute her over the death of George Rundle? Because if you are then we don't stand a hope in hell of getting her back to face charges in New Hampshire.'

Trainter rubbed his chin. 'You get first bite. Would be ungracious of me to steal your prize.' A generous gesture. But for good reason. Trainter didn't want another long-winded case clogging up his already bogged down prosecution timetable. However much he felt the weight of the albatross around his neck.

'This all okay with you Bobby?' Dick realised his omission and turned to consult with his scout. 'You going in first? You be all right seeing her? Won't do you no harm will it?' Dick was embarrassed by these afterthoughts.

Bobby nodded assent.

'We're going to be right behind you. Can't have a dramatic admission without witnesses. That'd be a waste of a journey.'

Chapter 30

Bobby wore a suit. Buttoned up as if he'd been stage-dressed for the part. Silk tie with a ludicrously large knot. Shoes he had polished for most of the previous evening.

The gate at 16 Church Cliff Avenue dragged across the cracking path that led to the front door. Bobby Clayman had pushed it. The squeal of it opening was heard by both women inside. From both encampments.

There was a broken bell and a tarnished knocker. Bobby rapped the door with his knuckles. It was how he felt.

Debbie emerged from her room, gave a sideways glance to check her sister hadn't ventured out also and headed for the stairs. She needn't have been concerned. Sarah ignored callers.

At the door Debbie checked on the visitor by lifting the grubby net curtain at the small adjacent window. 'Bloody salesman or one of them morons,' she moaned to herself. A sense of disappointment. Every caller was Ron coming to rescue her.

Bobby felt a presence. Heard the scratching movements inside. Struck the door again.

'Okay, I heard you.' Debbie was ready to dispense with this guy quick. She pulled at the door. It held for a moment, where warping made it stick, and sprang open, vibrating.

Not a bad looking man. Smart. Money maybe. Debbie surveyed Bobby Clayman before she spoke. 'Yes?' She wouldn't sound interested though.

Bobby froze with the opening of the door. Expecting to be face to face with Sarah. Face to face with the woman he had befriended, dated, taught how to shoot a pistol, framed him, killed the Roberts kids. From the times behind the curtain. That's how he saw it. His breakdown - a heavy, fabric drape drawn closed, that he wouldn't dislodge.

'Yes?' Debbie persisted. Unnerved by the eerie silence. She looked beyond Bobby. A group of men similarly dressed. Even Trainter suited up. Further evidence this was a door to door sales campaign or a swoop by some religious sect.

Bobby swallowed as if clear a blockage. 'Sarah. Is Sarah at home?' A mouse of a voice. But singing from New England. Quite a contrast to Debbie's clacking dialect.

Debbie was startled by the enquiry. Expecting the first line of some sales pitch, or a suitable quotation from the Bible on which to base a crusade. 'Sarah?' Dumb sounding response.

'Is she there?' Bobby sang.

'You got business with her?' Debbie was still thrown. The other men were milling at the gate.

'Yeah. I've got business with her.' Almost through the teeth. Bobby's eyes didn't flicker.

Debbie pushed the door slowly until it stuck, but not closed. Her deliberate tread up the stairs boomed in the stark hallway.

'Door!' A slap on her sister's bedroom door and she was gone. Swallowed up by her crowded refuge. Vicky safely asleep.

Sarah rarely ventured to greet callers, but there was fresh interest after her interview with Margaret Moncton. She even straightened loose hair as she passed the mirror, and pushed down the creases in her ugly green skirt from where she had been sitting on the bed.

At her pull the front door bounced open.

A cauldron of emotions. Cartoon pause of two adversaries held primed, ready to run into each other head on. Steam hissing.

Sarah gulped, eyes threatening to leave their sockets. Her mouth twitched and her bowel went into spasm. Racing through her mind frantic explanations. Her head shook from side to side with every dreadful notion.

Bobby's stare missile homed. Long breaths through his nose. Gushing air. Controlling a deep-rooted urge to squeeze a plea for forgiveness from out of her quivering mouth.

No words.

Sarah was too numbed to speak. Muscles locked. Slamming into a wall. Almost unconscious.

On the path the policemen waited. Watched the speechless stand-off and silently urged the nanny to yell out her guilt.

She looked primed for it. Surely she would. Dick gritted his teeth. A bobbing head. Trying to work her with his mind. Like propelling your horse home in the big race.

Leaving the door ajar Sarah retreated upstairs. Meandering in a delirium born of ghosts and consequence.

Seeing the cause lost the scrum of detectives bore down on the swinging front door, oblivious to the reeling Bobby Clayman stuck rigid by the numbing encounter.

Trainter clattered up the stairs to intercept Sarah before she reached her bedroom, and coaxed her back down to the hallway. A guiding hand and a garbled caution. Not usually his job.

'You'll need your coat. We're taking you to the station where we will be asking you some questions. You will probably want some legal representation, and if you don't have a solicitor to call we can provide one for you. Do you understand?'

Sarah managed a jerking nod as she was helped into her overcoat. Still struck dumb. Awful ideas swimming in her head.

Debbie had heard very little despite having an ear pressed against the door of her room. Hearing the heavy boots on the stairs and the persuading words ushering her sister back downstairs, she opened her door a few inches. Caught the conversation in the hall. Crept to the landing banisters to see the going of her bitch sister. Things were looking up. Perhaps they would keep her. She gave the sleeping Vicky a triumphant grin as she slid back into her room.

Trainter was unsure of the procedure. He had, in the absence of a legal representative, dragged Simon Jefferson in from Windrush, Gibbons and Jefferson just up the road.

Jefferson wasn't strictly a criminal lawyer but it was enough to satisfy requirements. In the confined space of the interview room he permitted Dick Kaltenbach to attend despite his hazy knowledge of conduct in such cases. WPC Wilmot was the obligatory female, and with the five of them stuffed around the desk it was congested.

Bizarre became comic when Trainter attempted to rig up the twin-decked tape recorder. Plastic doors flapped and lights fluttered but he could make no sense of the contraption. WPC Wilmot took over when the Inspector was about to throw the cassette out of the window.

'Please confirm that your name is Sarah Doreen Bickles, residing at 16 Church Cliff Avenue, Lyme Regis, Dorset.' Trainter sat proud at the table. One eye on the darting red light of the recording indicator.

Sarah kept her head bowed. Jefferson leaned down to listen to her reply, unsure it would be picked up by the microphone. No one round the table heard her.

'She confirms.' Jefferson's verification satisfied Trainter.

'Get her to speak up, will you, Simon. We can't have you translating under-the-table mumblings.' Trainter wanted to hold court with authority.

'I have been requested by police authorities in the United States, New Hampshire State Police to be exact, to ask you some questions concerning your involvement in a crime. Do you understand this, Sarah?' Trainter befriended. It was softly, softly now.

A head flicked up from table level. 'Don't know nothing.' Sarah blurted, much to the annoyance of Simon Jefferson.

'You know the crime I am referring to, don't you?' Trainter smelled success.

Jefferson caught hold of Sarah's arm. 'You don't have to answer these questions.' Whispered away from the tape recorder.

'Yeah.' Sarah ignored the solicitor.

'The murder of John...Stella...Lucy Marie and Tommy

Roberts.' Trainter solemnly announced. Tolling tone, as if tolling a funeral bell at the mention of each name.

'Told 'em it all over there.' Sarah dismissed. Brave voice. A stubborn defiance. Jefferson cringed.

'Things have changed and the case is moving in a new direction. Lieutenant Kaltenbach here, who I think you know, is looking along a different bearing.' Trainter nodded towards the American detective.

Sarah shrugged her shoulders and peered out of the window. She didn't know what Trainter was on about. All she knew was that she had to close the hatches and tie down the loose material. Hibernation was the tactic. Show no interest and offer no information. The body language of an obdurate schoolgirl and the grunts of an indifferent lover.

Dick Kaltenbach wanted an immediate reaction. His first ploy of sending in Bobby Clayman hadn't worked, but he hadn't finished with the shock tactics.

Trainter pulled out a pack of photographs. The dead. Tommy amidst the brooms and the buckets. Pale and contorted. Not a boy at all. A discarded doll, broken and disowned. 'Did you kill Tommy Roberts?' Trainter pushed the first photograph across the table. Under her nose. Jefferson's eyes bulged and he held his mouth.

She hadn't seen him inside. It had been like a conjuror who slides his sword into the black box where his assistant has been locked. Holes in a door and the swilling blood. It hadn't been Tommy at all. She hadn't killed him. 'No.' She'd convinced herself.

'Or Lucy Marie, or John Roberts, or Stella Roberts?' More gruesome pictures slid across the table. Jefferson's head rocked.

'No.' It wasn't a problem now.

'Sarah, you did kill these people didn't you? Look at them. You shot John Roberts first, out in the woods. Him dead there was nothing to worry about from the others was there?' Trainter obeyed Dick's script. 'Two small kids. Tommy in the cupboard and Lucy Marie out at the lake. And their mother you gunned down in the house. Blew away half her face.'

Sarah remembered that. What a feeling that was.

Dick watched from his seat. Watched every movement and every expression. Trainter was doing a good job. He was surprised how intimidating the Inspector sounded.

'No. I didn't.' It wasn't what Jefferson wanted, but it was negative enough.

'Do you remember that day? Do you remember the slaughter of the entire Roberts family?' Trainter goaded again.

'Not me. Weren't me.' Sarah's eyes danced around the room. Frivolous glances that picked out cabinets and doors. A plane above the accusing photos.

'You were first there. First to discover the bodies. Isn't that so?'

Bodies? That's how they were. All the intimidation and bullying. All the conspiring and degrading. But now they were just bodies. Bagged up and disposable. Dead meat with nothing to laugh at. She'd seen to that. Sarah fought not to show her satisfaction. She knew that not a twinkle of these comforting thoughts should creep out. An audience too interested.

'Weren't you the one that found the family dead?' Trainter tried again.

'Dead. Yeah, they were dead.' Matter of fact. No emotion.

'And it was you, the only person there, who killed them. Wasn't it?' Trainter shuddered forward in his chair. Only inches from Sarah. 'You killed them didn't you? Had your reasons I bet. Deserved it perhaps? Tell us what happened. Take your time. Let it out. Make it easier for you. Driven to do it no doubt. If you explain, I'm sure we'll understand.' Fatherly and forgiving. Old tricks and counterfeit concerns. A policeman's upbringing. Judas counselling.

Greeted by a tsunami of silence. Concrete defiance.

Trainter reshuffled the pack. Cards held to his face as if protecting a hand. They were all trumps. Each photograph as brutal as the next.

'Lucy Marie?' Trainter pulled out his lead and snapped it on the table. Pushing it under Sarah's nose.

Dick fidgeted in his seat. He wanted to rub her face in it. A disgusting pet who had soiled the carpet. Sarah, clasped hands. Mute. He'd get her to talk.

Lucy Marie dragged from the lake. A Barbie doll in her own right. Discarded in a child's game. Legs buckled. Arms, pasta cream, clutching pond weed. Groping beyond death. Face torn. Nibbled flesh. Fish bait.

'Well?' Trainter twisted the photo in front of her.

It meant nothing. Sarah glanced at the Inspector without lifting her head. White crescents cradling snooker-black eyes.

'Lucy Marie. Did you do this to Lucy Marie?' Trainter prodded. Finger stabbing at the girl's foundered body.

'Not me.' Scowled from her cavernous face. Flicking back the photograph, with fingernails as if scattering dust from the table top.

Sarah shook her head. Long sweeps as if to free a frozen neck. Brushing away triumphal notions. Clearing her head with deep inhaling and gushing exhalation through her nose. Audible rushes of air. 'Not me. You got 'im. You got Bobby. Weren't me.' Sarah scuffed her shoes under the table. Smoothed her dress. Dismissing, even in her own head, such ludicrous accusations.

Jefferson watched. Then studied the inquisitors. He wasn't bad at picking up body language. His client had locked a steel door and was ready to deny anything. Her accusers recognised a barricade when they reached one.

'We'll take a break.' Trainter needed advice. 'Be back here in half-an-hour.'

'She's not cracking.' Trainter blurted as they headed for the canteen. 'Cow's not going to talk.'

'Don't look promising.' Dick was in agreement. 'You want to bring up the Rundle business to sidetrack her?'

'I'm having my doubts about that.' Trainter piled in three sugars and stirred vigorously, spilling waves of coffee with every circuit. 'With the Bassnett case being reopened I need to tread carefully. Don't reckon on raising that now. Too much dust at the moment. Keeping that in reserve.'

'Feel like Custer. Running out of ammo. The old crow ain't looking like surrendering with her hands in the air. What we got left to fire at her? Jack shit, that's what.' Defeat and the hint of dejection. Dick slouched against the wall, hands in pockets.

'I'll keep her here for another five hours. Tell Jefferson we need to complete some spurious enquiry. Won't matter to him. Might break her. Being cooped up in the cells could loosen her tongue. It's happened before. Some of the most unlikely villains have squealed when faced with only a few hours in the slammer.' Trainter gulped the last of his bitter coffee. Screwing up his face and chewing at some void in his mouth, as if to purge the awful taste of the canteen brew. He had more faith in this new plan than those listening.

'Give it a go. Can't lose. But I ain't holding out much hope.' Dick was resigned to failure, but he'd play along.

Chuck was no company for Bobby. They sat together, but alone, in a corridor at the police station. People came and went. On Trainter's face a bulldog grimace. On Dick Kaltenbach's the glumness of resignation. No questions were asked of either officer as they flitted between interview and refreshment.

Sarah sat on the metal-framed bed. Springs twanged with any movement. Jefferson helped himself to the single chair at a wooden table, barely two feet square decorated with tattoos of biro doodles. He spread documents out in front of him and sorted through them.

'No comment.' Jefferson spoke without looking up. 'No more. Nothing needed but that.'

Sarah's nod invisible to the solicitor's shifting eyes.

'That clear?' Jefferson didn't like being ignored.

'Ain't going to say nothing.' The begrudging response of a chastened child.

'We'll sit this out and hope they haven't got enough to detain you. Hopefully you'll be going home soon. Even if it's bail. But that'll only be a formality if there's a UK allegation.' Jefferson moved papers as if involved in a game of patience. He was just about treading water. More time and information before he could swim.

Neither spoke nor exchanged glances. Hours passed.

'Get her back in here, Wilmot.' Inspector Trainter snapped, despite his tiredness. 'Let's hope she dried out down there and will crack when we restart. Won't keep her overnight if we draw a blank.' Trainter pulled a no-nonsense face to Dick Kaltenbach who walked alongside him. 'She's loose if she's still playing hermit crab.'

Sarah never spoke again. Trainter had laid out the condemning photographs, had questioned her once more about the appalling crimes and the contorted corpses, asked her to reconsider her stance and appealed to her lawyer to reason with his client. Becoming a sermon. Losing the sting and the agility of penetrative interrogation.

'Interview concluded ten seventeen,' Trainter announced after close scrutiny of his watch and some mental arithmetic. Twenty-four hour clock was a curse to him. 'Tapes, Wilmot.'

Trainter sealed the tapes in separate envelopes and gave one to Jefferson. Who hoisted his client to her feet. 'Any charge, Inspector?'

'Not as yet.' A guarded reply that couldn't camouflage the heavy defeat.

Bobby saw her leave. Scuttling past at the elbow of her solicitor. Just the once he exchanged glances with Chuck Nolan. Both had their own concerns about Sarah's unhindered departure.

Dick Kaltenbach followed. Hands in pockets, head bent. Stopped to stand over the two men. 'No luck. She ain't talking.' His eyebrows lifted. A shrug of the shoulders. *What can you do?* Stuck on his face.

'Did your best. No argument that you didn't explore this

fully.' Chuck pulled himself to his feet. Stretched in an effort to wake his sleeping joints. 'She give us anything?' Chuck gave Dick a quizzing look. 'Clear up some of our concerns?'

Dick, aware of Chuck's direction, shook his head slowly and deliberately. 'Gave us nothing. Wouldn't say a thing. Some weak denials, but no new material. Told Trainter that we'd got our man anyway.'

Bobby edged towards the police station door. Uncertain. Waiting to be led somewhere else. Moving on.

'Hotel then.' Dick announced. 'Day of rest tomorrow and then back to the good old US of A, day after.'

Chapter 31

'Trainter said he'd drop by for a drink.' Dick found Chuck freshening up in his room. 'Said I'd see him in the bar around seven. Didn't want a late one. We need to be up early for that flight.'

'More shit beer.' Chuck struggled with the top button of his shirt. 'I suppose one last taste of the deadly broth won't be too disastrous. That's as long as I don't end up crapping swamp water. Serious danger to your health that stuff, I reckon.'

'You can get them in. I'm sure it's your shout.' Dick declared. 'Don't think we'll bother Bobby. He ain't what you'd call fun to have around.'

'Suits me fine.' Chuck still held on to some doubts about Bobby Clayman.

Bobby heard both men make their way downstairs. He padded around his room in his dark trainers, checking his reflection each time he passed the mirror. He was nearly ready. One final adornment. He lifted the lid of his case that sat on the bed. Pulled it out from under some soiled clothes. Fixed it to his belt. It fitted perfectly. Hands free. Now he was fully dressed.

At the door of the bar Bobby paused. The three policemen were swapping anecdotes and chortling into their beer. They didn't see him slide through the hotel lobby. Nobody remembered seeing Bobby Clayman leave or slip through the wet streets of Lyme Regis.

And no one saw him slither through the gateway of 16 Church Cliff Avenue or approach the house. New England stealth.

The Yale latch uttered barely a click as Bobby slid his razor blade through the door jamb and into the mechanism.

Only the slightest creak on the stairs. A landing in sombre darkness.

Sarah Bickles was fathoms deep. Sleep driven by the ordeal of that day. And from that overpowering depth came the visitors. Images and events stirred in a cauldron, buffeted and massaged by fantasy and fever.

A child in white sat on descending grass at the edge of a smooth lake, dropping petals on to the glass surface. Exotic metallic birds dived and soared in silence. Each petal tossed was a pink coracle floating away, powered by a muffled wind. Leaving no trail. No ripple on the mirror lake. Sarah struggled to move. Stricken by a dream's own crippling mechanism that cements you in place. Behind her she could hear children playing. Rupert and Tommy. She knew the voices. If only her head would turn. No rotation. Numbed impotence.

As if taking on a different identity she watched the boys pointing to her own statue back. Giggling and whispering. Jumping on the spot with the pleasure of their own humour. Laughing until blood pumped out of their eyes down to their ankles. The watching body was not rigid and immovable. At the twisting of the head she now saw Stella Roberts in the log cabin, at the sink. A broken face. Grey as slate. Moving mechanically. John Roberts was also there, but she only heard the barking of his voice. Boasting bold manoeuvres and predatory ambushes in a disintegrating market. Jumble and nonsense.

In her hand cold steel. Her gun snuggled there. Momentarily until it melted. Leaving a gooey deposit. Coagulating blood. Stella cackled from the kitchen sink and the playing boys mocked. And the child from the lakeside stood blank and ivory. Petals now charred brown and rotting on a stinking green, stagnant lake. The child decayed before her eyes and stabbed a skin-flapping finger; pointing to the pickup truck, chrome-wheeled and rocking with the bass of country music.

Knocked back into an insect-writhing grass she saw him bearing down. Bobby Clayman came heavy at her, wielding a huge scimitar. Flashing blade hanging above her. She grabbed at the air between them. Stretching to hold him off. The images disappeared into a black blanket that shrouded her head.

'Looked in his room as I went up.' Chuck explained to Dick. 'Wasn't there. Hope it don't mean nothing.'

'Let it go, Chuck. He ain't goin't' run now.' Dick showed his lack of concern by taking each stair slowly. 'Got some air, I expect.'

Chuck would have bounded up two at a time. 'We ain't goin' home with someone to crucify, are we? He realises that. Must have crossed his mind to run from this.' Chuck held on to his top lip with his teeth.

'Bobby.' Dick called outside Bobby's door. 'You in there?'

Chuck strode around. Circles in the corridor outside.

Movement from within. 'What's wrong?' Bobby held the door ajar and spoke through the opening.

'Ah, just checking. You all right?'

'Yeah. Something up?' Bobby's bland voice enquired.

'No. A little concerned. Chuck came up earlier and said you were missing. Didn't want you getting lost or anything. No problem.' Dick wanted to strangle his colleague.

'I'm fine. Popped downstairs. Check on the papers. Didn't want to disturb you in the bar.' Bobby threw that in to establish he'd been about the hotel.

'Well, goodnight. See you in the morning. Bright and early. Seven I'm afraid.' Dick smiled through his embarrassment. He felt a fool that he'd even considered Chuck's theory.

Heathrow was a termites' nest. Dick organised tickets and formalities whilst Chuck watched Bobby. As a dog, ever-attentive to his master's movements. Watching. Watching subtle differences. A detective's eye. Something he couldn't fathom. Bobby was walking with more spring. No dull lope. Glazed eyes as if bathed in healing waters. A sharpness. An awareness. An impala waiting to bound away? Chuck was sure he caught Bobby smirking. Perhaps even a grin. Was there an escape plan? About to desert?

'Pleased to be getting out. Going home. I expect.' Dick decided when Chuck mentioned this to him. 'Must be as glad as we are to be returning to some decent beer.' Dick offered a reassuring smile.

'Ain't goin't' be a great homecoming for him, is it?' Chuck hastened to add. 'We aren't bringing us home the fatted calf are we? He's still goin't' be number one on our list, ain't he?' Whining like a kid begging a favour.

'Just 'cause we missed out here, it don't mean we've given up on this angle. She's no innocent. Take my word for it. If you'd been in that room you'd have seen it. Not transparently vicious like. More the sly malice of the mink than the panther. Harmless enough for the most part. For me the scales tipped over. I'm sure our odd job man, Bobby Clayman, is only a sleepy chipmunk.' Dick collected his hand luggage as he spoke. 'Enough of the animal analogies.' He hailed Bobby from his seat in the departure lounge.

'Not convinced myself. Know there's goin't' be trouble if we don't make a spectacle out of someone for these murders.' Chuck raised his voice to make the last word audible to Bobby as he joined the two detectives heading for Gate 14. Springing along behind. Bouncing on the moving walkway. The weak sun picking out a devilish smile that he wouldn't let the two police officers see.

She woke to the whimpering of a child needing food. Vicky's faint but insistent cries demanding breakfast. She couldn't raise herself immediately. A night of fitful sleep. No evidence of her sister. No clumping footsteps or muffled movements from beyond the wall. No occupation of disputed territory, the kitchen. A step onto the landing confirmed this. Bedroom door firmly shut.

The American Airlines' plane proud and glinting. Titanium fuselage and wings polished to a stainless steel sparkle. Just like American toasters of the fifties. Somewhat garish, but a glitter wreckage easier to spot on the side of a hill. Not a deliberate ploy. More big car and brashness. Bobby liked the livery, and from his window seat over the wing was engrossed in the reflected images thrown in confusion by the taxiing plane.

It was well after eleven and no sign of her sister stirring. Vicky's bawling snuffed by sleep. She dressed to go out. Still no telltale sounds from upstairs. Over four hours. She examined her cheap watch, and with her forefinger traced the time from when her sister usually got up. She searched the stairs through curious eyes. From the well of the hall she could see the closed door. Barely a glow from the gap below. Curtains still drawn. Only a pace to the pathway. Scarcely a step forward. But. She slapped the front door closed with a shudder. A lazy clack. She climbed the stairs slowly. Hauling her shabby body. Levering from the handrail. It made no sense. A compelling enquiry.

'The coast. Bognor or somewhere.' An elderly couple eager at the window of the jet. Pointing through the plastic lens. The amusement of old age.

Bobby looked. He could make out the patchwork fields finishing at a ragged coastline and a thin band of straggling beach. Grey sea flecked white by a whipping wind.

And below, the curving arm of the cobbled groyne. A glistening slug tormented by the stinging flack of a fletcher ocean. Lyme Regis under attack. A relentless wall of water.

She listened again. A clock tocked to itself. Loud silence.

333

The round doorknob filled her hand. Responsive to her rolling turn. Foul gloom filled the fine crack as she pushed it open. Her sister was in her bed. No movement. A lump of a body beneath bedclothes. As much as the filtered light allowed. A wider gap and weak landing illumination wasn't enough. She skirted the bed. Scuffing the carpet with deliberate steps. Back against the wardrobe. Reaching for the curtains. Close enough to smell the dust. Light invaded the dingy bedroom. Hardly any sun, save for a rogue beam that ignited in brilliance a solitary pewter plane climbing south.

'You there?' Polite enquiry. Unsure if she welcomed an answer. Vicky sprung awake. Sarah turned and edged to the foot of Debbie's bed. Rested her hands on the wood frame. Her sister's face a bleached sail in the wild blue quilt.

Vicky peered from her cot, gripping the bars. Puzzled and hungry. Nappy full. Her mother lying storybook still. Her aunt staring.

Sarah leaned forward. Saw Debbie's ivory cheeks edged with the black and blue of bruising. Frozen mouth about to speak. Dead. Glacier eyes about to see. Dead. Odour of old blankets or a dank wooden shed. Dead.

And stuck through all the black blood map and the thickness of bedding, as if held as a trophy in her lunging, desperate hands, a huge blade protruding from her chest. Glinting silver teardrop at the butt; Bobby's deerskin-handled Bowie knife. Excalibur.

Sarah sucked back some gurgling saliva. Recognised the events of the night. Narrow escape. Turned to Vicky's nodding head and into her spaniel eyes. Let out the merest hiss of satisfaction.

Chapter 32

Lilly Moncton, petal-pink dress oozing the chalky aroma of soap, studied her nails, yet didn't study them. She had finished playing on the swing that nestled between the two sprawling yew trees. It continued to swing randomly following her abrupt dismount. Up, nearer the house the new nanny sat watching. Lilly felt uncomfortable. There was something about the woman's eyes that made her uneasy. Her podgy sister, Grace, waddled towards her as if seeking refuge in the heavy shade. Dim eyes, languid movements.

The nanny surveyed, with cold unnerving eyes, the two figures lurking at the far end of the garden. Next to her a pram vibrated as Laurel Moncton reached for the hanging row of rattling plastic discs. Chubby legs squirming from tight padding of her disposable nappy. And in a pushchair monotonously rocked by her extended hand, nanny Sarah Bickles encouraged Vicky to sleep.

And in her scrapbook head nanny chortled at some crazy thoughts. And her mouth curled with a snapshot grin. And she had those little girls misbehaving at the bottom of the garden, in her laser sights. Just waiting.

Other books by Michael James

That'll Teach You!
ISBN 0 9537373 0 6

A powerful and shocking account of an abused schoolgirl's vicious allegations, a police witch-hunt, a school's treachery and a teacher's struggle for justice.

> *A frightening story of lies and deceit, yet of fortitude and courage.*
> **Judy Finnegan** (This Morning GMTV)

> *This book will give any male teacher the shivers and makes unsettling reading.*
> **Times Educational Supplement**

nanny